SKIN AFTER SKIN

A PSYCOP NOVEL

SKIN AFTER SKIN

A PSYCOP NOVEL

Jordan Castillo Price

Skin After Skin
A PsyCop Novel
PsyCop #8

Print edition published in the
United States in 2017 by JCP Books
www.jcpbooks.com

This book is a work of fiction. The characters, incidents, and dialogue are drawn from the author's imagination or are used fictitiously.

ISBN-13: 978-1-935540-92-2
Cover art by Jordan Castillo Price
Audio edition available

Special thanks to Tony Edmondson
for allowing Crash's neighbor
to borrow his name

PART ONE

The One Who Got Away

CHAPTER 1

Psychics were once viewed with as much skepticism as Nigerian email scams and the Bermuda Triangle. But at the tender age of ten, I was assailed by scientific proof of psychic ability from every media outlet.

By the time I was thirty, I owned a metaphysical emporium of my very own, but I wasn't always this evolved. Convincing me all the drama was more than just an elaborate fraud? It took a few years....

Do you believe in Santa Claus? The Tooth Fairy? The email claiming you won a humongous jackpot in some lottery you never actually played? Of course not. Our culture is built on fables and fairy tales, and we're bright enough to understand that they're allegories and metaphors...usually. So why everyone gets behind this whole "psychic" hoopla is beyond me.

"I had another dream last night," Pilar was saying. "God, Crash, I hate it when you roll your eyes."

Don't get me wrong, Pilar is my best gal-pal. But if she was psychic, then I was the poster boy for chastity. Even though she'd helped me keep the primo parking space at my apartment by carpooling, I couldn't simply sit back and pretend she wasn't being ridiculous. "I'm doing you a favor. The eye-roll means you sound like a dumbass."

"Nice."

"I'd point it out if you had spinach in your teeth, too. That's what friends are for."

She turned down the stereo I'd turned up mere moments before. "Anyway. It was at Luscious. The salon seemed pretty much like it really is, the chairs, the lighting. I don't remember if you were there, but you must've been. Mostly I remember Ralph. So, I was trying to work, but Ralph kept moving me around to different chairs. My client had long, thick hair, and the color was taking forever to come out at the shampoo bowl. It just kept swirling down the sink, blood-red, running down the sink, like something out of Psycho."

"Psycho was shot in black and white."

She ignored me. "And just when I thought I was making some headway, Ralph would come along and say, 'No, no, no, this isn't right at all. I need you in chair three,' and he'd make me leave my client at the sink and move my station. Every time, he moved me to a worse chair, until I was practically at the back door—there was this huge back door that led out to the alley, you know, where the client consultation room actually is, only it was sort of like this door that led out to the gym in my grammar school."

"Further evidence that dreams are basically the backwash in the dregs of your psyche."

"This door was huge. Big and rusty and old—not just distressed to look old, like the rest of the shop. It was actually really beat up and scary. And I knew that if I couldn't get this red dye out, Ralph was gonna come along and move my station again. Only the next time, he'd move it right out the door."

I lifted up my sunglasses and slid her a sideways look, and was surprised to see actual distress in her eyes. "What're you saying, you think Ralph's angling to get rid of you? Based on what, a dream you had last night? A *dream*? Come on, we both know you're way smarter than that."

"Gee, that's really comforting." She turned up the stereo and muttered, "I have no idea why I ever tell you anything."

"Because I won't feed you a load of crap just to make you feel better...and when I say Ralph would be crazy to mess with you, I totally mean it."

"Aw."

"It's true. Ralph might be a prima donna, but he's no idiot. You're the Updo Queen. Nobody else has an eye like you—nobody. Your bridal parties look like a million bucks and they all love you for it. No one's getting edged out the door. We have an oddball staff meeting and you had a stupid stress dream because you set your alarm half an hour early and it disrupted your sleep cycle, end of story."

"I dunno what you've got against Psych, anyway," Pilar said. She parked at the far end of the lot and killed the engine. "Maybe you're jealous."

"I don't waste my jealousy on products of pop culture's imagination. Besides, if Big Bad Boss-Man needed to edge someone out, don't you think he'd go for one of the Juniors?" Half the lowest ranking stylists wouldn't last out the year. It was easier to keep from getting too attached by thinking of them en masse.

"Yeah," she said wistfully. "Hopefully not Matthew. He's cute."

"Gay," I said.

"No kidding," she replied with a huge undercurrent of *duh*. "I dunno. Maybe I'm just spooked because I've been looking at want ads lately. Like seriously."

"Can't hurt to look—just make sure you don't get caught. If Ralph decides you're disloyal, well...that's another story." I hopped out of the car while Pilar was busy rocking herself out of the front seat.

There are all kinds of euphemisms for fat. Voluptuous, pleasingly plump, Rubenesque...more to love. In the beauty industry, some people try to celebrate fat with body-positive images of slightly larger models and chic plus-size clothing lines, while others are offended by the mere notion of extra weight. I don't take a personal stance on the matter. I also knew better than to offer any advice, since I could live on burgers and fries without gaining an ounce. Keeping my mouth shut wasn't easy. It pained me to see someone as cool as Pilar struggle with tasks other people took for granted...and it was a good thing her dreams were nothing more than a release valve for her worries. As fantastic as she was at her job, unfortunately it wouldn't surprise me if Ralph thought the Luscious image suffered from the fact that she wasn't stick thin and conventionally gorgeous. Plus, I'd bet if anyone was jealous, it was Ralph—subconsciously jealous that Pilar could style circles around him, even though his job was running the salon, not cutting hair. And while her expertise made the salon look good, her personal struggle with weight did not.

We gathered in the consultation room, Pilar, me and the other stylists, and we dished dirt about who looked crappiest in the latest issue of *Coif.* Ralph was conspicuously absent—and Luscious was his salon—but none of us were surprised. To be honest, I enjoyed studying Ralph to figure out what made him tick. Keeping to his own internal schedule was a perk of being the boss, but during the year and a half I'd been in his employ, not once had I seen him keep a client waiting. The waiting game was only played with employees. It might have been a demonstration of power, or maybe it was something more nuanced than that. A way to keep us on our toes, off-balance. He wasn't consistently late; he could just as easily have been crazy-early, sitting there by himself for an hour, taking mental note of who showed up when. But there was no way of knowing without being on time...unless you had a pal on staff willing to shoot you a quick "get your ass in here" text. As far as I knew, other than Pilar and me, at Luscious it was every stylist for himself.

"I heard Ralph's gonna give us a big surprise," one of the Juniors announced dramatically. While Pilar's backdoor dream niggled at me, another Junior turned to the window that overlooked the salon floor and said, "Ooh, I wonder if that's it."

One thing I'd give Ralph Maldonado: he knew how to make an entrance. He swept like royalty across the dimmed salon floor with a towering stack of boxes in his arms. He appeared to be hurrying...but I wouldn't have been surprised to see him tucked out of sight waiting for the moment in which his hurrying would have the greatest impact.

"Look alive, people, look alive," he said as he burst into the room. Two of the Juniors hurried over to relieve him of his burden of boxes, while another actually pulled out a chair for him. Maybe that kid would be the next to go...the art of brown-nosing is more subtle than you'd think, and taken too far, it only embarrassed us all. Ralph shuffled a box pile toward the nearest Junior with exacting carelessness, then planted his hands on the back of the proffered chair. "Take one, pass 'em around. There's plenty of goodies for everybody."

Pilar shifted forward in her seat. We often discussed whether or not we should eat on staff meeting morning. Have breakfast, and chances were you'd be greeted by a catered brunch. Abstain, and sit down to nothing but a bottle of tepid vitamin water. I didn't care—I could eat or not eat, and it was all the same to me—but if Pilar skipped a meal, she got woozy. Apparently today we were being fed, so hopefully she hadn't stopped for an Egg McMuffin on her way to my place.

Ralph beamed as the pristine flecky off-white boxes made their way around the table. I only stole the quickest glance, since it would ruin everything if he knew I was totally onto the man behind the curtain, and that I enjoyed watching him perform. Ralph's dark hair was still wet, as if he'd just dashed out of the shower. It was overlong and careless, though he trimmed it every week, and a few threads of gray had been allowed to peek through at the temples. His teeth were bleached to perfection, but one of his eyeteeth was too prominent. And though his beard was a precise three-day growth, his neck was flawlessly smooth. Very handsome. Very rugged, too—at least if you weren't looking terribly hard at all the details. A less attentive observer might think he was rumpled, and even fairly butch. I saw a gay morning routine that must've taken hours.

"Iris Moon doesn't open until dinner on weeknights," Ralph said dramatically, "but as a personal favor to me, Chef Sable came in special this morning and whipped up something just for us."

Pilar was holding very still in an attempt to keep from devouring the box, sustainably-sourced cardboard and all. I had to admit, my curiosity was piqued. Iris Moon was one of those places where it took half a year to get a reservation, and then you ate what the chef put in front of you and pretended you understood it. That sort of food intrigued me, since it was more about social currency than sustenance.

Once everyone had a fussy origami box in front of them, Ralph gazed around the table, surveyed his kingdom, and said with an expansive sigh, "Enjoy."

I hefted my box. It was the size of a small Chinese takeout container, and it felt like there was something substantial inside. A giant scone, or maybe a tart. It didn't smell like anything—but between the ionizers and organic oils strategically daubed throughout the salon to mask the lingering whiff of perm, normal food smells didn't stand a chance. The room filled with the sound of paper as we all pried at the origami. One of the Juniors breached it first and gasped in delight. I quelled a smirk, found a fold in the cardboard, and attempted to pry it open. Not too quickly. I like to play it cool. But as the box confounded me yet again, I did find myself picking up steam so as not to be the last one to get to my treat. Especially once I felt Pilar go still beside me as her box yielded to her skilled fingers.

And there it was, the magical seam. I thumbed it open, peeled apart the cardboard, and looked inside. I had to press the side of my tongue between my molars to keep from laughing.

The last Junior to get his box open was the one to voice the question we were all wondering. "What is it?"

"That," Ralph explained with great showmanship, "is an absinthe gel reduction with nitrogen-seared bergamot."

We each gazed at the leaf-topped gumdrop sitting at the bottom of our box, nestled there on its heavy cooling pad. I was amused. Pilar was probably pissed. The Juniors were suitably impressed, though. They lifted their jellies out of the boxes with hushed murmurs of reverence and awe, held them to the light, and inhaled their bouquet.

"Hopefully it's concentrated enough to pack a buzz," I said. I popped mine into my mouth whole and gave it a good chew. It tasted like unsweetened licorice had a gummy baby with rubbing alcohol then covered it in menthol. Tears sprang to my eyes. I took a deep breath and said, "Clears the sinuses."

"There's a kick to them," Ralph agreed. I noted he didn't touch his.

Pilar didn't either, though she did try to be diplomatic by saying, "I'll save mine for later."

The rest of the Juniors oohed and ahhed as they ingested their jellies with tiny, precise nibbles—just like they minced words around him. On one hand, Ralph enjoyed safety. There was a comforting predictability in knowing your minions would never dream of an uprising. The other hand? It was busy toying at the inseam of my jeans under the table. Devotion is flattering, no doubt, but it doesn't tickle the testes like a hint of rebellion.

Ralph was easy on the eyes and fun in bed, and I liked to think I was too, but both of us knew our occasional ejaculatory dalliance would never go anywhere. He was the boss, after all, and I was the insubordinate subordinate. Ralph was nothing if not savvy, and he was way too canny to get seriously involved with an employee.

"Oh my *God*, this is so *good*," one of the Juniors enthused over the gumdrop, batting his dark eyelashes at Ralph. Matthew was fresh out of school and only a few years younger than me, half Portugese and half sultry Puerto Rican, dewy-eyed with innocence. Ralph had taken a tumble with him, too. Then again, Ralph regularly did everyone else there with a dick, and the dykey goth receptionist, too. Hopefully Matthew's breathless enthusiasm was only schmoozing, and the kid knew better than to fall in love. And if he didn't, well...life would chafe a thicker skin onto him soon enough.

"And now that I've plied you all with candy," Ralph said, "It's time to get down to business." Ralph Maldonado is melodramatic and gloriously queer, but in the end, he's also a shrewd businessman.

He started, as always, by reiterating the salon's mission statement: *We delight our clients by making them feel comfortable and welcome. Through technical excellence and cutting-edge technique, we establish ourselves as industry leaders.* Although the words were hand-lettered in broken calligraphy around the consultation room's chicly distressed crown molding, he didn't so much as glance up at them. He'd written the spiel, and whether it had come from his idea of what a salon *should* be or the depths of his heart, I think he'd repeated it enough by now to actually believe it himself.

He ran through some typical things, an awesome mention in the Reader, a reminder to keep f-bombs to a minimum, and a scolding to desist from wearing tank tops as some clients don't appreciate a man's hairy armpit in their face. "And next on the agenda," he said, "Square Days."

Pilar and I groaned. The Juniors joined in, once Ralph's body language indicated that bitchery was permitted.

"Do we have to?" Pilar asked. "Last year we lost a whole Saturday's worth of business, and for what? The raffle sucked, and we ended up cutting for a bunch of cheapos who didn't even appreciate it. No return clients, not one. Do you know what I made for tips that day? Eight dollars...and twenty-three cents."

Picking up a tip envelope and hearing it jingle is never a good sign. I added, "If you sign us up for Square Days again, I'm gonna have to call in sick. Just sayin'."

Ralph raised a hand in placation. "Look, no one's overjoyed about Square Days, but the Lincoln Square Chamber of Commerce is counting on us, and I already told them we're in. It's just a matter of ironing out the details. Swing by my office if you want a say in how our participation will look, Mr. Ash...since calling in sick is most definitely not an option."

I scanned his eyes to see whether a fellow Chamber member had threatened, cajoled or flattered him into a commitment, but I couldn't quite tell which. I supposed the "why" of it all didn't make much difference. He was the boss. And when he said *jump*, I might hem and haw about it, but in the end, I would grudgingly hop.

Maybe Ralph was in the same boat and he was answering to a higher power, too. I wasn't entirely clear on what the Chamber did, but I did know Chicago was an Old Boys' Club. If Ralph wanted Luscious to thrive, playing by their rules would make it a heck of a lot easier.

Who says love makes the world go 'round? Money, power and favors was more like it. Those gumdrops, for instance. Could I put a price on them? Not individually. No doubt they were normally part of a froofy twenty-course meal. Even if he paid for the stupid little jellies, he'd probably burned one massive favor to obtain them, as well. To what end, though? Sure, Ralph likes to make an impression. But why waste it buttering up the staff?

The lighting shifted from out front as a receptionist flicked on the overheads and began readying the waiting room for the morning's clientele. Ralph stood up and glanced through the glass at his domain, and the rest of us pushed away from the table. I lobbed the origami box into the trash, and was already at the door when Ralph added, almost as an afterthought, "Oh, and in the spirit of technical excellence, I'll be bringing in a dedicated colorist to the staff. He starts tomorrow."

What?

I whirled around to ask him if he'd swallowed too much absinthe jelly that morning, but he didn't meet my eye. Somehow, I reined in my fury. Pilar had gone still again, I noticed. One of the oblivious Juniors declared Ralph's announcement "fa-bulous," and the others all chimed in.

Figuring I'd only be shooting myself in the foot if I mouthed off now, especially in front of the other stylists, I decided to give myself some time to think on what I'd say to Ralph about this whole "colorist" business. Maybe words wouldn't even be necessary while I was wringing his goddamn neck.

CHAPTER 2

Since I had an eleven o'clock touch-up and a twelve-fifteen cut, I'd calmed down considerably by the time I finally cornered Ralph. Unfortunately, it also meant my anger had shifted into something that felt distinctly vulnerable. Ralph made money no matter which of his employees did what, but me, I earned my biggest tips doing color. Between credit cards and rent and car payment, I'd be sunk without those tips. For the duration of Square Days, it was a mere inconvenience. Permanently, though? No can do.

Ralph was scowling over his laptop when I closed his door behind me, not with a slam, but a gentle click. He half-glanced at me and said, "Square Days are non-negotiable, Mr. Ash."

I crossed my arms and made a scoff-noise. "You think that's what pissed me off?"

After a few moments of me not budging, Ralph steepled his fingers and graced me with his full attention. "No?" he asked with exaggerated patience. "Then indulge me. What's on your mind?"

"You can't skim off my best clients and toss them to someone else." Blunt? Sure. But I've always thought bluntness was one of my better qualities.

Too bad telling your boss he "can't" do something has so much potential to backfire. I could see the shift in Ralph's eyes as he realized I'd come to butt heads, and especially that I wasn't gonna back

down. He liked it when I was spicy, not unpalatable, and the line between the two was constantly shifting.

I didn't backpedal, exactly. But when his body language told me
I was treading on dangerous ground, I did soften my approach. "You
know that's where all the tips are."

Ralph indicated a chair with his eyes. I briefly considered towering over him for the sake of making my point, but in the end, I
chose to sit. He said, "Our new hire is a certified specialist from the
American Color Institute. Having him on staff bumps up the entire
salon. Imagine this: a forty-five minute cut who tips like a two-hour
color. Now multiply it by the heads you do in a week."

"That's future-talk. I'm looking at next month."

"Really? Are you sure? I sign your paychecks and I can guess your
tips. Unless you've got a coke habit I don't know about, a lean month
shouldn't kill you." What I had was an overpriced pad that cost a cool
two grand and a car payment that made me wince. Not to mention a
newfound love of the Limoncello Collins, a cocktail that went for at
least twelve bucks, plus tip—and I took great pride in being a generous tipper. "Just hang in there," he said. "Pretty soon, for far less work,
you'll be bringing in more dollars."

Or, I could go find another salon that was hiring and take all my
clients with me. I knew better than to threaten, though. Ralph might
come off all charming smiles and absinthe gumdrops. But I could tell
just by looking at him, if I ever backed him into a corner, he'd show
his true stripes. And they wouldn't be pretty.

He was starting to get irritated with me too, but that didn't mean
I was willing to let the matter drop. I kept everything as neutral as
I could possibly make it—my voice, my posture, and especially my
face, as I tried to gauge whether I should appeal to his vanity or his
sympathy. "There must be something we can work out."

Ralph's annoyance shifted all right, but not in the way I expected.
One minute he was all business and condescension, and the next, his
Vibe was through the roof.

Pilar claims she's blind to Vibe—but come on, that's not possible. The "let's be more than friends" look is as plain as the nose on
someone's face...or plainer, depending on how much work they've

had done. She's dumbfounded that there's a facial expression that's completely invisible to her. And I don't buy that she's never on the receiving end of it. Plenty of folks dig a little cushion for the pushin'. "Is it like a smile?" she often wondered—and yeah, sometimes it was. But some guys had Vibes so serious you'd swear their pet hamster just got stepped on. Maybe it was more in the length of eye contact. Or maybe it was how they moved, since I'd scoured Google plenty of times to give her a perfect example, only to find a bunch of posed and lifeless jpgs. Spotting the Vibe was like artistic nudity versus porn: I might not be able to tag it with a definition, but I knew it when I saw it. And Ralph was sporting some classic Vibe.

I sprawled back in my seat, gazed at Ralph evenly over the expanse of his desk. Square Days was one day of discomfort and lost wages, but this new colorist was a dealbreaker. There had to be some way to get him to reconsider.

The Vibe intensified—flashing eyes and a tuck of the chin in this particular instance. Maybe that's an Italian thing, or maybe it's just Ralph. "When's your next client?" he asked—and even his voice was Vibing.

"Ten minutes—if that clock's right."

Ralph's mouth quirked into a naughty smile and his dark eyes twinkled. Apparently he saw the time limit as a challenge rather than a constraint. He rounded the desk and sank down between my knees. When I didn't reach for my belt buckle fast enough, he did it for me. "You've only got ten minutes," he told me. "So you'd better start convincing me."

I'd hoped to convince him by arguing logical points, not stroking his dick. But I couldn't really afford to land myself on his shit list.

I sat very still, just watching him, until he hesitated. I allowed the threat of my stillness to imply the possibility that maybe he'd crossed a line. Imagine, him mashing on an employee in an unwelcome advance. He'd be in deep shit. But before he could experience more than the preliminary spike of panic at the thought that he'd misjudged the situation, I grabbed him by the hair and jammed his face between my legs.

I enjoy being fantasy fodder. Who doesn't? Once in a while,

though, I worried I might take things too far. Sour the mood. Say or do something a little *too* nasty. But even without the Vibe to go by, what with Ralph's mouth grinding against my half-open fly, I could tell I was rocking his world by the way he grabbed at his crotch to reposition his sudden, startling boner.

Most people establish dominance by showboating and making lots of noise. I find my point hits home better when I make people strain to hear me, the epitome of calm. "Did I say you could touch yourself?" I murmured. Ralph's breath huffed in and I knew I'd hit the nerve on the first try. "Don't be stingy. Both hands on me. And your slutty mouth, too."

I'm a giver. It took some mental maneuvering to sit there and do nothing but raise my hips while he yanked down my jeans. It took even more restraint to censor myself from telling him his mouth felt pretty darn sweet. I'm chatty, both in and out of bed. Normally I'd be moaning and groaning and singing his praises. Maybe Ralph was just sick enough of brown-nosing that he didn't need any kudos in the sack. Or maybe he just knew he was good.

He lavished his whole focus on me, sucking, stroking, moaning with delight around the girth of my stiffening dick. And then he sucked even harder.

Yes. There it was, only moments later, the glimmer of release, beckoning me. In the background, the noise of the salon—phones, hairdryers, the rise and fall of conversation—only spurred me on. The Spanish Fly magic came from knowing we were one unlocked door away from company. Anyone could barge in: a customer, a health inspector, even Ralph's mom, looking to see if he could fit her in for a quick touch-up.

"Like that dick?" I asked. "Huh?"

He replied with something that sounded like *hohmiwa*, punctuated by the prod of my hard-on, and my hand floated toward his face to stroke his cheek. At the last second I caught myself and grabbed hold of his hair instead. I was so close now that I could say basically anything without killing my own buzz. And maybe the thought of putting arrogant Ralph in his place even made my grand finale loom that much larger. "That's it, take it. Take it deep. Don't even think about being selfish, don't you dare."

Gargling his approval, he went at me even harder. My tipping point was close—and Ralph's was too. He didn't want me to noodle him between the thighs, though. He wanted me to tickle the lurid corners of his brain. He wanted raunch. "Is that all you got?" I snarled—as if I wasn't ready to pop. "Come on, you dirty little slut. Don't hold back. Do it. Do it right."

He warbled around my dick and dropped one hand between his own legs, chafing the outside of his slacks with the heel of his palm.

"Did I say you could touch yourself, cocksucker?"

He hesitated—too much? No, didn't feel like it. He was definitely still in the groove. But he ignored that comment and kept on rubbing himself, so I let it slide. "Look at you, Mr. Big Shot, down on your knees. Just the way you like it. Slut." He lost his rhythm because I'd hit the magic button that had sent him into a frenzy.

No way could I last with Ralph gobbling my dick like that, so I let loose with whatever popped into my mind while I savored all my pent up frustrations coalescing into a delicious ache deep down inside. "You call that a blowjob? Huh? You call that a fucking blowjob?" So close. So incredibly close. Just a little more. "Suck...my...cock, *bitch*."

He yanked my balls and sucked so hard it hurt—and oh my God... "I'm coming," I gasped. He pulled off just in time for me to spurt while he jacked me. His grip was ruthless on my spit-slick shaft. It dredged up a load from the very bottom of my balls and sent it flying over his shoulder.

Once I'd shot myself dry, Ralph stood and let me collapse back in the chair. I breathed shakily. His eyes held mine with a gaze so intense I couldn't have looked away even if I'd wanted to. Not smiling, but somehow pleased. He loomed over me, looking down, while I sprawled there like a wrung-out towel. With one hand, he reached into his pants. A few quick strokes was all it took. He sighed. His gaze softened, and the hint of a smile teased the corners of his mouth. I felt myself smile in return. I may not always agree with Ralph, but once I get my rocks off, everyone's my best friend. I chalk it up to endorphins.

"You're always so much fun," he said as he reached out to stroke my cheek—or so I thought. I was too post-eruption logy to turn away in time before he brushed a smear of jiz across my lower lip. What the hell? The one time I'd dared come in his mouth, he'd read me the riot act. When he turned to grab a tissue off his desk, I knuckled his spooge away. Maybe I was generous with my charms, but that didn't mean I was a free-for-all.

Ralph shoved the tissue down his pants, swabbed it around, then pulled it out and lobbed into the wastebasket. With absolutely zero pretense that my actual haircutting skills had earned me some special consideration, he said, "Upping your salary would be the best way to keep your income steady once I bring on the colorist. But there'd be additional duties involved."

Seriously? I'm no prude, but a steady arrangement of play-for-pay definitely wouldn't end well for either of us.

When I responded with a raised eyebrow, he said, "Don't flatter yourself. You'd earn your keep as Senior Stylist."

Oh.

Senior Stylist, and me just a few years out of school? Hell, yeah! I totally hadn't seen *that* coming. If the Senior Stylist job went to anyone other than the owner, it was someone with a dozen years of experience or more. Someone like...Pilar.

My heart sank.

Ralph's phone rang. He answered, started buttering up one of his suppliers to see if there was any kind of special deal he could cut for his next big product order, while I tried to figure out how I could ever give Pilar that kind of news and still live with myself afterward.

If the Juniors all reported to me, they might learn a thing or two. I was great at keeping my clients happy—but so was Pilar. Plus, she had a decade's more experience behind the chair.

"Hold on," Ralph told his distributor. He put his hand over the receiver, looked at me with obvious annoyance, and said, "Well?"

"I'll think about it."

Apparently, he'd expected a peon like me to lap it up without question, and I hadn't scored any points with him by hesitating. He curled his lip, turned away, and resumed his conversation as if I'd already left the room. Or as if I was too insignificant to matter one way or the other. As I did a quick check for telltale cumstains while I tucked in my shirt, the thought occurred to me: *Who's the bitch now?*

CHAPTER 3

However convincingly I try to claim the Juniors are basically the same, of course, they're not. Matthew Espinosa was the dark-eyed beauty who'd claimed the absinthe gumdrop was yummy. He was also the one to shoot me a quick Vibe when a lull in his schedule coincided perfectly with a cancellation in mine. We forged out on an "errand" with no intention of going any farther than the parking lot behind the funeral home, where he tried to talk me into a quick hand-job. Since I'd just left all my gumption in Ralph's office for the cleaning lady to mop up, I said, "Nah, 'sokay."

He looked at me as if I'd just turned down a hand-job. Which...I had. "What-*ev*-er." He pulled out his phone. I did the same, and we both called up Tanngo, the latest and greatest gay hookup app. He left-swiped as fast as the photos scrolled by. "Too serious. Too fake. Ew—too much like my weird cousin Dominick."

"You're awfully picky for someone who just angled for a car handie."

"Yeah, but I *know* you. With strangers, you gotta be more careful. Never know what kind of creeps are out there."

I was pretty sure I did; I'd just allowed one to suck my dick.

I scrolled through the same list of guys—I was more liberal in my right-swiping than Matthew was—and went on to check my inbox for the possibility of an after-work date. I was only half-reading the messages, though. Mostly I was still processing what had just happened in Ralph's office. Not the sex part—I understood that just fine. But I didn't know what to think about the part where he dangled a promotion in front of me.

"Could you see me as a Senior Stylist?" I asked.

"Bitch, please."

I deleted a few dick pics and switched to eBay to see if any interesting vintage T-shirts had surfaced. "I dunno, I think I'd be good at it. My customers are always happy."

"Yeah, but that's customers. I've seen you try to explain something to another stylist—you don't have the patience. The minute someone can't keep up, you're all like, *What's the matter with you, son? Been dropped on your head?*"

If it meant a big raise, I could cultivate patience. Take a weekend workshop or an online course. Management skills, communication. I'm a quick learner. I'd adapt.

Problem was, the salon already had someone who was good at all of that, and more: Pilar.

Would our relationship weather the strain if I accepted the title that was rightfully hers? Theoretically it would, but with hurt and pride and money involved, quite possibly it wouldn't. Maybe if I didn't accept the offer, neither one of us would get the job. And wouldn't it make sense for at least one of us to not be broke?

We'd retreated back into the salon when reception buzzed to see if any of us were up for a walk-in. Pilar was in the midst of a consultation, one Junior was unrolling a perm and the other was leading his client from the shampoo bowls. Matthew was detailing his station while I restocked my product. He eyed me like he was willing to race me to the front, then started sweeping hair double-time. If I had to fight him for the walk-in, I would. Just because we'd spent our break together didn't mean he should expect any favors from me.

He caught me by the sleeve as I strode by. I half-turned, thinking I'd be perfectly willing to fight dirty if it came down to that. But judging by his smirk, the threat level was low. "Dibs on the hottie in gray," he whispered, and released my arm.

Not one walk-in greeted me in reception, but two. The hottie in gray was definitely a looker. Businessman. Suit. Nice head of chestnut hair in moderate need of a trim and some shaping. Thirty-something and a killer set of cheekbones. But the moment we locked eyes, my gaydar told me to pass. Not only was he straight as an arrow, but he wasn't particularly keen on having a gay guy pawing at his head.

My walk-in was indecisive and bored, and the consultation was tedious. She nixed everything I suggested, and eventually I had to admit defeat and pull out my old standby move. I offered to "frame her face." Basically, a trim. But when someone's impossible to please, it's best to do as little harm as possible. Meanwhile, one chair over, Pilar had transformed her client from a schleppy middle-aged dad to a dapper guy I'd totally swipe right.

No face-framing there. I felt guilty for even considering Ralph's offer.

In haircutting, there are only so many angles. Unfortunately, in life, the potential angles are infinite, and I needed to discover the angle that would leave the least amount of collateral damage behind. Once the last client was out the door and the Juniors were busy arguing about where they should meet up for drinks, I asked Pilar, "So who d'you think would make a better Senior Stylist. Me, or you?"

She indicated the campy junior stylists with a sweep of her eyes. "Those drama queens would probably stage a revolt if either of us took the reins. You seriously think you'd be able to mentor them like Ralph does?"

As Ralph made his end-of-the-day rounds to check in with his staff and distribute the tips, I saw how he made the Juniors wriggle and swoon. Pilar was right. Ralph was the one those kids all wanted to impress, not me. Maybe it would be best to forget about the whole Senior Stylist offer and let it drop. I planned on avoiding the topic, or at least stalling Ralph, until our eyes locked. No Vibe, not anymore. Instead, Ralph was wearing his Boss Face. Great.

I batted my eyelashes a few times, hoping he'd think I was still amped about the office beej, maybe sniffing around for a do-over. He glanced me up and down and I shifted my hips. When he answered with a knowing smile as he sorted through his stack of envelopes, I realized I'd better ease off the throttle. After all, I didn't want to end up sprawled across his desk. I was only trying to avoid the Senior Stylist conversation.

"Can you stick around for a few minutes?" he asked.

I wasn't sure if he wanted to talk business or pleasure after the rest of the stylists cleared out, but either way, it was a relief to tell him, "I rode in with Pilar."

His brow furrowed in annoyance as he glanced toward the parking lot to verify my car wasn't there, but before I needed to stifle myself from asking if he thought I was lying, one of the Juniors actually came to the rescue by shrieking, "Dibs!"

Everyone turned toward the front window, where a man had paused to press his face against the glass, shielding his eyes from the streetlights to peer into the darkened lobby. Intriguing. It was a black guy in a glitter-vinyl motorcycle jacket and painted-on jeans. He had a short retro mohawk—and heaven help me, I'm a total sucker for a mohawk. Not those lame fauxhawks that are just vaguely mohawk-shaped wedges done up with hair paste, but true 'hawks with buzzed sides, 'hawks you couldn't conveniently rinse out when you had a job interview or court date.

Dibs or no dibs... black mohawk dude was mine.

"I'll go tell him we're closed," a Junior grandly offered. Apparently *dibs* was not sacred, even among them.

Ralph was already striding toward the door. "Not necessary. And since you're all here..." he undid the lock, leaned out and invited mohawk dude in. My gut went topsy turvy. No reason it should have since the body language was all congenial and the dramatic anticipation was typical Ralph. But sometimes my gut keyed in on a telltale gesture before my brain caught up with it, and whatever subliminal flicker I'd just perceived, I knew something big was churning beneath the surface. Ralph settled his hand on the mohawk guy's low back and guided him toward the chairs where his rapt audience awaited. "Everyone, meet the newest member of the Luscious family—Red Turner."

"A colorist named Red," Matthew exclaimed—then he and two other Juniors intoned, "Ca-yuuu-ute."

Red took in the room in a single, cool glance. "Words are just words. They don't have any special power, but the intent behind them does." His voice was like silk. Hypnotic and low, and stunningly deliberate. "I've always been fascinated by color."

It was an intriguing reply to a ridiculous remark, an invitation to delve deep and forge a real connection—but the Juniors didn't do serious. One of them shot back flirtatiously, "Well, I know what *my* new favorite color is." The one who had dibs? It didn't much matter. "Who doesn't adore red?" another chimed in, while a third giggled like they'd both been phenomenally witty. Although Pilar was the only woman in the room, she was also the only stylist who didn't squeal like a giddy thirteen-year-old girl. She walked up to Red, offered him a normal handshake and said, "I'm Pilar. I look forward to working with you."

Red was so inscrutable, it was impossible to say if he was impressed by Pilar's restraint, or threatened by it. Her introduction had left me as the only one in the room who hadn't yet said anything, and I knew I'd need to choose my first words carefully. I wasn't about to suck up to the guy like I was desperate, and yet I really did want to convey my interest. I was just about to tell him it was a *pleasure* to meet him when Ralph noticed he was still carrying my tip envelopes and handed them over to me.

Unprepared for the weight, I grabbed wrong, which caused the envelopes to slip through my fingers. One hit the floor with a metallic clatter of change that rang through the closed salon. The Juniors went wild, and one sang out the "jingle jangle jingle" part of some ancient country and western song. Another fell into the dance that went with it, slapping a hairbrush against his ass like a tambourine.

And Red? A flicker of pity flashed across his face. Maybe. Or maybe I'd only imagined it.

I had better things to do than worry about the dismal first impression I'd made. The night was balmy, the company convivial, and a half-dozen Limoncello Collinses had left a taste in my mouth like delightfully boozy lemon drops. The sidewalk dipped when I slunk out of the cab, though not too steeply. The cabbie waited until I let myself in. He could've driven off—but I truly was a spectacular tipper.

As nights out go, it was pleasant. Not profound. Not earth-shattering. Not a night I'd find myself reminiscing about in years to come. But I'd run into an old pal from a gym where I'd done a two-week trial membership. He was free, I was free, and a good time was had by all.

The ring of my land line was audible from the hall as I attempted to finesse my key into my lock. It wasn't my gym buddy wishing me a good night, not unless he'd suddenly developed a bunch of sentimental feelings toward me that were entirely absent while we were picking up splinters on the hardwood floor of his front hall. It was too late for Pilar, who turns in shortly after she browbeats her kid into bed. And Ralph stopped calling after the first time he'd landed me in the sack.

Maybe it's Red.

No, I hadn't given him my number—and, in fact, he didn't even know my legal name. Although...a resourceful enough guy can figure these things out. Just as I wondered what sort of line he'd lead in with, my machine beeped and a familiar voice said, "Okay, I know it's late...."

My mother's voice. Dang it.

Not a hot black mohawk guy, not at all.

Maxine asked if I wanted to try a new Italian place for dinner next weekend, then added, "...and before I forget—Dumpling tore through another collar, so I'm going to see if there's anything more dog-proof than the last four collars he ate. You know that new pet warehouse in Schaumburg? It's huge. I just thought I'd check and see if you needed anything for your aquarium." I stared at the blinking green light and wondered if she could sense me standing there too tipsy to talk, or if she thought I was still out getting spit-polished. "I'm heading to bed myself. Email me if you think of anything. Good ni-ight."

A little singsong, but not her traditional full-on "good ni-ight Lit-tle Peanut" that she presumed would mortify me if it were ever paraded out in front of a fuck-buddy. Not that I'd actually care, but I did appreciate the fact that Maxine respected me enough to be discreet. And also, that she was offering to bankroll my aquarium. No one walks into a pet store, looks at the fish and thinks, "I know, I'll pick up this massive stinking timesuck money pit—it'll be fantastic." But unless you're a true fish-lover, that's what it amounts to. Still, I supposed it did me good to have something to come home for, aside from a fresh change of clothes.

No doubt there was some chemical, some food, some gadget the tank was in need of. It was always running out of something. I grabbed a hot wing from the fridge and ate it cold as I strolled in and headed for the massive 120-gallon aquarium wall that was the focus of the room. Between the filters and the plants, there was plenty of movement in the water even when the fish were hanging out in the scenery. That's probably why I didn't notice right away. No, I was pawing through the cabinet beneath, one-handed and gnawing on a drummy, overjoyed at the prospect of my mother picking up the tab. Filters don't grow on trees—well, maybe the carbon part does—and my big ol' tank gooped them up faster than you can say "slimeball." Only when I glanced at the filter in question did I notice my keyhole cichlids were missing. Which was impossible, since they were the biggest critters in the tank and the top of the food chain.

And then I looked up.

Even though I knew damn well what I was seeing, my devastation took a long moment to sink in. I kept thinking it was impossible, just impossible. Clearly, though, the worst possible scenario had indeed come to pass. My four keyholes had formed a cloudy-eyed flotilla at the top, peppered here and there with the iridescent bodies of the smaller cichlids. And bumping up against the foamy corner of the tank, rocking in the jet of the filtration system, was the massive plecostomus I'd had since I was twelve.

His name was Iggy.

Once I'd swallowed down the limoncello-tinged hot wing that kept trying to creep back up my throat, I pressed my forehead against the glass and realized the tank was hot to the touch. That would explain why the translucent ghost shrimp had gone opaque, cooked in their own juices.

I pulled my vodka out of the freezer and drank a few slugs from the bottle while I sat cross-legged on the floor and gazed upon my tank of death to try and make sense of what had happened. The heater was on its normal settings, so that ruled out the possibility of the last guy I'd brought home monkeying with the equipment. Simply a malfunction. No one to blame, or at least, not him. Maybe if I'd been home, I would have noticed the first fish floating up to the surface in time to save the others. Then again, why would I? I only paid attention to the tank when it was time for food or cleaning.

The room was swaying pretty well by the time I scooped everyone out. I would have flushed them, but since I was worried Iggy would clog the toilet, instead I gave them all a back alley funeral courtesy of the dumpster, then came inside and shut down all the filters and jets. Given how late it was, how much I'd had to drink, and how many times I'd shot my load that day, you'd think I would pass out the second my head hit the pillow. I didn't, though.

Funny how quiet a house can be without the hum of an aquarium to keep you company.

CHAPTER 4

Luckily Pilar didn't mind picking me up again. I'd had so much to drink the night before, I might not have passed a breathalyzer. And my headache was so ruthless, I answered with distracted grunts while she made guesses as to where the new colorist would be stationed, and how many clients he'd likely see each day, and whether she should try to score some more specialized training. Halfway to work, when it was clear I was incapable of holding up my end of the conversation, Pilar took pity on me and stopped trying. But the Juniors didn't know I was in no mood for banter. Three of them were lingering in the parking lot that morning, clustered by Matthew's Miata. The conversation looked saucy. Lots of big gestures and campy faces.

It's a love-hate relationship between me and the junior stylists. Sometimes it's fun to listen to them out-snark each other, and sometimes they grate on me. That morning, I really wasn't in the mood. Even so, I couldn't just breeze by them without an acknowledgement. Playing well with others is part of surviving this cold, cruel world.

When I slowed and made eye contact as if I was interested in their conversation, Matthew shifted to allow me access to the inner circle. "We were just sizing up the fresh meat," he told me. "I say Red Turner likes his men pretty and submissive."

"Power bottom," another Junior said.

"Now, y'all need to understand the black man," the last Junior declared. Presumably, he did. Trevor Sims was at least half black, though I wasn't sure which of his parents was which since the only photos he kept around his station were of Gwen Stefani. One thing I did know—he had some badass dreads and he might sound ghetto when he was trying to prove a point, but he'd grown up on the safe suburban lanes of Schaumburg, not the projects of Cabrini Green. "Ain't no way he let a white boy get all up in his bidness."

Did he seriously just say that? For the sake of diplomacy I nodded as if he had a point. Normally I'd be quelling the urge to laugh in his face…but with the image of Iggy's corpse thunking into the dumpster haunting me, I wasn't feeling particularly jocular.

"Ex-cuse me," Matthew sang out with exaggerated Latino flair. "But everybody knows chocolate goes best with caramel." Ugh…says the guy who claimed the absinthe jellies were delish. He turned to me and asked, "What's about you, Crash? Hoping that yummy piece o' man's got a taste for some vanilla?"

I wasn't about to confide that Red rocked my world just by walking into the salon. Knowing when to keep your mouth shut is another good way to stay tactful. But when I didn't dignify the remark with an answer, Trevor said, "You tryin' to play it cool, but we all seen that tattoo on your chest. Everybody knows you like the dark meat."

Matthew bumped me with his hip. "C'mon, son, dish. Dud, or stud?"

It was tempting to school them about the significance of my ink. The black Virgin on my chest was a tribute to someone I'd lost way too early. I could've sworn I'd already told them, though—and the meaning probably blinked right out of their empty heads. So instead, with lofty indifference, I said, "I haven't decided."

That proclamation set them all to ooh-ing. What can I say? Even when I'm hungover, I know how to play to my audience.

Ralph spent the morning marching Red around the salon and giving him the VIP treatment. Today our new colorist was dressed more plainly in black T-shirt, black jeans, studded belt. The look was understated punk, and he rocked the subtlety perfectly. I watched the Juniors checking him out with unabashed interest. Meanwhile, Matthew's stupid "vanilla" remark had me thinking of all the Juniors in various flavors of mocha, caramel and buttercream.

Lameness. In this day and age, was race even a thing anymore? Not unless Matthew or Trevor needed to play up their imaginary street cred. We all spoke the same language, lived in the same neighborhood and peed in the same urinals. All of us were twenty-something gay Chicago stylists. If that hyperspecific demographic didn't outshine something as trivial as skin color, I don't know what did.

And besides, I might be white, but I'm most definitely not vanilla.

Red got himself situated in time for the steady stream of customers Ralph had packed into his afternoon schedule. As far as I could tell, he didn't lead in with any of the banal chitchat we all resorted to: Anything exciting going on today? Got any kids? How about that weather (or news item, or sports team)? In fact, once they'd sealed the deal on which color he'd be conjuring on their heads, it looked as if Red hardly spoke to the client at all. Maybe he didn't need to. After I saw the stunning champagne blonde leave the shop veritably sparkling, I suspected his work was enough to speak for itself.

I wasn't the only stylist keeping one eye on him, and I'm not just talking about the sharp intake of breath from a Junior when Red bent over to pick up a dropped foil. Pilar eased close while she was sweeping and murmured, "He writes everything down in a little notebook. Meticulously. And he measures everything too."

Seriously? I knew my proportions well enough to eyeball my mixtures. I'd always thought measuring that way saved a lot of wasted product and unnecessary cleanup, but now it made me feel as if I'd been cutting corners. Even if I was the only one who could see those corners, it still might explain why Red was at the top of the pack while I fell somewhere in the middle. And being offered promotions for being fun in the sack didn't count.

Pilar went up front to pick out a conditioning mask, leaving her client to preen a few minutes in silence. I was busy taking a disappointing inventory of my station (and my life) when the client reached over, tugged on my retro wallet chain and asked me in a loud whisper, "So Pilar can't do my color anymore? I have to go to that new guy instead?"

She seemed distressed. "Right," I said. "The colorist."

"But I want Pilar. She's been doing my hair for three years."

And now the pushback was about to begin. Stupid Ralph. And now the new guy would bear the brunt of the resistance. "It's his specialty."

The client leaned in and loud-whispered, "Maybe with black hair." I then took a good look at her. How could someone so normal say something so asinine? My surprise must have registered in my expression, because she backpedaled with, "I mean African American."

Here's the thing about black people's hair. It *is* different from Caucasian hair. It's drier and coarser and takes forever to grow, and working with ethnic hair is a skill most white people don't bother to cultivate. "We don't need to be worrying about black folks touching our hair—it's the other way around. Do you have any idea the amount of skill and training it takes to become an ACI specialist? There's probably a thousand stylists in this city alone—but there's only a thousand certified specialists in the entire freaking country. He's dumped a bunch of time, money and effort into his training, and he's passed a bitch of an exam that really separates the boys from the men. He's the guy people come to when they've seriously messed up their hair. Covering that gray? I think he can manage."

I could have kept going and told her that no hair color in the world would stop her from looking like a wrinkled old bag, but I restrained myself. Having it out with a client in the middle of a salon might be cathartic, but it wouldn't exactly bolster my reputation. It took a while, but eventually my disgust dwindled down to annoyance, and finally a vague miffed feeling that gave way to thoughts of where I wanted to eat dinner. I'd forgotten all about it by the time I climbed into Pilar's car and buckled myself in.

She drove like she was wearing a lead boot on a concrete foot. For all I knew, maybe she had somewhere to be and she just wanted to get home. Except the way she had her face all scrunched up—emanating waves of pissiness—told me a different story. She pulled up in front of my house with a screech. I was about to ask what the damage was, but there was enough good history between us that instead, I asked, "Do you want to come up?"

She chewed on her reply for a while, then finally said, "What the hell, Crash?"

"Hard to say. Be more specific."

"Where do you get off turning my clients against me?"

"Who, the frowny racist?"

"Julia. Her name is Julia, and she comes in like clockwork, every six weeks. She tips decent and she's referred half a dozen of her friends to me."

"Which is why I didn't read her the riot act, like she deserved. Look, until we can convince Ralph to start giving the straightforward color jobs back to us, Red's going to be the one handling her color. It's either that, or she switches salons entirely because she can't handle being touched by a black man."

I expected Pilar to stick up for her client—all that customer loyalty would have bought that nasty woman understanding she didn't deserve—but instead Pilar narrowed her eyes and said, "Are you doing him?"

"Red? As if! I haven't said ten words to the guy. He hasn't so much as glanced in my direction. Hell, I can't even tell if he's gay."

"Of course he is." If you've spent any time at all in the industry, you know that the straight male hairdressers can be confusingly nelly, so before I could protest, she added, "He's got a little triangle tattoo on the inside of his wrist."

"And I've never once seen him Vibe? After being in the same shop with him all week? Preposterous."

"My God. It really is that easy for you to get laid." Pilar seemed like she was calming down. She's not grudgy, which is yet another thing I dig about her.

"Look," I said, "call your client, offer her a free conditioning mask on her next visit and tell her I'm an asshole. I don't give a shit. I've been called worse. I'll even spring for the mask."

"The sixty-nine cent mask."

We both knew the value part of the deal was a free pass to trash-talk me for the purpose of retaining her client.

I suspected she'd even take me up on it.

The more I thought about Pilar speculating about Red and me scoring, the more it bugged the crap out of me. Not because it was presumptuous, but because it hadn't happened. All week, I'd been playing it cool. But there's playing it cool, and there's ridiculous.

That man needed to take notice.

The next day, I strapped on my sexiest buckled combat boots and spiked my hair to perfection. Judging by the lingering looks I received from the customers, the Juniors, and even the UPS guy, my efforts had not been in vain. Would my arches be killing me by the end of the day? Likely. But hopefully I'd have my feet up soon enough...and not on a footstool, either.

Salons are a funhouse of mirrors, so all day long, chances presented themselves for me to catch Red's eye. Unfortunately, nothing panned out. I never caught him looking at me, or anyone else, for that matter. Every time I glimpsed him, he was either working on a customer or jotting something in his little notebook.

In other words, working.

Who could blame him? Luscious might be same-old, same-old to me, but Red was the new guy. It must have been intimidating. He couldn't afford to slack off—the position had been created specifically for him, so he'd have to prove his worth. He appeared to be earning his keep. I couldn't recall when I'd last seen someone as profoundly focused, and eventually I resigned myself to the fact that trying to flirt with him in the salon mirrors would get me absolutely nowhere.

Catching his eye at work turned out to be such an exercise in futility, by the end of the day I actually got distracted by my aching feet and forgot about my grand scheme to get down his pants. I was in the stock room topping off my home supplies when a shadow fell across the rack of toners, and I realized I wasn't alone. No mirrors—but the silhouette of a mohawk was a dead giveaway.

I glanced over my shoulder and found my quarry paused in the doorway. "C'mon in." I gestured to the spot directly beside me. "I won't bite...unless you dig that kind of thing."

I normally get one of three responses to an invitation like that. A giggle, an eye-roll, or on a good night, some flirty banter in return. What I got from Red was a slightly raised eyebrow.

"A non-answer just leaves it all to my imagination," I warned him.

He came in, leaving a generous amount of space between us, and began checking the expiration dates of the semi-permanent jewel tone dyes. "Fresh product," he said.

I ogled the delicious curve of his ass. "I'll say."

That earned me a tolerant headshake. It was a step up from the eyebrow.

"It's late," I grabbed a tub of lightener in one hand and developer in the other, "so whaddaya say we blow this pop stand...."

Red snapped around, wide-eyed, and I considered how I wanted to finish that thought. But before I could add a suitable innuendo, he plucked the developer from my hand. "What are you doing?"

"Trying to get to know you better."

He brandished the bottle. "With this."

"Touching up my...." Oh damn. I'd grabbed the 40-volume developer instead of the 20. Anyone who's had a 40 directly against their scalp knows it stings like a bitch.

Red handed me the correct developer and walked away without another word.

Sonofabitch. Why bother with sexy combat boots if I was going to make such a rookie mistake in front of him? Awesome footwear can only go so far in making someone look good.

I'd been hoping to make an impression that day, and I had.

A lame one.

CHAPTER 5

As if the week wasn't challenging enough, Square Days came around all too soon.

I'm not what you'd call a morning person. Working nights and weekends? Fine. It came with the job. Prying me out of bed before ten on a Saturday, however, was nothing short of sacrilege. Not that I'd curtailed my Friday night in anticipation or anything, but I was well within my rights to complain. I hit the snooze button three times before I managed to get myself together and head off to face the music.

The oompah music.

Beneath all the fancy boutiques, Lincoln Square is built on a German foundation—and on Square Days, kraut flies.

I wouldn't have thought I'd have the stomach for food quite so soon in the recovery process, but there's something about the aroma of seared flesh that beckons to me, hangover or no hangover. It was barely eleven, but Schnitzelhaus already had an outdoor grill cranked up to decimation levels. Even two blocks away, it made me salivate like crazy. Too bad there wasn't enough time to grab a bratwurst. Thanks to the street fest, our lot was stuffed to the gills and I'd had to park half a mile away.

Even still, I got there before Pilar. I'm guessing she'd needed to walk too. And the poor thing wasn't exactly a good sprinter. "Well,

what's everyone waiting for?" Ralph called into the darkened salon.
The Juniors were tittering together in the corner. I ambled toward
the meeting room and joined the new colorist where he sat at the
round table, hands folded, the picture of poise in a natty fedora and
shades. Shit. Did a look exist that he *couldn't* pull off?

The Juniors ignored him. They were busy ooh-ing and aah-ing
over the big Schnitzelhaus box. "Fresh meat," Trevor said.

"Sausage fest," Matthew squeed. He batted his eyelashes at Ralph
and said, "Is all that delicious meat for us?"

Ralph made a gesture of subtle, careless grandiosity. "Help
yourself."

Matthew opened the box, and his face fell. Briefly, but I saw it.
Poor kid was cursed with a big-eyed open book of a face. If he was
lucky, someday he'd outgrow it.

"Potato pancakes," Ralph said.

"No meat?" Matthew was aiming for cute, but mostly he sounded
disappointed.

Ralph broke off the corner of a potato pancake and popped it
into his mouth. "Didn't I mention? I'm leaning vegetarian."

"Ooh, good Karma," Matthew said.

"Girl, whatchoo know 'bout Karma?" Trevor catcalled.

"What's there to know? What goes around comes around."

"Puh-lease," Trevor said." You probably think you're reincarnated,
too. You worried you gonna eat your dead grandma by accident if
you have yourself a burger?"

Ralph stemmed off the ridiculous argument with a wag of his
finger. "Now, boys. You know how tedious I find politics and religion."
He held out an open box. "Why don't you take the inaugural pancake,
Matthew, and tell us all what you think."

Matthew plucked a fritter from the box with his pinkie extended, took a bite, and declared it *FA-bulous*. Then again, he probably
would've said the same thing if he was chomping on a big mouthful
of the box.

I crammed one in my mouth. It was greasy, bland and cold.

Ralph extended the box toward Red and gave him a look—one
that I knew all too well. Chin tucked, eyes wide, gaze gone smoldering.

Ralph's hungriest Vibe.

"No thank you," Red said.

Ralph cocked an eyebrow. "But I bought them especially for you."

"I'll save mine for later."

In the moment of uneasy silence that followed the outright re-fusal of Ralph Maldonado's largesse, the alley door banged open and Pilar limped in, red-faced and wheezing. "I had to park like a mile away," she panted.

Ralph scowled. "And now that Ms. Rocha has finally graced us with her presence, I can walk us through the day's game plan."

The shift was off to a stellar beginning.

Since it was Square Days, we had no regular bookings. The plan was to woo potential customers with cheesy ploys like coupons, live demos and a raffle. Everyone took their assignments with a fair amount of grumbling and eye-rolling because historically, Square Day tips were sucky to nonexistent, and even the Juniors, fresh out of cosmetology school, felt they were above cutting hair on the street like a bunch of performing chimps. The only employees not expect-ed to shill on the sidewalk were the receptionists, who'd hopefully be busy cramming the books with scads of new customers. The rest of us got our time divvied up between handling walk-ins and pimping out the salon to anyone who'd listen.

"Before you head out, people...." Ralph turned and opened a cab-inet with deliberate casualness, and pulled out a stack of black gar-ments. "This year, we're doing uniforms."

The word hung in the air as every last one of us stared in horror. If I wanted to wear a uniform, I'd fill out an application at Burger Barn, but somehow I managed to choke back my indignation. I knew better than to call out the alpha dog in front of his pack. I'd just have to figure out how to punish him later...in a way that didn't give him a chubby.

He handed out the beauty smocks. Black on black, with piping Ralph insisted was "ocean," though normal people would call it tur-quoise. He must've been feeling generous toward me since he'd had the name *Crash* embroidered over the heart, and not *Curtis*, the name on my birth certificate.

He got to the bottom of the pile and gave the last one to Pilar. Instead of the shirt he'd given everyone else on the team, he handed her a slip of fabric with dangling ties. An apron. "They didn't have your size," he said. With evident satisfaction.

Fucking hell. Like her day wasn't shitty enough.

Ralph left us to go coach the receptionists before anyone said anything they regretted. The Juniors rallied, playfully teasing one another as they wriggled into their new smocks. I steered Pilar aside and said, "You okay?"

"Fine."

Clearly not. But there was nothing either of us could do about it.

I trooped out to the street to start pushing raffle tickets while Ralph did a demo on a hair model. Grudgingly, I had to admit that it did make sense for the stylists to be in uniform so we didn't come off as primped-up gay panhandlers. The apron thing was still pissing me off, though. Even if the ocean-piped smocks didn't run big, he could've done Pilar's in plain black. I'm sure it had occurred to him. The man's always thinking.

The raffle was yet another genius way Ralph could make himself look munificent while scoring the better part of the deal. For a mere dollar, some lucky bastard might win a wash, cut and style, a seventy-dollar value. All they had to do was provide an email address to be notified if they'd won...and arrive precisely at six o'clock to collect.

The last two Square Days I'd worked, neither of the winners had even shown. Ralph raked in a few hundred bucks selling tickets, and his email marketing list grew that much fatter.

I watched him work the crowd as he primped his model's new cut. She looked fabulous—but she was one of those hot chicks who'd look fabulous in most anything. Not that I'd ever impugn Ralph's cutting skills. I just knew his business acumen weighted the equation in his favor.

As I watched Ralph and pondered how I might make lemonade out of Square Day lemons, I felt a tug at my smock. An old woman in a babushka was squinting at my embroidered name. She asked with the lilt of an accent I couldn't place, "He can really charge *seventy* dollars for a haircut?"

"He can and he does. Feeling lucky?" I flashed a fan of lottery tick-ets. "Maybe it's your day to win a new 'do." When her brow creased in doubt, I added, "Then you'll have a fun story to tell all your friends about winning an outrageously priced haircut."

Absurdity. Whimsy. Funny how I keyed in on those things to appeal to her since my own life had been sorely lacking them. "I would pay a dollar for that," she decided, then started rifling through her ancient naugehyde purse. She searched. And searched. I started to think it would be easier to simply give her one, but people can feel slighted if they think you're acting out of pity, so I did my best to tune out the Juniors hawking their tickets with campy, overdone enthusiasm poorly masking their disdain for Square Days, and I waited. She found some change and began counting. Dimes. Nickels. Pennies. Shit, what if she didn't even have a dollar to her name, what then? I rued the last time I'd lobbed my shrapnel into the "take a penny, leave a penny" tray at the deli. I was trying to figure out how to offer her a discount when she smiled triumphantly and pulled out a final quarter. "I try to save these for laundry," she confided.

I bit my tongue and smiled. "Here you go. Fill it out and put it in the hopper. We'll shoot you a text if you win."

"A what?"

"A text message."

She looked puzzled.

"To your phone."

"On my answering machine?"

"Your cell phone." I turned over a ticket and showed the part she'd need to fill out. "Name, email, cell. That way we can let you know with-out you having to go all the way back home, check your messages, and come back to get your haircut."

"I have no cell phone."

Then her email wouldn't be much use either. "Here, look, let me just give you your money back, and we can—"

"Absolutely not." Her eyes sparkled and she shot me a knowing grin, which revealed half her teeth were gray. "This is the winning ticket."

"Thing is, we draw them just before six, and if you don't text back a confirmation—"

"I will be here when you draw it."

Through the crowd, Pilar shot me a curious look, wondering what I could possibly have to argue about with a raggedy old lady. I decided it was most expedient to just take the damn dollar. "Suit yourself, sweetheart. Good luck."

CHAPTER 6

As the day progressed, the previous night's booze burned off and my head eventually cleared before it was my turn to man the chair on the sidewalk. Ralph plucked a high school girl out of the crowd for my demo. While she wasn't as drop-dead gorgeous as his model, her sun-kissed hair was thick and unprocessed. The whole idea of roping someone in off the sidewalk and styling them in front of a milling audience is unpalatable at best. Not only was it so chilly out it was difficult to hold my shears, but there's no privacy to do a real consultation. So when my demo client said she didn't know what she wanted—and asked me if I thought she should go short—I used all the charm I could muster to coax her into something that basically amounted to a trim.

"You don't have to sacrifice length to add texture," I said sagely. "Some angle cut layers would give you terrific movement." She was just about sold. I teased a strand of hair from her temple with my pinkie and checked the length, then looked deep into her eyes and said, "It'll really frame your face."

Her breath caught. Her eyes went wide. Her expression shifted into a Vibe that many a horny young quarterback would love to receive. "Okay. If that's what you think."

"Don't worry, kiddo. You're in good hands."

My prom queen was happy with her trim, and as the afternoon

progressed, the Juniors made a good show of pruning split ends and cleaning up fringe. I managed to slip away to charm a few wieners out of the guy working the Schnitzelhaus outdoor grill, and when I got back, I saw Pilar had emerged from her inside shift to man the demo chair. A black cloud of pissed-offedness hung over her, maybe from the shitty apron she'd been forced to wear, or maybe her proximity to the man who'd done the forcing.

Whatever the cause, she was in no frame of mind to cut hair. That was for damn sure.

Ralph scanned the crowd and beckoned to one of the women who'd been hoping for a free cut. My heart sank as his choice stepped onto the sidewalk. The woman looked like she hadn't smiled anytime during the last decade, and her hair was baby-fine and wisp thin. The type of hair you really needed to work at, even under ideal conditions. But outside in the wind with a mob of people-watching? Brutal.

Annoyance flickered across Pilar's face, but if you didn't know her, it just looked like she was squinting against the wind. She introduced herself to her client and their consult was all professionalism. No shampoo, not for the demos, just spray bottles. Pilar spritz-dampened the hair and started twisting up her sections. All the while, Ralph kept one eye on her while he worked the crowd, doling out promo postcards. He was not nearly as good at Pilar at schooling his expression. His sick glee was evident.

"So, do you have kids?" Pilar asked. Which earned her an earful about how the woman's daughter was wasting all her time texting when she should've been doing her homework. Since Pilar could commiserate, they were able to form a tenuous bond. It cost her, though. Her son was the light of her life, and to bitch about his video gaming to some stranger just for the sake of seeming empathetic was as much of a downer as wearing a two-bit apron and cutting hair on the damn sidewalk.

Did I believe in karma? Not the way some folks do, with a giant cosmic scorecard keeping track of all our best and worst moments. But I have noticed it's when you're at your most vulnerable that life tends to bite you in the ass. Despite everything that was stacked against it, Pilar's cut was going well until the wind picked up a strand of cut hair on the sidewalk and trailed it through the client's direct line of sight. When the woman saw it, she completely lost her shit.

"How much hair are you taking off? I told you I wanted shoulder length. That's at least three inches, you stupid cow!"

Pilar went still, eyes bulging. Then without a word, she yanked off her horrible black apron, threw it on the sidewalk and marched back into the salon. The crowd shifted uncomfortably and the folks around the perimeter started to bail. Me, I kept my eye on Ralph. He was the owner, and it was his call. Either he'd need to appease the odious bitch or tell her to go fuck herself. And I was curious how he'd handle the situation.

But the spineless weasel did neither. With a careless flick of the hand, he said, "One of you finish the cut," then turned back to the potential customer he'd been wooing as if nothing had just happened, which left Matthew, Red and me to sort out the debacle ourselves.

One thing I knew—I'd be damned if I gave that woman a haircut. She didn't deserve it. Matthew turned his most beseeching big-eyed gaze to me and mouthed the word *please*. He wasn't exactly delivering it with a Vibe, but there was definitely the implicit promise that if I handled this ugly situation so he didn't have to, he'd make it *very* worth my while. Red regarded me too, with nothing but a stony silence.

"I'm going after Pilar," I said.

Matthew looked like he might burst into tears.

Red nodded once, almost a shrug. "Then I'll finish the client."

Oh, la-di-da. Not only was he the polar opposite of melodramatic, but he actually enjoyed rubbing his calm composure in my face. Well, I wasn't about to give him the satisfaction of gawking at how smoothly he could handle a problem customer. I went off in search of my friend without a backward glance.

She'd blockaded herself in the storage room. It must've been an office in a previous life, given that it locked from the inside. We all knew Ralph had the key, but I understood that the gesture was symbolic, especially since Ralph showed no signs of running after her. I tapped on the door and said, "It's me."

"Go away."

"Not gonna happen. So either you let me in or we yell this conversation through the door. You pick."

The lock clicked open. I let myself in.

The narrow storeroom houses all the obsolete equipment Ralph couldn't quite bring himself to part with. It's crammed with shelves of old gear, half-used product and a styling chair with a defective hydraulic pump. Pilar perched on the seat and knuckled away angry tears while I tried to find somewhere to lean without getting a curling iron up my ass. "You're the most talented, hard-working stylist I know," I said.

I was attempting to make her feel better, but for some reason, that statement just turned up the waterworks. Her face scrunched as if she could will the tears to stop flowing.

"It's true," I said. "You cut circles around everybody else."

"And you know what? It doesn't fucking matter."

"Yeah, it matters."

"I hate it here, but where else can I go? Even if I dipped into Nick's college fund, I wouldn't have the kind of money it takes to open my own shop. I definitely don't have the energy to run it. And Ralph will make sure I can't go anywhere else."

"How's he gonna stop you?"

"A few months ago I put out some feelers about moving on, and get this: he said if he couldn't have me, then no one could. That's practically a guarantee that if I try to leave he'll slag me off to anyone who'll listen. You know how charming he can be, and people in the industry don't look any farther than that. Ralph's word is gold. If he spreads it around that I'm the problem, then forget it. My career is done."

"That's crazy. Your clients love you. Someone'll give you a chance."

"Oh yeah? Remember Gail? She used to book out three months in advance. She thought the same thing, but no one would hire her—no one would even rent her a station—and now she's working at ClipLand." I shuddered. I'd turn tricks under the viaduct before I donned an orange-checked ClipLand smock. "Anyone who crosses Ralph Maldonado might as well find a whole new line of work."

"There's no way his opinion carries that much weight. You know what? Fuck Ralph."

"Easy for you to say." She laughed bitterly. "That's all you need to do to get him on your side."

I stopped. I took a breath. And I counted to ten. Anyone else, I would've ripped 'em a new one, but not Pilar. Especially not after the humiliation she'd just endured. "Let's not go there," I said softly.

"I guess it's not like you can turn him down. You'd end up sweeping hair all day."

"I am perfectly fine. And since when is my private sex life the topic of this conversation?"

"Oh, come on. I know you fucked each other last night. You drove yourself to work, and he's been prancing around with that disgusting just-got-laid swagger of his."

"You don't know shit. I slept in. And that's just the way Ralph walks."

"Gimme a break. Contrary to popular belief, I'm not stupid." She heaved herself up and turned toward the door. "I'm outta here. If Ralph has any problem with it, he can keep my day's tips." Which wouldn't even buy enough pizza to feed her and her kid, and both of us knew it.

Square Days was winding down anyhow. Over by the chairs, Matthew and Trevor were finishing up the final walk-ins, and the crowd out front had thinned as the spectators wandered off in search of dinner or music or copious German beer. On first glance, I thought Red had ended up with yet another demo cut, but then I realized he was putting the finishing touches on the baby-haired harpy. I hardly recognized her with her sassy, piecey crop. I eased up to Matthew and said, "All that fuss and she ends up going short-short?"

"It was off the hook," he whispered dramatically. "Red put the whammy on her."

"Really."

"Big time. Before he started to cut, he crouched down in front of her, looked her in the eye and said something, and she went all still and quiet. I think she's hypnotized."

More likely the woman had a pathological aversion to heavy people.

I was more than ready for quitting time when Ralph ambled over. Was he post-fuck swaggering? Hard to say. He leaned in and murmured, "The fun never ends, does it? Why don't you draw our big winner so we can pack it up and call it a day."

The kitty was jammed with raffle tickets—if nothing else, Ralph's email list would get a big boost. I shoved my hand down deep in the box and stirred it all around, grabbed a ticket, pulled, and handed it to Ralph. He squinted down at it. "I can't read this, pull another."

"Lemme see." I had no idea why I even cared. When Ralph hesitated, I whispered, "You can't let it look like you're tossing one aside. People are really invested in the illusion that the world is fair."

He handed me the ticket. In stilted, old-fashioned printing, it read *Olga Kylsey*.

"Pick another one," Ralph told me. "There's no email. It's disqualified."

"What difference does it make?" I had no idea how to pronounce the surname, but I'd lay a wager on the fact that not many folks in the crowd could lay claim to that first name. "Olga?" I called out. "Is there an Olga in the house?"

"Fine. Text her and get it over with so we wrap this all up."

A phone number was listed—one that I strongly suspected was a landline—but the text wasn't necessary. My little old lady in her babushka was already picking her way through the thinning crowd, gray teeth bared in a triumphant smile.

CHAPTER 7

Ralph leaned in to whisper in my ear. To the sparse crowd, it would look like a convivial chat. But I knew him well enough to pick up on his seething resentment when he said, "Is this some kind of joke?"

"You watched me draw the ticket. What are you saying, I cheated?" I'd be damned if I let Ralph touch that weird little old lady. "I sold her the ticket, I'll stay and do the cut."

There was no pleasing Ralph one way or the other. Maybe my offer to stay late had deprived him of something to bitch about, who knows? He should be grateful—he'd be able to go have an actual Saturday night—but I knew better than to expect gratitude from the likes of him. In a spirit of one-upmanship, I acted as if there was nothing I'd rather do than stay late for no pay on a weekend, and ushered Olga into the salon. "What did I tell you?" I said to her. "That'll be the most interesting dollar you've ever spent."

Call me contrary, but because everyone was so busy running around getting ready to fly, I took sadistic pleasure in taking my time. And my customer? It felt like she was in on the joke.

I showed her to my station, turned up all the lights that had been dimmed for the night, and offered her a glass of wine. She wouldn't have been more shocked if I'd proffered a line of coke. "Don't worry, I'm not trying to get you wasted. But all the fancy ladies go for the wine. Sometimes before noon."

"With a haircut, they give you wine?"

"Or infused water. Or tea. But hell, if it were me, I'd take the wine."

Her eyes sparkled. "Then wine it is."

Normally the receptionists handled the beverages, but Luscious was a ghost town now that Square Days had drawn to a close. When I turned toward the fridge where a passable chardonnay was chilling, a figure emerged from the shadows, startling me so bad I nearly dropped my comb. "I'll handle the wine," Red said. "You do the consult."

"You don't need to stay late," I said.

"I don't need to, I want to."

"Why? Trying to prove something? I'm not the one you need to impress."

"No. You're not." He said this as if it was the most obvious thing in the word, which made me feel like a complete ass for bringing it up.

Well, screw him. I turned back to Olga. "Let's lose that babushka and talk about your cut."

She slipped off the kerchief and unveiled a single gray braid slicked back with a scattering of hairpins. There was some thinning, but not too bad. Dissuading her from a perm was my main concern. If we had to do a perm, we'd be there all night. "You strike me as someone who appreciates a classic look."

She was listening, but the flattery didn't quite take.

"Something that's not too much fuss, ready on a moment's notice. Versatile." That garnered a slight frown. Was she unfamiliar with the term? Sure, she had an accent, but her vocabulary seemed expansive enough. When in doubt, leave a woman the option of a ponytail. "Something with enough length to pull back."

Red joined us and handed the wineglass to Olga with a nearly imperceptible flourish. They locked eyes, not with the leery apprehension I'd expect an immigrant to give a mohawked black man, but with one of those instantaneous clicks of understanding. I backed away a couple of paces, and he planted himself directly in front of her, crouched at her feet so she was looking down at him, stared up into her face and said, "Tell me a story."

Her gaze immediately shifted and went distant.

Holy shit. Maybe Matthew was right and he really was some kind of hypnotist.

"Tell me about a happy time. Nothing too big, nothing formal. Something quiet. Easy. Whatever pops into your head."

Olga blinked slowly. Once. Twice. Then haltingly began. "My daughter got a good job. She took me on a trip to the old country. We had coffee on the sidewalk, and it was so terrible, we laughed." She sighed wistfully. "So long ago."

"Now tell me," Red murmured, "not how your hair looked, not how it actually was, but how it felt."

"My hair." They were both speaking in low, private tones now, as if this memory would be diluted if they shared it too freely. "The wind. It tickles my scalp. It feels...free."

Without dropping her gaze, Red reached up and tugged the elastic from the end of her braid. "Free. I like that. Let's get your shampoo started while you think about the wind in your hair."

He took Olga by the hand, courtly, and led her to the sinks. Once he had her situated, I nudged him out of the way. Staying late with no compensation was my punishment, after all. Not his. "I got this."

He did back off. But he shifted his focus to me. I never really got the saying *Watch out for the quiet ones*, not deep down in my gut, until I found myself under Red Turner's knowing scrutiny.

I ignored him. "How's that water temperature?" I asked Olga. "Too hot? Too cold?"

"Warmer."

"You got it."

I'm not the type of guy you can rush by staring at me. In fact, if anything, it makes me more deliberate about taking my time. Not only did my newest client get a shampoo, but she got one hell of a scalp massage—the longest one I'd done all week. Red just kept right on staring, like there was nowhere he'd rather be on a Saturday night.

Olga was practically in dreamland by the time I got her all scrubbed up and situated in the chair. "So, what are we thinking?" I asked. "Shoulder length?"

"Wind in the hair," Red murmured.

Wind in the hair. Layers. On the client who wears a single braid and clearly trims the ends herself with kitchen shears. The free client. Fine.

I met his eyes in the mirror. At the rate we were going, this stand-off would last half the night. And I was totally up for it. I combed through and sectioned with elaborate care while Red simply watched with his fathomless gaze. When was the last time Olga had layers—if ever? She was getting them now. And I fussed over every damn one.

By the time we were done, the oompah music by Schnitzelhaus was quiet and Olga's hair looked like the model's on the Patently Platinum bottle. I spun her toward the mirror, aimed a short blast of the blow drier in her general direction, and said, "Wind in your hair."

She gasped. "Is that...it doesn't even look like me."

"It's you, all right." It totally was.

It also was the best cut I'd done all day. Hell, probably all week.

Take that and stare at it, Red Turner.

But of course he couldn't leave it at that. He had to make sure he outdid me. We led her to the door, and as he unlocked it, he asked, "How'd you get here? Drive?"

"I walked."

"It's late. I'll walk you home."

Like I'd let *that* happen—give the cut of my life, then let him steal my thunder. "I drove. I'll take everyone home. How's that?"

"That's great," he said. "I'll get my things."

The walk to my car turned out to be just as long as the walk to Olga's apartment in a butchered Colonial deep down a tree-lined side street, but it gave me the chance to be courtly and open the car door for her. Apparently the haircut had shaken loose some memories. She prattled on about her trip. The sights, the sounds...the food. Once we said our goodbyes and got Red re-settled in the front of the car, she pointed at the greasy box of potato pancakes in his lap and said, "Don't heat those up in the microwave. Use the oven. It takes longer, but you'll thank me later."

Since I was in courtly mode, I didn't just wait in the car to make sure Olga got inside safely. I walked her to her door to emphasize what a gentleman I was. Plus, it gave me some distance from Red—who was one of the most maddening guys I'd ever met. And I've met plenty of guys.

What the hell was his game, an attempt to prove he was better than me? Or an elaborate ruse to kill my Saturday night?

"Thank you for a lovely evening," Olga said.

I nearly jumped. I'd fallen so deep inside my own head I practically forgot she was even there. "Just making sure it was the best dollar you've ever spent."

She glanced back at the car—not that we could really see anything from the porch—and said, "You're a cute couple."

"Him? And me? Oh, hell to the no."

She flashed her little gray teeth in a smile. "Ah."

"Totally not my type."

She didn't even bother to argue. With a placating nod, she slipped inside. "Good night."

I stood there for a moment to collect myself. Or maybe to glare at her closed door while I considered dumping Red at the closest El station. But of course I wouldn't. I needed to prove how fucking gracious I could be.

There was no chitchat when I got back in the car. Red gave me his address and we drove there in silence. Normally I'd crank up the tunes and enjoy the custom speakers, but I didn't want to give the guy an engraved invitation to impugn my musical taste. Which was totally unimpugnable.

I steeled myself for a zinger when I pulled up in front of his building, and I got one, all right. But not the one I'd expected. "You must be hungry." He dipped the potato pancake box at me. "Do you want to come up?"

My gut did an acrobatic maneuver at that age-old invitation...but then I realized a Vibe was nowhere in evidence. I'd let Olga's "cute couple" comment get to my head. Not every invitation to come inside involves coming inside. And sometimes a pancake is just a pancake.

Whatever he was playing at, I refused to let him get the best of me. "Sounds delightful."

His apartment was sparse in a just-moved-in kind of way. New appliances, spotless wood flooring, tastefully restrained. I parked myself at the kitchen counter and waited for him to break the ice.

He was one cool customer, I'll give him that. He turned on the oven, arranged the horrid little pancakes on a baking sheet and got them all situated before he turned to me and said, "Iced tea? Water?"

Who the hell offers a guest *water*? I countered with, "Wine? Vodka? Anything with alcohol, actually. I'm easy that way."

"I don't drink."

Fantastic.

I sighed and accepted some tea, and told myself I wasn't curious as to why he didn't imbibe. He seemed awfully young to be on the AA bandwagon. Some kind of straightedge punk rock philosophy? Could be alcohol just didn't agree with him...though if that were me, I'd simply figure I hadn't yet found the right booze. Easiest thing would be to simply ask. But I wouldn't give him the satisfaction.

He poured me the tea, and took water for himself. Oh, touché. He parked himself beside me at the breakfast bar without a word, the picture of ease and grace, as if he hadn't just sat in excruciating silence for the past ten minutes. And finally I decided I was doing myself a disservice if I didn't take this opportunity to get inside his inscrutable head. "Tell me something," I said, and he shifted his focus wordlessly to me with the faintest cock of an eyebrow. "Why'd you stay late tonight? Scoring brownie points with Ralph?"

A minuscule laugh twitched his shoulders. "I doubt it."

"Then, what? Exploring your inner masochist?"

"What makes you say that?" He turned on the stool to face me full-on, and the weight of his undivided attention made me clench my toes so he didn't see me squirm. "Seemed to me like you *wanted* to do that woman's hair."

We all want things. The question is, what? Me, for instance, I'll go way overboard to prove a point. Even if I only have a vague idea of what that point might be. I shrugged off the question and steered the inquisition back at him. "And you?" I asked. "What do *you* want?"

"To see the salon thrive."

"Not generally—specifically. Why are you here? Right now. With me."

"My intention was to be supportive."

I snorted into my tea. "Says the guy whose presence made the cut last twice as long as it needed to."

"If you didn't want to be there, why did you offer?"

"Because I was the one who sold the ticket, that's why. I talked the old lady into buying it, so I had to pay the piper."

"You didn't have to. You chose to."

"Same difference."

"Not really. We all experience pain—but we choose to suffer."

Clearly, he had his double-talk well rehearsed. I, however, was unwilling to concede. "Going a whole Saturday with squat for tips, shilling tickets on the sidewalk, then spending the time I could normally be getting lit or getting laid giving a free haircut? No way did I *choose* to suffer that."

"If that's how you saw your day, it's not for me to judge. Me, I got to interact with the community, and meet new people, and help grow the business I came here to work with. Ralph has a strong vision for Luscious and I'm fortunate to be a part of it."

The oven timer buzzed. I was saved by the bell from telling him to take his high and mighty self-righteousness and fuck off. He put a plate in front of me and I tried a greasy pancake. They were slightly better warmed up, but only slightly. Was he seriously going to eat his? "Talk about choosing to suffer," I said. "So the boss wasn't kidding when he said he bought them just for you. Vegetarian? Don't answer that, of course you are."

A tiny smile played at his lips, and the grease only accentuated it. In just a split second, a fraction of a heartbeat, a series of fantasies unspooled. That generous mouth wrapped around the head of my dick. Our oily lips sliding together around trembling, sated gasps. A flutter of contentment as he said my name, and smiled.

Who knew I'd be raring for a hate-fuck? And now that I'd glimpsed that thought, I could hardly unthink it. It made perfect sense. Why else would he have invited me up? (And don't give me that shit about being *supportive*.) More importantly, why else would I have accepted?

Too bad we didn't have any booze to lubricate the situation. I watched him carefully. He ate another pancake and watched me right back.

No Vibe. None whatsoever.

Booze or no booze, the guy didn't reciprocate my lust. And the depth of my disappointment startled me. I glanced down at the inside of his wrist, and there among a few bangles and strands of wooden hippie beads, I saw the tattoo. An inverted triangle with little angel wings.

"Are you gay?" I blurted out.

"I am." He didn't bother to ask if I was too. Either it was obvious, or he didn't care. "Now you tell me something personal. All afternoon, I watched you play it safe with each and every client, barely dusting the ends, and rushing through as quick as possible even though you weren't getting paid by the cut. Like you didn't care about the cut itself, you just wanted to get it over with. It doesn't make sense. If you don't like to cut hair, why are you a stylist?"

There's hate-fucks, and then there's homicide. I pushed away from the counter and grabbed my jacket. "Let's get something straight, pal. You don't know the first thing about me." I stomped out the door, livid. How dare he?

I thundered down the stairs and out to my car.

Really. How *dare* he?

Safe was the Juniors, plying the clients with compliments to make up for their rudimentary skills. Safe was leaving as much length as possible to avoid a freakout like the one Pilar endured. Yeah, maybe today I went basic, but that wasn't *safe*. That was practical. That was smart. None of those walk-ins would come back for a real cut. None of them would refer their friends. They were just out for Square Days and thinking to kill two birds with one stone and take advantage of a big coupon. So why should I expend the effort of opening my heart and soul to them if they were only in it for a quickie? Better to give them a decent trim they wouldn't hate.

Because...it was safe.

Fucker.

I climbed back into my car, which now smelled like old lady and cold potato pancakes, and headed home.

CHAPTER 8

I wasn't too hungover by the time I met my mother for dinner the next day at the new Italian joint she'd been jonesing to try. But between the sub-par Limoncello Collinses I'd subjected myself to—making them at home is no mean feat—and the potato pancake I kept burping up, I'd tossed and turned half the night. Even with the whole damn bed to myself.

"And there you are," she sing-songed as she swept into the restaurant lobby. She uses bubbly, expansive gestures in everything she does, but always manages to seem vaguely contrived. It's not because the sunny grandiosity is a put-on. Her actual personality's just naturally stilted. "Handsome as ever."

I held still for the obligatory mom-hug: a squeeze followed by a timely rappel. Catch and release.

The maitre d' warmed to her awkward breeziness as people in any service industry usually did, and he escorted us to a table with a decent view. We got ourselves situated and started in on the pleasantries. Same old, same old, beat for beat. I wasn't there for the news, though, I was feeding my urge to see her with my own two eyes and make sure she was still okay. Not that I get all Norman Bates about it. I was away at school when my dad keeled over, and I needed reassurance that my remaining parent wasn't pining away or adopting random rescue animals. It was a pleasant enough way to while away the evening and enjoy a decent meal. Plus I had nothing better to do, since the bar scene's kind of dead on Sunday nights.

Discussion ensued. Catch-up on my cousins' latest news. Complaints about her Pilates class. A blow-by-blow description of a jewelry party where she made the atrocious beaded hemp thing on her wrist.

We were well into the entree before she had a chance to start harping on my love life. "So...have you met anyone lately?"

"Oh God!" I flung myself back so hard my chair rocked on its hind legs. My melodramatic gestures come a lot more naturally, so much so that they're practically invisible to Maxine. "I am single. I like being single. I intend to stay single."

"In your line of work you meet people every day. Quality people who can afford to spend money on themselves."

"Oh, I meet people all right." It was tempting to bitch about Square Days, but I stopped myself. She's always covered it with a forced brightness, but I could tell she was chagrined I chose to be a "hairdresser" (as she calls it, never a stylist) and not a college professor, or an accountant, or an astronaut. "But I don't need a partner to validate me."

"I never said you did."

"I want to go where I want to go, and do what I want to do. No yes, dear...no, dear...did you take out the garbage, dear. That's my idea of hell."

She rolled her eyes the whole time I spoke, and when I stopped for a breath, interjected, "He doesn't have to be boring."

"There is no other half. I'm not broken. I don't need a man to complete...me."

A busboy clearing the table behind my mother caught my eye. My age, maybe younger, but with a swarthy broodiness that made him seem sullenly ageless. He flashed me an angry look—and it morphed into a Vibe that threatened to ignite the very air between us in a flash of frustrated longing.

Maxine prattled on, blissfully unaware. She was lucky her hair didn't go up in flames, and not just because she used ten times as much spray as she needed. "Now you're just being argumentative. Of course you're not broken. Being in a relationship isn't about completing yourself. Loving someone isn't a weakness."

"Uh huh," I said absently. The busboy blasted me with another look. He twisted, tray in hand, and his stiff white dress shirt gave a tantalizing hint at the planes of his chest. It would be hairy. I could tell by the lushness of his five-o'clock shadow.

"I can't imagine my life without your father. And without him, I wouldn't have had you."

That argument was so irrelevant I wouldn't even know where to begin. Especially when the waiter's dark eyes raked down my chest and lingered on the tabletop as if he wanted to scorch a hole straight through it that led to my groin.

He turned toward the kitchen, and I found myself up and out of my chair as if an invisible tether connected the two of us and he was dragging me right along behind him. "Hold that thought."

Maxine pushed back from the table as if to follow. "What's wrong? Are you okay?"

"Fine. Just need to hit the powder room."

Or...hit something else.

The busboy parked his tray by the kitchen door with me hot on his heels. One thing Maxine had right, being a stylist gave me plenty of opportunities to meet people, even when I was nowhere near the salon. I slipped a business card from my pocket—a special one with my personal number scrawled under the salon's—and followed him up the staff hall. I debated whether to be so blatant as to tell him I couldn't wait to run my fingers through his hair, when he turned on me and flattened me against the wall. Not with a kiss, either. My card fluttered to the ground.

"What the fuck is your problem?" That's what his mouth was saying. But I wasn't worried. The Vibe was palpable.

"No problem. Just thought I knew you from somewhere." I pulled an Italian name from the air. "It's Salvatore, right?"

"No."

"Oh. Sorry." His mouth. Yeah, baby. Hot, hot mouth. "My bad."

He released my shoulders and stepped back, but there was a pause in between, a brief but telling pause, in which he could've given me a little grind first. He didn't. But I knew he was just dying to rub our naughty parts together. "You stay away from me," he growled. "I ain't no fag."

"Got it." I barely restrained myself from raking my eyes down that white permapress shirt again, though I couldn't keep the lilt out of my voice when I shot him the parting line, "Though who am I to judge?"

I hit the bathroom and rinsed my hands before I rejoined my mother. Maxine would notice something like dry hands. She notices everything, actually. She just doesn't put it all together. Probably too busy trying to figure out how to convince me I needed to be saddled with a significant other.

I seated myself, and she asked, "When was the last time you actually had a conversation with someone you didn't have to shout over loud music?"

Not-Sal's friendly warning probably didn't qualify. Neither did the banal chitchat I used for putting customers at ease. I supposed I'd been subjected to a pretty big earful while I choked down those potato pancakes. "Just last night I had quite an extensive dinner conversation."

"And?"

And Red had accused me of playing it safe. Being an underachiever. Phoning it in. "And nothing. It was mostly work stuff, I guess."

A frown of disappointment flitted across her face, but she covered it fast with a trademarked baring of the teeth that was nearly as much grimace as smile. "Isn't that nice?" She snatched up the dessert menu and quickly added, "Should we split a tiramisu? I'm dying to try it but I shouldn't eat the whole thing myself."

She plowed ahead with an animated reading of the cake's description, and all the while, I pondered her abrupt shift in mood. Saddened that my "deep conversation" had produced absolutely zero romantic sparks?

Or disappointed that the person privy to my deep and intimate thoughts was naught but a lowly *hairdresser*?

ॐ

By the time Monday rolled around, Pilar's outrage had shifted to worry. She second-guessed herself all the way to the shop, carefully reimagining pithier comebacks and better reactions to every sleight Ralph could dish up.

"Haven't you known me long enough to realize I have the least comforting shoulder you'd ever cry on?" I finally said.

"Long enough to know you're more sympathetic than anyone else at Luscious."

True. Plus she hadn't been the only one to come out of Square Days with a bruised ego. I wasn't about to drag out the whole Red conversation and dissect it, though. Not that I didn't trust Pilar, I just had no desire to salt my own wounds.

"Maybe I should try to line up another job while I'm still in Ralph's good graces," she said, "before he has a chance to smack-talk me to every other salon in the city."

"Then you'd better figure out what you plan to say when it all gets back to him before the day's over."

"I need to work on a good excuse. Tell him Nick has some kind of *thing* after school. I need a salon with different hours so I can drive him."

"Everyone'll see right through it. He's old enough to take the bus."

"Or that I plan to move. And start applying to salons out in the burbs."

"And when you didn't actually follow through and relocate, the shit would hit the fan." I had no illusions that Ralph wouldn't fuck with her reputation even after she'd flown the coop. "Lying doesn't get anyone anywhere. You need to start saying what you mean."

"Easy for you. You're a man. When you stand up for yourself, you're being forceful. If I do it, I'm a bitch. Women have to sugarcoat everything we say so our opinions don't offend anyone."

"Sounds an awful lot like an excuse to me."

We pulled up to the salon. "You know what?" she said. "You're right. Your brand of sympathy does suck." Ralph's insufferable Prius was already in the lot. I could practically feel Pilar's guts twisting up in knots from the mere sight of the man's car.

"This dynamic can only bother you if you let it," I offered.

"You don't know what you're talking about. No one would ever go out of their way to make you question your own worth."

Oh, you have no idea.

Thanks to the coupons we'd blanketed Lincoln Square with, there wasn't time for navel-gazing. The receptionists were deluged with calls, and walk-ins crowded the normally-serene waiting room. Some people hate chaos, but I got a little buzz off the energy. It felt like one of those all-in-one foil popcorn pans, heating up, growing, expanding, ready to burst open with steamy goodness. And Red was equally busy, occupied with a corrective color that would keep him well out of my hair.

The babble of a full shop rose and fell, punctuating the pretentiously atonal spa-like music Ralph piped in. I found my groove and delivered on three precision cuts, when an incoming text threatened to break my stride. One of my regulars.

Stuck at work, gotta reschedule. Sorry.

And a smiley-face.

No big. Wasn't there a lobby full of walk-ins just dying to make my acquaintance? I had myself convinced things were unfolding just as perfectly as they possibly could—that it was all a big synergistic lovefest—when I realized some of the raised voices I'd been half-hearing had a distinctly uncomfortable edge.

"Why are you crying?" a woman demanded. "There's nothing to cry about."

The palest, frailest receptionist darted past me, face buried in her hands, on a beeline to the staff toilet. Matthew met my eyes in his mirror and mouthed "Oh-em-gee." Trevor, who'd also been heading up front, suddenly veered away as if he remembered something very urgent that needed doing at the other end of the salon. Which left me charging into battle all by my lonesome.

Well, why not? I'm not one to back down from a fight.

An uptight professional woman in her thirties—brown hair, corporate skirt suit, big stick up her ass—stood at the receptionist desk with her hands on her hips. She blinked incredulously at the seat vacated by the weeping girl. The other receptionist was busy talking through her headset and focusing very hard on her scheduling software. From my point of view, I could see her phone wasn't actually on.

What a bunch of babies.

I sashayed out and looked the pissy woman right in the eye. "Are you being helped?"

"No. I'm not."

First impression: what a bitch. But that morning's car talk was so fresh in my mind, I immediately adjusted my attitude and told myself she was merely being honest. Unless she was in the market for drama queen histrionics, at that very moment, technically no one *was* helping her.

"Let's see what I can do." I parked myself primly in the receptionist's chair, cranked down the ergonomic seat a couple of pumps to stop my knees from whacking up against the underside of the desk, then squinted at the schedule. It had been a while since I'd trained on it, but come on. A spreadsheet's a spreadsheet. "Did you need an appointment?"

"I need a trim. And I have an appointment. Right now."

"Name?"

"Brinkman. Carolyn."

CHAPTER 9

A search for the name *Brinkman* got me nowhere. It wasn't as if appointments never fell through the cracks, but I'd get farther faster if I knew which stylist's column I was looking for. "And who were you scheduled with?"

"I don't know." Not bitchy, I reminded myself. Just phenomenally blunt. "Doesn't the computer say?"

It would. If I knew where to look.

"One of the cheaper stylists. I just wanted a trim, it doesn't make any difference."

"Ah, but it does. Different stylists have different fees depending on their level of experience and expertise."

"But it's a *trim*. How involved can that be?"

I met her eye. She gave off some pretty hardcore eye contact. Maybe the receptionist quailed under this woman's unvarnished bluntness, but the contrarian in me was starting to find its rhythm. I levered myself across the stretch of the desk, leaned toward her, dropped my voice, and poured on twice the charm I would use in an actual seduction. "If a trim was just a trim, you'd have it seen to by the minimum wage staff at ClipLand. No, you come to Luscious for a reason. To pamper yourself? Imbibe the free wine? Or to make sure you drop a big enough chunk of change on your 'trim' to make sure you feel important?"

"I come here because one of those franchises gave me really a weird haircut," she said stiffly. Dang. I'd gone too far. Oh well, wouldn't be the first time. Or the last. I settled back in the seat, looked at the screen and spotted her name—basically under my nose—but it wasn't color coded by stylist like the ones around it. And there was a little pencil icon beside it. A note? I clicked.

Problem customer. Trevor - NO. Matthew - NO. Who???

So, the Juniors weren't any fonder of her than the weeping receptionist was. "Look, I'm not a junior stylist, but I just had a cancellation." I slipped her the fee schedule and pointed at my tier. My rate was only twelve dollars more—but on Mondays, twelve bucks will get you a wash, cut and blow dry at ClipLand. "It would be my absolute pleasure to show your hair some TLC."

She didn't even glance at the price list. Instead, she was staring at me. Puzzled. And all the annoyance had gone out of her. "Yes...I'd like that."

I indicated the way to the shampoo station with a flourish. "Then step this way, Miss Brinkman. Or is it Mrs?"

The rhythm of the conversation faltered briefly, then she answered, "I'm married. But technically, it's Detective."

Huh. As I lathered her up, I studied the faint line between her brows. I spotted a glimpse of a heavy badge on her belt, too. And...a gun. No big surprise that at mere sight of her, the Juniors had tinkle running down their legs. I twisted a towel around her wet hair, walked her back to my chair and suggested, "Wine?"

"I'm on duty."

"Tea, then." I signaled the receptionist to hop to it. The phone-faker, not the crybaby. Miss Weepy was still in hiding. "Cream? Sugar?"

"Plain."

Just like her hair. I combed through and considered the unprocessed color, the previous cut. Everything about it was utilitarian, and frankly, she should have gotten a good enough result from ClipLand if her needs were that basic.

"So you just want a trim," I reiterated. "How much?"

"To my shoulder."

I walked around her, studying. It was tempting to encourage her to "frame her face." A little softness can work wonders. And yet....

Maybe she didn't want to be soft. Maybe severity was her thing.

Who really knows themselves? I saw plenty of women wearing hair that served them well in their twenties and thirties, but they were forty-something now and starting to look like they were overcompensating. On the other hand, I encountered plenty of folks hopping on the latest trend whether or not it flattered them.

There was something about this gun-toting woman who made people cry, something that had me wondering if maybe there was a story in her that she needed to revisit. If she ever fantasized about the wind in her hair. I positioned myself in front of her, combed through, and checked the current length. "Are you sure you just want a trim?"

"That's all. I need to be able to pull it back."

I watched her as she spoke in case her body language told me another story. Hard to say. "I can texturize it, give it more movement, and still leave plenty of length."

"I don't want stray hairs getting in my eyes."

"Gotcha. No fringe." It really did seem like the only thing she needed was a trim. But was that just wishful thinking on my part? The feeding of some impulse to play it safe? I glanced at Red, writing in his little notebook with his profile to me. From that angle, the curve of his ass was breathtaking. Jerk.

I turned back to my new client, ran my fingers through her wet hair and sought out the angles of her last cut. "Just a trim..." I said under my breath, and then on impulse, added, "but how about some color?"

She stiffened. "I tried going blonde once. My hair turned orange."

"At a salon? Or at home?"

"What difference does it make?"

"All the difference in the world. If you think I get this platinum by bleaching the crap out of it, think again. All that would get me is a fried head of hair. It's all about the toner and the maintenance."

I sectioned her hair without any chitchat, telling myself it made no difference to me whether she considered my suggestion or not. I'd stand nothing to gain from it if she went blonde, not even the satisfaction of referring a tough customer to Red, since he was even more unflappable than me.

Whoever had done this client's last cut—Trevor, or maybe Matthew—had done well by her, even if they'd been shaking in their boots the whole time. It galled me that I couldn't show up Red by talking her into a choppy pixie or an edgy, asymmetrical bob. Something that extreme would make a big splash, all right. But in all the wrong ways.

In the end, I gave her exactly what she wanted. A trim.

I passed her the hand mirror and spun her so she could check the back, then turned her to face it head-on. The crease between her brows deepened. I stood behind her and ran my fingers through to demo that she was welcome to scrutinize as hard as she wanted— both sides were precisely the same length. She met my eyes in the mirror. It seemed we had an understanding.

I was expecting a curt thank-you when she surprised me with, "I wouldn't end up with a big head of orange clown hair?"

"With our colorist? Absolutely not." In fact, I'd bet my week's tips that whenever Red left his customers in tears, they were tears of joy. I stepped around and leaned my butt on my station, crossed my arms, and gave her a long look. "You'd totally rock the right blonde."

She frowned, but her body language suggested she was just flashing her particular brand of perma-bitchface.

No two ways about it, she'd be hot. "And the hubster...I'll bet he'd get a charge out of it too."

Her eyebrows scrunched. The cape rose and fell as she shrugged. "He probably would."

"Not that I'm recommending you should sacrifice your own preferences to cater to someone else. I sure as hell wouldn't. But knowing you can light someone up by simply walking into a room is a heady thing." I took up position behind her again, worked through some smoothing serum and blowdried while she sat and scowled. It was a companionable enough silence. Once her hair was dry, I primped it into place and gave it a light hairspray mist. "Well, Detective? What's the verdict?"

"It's fine."

Geez. Don't spare my feelings.

Her frown deepened. She met my eyes in the mirror. "I never saw myself that way—the way you do when you think of blonde. I was never 'the pretty one.' Only 'the smart one.' I'm not sure I'm ready for a change that big."

I gave the cut another primp. "It's just hair. It grows out."

We stared each other down in the mirror, both knowing full well that hair was oh so much more—but now I'd given her permission to start daydreaming about what it might be like to no longer be 'the smart one.'

Red had parked his customer in the lounge to wait for her color to process, and was currently topping off her merlot. Even though there was still a tender bruise in my ego where he'd jabbed me with his accusation of half-assery, I gave him the come-hither crook of the finger, and he joined us.

"I was just telling Detective Brinkman she'd make a knockout blonde. What's your *professional* opinion?"

God only knows whether I was daring him to contradict me, or if I was secretly hoping he'd agree. Bless me with his validation. Which I absolutely did not want or need. But he zeroed in on her like she was the only other person in the world, and he considered her a long moment before he asked her, "What do you think?"

"I'm not sure." She frowned. "No, that's not true. I'm afraid."

I bit back a scoff—everyone knows the best way to deal with a fear is to plow straight through it. But not Red Turner. He was the picture of finesse. He pitched his voice low and gentle. "It's okay, baby. Thoughts are just thoughts. What do you see?"

"I see...I see myself watching the kitchen timer tick down. I'm so excited, thinking about how I'd get this boy in my geometry class to like me, if only I looked like the model on the box."

"Shh." Red stroked her hair way more intimately than he had any right to. "That's the past. It was painful, I know. But you keep on re-living that? That's your choice. You're choosing to keep suffering."

The detective looked like she was gearing up to contradict him, but the argument never materialized. "I suppose." She thought about it some more, then gave a small, brittle laugh. "Actually, I can't even remember that kid's name."

"Because it's not about him," Red murmured. "It's about you. So tell me, now that you've got *that* out of your system. What do you see?"

She totally humored him, closed her eyes and thought hard. "I see myself looking like...a bitch. Which sounds crazy, I know, since I already do. Except I get away with it. As a blonde."

God damn. I saw it too.

She opened her eyes, and Red smiled at her without a lick of condescension. "Here's what I see. Cool beige tones. A hint of pearly silver. Oyster blonde. Very natural. Maybe even a little imposing."

I added, "Not an orange clown hair in sight."

She nodded cautiously.

"There'd be some commitment involved," Red warned her. "Conditioning. Special toning shampoos. Touch ups."

"Of course."

"Well then." He passed his business card to her. "Right now I need to get back to my client. If you decide on some new color, I'd be honored to be the one to make it happen."

Aaand...apparently that's how you make your nemesis look like some major hot shit, while you come off as merely "fine." And not in the way the Juniors say it when they're looking at someone's package, either.

"What about you?" Carolyn asked me. "Can I have your card?"

I handed one over. "Of course. I'd be delighted to give you another perfectly adequate cut."

She frowned at my card and mouthed my name as she read it, then looked back at me and said, "You're angry."

"Nothing so dramatic." I spun her chair to face the reception area and made a courtly gesture toward the desk. She didn't budge, just looked at me and waited for me to explain. I figured if there was a total stranger I could level with, it would be her. "The thing is, I've never aspired to mediocrity."

"Everyone has an agenda, that's just the way things are. All I needed today was a trim, and you gave me exactly what I asked for, without being fake about it. And to me, that's a pretty big deal."

I was just about done swabbing down my station at the end of the day when a text from the busboy rolled in. *Can I see U?*

I wasn't surprised. No matter how hard someone might carry on to the contrary, there's no mistaking the Vibe. The big question was whether he wanted drinks and small talk first, or if it was just a booty call. Me, I could go either way. I texted my address and told him I'd be home by eight, then got busy wrapping things up at work to make sure that timetable actually happened.

Ralph was coming around with the tip envelopes. He chatted briefly with everyone but Pilar. After her storming off on Square Days, she got the silent treatment. Apparently we were in Middle School now.

Some people just aren't happy unless they're miserable. I hated to take a cue from Red, who was floating around his corner of the shop in his own personal nirvana, but I really had no stomach for their melodramatic angst. Not tonight, with a hot Italian busboy en route from Arlington Heights.

The boss man approached me last. "Mr. Ash, could I have a moment?"

I was so busy ignoring the simmering tension between him and Pilar, he managed to catch me by surprise. Vibe? Hard to say. He was already heading toward his office. I followed and left the door open in hopes of getting home on time. Ralph strolled over to his credenza and began casually sorting mail. "Close that, would you?"

Fabulous. I nudged the door shut with my heel.

Once we were nice and private, he said, "Square Days."

Okay. Where was he was going with that? I waited for a beat—evidently nowhere. Although I really wanted him to spit out whatever he had to say so I could leave, I couldn't really dredge up much of a reply. "Yeah?"

He spun around in a turn that was only subtly dramatic, and tapped a fan of envelopes on his desk. His expression was set in the same intense semi-smirk that was usually laden with Vibe. Except tonight, it wasn't. "You stayed later than me on Saturday so I didn't get a chance to give you your tips. They feel pretty sparse."

"Figures. Can't say I've ever walked away from Square Days with enough cash to cover both cab fare and my first round of drinks."

"And so you started here."

"Started what?"

"Drinking."

"What," I said, "you're monitoring the wine now?"

"Just happened to notice an open bottle this morning that wasn't there when I left."

"I offered the customer a glass. Like I always do—like we're *supposed* to. I'm not a big wine drinker anyway."

Ralph looked me up and down as if he didn't quite believe me.

That didn't sit well. I'm no liar. "Plus, I drove."

"Did you?" He tamped together the carefully arrayed tip envelopes, all the while smiling that tiny, odd smile. Remembering Pilar showing up separately, her face the color of a candy apple from her mile-long sprint? Or thinking he'd caught me in a lie?

"Ask Red, I took him home."

Ralph's eyes narrowed, and suddenly I realized why he'd been pissy with me for taking that final customer and encouraging him to leave. Not because I was stealing his thunder, but because he'd been hoping to stick around and get me to polish his rod.

Ralph Maldonado, jealous? Wonders never cease. I'm under no illusions, however, that he's particularly attached to me. It's more like him threatening Pilar over leaving the salon. He'd wanted me to help him blow off some steam after Square Days, but I didn't go home with him. And if he can't have me, no one can.

On principle, I wasn't about to tell him nothing had happened between his fancy colorist and me. I neither confirm nor deny my conquests. Period. But having my character questioned was insulting. I don't boink my fellow stylists inside the shop. And if I want to get my buzz on, I wouldn't sneak wine at Luscious like a teenager lurking around mommy and daddy's liquor cabinet. I'd pony up to the bar and start a tab, like a grownup.

"I didn't drink the wine. It's for clients—you told me that on day one. No need to say it again."

"And Red?"

"Unless he stood by the fridge and chugged it while I wasn't looking, neither did he."

"You didn't smell it on his breath?"

As if I'd fall for a transparent ploy to get me to admit I'd tasted it on his mouth. "I hardly know the guy, but if you think he's the one raiding the fridge, you're barking up the wrong tree. If anyone goes by the book, it's him." I held out my hand. "So are you holding my tips ransom, or can I get going?"

Ralph gave me a cold smile that never reached his eyes, and forked over my thin envelopes. "Of course."

CHAPTER 10

A taste like furniture polish was heavy on my sandpaper tongue when I pried open my eyes the next morning. I really needed to get a better handle on how to make a Limoncello Collins myself. That, or choose my company more carefully. The busboy had thrown a fit when I suggested we head out for a nightcap, even though I reassured him my normal watering hole was not technically a gay bar. Because he insisted he wasn't gay.

Sure, he'd feasted on my dick like a starving man, but we didn't kiss, so it was totally not gay.

Whatever.

He'd fled sometime after the big event and I was currently alone. If he'd left behind a dent in my spare pillow, I'd erased it with all my tossing and turning. Too much booze. Too little comfort.

I like a good roll in the sack as much as the next guy, but something about this one rubbed me wrong. He was totally hot to trot, but the way he interacted with me, I could've been anybody. No pillow talk. Zero. Zilch. Once all the grunting and moaning was over, we had nothing to say to each other. Literally nothing. So I had pretty low expectations when I checked to see if he'd texted any parting remarks. Instead I found a voicemail from Pilar waiting for me.

"Hey, I got an interview at Cashmere so I'm calling in sick. Can you take my 12:30? I couldn't get her rescheduled, but everyone else should be okay.... Cross your fingers for me."

I stared at the phone as I considered what this message meant to me, other than a heads-up to drive myself in. Did I even want her to get the job? It would shift the whole dynamic at Luscious if she was no longer there. Ralph would need to hire another stylist—would he score someone with experience, or grab another Junior straight out of cosmetology school? And where would that leave me in the pecking order?

It was a pensive drive. First my date turns out to be vaguely disappointing, then my morning sounding board goes missing. Obviously I didn't expect Pilar to work at Luscious for the rest of her life—especially given the way Ralph went out of his way to shit on her—but there was no question that once she was gone I'd be one lonely soul.

All my stewing landed me at work before the doors were even open, so I popped over to the coffee shop across the street. Midmorning I'd normally have my pick of tables, but a cluster of tourists in matching T-shirts had the place stuffed to the gills. Tourists don't move like regular people. They're oblivious to everyone around them, wandering directly in the path of anything with purpose. And if it wasn't bad enough that I had to keep stopping to let various people drift by, across the chest of each ugly T-shirt was printed, *Rediscover: The Couple's Vacation.*

And I realized that at the tables, they were all paired off and holding hands.

Gag me.

As I waited for my cafe con leche, I attempted to look anywhere but the cloying displays of affection by keeping my eyes fixed hard on the bakery case. That's when I heard my name. Once. And again. Like maybe someone had called it a few times. And maybe that someone was none other than my nemesis.

"Curtis—over here."

I accepted my beverage with a sallow smile and turned to face Red. The day just kept getting better. And it wasn't even eleven o'clock.

Red put down a book he'd been reading and gestured eagerly at the empty seat across the table from him—the only empty seat in the whole damn shop. Normally I'd be thrilled to join him in a game

of cat and mouse, but I was tired. Hungover. Strangely disillusioned.
I glanced out the window. The murky skies had darkened, and now
it was misting. I could hardly go drink my coffee outside. My hair
would wilt, and I'd be damned if I went and hid in my car while I
waited, as if I was too much of a wimp to face up to Red.

And so I sat.

"No one calls me Curtis except telemarketers," I said.

"Not even your momma?"

"Not unless she's trying to make a point."

"I didn't mean to offend you."

If I was offended by anything, it was the *playing it safe* remark,
not the use of my proper name. "Did I say I was offended?" I stared
him right in the eye to show him I wasn't intimidated. Unfortunately,
neither was he. His eyes were dark and melancholy, with tantalizing
depths lurking just beyond my reach. With natural assets like that, I
could see how his penetrating gaze left his clients dazed and reeling.
"It takes a lot to piss me off."

"What would you prefer I called you?"

"Whatever tickles your fancy. After all, a word is just a word. It's
the intent that matters."

When I bait Maxine by quoting her to herself, half the time she's
so oblivious, she thinks we're just agreeing. Red was too sharp for
that. He recognized his own words, but by accepting them at face
value, he deliberately ignored my mockery.

He dropped the subject of my name and asked, "There's not a
referral program in place at Luscious?"

I was relieved he only wanted to talk shop. That, I could manage.
"Just loyalty reward type coupons. I don't bother giving any out, myself. If someone doesn't want to see me again, I'm not gonna twist
their arm."

I considered what I'd just said, and wondered if I was, indeed,
talking shop.

Of course I was. If I bared my vulnerable underbelly to anyone,
it sure as hell wouldn't be Red.

"Miss Brinkman decided to go blonde after all, thanks to you."

"Detective," I said absently. "She's a cop."

"That's one lucrative appointment. But Ralph seemed put out when I told him you'd done the referral."

Weird. You'd think our boss would be excited that I was a team player and was embracing the new guy. With our little chat about the customer wine fresh in my head, though, I couldn't discount the idea that Ralph presumed the embrace involved nightcaps and pillow dents.

"There's no referral system in place," I said. "We never needed one. And a friendly piece of advice: if you suggest a referral program, Ralph won't take kindly to you telling him how to run his business, whether you've worked in ritzier shops or not."

I could have added that as a gay man, Red probably shouldn't pique Ralph's jealousy by acting too friendly toward me in front of him. But that would be like standing up on the table and announcing I was boffing the boss, so I left him to figure out that tidbit himself.

An incoming text dinged, and I checked my phone. I'd never bothered to key the number in to my contacts but I did recognize the west suburban area code. I tapped it open....

And there was the busboy's dick.

A photo of it, anyway. Dark, slightly blurry. But I'd recognize that formidable Sicilian bush anywhere.

I closed the app and pocketed my phone without replying.

"Do you need to answer that?" Red asked. I didn't know him well enough to tell if the question was laced with sarcasm.

"It'll keep."

"So listen," he said, "the other night...it wasn't my intent to insult you."

Right. I'd hate to be on the receiving end when he was feeling catty. "By all means, say what you mean and don't sugar-coat it, I'm just saying it's not fair to judge my entire M.O. based on Square Days. I mean...it's *Square Days*. Oompah music. Lederhosen and knockwurst. Smocks and sideshows."

"And you felt like you were being forced to make a spectacle of yourself out there on the sidewalk. You worry about people soaking up more than you're willing to give. So you protected yourself by not caring."

"I care plenty, Sigmund Freud. I'm just not willing to waste a five-star performance on some freeloader I'll never see again."

"I understand," he said with such surprising gentleness I did a double-take to see if he was putting me on. I didn't think so. Then again, I hardly knew the guy. He watched me pondering my coffee for a long moment, and eventually said, "There are other ways to keep yourself safe. Mindfulness. Meditation."

"You're serious."

"Absolutely."

Of course he was. In fact, I couldn't even imagine a scenario in which the vegetarian with his high ideals didn't want me to plunk down cross-legged and chant *om*. Except I didn't quite see the connection. "What does that have to do with safety?"

"The thoughts we think—they matter. We're more than just our physical bodies. Sensitive folk like us, we got to stay grounded."

I scoffed. "No one has ever accused me of being sensitive. Not even once."

"I'm not talking the emotional sense of the word."

"Then you lost me."

He gave me a long look, lowered his voice, and said, "It's obvious you read people."

"And? Everyone reads everyone. It's called body language."

"It's called telepathy."

I laughed so suddenly I damn near shot coffee out my nose. I was shocked that someone as smart as Red actually believed in psychic ability—those bizarre statements Uncle Sam issued back when I was more worried about scoring my drivers license and flirting with college boys willing to buy me beer and stroke my teenage dick. "Sorry, no. If you've fallen for that dog and pony show, the word you're looking for is gullibility."

He slid his book across the table and said, "Read this—just the first few chapters—practice it for a week, and see if it doesn't make a difference in the way you feel."

I turned it face-up. *Mindfulness Methods*. Before I could roll my eyes over the vapidly blissful cover model meditating on a beach, my phone dinged again. I slipped it from my jacket, glanced at the 847 area code on the incoming message, and pocketed the thing without bothering to subject myself to another tedious dick pic.

Across the table, my coffee companion watched me with a cryptic half-smile. I'd give him one thing—our little chats made interesting conversation. Even if he did believe in fairy tales.

I did manage to work in Pilar's 12:30 without keeping the client waiting too long, but the woman cringed away from me like she thought I might shave her bald and pierce her septum. As if I'd waste a killer look on a frump like her.

Elsewhere in the salon, the Bitch was back in town, a.k.a my favorite uptight detective, Carolyn Brinkman. I found myself gazing longingly at the color station while Red sweet-talked Carolyn through the beginning of the blonde phase of her life in his patented low, reassuring tones. He wasn't flirtatious, not the way the rest of us were when we thought it might put someone at ease or coax a bigger tip out of their wallet. But he was so present, so focused, it blew right past flirtation-level and landed solidly in the realm of intimacy.

Must've been all that "mindfulness" he touted. If I didn't know any better, I might've been jealous of all that quality attention Carolyn was getting. Because my constantly dinging phone was now bulging with Italian sausage, but I could hardly call it intimate.

I was doing my best not to stare. After all, I didn't want Red to know I found him grudgingly fascinating, not when he didn't return the sentiment. I only had half an eye on them when they bolted up from the hairdryers and rushed over to shampoo like someone's life depended on it. And she'd only been processing for fifteen minutes, tops.

Since my new consult was still flipping through a style guide trying to make up her mind, I excused myself and went to see what was going on. Everything about Red's body language screamed *urgent*, but I did my best not to fan the flame. Even from a dozen feet away, I could tell Carolyn's hair was at the most brassy stage of lift. In layman's terms, clown orange. "Can I help?"

Red said, "She needs to go. Right now."

I was about to try and lighten the mood (if not the poor woman's hair) by asking if it was really life or death. But given her profession, it probably was. I hunkered down opposite him and said, "Give me the spray. You'll rinse her a lot faster with two hands."

"You'll be right out the door in no time," he murmured as we worked. "I'll give you my personal number. Soon as you can spare two hours, call me, day or night, and I'll have you as blonde as Grace Kelly."

"Are we almost done?" she asked.

"Trust me," I said. "You do not want to go walking around with traces of bleach on your head."

"I know." The furrow between her brows deepened. "But this timing really...sucks."

"We can tuck most of it into a scrunchie," I told Red.

"That's a plan." Right there in shampoo, he towel-dried, worked through a swipe of leave-in conditioner, and wrapped up as much of the brassy mess as he could.

We did our best, but the results were still appalling. Our stern detective looked worse than a teenager who'd attempted to go platinum with a quart of household bleach.

"Don't you worry," Red told her. "It might look bad now, but that's still healthy hair. We just need to finish what we started."

She caught a glimpse of herself in the mirror, blanched, and said, "For my professional reputation, I sure as hell hope so."

She rushed out the door without paying. The receptionists both pretended not to notice. "Any idea what the big emergency is?" I asked Red.

"She didn't say."

Maybe not, but her body language gave some pretty solid hints. The situation was ripe for a remark about my so-called psychic telepathy, but I just couldn't bring myself to wisecrack. Whatever had called her away was something urgent. Something bad. I returned to my current client who'd decided on a trim, told her I could add some layers that'd really frame her face, and got to work giving her the same basic haircut she'd walked in the door with. It was perfectly fine and she seemed happy enough, even though halfway through her cut, the dick pics started pouring in so fast and furious I had to excuse myself yet again to block the damn number, disgusted with the way Red managed to one-up me without even trying. He gave out his number to people having genuine hair emergencies, while I wasted mine on idiots with nothing better to do than keep reminding me of my latest underwhelming encounter.

Before the tip envelopes were passed out that night, I made a point of demonstrating that I could be just as considerate as Red by handing him one of my special personalized cards. "In case you need backup with Detective Brinkman, feel free to give me a ring. Contrary to popular belief, I really do enjoy hair."

"Thank you." Red pocketed the card.

Damn it.

Now I couldn't even get off on making cutting remarks—not when Red blithely ignored all their sharpest edges.

CHAPTER 11

When I gave Red my number, I didn't think he'd actually call. Too self-sufficient. Too proud. And yet I stayed in that night, so perhaps I did have some inkling he'd tap me. Could have been some kind of reverse psychology at play: by reaching out, he was reinforcing his vast capacity for independence by demonstrating that he thought it was completely appropriate to call at quarter to twelve without reminding me to bring massage oil and a party-sized box of condoms.

Though he did request a bottle of wine.

Not for him, of course. He didn't drink—so he said—but I picked up three bottles just in case he changed his mind.

He buzzed me in, met me at the door and took my coat. "Thank you for coming." Tonight, on his home turf, his body language felt different. His posture was nowhere near as rigid as it was at Luscious, and when he absently massaged the back of his neck, the gesture felt vaguely vulnerable. "Carolyn's on her way. She was pretty upset, and I thought it would be a comfort to her, having you here." He and I must have had entirely different definitions of the word *comfort*. He stowed the wine, then beckoned me over to the breakfast bar. "Come take a look."

Though he'd painted the standard-issue white walls a sunny yellow and added some colorful Asian floral prints, the place was still underfurnished. The only thing on the countertop was a tablet. I planted my elbows beside it, opposite him. He woke it up to a news video, hit play, and the broadcast stuttered to life. A grim female reporter stood in front of a police station with a crowd milling all around, though at first glance it looked like all the action was newscasters getting in each others' shots.

The reporter said, "Chicago police have a suspect in custody linked to the disappearance of at least three young women. Fifty-two year old Edgewater resident Hugo Cooper is being held without bond. Sergeant Owens of the Twelfth Precinct has stated that while the investigation has been expedited to the PsyCop Sex Crimes Unit, he declines to confirm any details about the victims at this time."

"There." Red tapped the pause and pinch-zoomed in. "On the stairs, with that big man. That's her in the background."

"Back up." I said. He reversed a few stops and we watched it again. The woman he'd spotted was wearing a beret—and a black suit is a black suit—but something about the way she tugged her jacket down was definitely familiar.

"That's it, just those couple of seconds?"

"That's it. But her job, the timing, the hat...."

True. I tapped back and watched it again. The guy she was with herded her like a bodyguard. He did his best to keep himself between her and the cameras. He was big, but there were so many news crews surrounding the place, he couldn't block them all.

I zoomed out, backed up, and watched one more time. "Hard to tell with those stairs if that's her walk." In the sidebar, breaking news loaded with the title *PsyCops Question Killer*. The suit in the video-still looked suspiciously like Carolyn's broad-shouldered handler.

I tapped in.

"At this time I can confirm that Mr. Cooper abducted at least three women from a local shopping center, assaulted them, and held them in his home for a period of time we've yet to determine." The broadcast's lower third identified him as *Det. Jacob Marks CPD PsyCop Unit.* He didn't look anything like the shysters you see on talk shows claiming they could read your past lives and predict your future. More like someone Central Casting had sent over to play a psychic cop on TV. Smart, classically handsome, and just intimidating enough to bully any skeptic out of his good common sense. "One victim escaped and alerted a neighbor. She's currently being treated for her injuries." He paused, frowning...finding his "official PsyCop" character's motivation. "The bodies of two more women were discovered at Cooper's home. We're not at liberty to release any names until we have a positive I.D. and contact the families, but right now our top priority is identifying the victims."

The doorbell rang. Red and I both flinched like we'd been caught doing something illicit. I X-ed out of the page while he buzzed Carolyn in.

"A PsyCop?" I hissed. "How is it even remotely possible that woman is a PsyCop?"

"What do you mean?"

Her quiet footfalls were approaching fast. "I dunno. She's not all woo-woo incense and double-talk."

"Don't you read the paper? Every PsyCop team has a non-psychic partner to balance out the psych."

"I do my best to avoid polluting my mind with government propaganda," I muttered, but mostly I felt embarrassed that even for a moment, I'd entertained the thought that Carolyn was one of those phony crystal gazers. In fact, I was kind of relieved they'd hired someone like her to rein in Psychs like that other guy. Those were the ones to watch out for, folks so persuasive they could sell salt to a slug.

There was a tap on the door. Red ushered her in.

Carolyn had changed into jeans and a sweatshirt, but she was still wearing a black beret. "Thank you," she told Red, then noticed me lingering by the kitchen counter. "Do you live together?"

"Him and me?" I scoffed.

Red said, "I asked Crash to come over in case I need a hand."

"That's not why, not really," Carolyn took off the beret and twisted it in her hands. "But never mind. It doesn't matter. I'm relieved you can deal with this." She gestured at her brassy, unfinished hair. "I can't show up looking like this again tomorrow. I won't."

She was as blunt and unvarnished as she'd ever been at the shop, but knowing she'd been wading through dead bodies all afternoon put a whole different spin on her attitude. The only bodies I ever saw were the live ones in my bed. Even my dad's funeral had just been a restrained memorial service after his cremation. But judging by the way she moved now—gingerly, like she'd just fallen down a flight of stairs but didn't want anyone to know she was all banged up—I was certain she'd seen something she could never unsee.

Red guided her to a dinette table where all his gear was set up, sat her down and swaddled her in the cape. "We'll take good care of you. I promise."

Her face twisted. Reddened. "How long is this going to take?" she croaked out in a tiny voice. "They want me back at the station at six."

Damn it. I hate crying. "How about some wine?" I said briskly, and proceeded to slam through the cabinets before anyone even took me up on it. No wine glasses. I grabbed a pair of tumblers instead, sloshed some Pinot Grigio into each of them and shoved one into Carolyn's hand.

"Do you want to talk about it?" Red asked.

"No." Carolyn sipped the wine once, twice, then chugged down a few big gulps. "I don't know. Maybe."

Red handed me a comb. "Detangle her while I mix the lightener."

"Today was…." She hesitated, searching for words.

Red nodded. "We saw the news."

Carolyn's shoulders slumped and she stared into her tumbler.

I combed through gently. Carolyn's hair was still strong, but she herself felt brittle, like the wrong move would cause her to snap. Between strokes, I let her linger over her wine in peace. Filling the space with chitchat would've been ridiculous. No one should have a murder shoved in their face, then be expected to mouth banal pleasantries about their kids.

Red handed me an applicator brush, and I mirrored what he was doing, section and apply, section and apply. It went fast with both of us working, and with my focus on matching him move for move, I didn't notice the quiet until Red broke it. "Anything you need to say won't leave this room."

Corny as it might be, I was touched he included me in that assurance. But I was beginning to suspect Carolyn wouldn't take us up on the offer anyway when finally she said, "You'd think the worst part would be the crime scene. But it was the...." She shuddered. "I can't even call it a man. More like a *thing*. The thing responsible for those deaths. Talking to him. You know why he did it? Not because he was disempowered, not because he was in pain, not because he had trouble relating to people and the situation had spun out of control. He killed those women simply because he could."

We weren't in a salon and there was no mirror where I could watch her expression to gauge how she was doing, but I didn't need to see. Not with the agony so plain in her voice. I dropped a hand to her shoulder and squeezed. She leaned in, briefly. I suspected that was more reassurance than she'd normally let herself receive from a stranger. Maybe Red was right. Maybe I was a comfort.

She went on. "That poor girl. The one who got away. What kind of life can she have now? How can she ever trust anyone again?"

Thankfully, Red didn't proclaim that it was easy-peasy and all the victim had to do was *choose* to be happy. He finished the last section, tucked everything into place and covered her head with a cap and a towel wrap.

It wouldn't be long with her hair half-lifted to begin with, but without the distractions of the salon—no music, no chatter, no fluffy magazines—our wait might really drag on. Red pulled the other chair around so it faced Carolyn, planted himself in it and took both her hands in his while I boosted myself onto the kitchen counter just a few feet away. He gave her hands a squeeze and said, "Tell me a story. Back when you chose your path and you felt like you made a difference. Tell me about that."

She finished her wine. I reached for the bottle to refill her glass but she waved it away. "I can't show up with alcohol on my breath in the morning. Everything I do will be under the microscope as it is." She turned back to Red and looked deep into his eyes. "I thought I'd make a good attorney. No one expects you to be likable, just smart. If I could stop people from being falsely accused, railroaded...." Her face twisted again and she pinched the bridge of her nose, hard. "You can't pick and choose your clients. Not when you're a public defender. It was wearing me down, no doubt, but the last straw was a monster who beat his own grandmother because she wouldn't give him her ATM card. Broke her arm in two places. That piece of human garbage sat on the stand and lied through his teeth. Eventually, he walked. That smug little creep walked."

We sat and took that in, Red and me. I was grateful that the worst thing I'd be called upon to do in the course of my day was give someone an unflattering cut I couldn't talk them out of.

"Now how about someone you helped?" Red asked. "Tell me *that* story."

Carolyn didn't have just one story—she had more than she could count. People falling victim to predators. Mostly women, but not all. People whose stories were swept under the rug because they weren't as powerful, as charismatic, as believable as their assailant. People who finally had someone step up and hear them.

We rinsed her over the bathroom tub. She'd lifted evenly to a sunny level 9. While I toweled her dry, Red mixed up three different toners, the dusty cool pastel shades that would counteract all the yellow. Everything was meticulously measured, and every last measurement was jotted in his little notebook. He layered the tones, pearly grayish greenish violets. Usually I'm sad to see those muted pastels swirl down the drain leaving nothing but blonde behind. But even wet, I could tell Carolyn's subtle ash tones would be absolutely perfect.

We'd hit the wee hours of the morning by the time Red conditioned, but he took an extra few minutes to blow out the new 'do. Even puffy from exhaustion, with all her makeup cried off, our PsyCop still looked stunning.

Red offered to call her a cab but she said she was fine to drive. She'd only had that half glass of wine. So had I. And the rest of the bottle would likely go stale in Red's fridge, unless he ended up pouring it down the drain. He rebagged the two untouched bottles and held them out to me. "Don't forget these. Unless you want to stay."

The Vibe was subtler than a henna rinse on a redhead, but it was there. What started as a grab for the bag ended up with me catching his wrist, tugging him up against me and fitting my mouth to his. He gasped. The inhalation played over my lips and sent a shiver down my spine. But then he stepped back and left me swaying there, near-ly-kissed and alone.

"That's not what I meant," he said. "It's late. I was offering you my couch."

As he spoke, he chafed at the tattoo where my thumb had brushed over his pulse point, and I could see I wasn't the only one all a-tingle. I closed the distance between us and said, "It's okay. Whatever happens here, stays here, remember?"

"Nothing happening here."

So his mouth claimed. But his eyes spoke volumes.

I could drown in those eyes. A parade of delights trooped through my imagination, all the ways I wanted to make this man call out my name while his body convulsed with pleasure. Again, I bent my mouth to his. This time he was trapped by a chair so he couldn't back away. He turned his head instead, and my lips grazed his jaw. "I'm sorry," he said.

"You can stop playing around. Your hard-to-get act has done its job." I nudged him in the hip with the fly of my jeans. Not quite a hump, but still, a promise of things to come. And come. And come. "I'm officially interested."

He pressed his forehead to my shoulder briefly, then nudged me away. "And I'm flattered, but ain't nothing going down here tonight."

Since I can usually get in someone's pants with little more than a come-hither look, I found myself rusty in the art of seduction. But that didn't mean I wasn't enjoying the skirmish. He was so disci-plined I'd nearly missed the fleeting Vibe, but now that I'd caught a whiff of it, I couldn't back down. I followed him around the kitchen island and caught him by the belt loop. He stopped walking and I squared off in front of him. "You know it's gonna be good...so why deprive yourself?"

Red reached for my face and cupped it between his hands. Not to kiss me, but to gaze deep, deep into my eyes. For a gesture that didn't involve jacking, licking or fucking something, it was stunning-ly intimate. Hints of a subtle fragrance tantalized me. Sandalwood and amber. Unblinking, calm, and phenomenally serious, he said, "Because I'm seeing someone, and I won't step out on him. So that's how it is."

He let it sink in for just a moment, then released my head.

So. That's how it was.

I turned away, gathered my bag of wine, and showed myself out.

CHAPTER 12

Luckily I'm not much of a wine person, or I would've been tempted to drink myself to sleep with the two remaining bottles and wake up with a real head-splitter to show for my trouble. Since it was so late and I was so beat, it was enough of a nightcap to beat off in the shower while imagining that Red's invitation to sleep over had come from an entirely different *intention*.

It really wasn't the same without him.

I'm not one to wallow over a left-swipe, but Red's rebuff hit me hard. We had chemistry. We had an intense shared experience. Compound all that with the tantalizing slow build, and no wonder I was a goner. My mind replayed the sensation of his breath caressing my lips. What would have happened if I'd eased forward that tiny bit and pressed my mouth to his? And when would I get another shot—if ever?

If Red was uncomfortable with our near-miss, he didn't show it, so I played right along. I wouldn't be such a copycat as to adopt his "tell me a story" line, but over the next couple of weeks, I did spend extra time shooting the breeze during my client consults. I ended up giving some pretty interesting cuts. Anyone who seemed even remotely interested in color got an enthusiastic referral to our hotshot colorist.

It kept both Red and me nice and busy. Even so, there's a dead zone in the afternoon around three-ish where the salon is a ghost town, a gap where we stylists can duck out, put our feet up and check Tanngo...well, not Pilar. Probably not Red, either, since the thought of him hooking up with anyone who dashed off a "wanna suck U dry" message was beyond ludicrous. Not that I didn't entertain myself by casting him and me in that particular lurid fantasy, in full, graphic detail. I even gave him a little finger-wave when he caught my eye mid-daydream.

As usual, he allowed my flirtiest look to roll right off his back, even though we both knew he saw it. Initially, it had been frustrating, but lately it was starting to feel like more of a challenge. A harmless one at that. Innocuous enough that when he beckoned me toward the conference room with a nod, my heart only skipped a few beats.

"So," I said as I followed him in. "You've finally come to your senses and dumped Mr. Wrong? Feel free to cry on my shoulder. Either one. I'm told they're both pretty fetching, though I'm partial to the one with the sugar skull tattoo."

He acknowledged the flirt, marginally, with the ghost of a suppressed smile. "No shoulder required, but I could use a hand." He passed me a trimmer, then turned toward the wall sconce and brushed his fingertips along the back of his head, the shaved part at the base of the skull between mohawk and ear. "I've got a few strays driving me crazy."

I knew all kinds of creative ways to drive a guy crazy—but random tufts of hair were nobody's idea of fun. No one I'd ever met, at any rate. Lighting wasn't ideal in the conference room, but I grabbed him by the head and angled it so I could see exactly how much missed hair we were talking about. A tiny stripe of stubble curved its way around his occipital bone, wended up the lower part of his skull, then tapered gracefully away. A mere hint of an imperfection. Surprisingly hot.

I ran my thumb along the hairs, when what I really wanted was to follow it with my breath, my tongue. I wanted it so profoundly I actually felt as if I'd physically done it.

I shivered. So did Red.

It was a situation ripe for innuendo, but no words sprang to mind. I guided him to a chair and tilted his head toward the light, taking much more time and care in my analysis than the tiny swath of strays actually required. It wasn't a matter of perfectionism...I'm sorely lacking in that quality myself. It was more that this seemingly negligible request was actually rife with trust. Helping people is easy. Accepting help? Well, that's something else entirely. There's vulnerability that comes with admitting a weakness, a mistake, and I suspected Red's mistakes were rare indeed.

"I should grab a cape," he said...and was it wishful thinking, or did his voice sound a little thick?

"No need," I murmured. "You're in good hands."

People underestimate the head as an erogenous zone. Their loss. The scalp is flush with nerves, deliciously sensitive. Ostensibly, I was positioning him. But my fingertips were busy forging that elusive intimacy we only share with stylists or lovers. Sometimes my clients actually moan when I caress their scalps. Red didn't. Not aloud. But I convinced myself he wanted to.

When I thumbed on the cordless trimmer and it buzzed in my hand, the tingle went straight to my balls. The urge was strong to catch my breath, but since there were no mirrors to give me away, I settled for a slow, calming blink that he couldn't see. There's some vulnerability in admitting you need help, but even more in wanting something as badly as I wanted him.

I touched the humming blades to his scalp, whisper gentle, and caught the stray hairs in my palm as they fell. As promised, I was phenomenally precise. Not a single hair escaped down his collar. But I couldn't resist finishing my work by doing something I'd never do to an actual customer. I leaned down so that my lips were nearly grazing his scalp, and I blew.

This time, I did make him gasp.

"Curtis," he chided.

"Just being thorough."

He stood and ran his fingers over the spot, but he couldn't rub away the touch of my breath any more than I could erase the scent of sandalwood that was lighting up my senses. It was more than just some cheap head-shop cologne. There was warmth and depth from the way it mixed with his body chemistry...and now I was the one being driven crazy.

"Can I ask you something? Personal?"

The answer hovered at the tip of my tongue...whatever you're into, baby, I'm one hundred percent up for it. "Sure."

"Did you have a chance to check out that book?"

Uh...anything but that. "Can't say it made a big impression."

"How many of the exercises did you try? Because different methods work for different folks, and that book has a little bit of everything." Which was a lot more meditation than I cared to try. "I'm not trying to pressure you, I'm gauging your interest. There's a get-together tonight...if you want to check it out."

"A *meditating* party?"

"More of a group session."

"And you're inviting me to go. With you."

He touched the spot behind his ear. The one I'd blown on. "As my friend."

"As your friend."

"I told you, Curtis, I'm seeing someone."

"And he's hotter than me? No, seriously, I've been working out pretty hardcore lately, really focusing on my abs and pecs. Lock the door and I'll show you."

He semi-smiled. "I believe you." Now that I knew him, I could tell he was Vibing, loud and clear.

"So if I go to this thingy with you, I get to pick the place for our next date?"

"Since I'm not single, it's not a date," he insisted, almost patiently. "I'm offering to introduce you to a practice you might enjoy."

"And how long would this thing take?"

"Two hours."

Me, and him, sitting there in each others' vicinity for two solid hours with nothing for me to think about but all the dirty things I wanted to do together? I might be able to hold a three-minute plank without breaking a sweat, but no way could I endure two hours of close proximity leading up to nothing more than a wave goodbye and a cold shower.

I turned to the wastebasket and brushed the bits of hair on my palm into the trash. "When you get an invite to a Tantric sex workshop, I'll gladly be your plus-one. But tonight I'll take a pass."

He smiled indulgently, only slightly disappointed. As he headed back into the shop, I considered the fact that I should probably tone the flirtatiousness down so he didn't mistake my sincere interest for mere shtick. Play the solid friend, the confidante, the port he'd most likely visit in a breakup storm.

I was mulling over the fact that a true friend would likely go to that meditation snoozefest when raised voices caught my ear. I eased out onto the floor and spotted an older woman having histrionics at the front desk over the big swampy-green stripe down the middle of her head, and that delightful client was none other than Pilar's beloved racist, Julia.

Red glanced over and said softly, "And here's a prime example of why you don't use home color unless you know what you're doing."

"I don't want your goddamn colorist," she hollered at the receptionist. "I want Pilar."

The cowering girl looked back to me as if I might offer to step in and save the day like I had with Carolyn. No chance—totally different situation. Maybe both customers were in touch with their true feelings, but Green Stripe's true feelings weren't made up of frustration and annoyance. The woman was exuding a noxious cloud of hate. "Totally booked," I said smugly. "There's my three-thirty now."

"*I'm* the customer. I'm *paying*, so I should get what I *want*. Pilar is perfectly capable of dyeing my hair."

Red approached the desk and said, "Actually, repairing a bad home job is a challenge even for me. I think it's best to let the owner handle this." He strode back to Ralph's office without another word while I escorted my client away from the fray. All the stations were quiet, stylists and clients alike, as everyone strained to hear what would happen next. Pilar met my eyes in the mirror and gave her head a subtle shake. She'd been walking on eggshells since her job interview, and this Julia explosion was a resounding crunch.

I set up my customer as if nothing whatsoever was happening and got down to our consult. Vaguely, I was aware of Ralph handling

Julia himself, all arrogant competence that invited zero whining. I also noted that he called Red over periodically for advice. I personally would be leery of upsetting the power balance by offering my opinion to Ralph. Then again, he wasn't in the habit of asking for it. Thanks to the mirrors, every discussion was another chance for me to gauge the dynamic. Red wasn't afraid of Ralph...and maybe he needed to be. I pondered a way to tell him so without signing myself up for two hours of nonconsensual meditative torture.

When all was said and done, Julia was in Ralph's chair for over three and a half hours. I'd turned over four customers by the time he blew her out. She didn't seem very happy. Her new color was too dark, and it made her look older. But I supposed it was better than green.

Afterward, Ralph took Red into his office and closed the door. Several of the Juniors said, "Ooh...." under their breath. I focused very hard on my current client's sideburns, and hoped I wasn't a day late and a dollar short with that warning.

The two of them were sequestered until close. The whole staff was expectant and subdued when they emerged from the office, Ralph with tip envelopes and Red looking...perfectly at ease. Then again, Red was the epitome of calm. Probably from all that meditation. Ralph, then. I knew him well enough to know when his outer aplomb was covering a jugular hit in the making. Maybe he was agitated under his cool veneer. Or maybe I was just seeing tension because I expected to see it.

"Customers need a firm hand," Ralph announced for everyone's edification. "That's just how it is. But it's important to see when something's on the verge of escalating and call me in while it's still salvageable."

"Absolutely," one of the Juniors said, and another chimed in, "Good job, Red."

I was bracing myself for Pilar to be called out for not training her client well enough to begin with when Ralph excused the staff for the day, then turned to me and said, "Mr. Ash, a moment?"

Pilar and I had carpooled. She checked her watch. "Should I wait?"

"Unnecessary," Ralph said. "I'll call a cab. Unless..." He nailed me with his shrewdest look. "Was there somewhere you needed to be?"

"Not particularly."

He smiled, but it didn't reach his eyes. "Good."

CHAPTER 13

Pilar filed out after Red and the Juniors, but she shot a final "what the hell's going on?" look to me over her shoulder before she left. I was curious about what Ralph wanted too, since the whole Julia fiasco had nothing to do with me. It was entirely possible that he was already over the incident—every now and then he let terrifying things roll off his back, maybe just to keep us all on our toes—so he might've wanted to see me about something else entirely. He ushered me in and I wandered over to an open box of product samples to avoid sitting down, and modulated my tone to a cautiously negligent, "What's up?"

"You're sure I'm not keeping you from anything?"

"No. Why?"

"I'm trying to triage the day. I was supposed to have the website updates completely proofed and ready for the webmaster, and instead I got sucked in to that repair job. Since you've got most of an English degree...." He trailed off and gestured to a bunch of printouts scattered across his desktop waiting for the red pen.

There'd been something weird in his body language, something that was clearly not a Vibe despite the enticement in his tone, and I was relieved to realize it was just the awkwardness of him asking me for real help with an actual project. "Sure, no problem. Where do you want me to start?"

He frowned. Disappointed. He'd expected me to have a prior engagement, and when I didn't, he was stumped. I realized Red must've mentioned inviting me to the meditation, which Ralph then construed as a date. And not in the way I'd playfully—and unsuccessfully—tried to turn it into one.

Ralph Maldonado, jealous. Will wonders never cease? I was slightly flattered, but decided it was best to sweep the whole thing under the rug. Trysting with Ralph was one thing. Encouraging him to develop a sense of ownership was another. I kept my expression affable, mildly disinterested, and businesslike while he handed me a stack of pages.

His possessiveness ebbed. He gave me instructions to cut the verbiage by 40-50% to make it more mobile-friendly, plus a list of keywords to leave untouched. I moved the samples that cluttered the tabletop, parked myself there and got down to business.

Persuasive speaking doesn't necessarily translate into catchy writing. Ralph's prose was pretty stilted. Luckily, I could zap a lot of his extraneous words and blame it on the need to simplify and condense. While he ordered Thai from a little restaurant at the edge of the Square, I whipped the *who we are, what we do* page into shape. Ralph poured us each a glass of wine. Not the shop wine, I noted. A Chenin Blanc from his private reserve. I took a small sip to wet my whistle. Wine. Meh.

"See what you think of that." I handed him the marked up copy and moved on to the *services* page, which was focused on getting bridal parties in the door. Pilar was the master of the updo. If she left, Ralph would definitely suffer. Or maybe it wasn't a question of *if*, but when.

Once I finished blending in the paragraph about what it meant to be a Certified Color Specialist, which had obviously been cut and pasted from the official ACI site, I felt a little prickle. The type of twang you get at the nape of your neck when you're being watched. Ralph sat at his desk, fingertips steepled, eyes on me. I quirked an eyebrow in response.

"I'm glad you could stay," he purred. It was half past nine and the windows were pitch dark. Overhead lights were off, and the desk lamp threw harsh shadows across his features. I was surprised it was already so late. My Pad Thai was cold and my wine was warm. I'd never thought I had it in me to own a salon, but working on the site, taking a long view of the business structure and marketing, I'd been deep in the zone.

"No biggie."

"Not hungry?" Ralph asked.

"Just focused, I guess."

He uncoiled from his desk, and nailed me with a look. "Maybe you're hungry for something...else."

Oh great, I hadn't successfully deflected his proprietary interest after all. And here I'd been enjoying myself. It's a sorry state of affairs when you'd rather write than screw, but there you go. I made myself shift gears. For someone whose ego has its own gravitational pull, Ralph can take offense too damn easily. Rebuffing his persistent advances would only land me in the doghouse, so I pitched my voice semi-playful and said, "Depends what's on the menu."

He strolled around the desk and unhitched his belt. "Picture this: me, a naive and trusting soul, trapped and at your mercy. And you, a predator who's schemed his way into the situation, salivating to gorge himself on my innocence."

The mobile-friendly version being, *Suck my dick, Mr. Ash.* Good thing I was fluent in verbosity. I adjusted my body language and stood. Aggressive, feet planted and eyes narrowed. "I've seen you looking at me," I said, low, with an undertone of threat. "You think you're being inconspicuous, but it's obvious you can't keep your eyes off me."

Ralph backed into his desk, and crossed his arms. "That doesn't mean anything."

"No? Then why are you always checking out my package?" I gave myself a thuggish squeeze. "I think you're hot for me."

"That's ridiculous."

"Oh yeah?" I glanced down at his crotch. The desk lamp threw the contour of his bulging hard-on into stark relief. The thing cast a shadow halfway to his hip. "Then why are you stiff enough to bust your zipper, huh? Show me that dick, and then try and tell me you're not dying for me to handle it."

He didn't meet my eye as he eased open his jeans. As if he was demure.

"Let's drop the act here," I said. Ralph's gaze flicked briefly to mine, and I realized I'd picked an uncomfortably ambiguous turn of phrase. For damage control, I sank deeper into my role. "I'm the one in charge, and I will do whatever I damn well please. And you? You're not just gonna like it—you're gonna beg."

Ralph's shoulders relaxed. I grabbed him by the dick and started stroking him off. It felt...mechanical. Because what I really wanted was to work on the website. Or to be at home listing my empty fish tank on Craigslist. Or, hell, even sitting around at that lame meditation gathering. Now the only thing to do was get the sex over with and get on with my night, so I sank to my knees and said, "Go ahead. Beg me to suck you dry."

"I can't...."

"You'd better." I jacked him hard, watching the ruddy tip sprout from the tunnel of my fingers, then recede. Over and over. "Or else I'll leave you hanging in the breeze, aching to feel my mouth on you, with nothing left for company but your own prissy hand." That threat rolled out easily enough, since it actually seemed like a pretty good idea. But I didn't bother waiting for him to come up with some good begging. I wet my mouth and took my medicine in hopes of finishing him as quickly as possible.

The key to a good blowjob is to act like you're into it. Like the busboy, for instance. He would've been content to suck me off half a dozen times if I'd had the juice. As it was, I think we hit round four before I got too chafed to keep going. He was dick-obsessed—that much was obvious even before he started assailing my cell phone with pics. Me, I'm not into dick for dick's sake. While I enjoy a good hard handful as much as the next guy, what really interests me is the brain behind the boner. Although, by that logic, Ralph Maldonado should've been my ideal fuck-buddy, since the guy's always thinking. And here, I was hoping to get him off and get the hell out of there.

Ralph shoved in hard and nearly gagged me. "Taking what you want...just like you always do." That's right, pal. Run with it. I set a steady rhythm. "You've got the world by the balls and it's still not enough. You have everything, you greedy pig: looks, brains, youth. And you're still not satisfied—you want more."

I took *him* by the balls and squeezed, just enough to amp up the mood. He grunted, and his thighs clenched.

"You want my hard cock up your ass."

Actually, in that particular moment, getting plugged was the last thing I wanted. I played my tongue stud over the base of his cock in hopes that he'd change his mind, reminding him how amazing it would feel if I flicked the metal ball over the head once he came, in that uber-sensitive moment where it's so good it practically hurts. But no. While he pulled out and started rummaging through his desk drawers for a condom, I did my best to rub myself into a convincing hard-on while he wasn't looking so my lack of interest wouldn't be so apparent.

He opened the wrapper, but kept his eyes on me. It felt like I was the one being peeled and exposed, not the slimy latex. I'd hoped to steer the fantasy into different territory. Make him jerk off for my pleasure, or hell, bend him over the desk and treat him to a few surprisingly heartfelt slaps. But he was tugging on the raincoat, and I had nowhere to backpedal.

"Tell me how much you want it."

What I wanted was to go home. And, damn it, I was drawing a blank. "Enough with all the talk, show me the action."

I kicked out of my combat boots, shucked off my jeans and held out my hand for the lube. He tossed me the bottle. Neutral silicone, no smell, which was good. Scent is a potent trigger for memory, and once I managed to sate Ralph's appetite and head home, I wouldn't want random wafts of fragrance reminding me, whenever I shifted position, how I'd misspent my evening.

The leather couch would be the easiest on my knees. I positioned myself with my ass in the air, realized he hadn't yet joined me, and finally broke down and said, "Get over here and satisfy me."

And so the fucking ensued.

Back when I was a restless tween, my parents sent me to all kinds of summer enrichment programs to keep me occupied. Maxine claims I was hyperactive, and if I was left to my own devices, I'd eat all the baking chocolate, set fire to the curtains, and let the dog run away. One of the camps was a pioneer day program. Scintillating activities like making cornhusk dolls and lurching around the grounds in a makeshift covered wagon. But churning butter—now that was one hell of an event. All us kids took turns plunging away at the butter churn, worked our skinny arms to the bone driving the stick in and out, in and out. We labored away at it for nearly an hour, which seems like an eternity at that age. And in the end, all we had to show for it was a bunch of waxy globs floating in a thin milky broth.

What an image. Good thing tonight's results would be contained by the condom, otherwise I might lose my Pad Thai.

I couldn't see a clock from my position, elbows dug into the armrest and one foot braced on the floor. But judging by the amount of variations of "yeah, fuck me harder" I had to come up with, we'd been at it nearly as long as the kids at the day camp. Not only was it ridiculously late—Red was probably even finished with his meditation and was home with his tablet and his herbal tea—but the thrusts had gone well past the point of discomfort and were starting to register as pain. And not in a titillating way.

I pushed myself up, dislodged Ralph from my posterior, turned onto my back and wedged a pillow under my ass. "Come on, you worthless fucktoy," I growled. "Bring it on home."

He slung my knees over his shoulders and assumed the position. I watched his expression as he sank in, hoping to find he was as bored with the proceedings as I was. But no. Sweat had deflated his carefully-mussed hair, and the fringe clung to his moist forehead. His neck was flushed. And there was such a delighted gleam in his eye, it was obvious he was enjoying himself.

I started whacking off in time with his thrusts. Hopefully once I shot, we could call it a night. I wished I could close my eyes, but then it would be too obvious I was pretending Ralph was someone else. Besides, I couldn't actually imagine Red banging me to the point of tedium.

"How good is it?" Ralph panted.

"We're close," I said. Hopefully speaking the words would make it so.

"Tell me." His balls whapped me in the rump with every stroke. "Tell me how good."

So good I wanted to fucking hurl. "Shut up and finish."

"Tell me." Whap. Whap. Whap. "Say it."

The rational part of me understood that I was supposed to dredge up more praise for his prowess, but the next thing out of my mouth had nothing to do with stroking his ego. Without thinking, I'd reached for him. Not to draw him down for a kiss, either. Instead, I'd grabbed him by the sweaty neck with my thumb dug deep. "Listen, you sick sonofabitch, either you come right now or I tear off your balls and cram them down your throat."

I let go of his neck so fast, you'd think I accidentally grabbed a hot flat iron by the wrong end. Even so, the strike tipped Ralph over the edge he'd been riding the past solid hour. His mouth dropped open and his eyelids fluttered half shut, eyes rolled back to show only whites. He arched and gasped, and plunged in hard as he spent himself deep in my sore ass.

Once he was *finally* through, I tried to extricate myself from beneath him, but he had me pinned. His eyes opened, and he gazed down on me with immense self-satisfaction while neither of us made a move to stop my grudging erection from dying. Maybe I should've been miffed we'd dropped the pretense that I was enjoying myself, but mostly I wanted to get the hell out of there.

Ralph Maldonado is not a cuddler. So it irked me when he lingered there in his afterglow. He folded himself across my body, tongued my lower lip, then spoke against the wetness. "I didn't think you had the rough stuff in you, Mr. Ash, but you wear it well. Make sure you read up on the technique before you try it again. You could have crushed my trachea."

Again? Delusional fuckhead. There would be no next time. Not that I could come out and say it, not with him clinging to me, all sweaty and sated. It was when I was schooling my features into the blandest neutrality I could muster that I noticed something even more disturbing: a scent. Earthy and lemony. And nothing at all like the subtle, trendy fragrances Ralph usually layered, sparingly, with the delicacy of a surgeon.

Sandalwood.

And it was coming from him.

I grabbed him by the hair and pulled his face down into the crook of my neck, and muttered something about me doing whatever I fucking pleased and him being grateful...but it was all just a ploy to get in a good sniff. Definitely sandalwood. I shoved him away, and this time he obliged and rolled off me.

I didn't allow myself to jump to conclusions. Not while I was busy fumbling into my jeans and trying to act like my ass wasn't on fire. At least, I tried not to—but it wasn't like I could force my brain to stop thinking. I'd done the deed with Ralph often enough to know he's got the stamina of a typical mortal. The only way he could piston me for that long was if he'd recently shot his load. And he'd been sequestered with Red in his office for the last part of the day....

Fuck. I should've squeezed his goddamn throat harder.

For a guy named Crash, I've had more near-misses than anyone deserves. Before I could lambaste him for enhancing his game with a warm-up show, a glint of plastic on the floor caught my eye. The torn condom wrapper. Specifically, the brand name printed on the plastic: Endura-max.

The inside of the fucking rubber was spiked with anesthetic.

Those things are meant for three-minute wonders, not regular guys. I'd tried one before, just to see what it was all about. Nothing titillating about numbing the tip of your dick, nothing at all. So if he looked smug while he was laboring away between my legs, it wasn't the sensation he was enjoying. That jerk had *planned* on hammering me to the point of pain.

After I'd stayed late and fixed his windbag copy out of the kindness of my heart, too. Fucking ass.

I pulled on my leather jacket. Ralph was busy primping in the mirror, finger-combing his sweaty hair so it didn't dry lopsided. "Cab fare's on the desk," he said, without bothering to meet my eyes.

I looked down at the pair of twenties. About twice as much as it would take to get me home.

In other words, twenty for the cabbie, and twenty for...services rendered.

I definitely should have wrung his neck while I'd had the chance.

I probably could've walked home powered solely by the steam of my own outrage, but I wanted to get there sometime before midnight. Everything's a fucking mind game with Ralph, and everything's a test. If I left the money on the table, I'd be admitting he'd gotten to me, but if I took it all, I'd look like a fool. I'd ended up grabbing just one of the twenties, the proper cab fare. Either it was the smart thing to do, or by splitting the difference, I'd come out on the bottom.

Not for the first time that night, either.

I rode home with my phone in my hand and my thumb hovering over Red's contact. The only thing stopping me from following through was the fact that for once in my life, I couldn't figure out what to say.

I was angry on my own behalf, sure, but it was the thought of Red getting spooged on by that loathsome prick that really upset me. I'd already been there, done that. But Red was special. Untainted. Then again, nobody's body language had seemed particularly alarming when they emerged from the office. Maybe nothing happened between them.

Yeah, right. That's why the smell of sandalwood still clung to Ralph's sweaty hair.

Hindsight is more than 20/20. It's a panorama of obvious with a heaping helping of "duh." Red had been practically insistent about me joining him in his meditation outing. What if his motive had nothing to do with meditation, and everything to do with sharing concerns about Ralph's unwanted attentions—and I'd gone and brushed him off?

Or what if the invitation had been precisely what it looked like on the surface, and nothing more?

CHAPTER 14

I tossed and turned all night. I toyed with the idea of staying home and spending the day looking for a new job. In fact, it was tempting to never cross that threshold again. But I'd be damned if I let Ralph know the previous night's fuck-a-thon even registered. Besides, I couldn't just abandon Red to that despot's tender mercies. So I dressed myself in my most badass, head-to-toe, form-fitting black—a long sleeved T-shirt, silver studded belt, and strappy bondage pants—and spiked my hair with precision.

I was bulletproof. I'd have to be.

While I wasn't *afraid* of Ralph—I could totally take him in a fight—I had the sneaking suspicion he'd somehow manage to screw me again. The next time we crossed paths, what could I possibly say? I'd been trying out and discarding various blasé remarks all morning, but it turned out all my mental rehearsal was all for nothing. Ralph had a meeting all the way out in Rockford and wouldn't be in that day at all.

With Ralph thankfully out of the way, I could focus on someone I actually cared about: Red. His morning clientele was business as usual. A striking bronzed copper, some hand-painted highlights, and several regrowth touch ups. My morning was spent wondering how on earth he could handle Ralph's noxious pawing, what with all his morals and ethics. In mirror after mirror, I searched Red's body language for signs of distress. Even accounting for the fact that he's as easy to read as the small print on a toner bottle, he seemed perfectly fine, despite the fact that he'd spent as much time sequestered with Ralph yesterday as I had.

I came up with half a dozen ideas about the way Red was handling Ralph's attentions. Could it be that meditation was powerful enough to blot out the experience? Or was Ralph still in the wooing stages, making Red feel as if his talent was valued more than his exquisite ass. No, I finally decided. There must've been some kind of contact. That sandalwood smell didn't migrate on its own.

During the afternoon lull, I let Matthew think he snatched a walk-in out from under my nose, then lingered in the storage room under the pretense of finding another blow drier. I'd had a peek at the schedule and knew Red was between clients, and I also knew the likelihood of him running out to his car to check Tanngo was nil.

Apparently I wasn't the only one who was observant. Red opened the door and said, "Okay, Curtis. You want to tell me what's on your mind? All day long you've been staring at me—and not like you're picturing me naked, either."

Shit. All the thinking I'd done, and no good way to say what needed saying. "So look," I blurted out awkwardly, "this thing with Ralph...you're not the only one." I paused to see how he'd react to that, but in typical Red fashion, he gave me nothing but a cryptic, semi-raised eyebrow. I plowed ahead. "He's the boss, and so he gets what he wants. And the rest of us have to put out—but, heck, we've got nothing to lose. You, though, you've got that whole relationship thing going on. It's not worth risking something so important just to appease him."

He frowned. A thinking-frown. Maybe.

"Skills like yours," I said, "you can work anywhere. You don't need him. Sure, he'll try to blackball you when you leave, but don't give him a chance. One word: lawsuit. Ralph's all about his reputation. He thinks about retaliating, threaten him with a big ol' sexual harassment charge, he'll think twice about coming after you." I warmed up to my little fantasy. "After *us*. And then? Me and you, we find ourselves somewhere else to work...heck, maybe start our own thing—"

"You're sleeping with Ralph," he said.

The doorknob rattled. A receptionist called my name. I ignored her and she went away. "The point being, I'd back you up, you're not alone."

When Red squared off in front of me and grabbed me by the face, my initial reaction was relief. As much as I was ashamed about the treatment I'd been putting up with, it felt good to finally come clean. Maybe even liberating. It wasn't until he said, "Ralph and you. Tell me about it," that I realized Red hadn't reacted with a sense of solidarity.

He was pissed.

"I...guess it started a couple of weeks after he hired me. I thought his flirting was harmless. Just his way of being charming. But then one night after closing things got out of hand, and he was so apologetic afterward I didn't think much of it. Until it happened again. And again. And every time, it got a little bit weirder. By the time I decided the only one enjoying our alone-time was Ralph, I couldn't figure out how to turn him down."

Distantly, as I related my story, I heard someone try the doorknob yet again. I ignored it. Because Red was holding me lover-close and gazing deep in to my eyes, and all it would take to bridge the gap between us would be for one of us to lean in. Yeah, he had a boyfriend. But would his boyfriend understand like I did what it was like to be manipulated and used? The fantasy I'd seeded began to blossom, him and me, free from Ralph and doing our own thing. I'd cut, he'd color, and we'd only deal with the customers we actually wanted to serve. Pretty up the Olgas for free, and tell the Julias to go to hell. And afterward we'd close up shop and head home. Together. All in all, a pretty awesome pipe dream. Until the lock turned, the door banged in...and Ralph Maldonado burst through it.

"How dare you?" he wailed—and it was impossible to say whether he was hollering at Red, or at me. At least until we broke apart and Red staggered back a few steps, and Ralph's eyes stayed on him. "After everything I've done for you—finding you an apartment, paying to move you out here, making a name for you—and *this* is how you repay me?"

Red didn't quail beneath Ralph's outburst. He squared his shoulders and faced it head-on. "Everything *you've* done for *me*? I left the only home I knew to bring my talent here—and you've got the nerve to act like I should be grateful." He took a trembling breath, modulated his voice, and said with deathly calm, "And what exactly is it you think is going on here?"

"Given what I just walked in on?"

"Curtis and I were talking."

"Oh, believe me." Ralph gestured at me in disgust. "I know this one's entire vocabulary."

"So he tells me. He's always been truthful, which I can't say for you. And I won't abide a liar."

Something shifted then, as if the ceiling opened up and epiphanies poured through. I finally pieced together the reason Red hadn't seemed distraught about spending hours in Ralph's office.

He hadn't been forced to cheat on anyone.

He'd been *with* his cherished boyfriend the whole time.

"You and Ralph?" I couldn't have kept the dismay out of my voice if I'd tried.

Ralph, meanwhile, realized Red was way more angry than he was, and decided to switch tactics and play on his sympathy. "So I made a mistake," he blubbered. His face had gone crimson and his eyes squeezed out crocodile tears. "You're always going on about forgiveness, don't I deserve another chance? You said you loved me—was that even true? Are you going to let this whore come between us?"

"Whoa," I barked. "Whoa, whoa, whoa. I'm the whore? Me? You're the one who can't keep his dick holstered."

"Curtis," Red interrupted, and I bit back a stream of insults that would make *even a whore like me* blush. "This isn't about you."

Damn straight. "Never mind. Let's go."

I pivoted toward the door, fully prepared to bank Ralph into the wall if he tried to stop me, but then I realized Red hadn't budged.

"Get out," Ralph shouted—not at Red. Just me. "Get the hell out of here, and don't you dare set foot in this shop again."

I looked incredulously at Red. "Aren't you coming?"

He gave his head a single, angry shake. "I can't."

"I had no idea the two of you were an item," I said, "so I'm not the one at fault here. You know that, right?"

Ralph stopped hemming and hawing, and looked expectantly at Red, who gathered himself, and with grim precision, said, "Every one of us...we are each responsible for our own actions."

I imagine it says something about my dubious moral character that I was stunned Red wasn't willing to tear out the door with me, hand in hand, whooping and laughing and dashing off into our newfound freedom. If he couldn't see that we were both the victims here, that we owed Ralph nothing, no explanations, no reparations, not one damn thing, then he was blinded by his own fucked up, self-righteous code.

I stormed out the door, past the receptionist—you'd better believe I wanted to give her something to cry about—and into the stations. I wrapped up my kit and snapped the photos off my mirror. My mother's dog in a ridiculous sweater. Me flashing my then-new tongue stud, and Pilar with a daith piercing that hadn't lasted a week. Sixteen-year-old me with my dad and the frumpy used Subaru he'd bought me. All this history, unceremoniously shoved into a messenger bag along with my shears and clippers and flat irons.

I took a deep breath and finally looked up as I slung my bag over my shoulder. Trevor, Matthew, Pilar. Plenty of history there, too. All of them stared at me in wide-eyed disbelief.

I'm sure I would be just as shocked, as soon as it really sank in that I was bidding Luscious a final goodbye.

PART TWO

A Spark of Empathy

CHAPTER 15

Three weeks later...

"Good mor-ning, my Lit-tle Peanut!" my answering machine chirped. I really needed to ditch that landline. Way too intrusive, and surprisingly pricy. Not to mention potentially mortifying. But thankfully Matthew was in the bath where he wouldn't hear Maxine over the roar of the oversized showerhead.

I mashed my face into the pillow and hoped my mother would just talk herself out, but her singsong voice went on and on, extolling the virtues of a spirulina cleanse she'd heard about on the Menopause Channel, or wherever it is she gets her daily dose of balderdash. The less embarrassing shit the junior stylist knew about me, the better. Not that our boredom hookups were in any danger, just that I didn't want him to give me any shit. Plus my first appointment was scheduled at the crack of nine, so I decided I might as well get it over with and pick up the phone.

"How's the new job?" Maxine asked, a little too brightly.

"Different. Very different."

"Getting there isn't a problem?"

"Not at all." Not if I took the bus, anyway. The very first day I was half an hour late trying to park, only to find my sideview mirror knocked sideways and brutally scuffed when I left for the day.

"And what about the safety alarm I bought you? Did you remember to put it on your keychain?"

"I think of it every time I handle my keys. And then I think of you." I also think of the way I pitched it right in the dumpster where it belonged, but I opted not to mention that.

Satisfied, she brought up the next item on her agenda. "It's the last day of the month."

"Did we have plans?"

"No. It just occurred to me that rent is due on the first."

My mother isn't a renter. She owns her house. It's the one I grew up in. As far as I knew, it was paid off...which meant that suddenly, out of nowhere, she's decided *I* need to be reminded to pay my monthly bills. "Yup. That's typically how apartments work."

"So...everything's okay?"

You gotta love how subtle she thinks she is. "If I was living in a cardboard box, I wouldn't have answered the phone, right?"

"Don't be mad."

In my peripheral vision, I glimpsed Matthew shuffling blearily toward the front door in wet hair and last night's clothes. He gave me a halfhearted wave goodbye, which I just as halfheartedly returned. "I'm not mad, I'm annoyed. There's a difference."

"I need to make sure you're okay. I'm your mother—it's my job to worry about you."

And apparently her main duty was to add insult to injury by inventing problems that weren't even there. I'd managed to dissuade her from driving into the city and checking out my new workplace by texting her a few carefully framed pictures. If she ever saw the salon with her own two eyes, she'd be trading in her spirulina smoothies for Xanax.

Parking aside, I personally dug the new neighborhood. True, there was a dangerous element. But it was way less contrived than Lincoln Square, and the only oompah came from snatches of bouncy mariachi. It was tempting to linger over my coffee. Instead of boring businessmen and even more boring tourists, I rubbed elbows with students and musicians and artists.

My own sensibilities had even started to shift. At Luscious, the stylists had been encouraged to look hip, but fastidiously put together, and never too edgy. Clothing with holes in it would earn you a stern lecture—or a bare-assed spanking that was nowhere near as playful as it seemed. But that creep Ralph was no longer the boss of me, and lately more and more casual "bar clothes" were sneaking into my daytime wardrobe. All the mirrors told me I was rocking my edgier look. Not that Red was there to enjoy it. He'd blown out of town after our tete a tete in the storage closet and hadn't looked back.

Screw 'im. Plenty more fish in the sea. Plenty of horny hookups on Tanngo, too.

For the first time since my ill-fated teenage gig as a supermarket bag boy, I didn't technically have a boss. A pecking order definitely existed, though. There were five stylists altogether, with a collective experience of over thirty-five years. Twelve of those years were on Gail Kessell, a fellow refugee from Luscious. Her entire wardrobe (including her hair) was black and red, her arms were two solid sleeves of kitschy ink, and she could stand for twelve hours in pleather rockabilly pumps with three-inch heels. On paper, Gail owned the indie salon where I now plied my trade, but the stylists working there weren't her employees. We rented the booths, supplied our own product and equipment, and scheduled our own appointments. It was a lot like being an entrepreneur—other than the fact that I had no control over the name of the salon.

CUTTERZ.

That's right. With a "Z." And all in caps.

Maybe one day I'd become inured to it. But right now, the mere thought of the cutesy spelling made my sphincter clench.

The thought of calling up still more of my clients from Luscious didn't feel so hot, either. Most of them claimed they'd get back to me just as soon as they had time for an appointment, then blew me off for one of the Juniors. This was not mere speculation. I'd coaxed the info out of Matthew with a hand-job and few pomegranate martinis.

It would be an understatement to say the intel was a major blow to my ego. I'd sincerely thought I shared a bond with at least some of those clients. Turns out they weren't really that into me, just the convenient parking and free chardonnay.

I got that the CUTTERZ location was nowhere near as

glamorous—and nowhere near as convenient. But my schedule was wide open and I'd even lowered my rates. Twice. And still, I couldn't figure out how to get business in the door.

As I approached the shop, coffee in hand, I noticed a big A-frame sign outside the shop. Black and red helium balloons tied to the sign were bapping against the building in the wind. I suspected someone with idle hands would set them free within the hour. In fact, the sign itself might walk away too—this wasn't Lincoln Square, after all, and it wasn't chained down. Foot traffic was fairly nonexistent with the shop tucked away on the second floor of the building, so I was glad to see Gail had done something to draw in some fresh meat...at least until I saw exactly what her irresistible offer entailed.

CUTTERZ $20 walk-in special! Ask for Gail!

Fucking hell. There I was, struggling to schedule clients at a bargain basement thirty-five bucks, while she undercut me by nearly half. Even worse, she was setting up the expectation that a haircut wasn't worth a round of drinks. There had to be some kind of diplomatic way I could dissuade her from screwing us all with her $20 price tag. I climbed the narrow staircase and scrabbled to come up with something less hostile than, *What the fuck, Gail?* but unfortunately I was drawing a blank. And when I opened the door and found my nine o'clock sitting in Gail's chair with her hair sectioned and her baseline already shaped, I nearly choked on my tongue stud to stop from blurting it on out.

My client was an airheaded middle-aged soccer mom who'd never worked a day in her life, so apparently it didn't occur to her that it was seriously uncool to park her ass in Gail's chair when she'd been scheduled for mine. "Hi, Crash! I love the new shop, the neighborhood is so artistic."

"Gail," I said calmly, "Mrs. Palmer was scheduled to see me."

Gail raised her meticulously thin eyebrows and gave me an *oops!* shrug.

The oblivious client piped in, "I just figured since you weren't here yet and I need to make sure I stop at the stationery store before lunch, Gail could do my cut this time." Same difference to her, maybe, but for Gail to agree to the arrangement was a major faux pas.

"Especially since you weren't here."

"It's five to nine. I'm early." I couldn't quite keep the anger out of my voice, either.

"Don't be mad," she said with a ludicrous pout. "I'll wait for you next time."

"You can have my next walk-in," Gail offered.

I hadn't even cleared the threshold and I was already angry enough to beat someone to death with a curling iron, so I turned around and walked right back out. I had to cool off before I told Gail exactly where she should shove her next walk-in. Red Turner would've told her how he felt in no uncertain terms, but me, I didn't know how to be angry without exploding. And what difference did it make what Red would have done? It was no use pining after him. He'd fallen off the grid and didn't want to be found.

As I thundered down the steps, lighter clicking furiously at the cigarette now clamped between my lips, a first-floor door opened and a woman called out, "Hey, Blondie, hold on a second."

I paused in the cramped vestibule. Between my coffee and my lighter, I had no idea how I thought I'd get out of there unless I planned on kicking the door down, and probably burning myself in the process.

"I hate to ask, but can I bum a smoke?"

The mood I was in, I wanted to bite her head off. But she was an old lady, and my downstairs work-neighbor, too. And she wasn't the one who'd just poached one of my clients.

My unlit cigarette stuck to my lip, and it bobbed as I spoke. "That ginormous neon palm reader sign in the window—is it yours?"

"Guilty as charged. Marketing. Back when I was your age, a cheap ad in the paper was all it took to get more bookings than I could handle. But now everyone and their brother claims to be psychic. Name's Lydia."

"Crash."

I pocketed my lighter and held out the pack. She tapped out a cigarette and handed it back. "C'mon in, if you want. It's cold outside, but I've got a back hall where we can smoke."

I wanted to refuse, but a peek out front told me it was crapping down sleet, and I didn't want my hair to sag. Plus, as much as I think official so-called psychics are a bunch of bullshit artists, the *Tarot Card Palm Reader* sign appealed to my nostalgic side, like the Ouija Boards of my childhood.

I followed her in.

Her store was smaller than CUTTERZ, a square room draped in black, punctuated with framed motivational posters of corny sayings. She had a pair of black couches that almost matched. The coffee table was scattered with well-thumbed copies of Astro Fortune and Lucky Numerology, and the far corner housed an altar type thing with statues of Buddha, Ganesh, and the Virgin Mary, all of them in sore need of a good dusting.

"This is the waiting room." Lydia pointed at a sign on the coffee table that read, *Have a seat—Your future awaits.* "Walk-ins can park themselves here and I don't need to pay a receptionist."

We crossed through to a black-painted door in the far wall. The next room was smaller, maybe the size of my den at home, and hung with beads and boas, psychedelic paisleys and tie-dyes. A round table draped in black and a few dining room chairs were the only furniture. "I do readings in here. Nothing else. The routine helps me get in the zone, and there's sound-blocking foam underneath the hangings. Just a tiny chime when the front door opens—and the Buddha's got a nanny-cam in his belly button I can see from my cell phone."

Through the reading room were even smaller rooms: a bathroom, a kitchenette, a bedroom sized more like a walk-in closet. A similar setup to CUTTERZ, in miniature. But there was an additional door off the kitchen we didn't have upstairs, and that door led to a stairwell. A damp, rusty stairwell to a scary meter room, but at least we could smoke in it. There was an old barstool on the corner of the landing. Lydia parked herself there, so I sat on the stairs.

She lit her cigarette, took a deep drag, and exhaled. "So you're one of the new hairdressers, huh?"

"Stylist." I suspected the difference was lost on her. "Did your psychic telepathy tell you that?"

"Just observation and common sense. I've seen you coming and going from the shop. Either you work there or you get your hair done an awful lot."

"Too bad you're not for real. I could use some psychic advice right about now."

The crow's feet around Lydia's eyes crinkled in amusement. "Who says I'm not real?"

"You tell me about your secret Buddha-cam but you still feel the need to peddle the psychic song and dance?"

"What can I say about letting you in on my secrets? You strike me as a good guy." And she struck me as someone who knew how to sweet-talk people to her advantage. I could probably take a lesson from her and use it to deal with Gail. "But the Psych stuff? That's not just a marketing scheme. I'm a certified level four."

"Okay, Psychic Lydia, if you're so perceptive, then tell me. Why did my colleague just put herself on my shit list over twenty lousy bucks?"

"I can't answer you as a Psych. You'd need an empath or a telepath to figure that one out. I'm a precog."

"Oh. That's convenient."

"I am picking up something, though: if you change your tune, I won't be the one to convince you." Which she knew by reading my body language, since in fact she could safely say that *no one* would convince me that palmistry was any more legitimate than spirulina cleanses or karma.

Lydia had my number, all right. I could definitely take notes from her.

CHAPTER 16

Confrontation isn't my forte—I enjoy it a little too much. But unless I wanted to start my professional life over in another city, I'd need to figure out how to work with Gail. First, though, I had to bring in some money.

I'd crunched the numbers. If I didn't take in two hundred bucks a day, come the end of the month, I'd be short. That would mean putting my expenses on plastic. And my credit cards were getting a vigorous enough workout as it was.

By the time I got back upstairs, my stolen client was already gone. I hoped Mrs. Palmer was happy with her fifteen-minute hack job. No, scratch that—I wasn't thinking out loud, so I might as well be *authentic*. What I really hoped was that she hated her hair and was kicking her traitorous self all the way home.

And I would indeed take the next walk-in, thank you very much. Sure, I was accustomed to $20 tips, not $20 cuts. But I couldn't let Gail get away with pushing me around.

I marched straight through the salon and into the bathroom to brush my teeth and douse myself with Febreeze. On a good day I'd wait until I got home to have a cigarette, but frankly, I couldn't even remember my last good day. To top it all off, when I grabbed the towel to dry my face, something fell out of it. Something big and brown and hard-shelled that hit the sink with an audible clack, then scurried down the drain.

I stared in dismay. If I ever brought home roaches in my clothes, no two ways about it—I'd have to burn my building down. Gingerly, I rehung the towel and blotted my face on my sleeve...and tried to ignore the sinking feeling that $20 tips were unlikely to happen in a second-story ghetto salon infested with vermin.

I was so busy feeling sorry for myself that the sound of my own name almost didn't register.

"I don't care about your special. I came here to see Crash. Specifically."

I knew that voice. That wonderful, bitchy voice. And I was so tickled to hear it, I didn't even need to *act* delighted when I burst forth from the back room to rain on Gail's parade. "Detective Brinkman. A pleasure, as always."

Carolyn had planted herself in a spot where she could take in all of CUTTERZ. Hands on hips. Frowning. Then she got a load of me and said, "I went through a lot of trouble to find you."

So sentimental. That's my girl. I gave her one of my new cards with only my name and my cell phone. No salon.

She tucked it into her suit jacket. "Do you have time to touch up my roots?"

"Always."

I ushered her over to my chair, and paused to give it a final whisk-down before she sat—sentimental or not, I didn't think she'd take too kindly to bringing home roaches either.

"So what's going on? Red's not taking my calls. His apartment is up for rent. Neither of you are at Luscious anymore."

I shook out my cape, checking for hangers on. None.

"It took three tries, but I finally got the receptionist to tell me where you were."

"And was she crying by the time you dragged it out of her?"

Carolyn scowled for a moment, then said, "A little."

We watched each other in the mirror as I combed through. She'd been keeping up with her home care. The ends were healthy and the cool tones looked fresh. She didn't pry. And I didn't owe her any explanations. And yet that night we'd spent at Red's place hung between us, an intimacy forged by circumstance. "It's complicated," I finally said.

"I figured."

Touching up regrowth is more exacting than people realize. You can't just slop the chemicals on. You only want to lift the virgin hair at the root, with as little overlap as possible. I was careful with Carolyn's hair, and not just because she'd tell me exactly what she thought if I didn't do an immaculate job. Unlike my other fair-weather clients, she'd jumped through hoops to find me. We had a bond now, and I was determined to deliver.

Gail butchered three $20 walk-ins by the time I rinsed. And we still had toning to see to.

I remembered which main toners Red used on Carolyn, and I could deduce the rest. And once I mixed, I made sure to key it all in to my phone for future reference. "Too bad you couldn't just read that crybaby's mind," I remarked as I painted in the cool beiges.

"What?"

"At the salon."

"Why would you say that?"

"Oh, you know how the news is. They love a good PsyCop story."

"I wasn't on the news."

I gave her a quick wink in the mirror. "And you're not the only one with deductive powers of reasoning."

Between the chatter and the blow driers and the sound system piping in pretentiously obscure underground punk, no one else could hear our conversation, but Carolyn dropped her voice low anyway. "Don't tell anyone, okay? As a favor to me."

"You know what they say. Only her hairdresser knows for sure." So she didn't want to talk shop. That was fine. But with my palm reader encounter fresh in my mind, I couldn't help but add, "It must be a real treat dealing with that so-called psychic every day. Strikes me as an insufferable know-it-all even without seeing the official certification claiming his mental telepathy is real."

Carolyn whipped her hair around so fast I dropped a glob of violet where it wasn't supposed to be. "My partner?"

"Big guy, bigger attitude? That's the one." As I blended in the toner, I could tell I'd rattled her more than I anticipated. "So...you two aren't an item, are you?"

"Of course not. I told you, I'm married."

Like that meant squat. But I knew when to back off—especially since this was the last client I wanted to alienate. I changed the subject and prattled on about the traffic and the weather, but it felt hollow, filling the space with meaningless words when I really wanted to troop out some "psychic" facts and figures and make her admit it was all a bunch of PR and spin.

Rinse, dry, smoothing serum, blowout. Perfect. I stood behind her and angled her head so the lights hit the color just so, and watched her carefully in the mirror. "Not to toot my own horn," I finally said, "But this touch-up is impeccable. So why the frowny face?"

She struggled with something for a moment, then said, "Can I meet up with you later? Somewhere more...private?"

Curiouser and curiouser.

The day wore on. I had two more clients scheduled. One cancelled and the other was a no-show who claimed she couldn't find the new salon. If I'd brought a laptop like one of the other stylists, I could have been putting together a mailing list or building a fabulous social media presence. But I'd been telling myself all that marketing stuff was beneath me since I had my loyal clientele. Right. Eventually I argued for another one of Gail's walk-ins. And I had the sinking feeling that not only would I eventually need to drum up all new customers at CUTTERZ, but I couldn't get away with charging anywhere near what I was worth. Not in a salon with roaches in the bathroom and an owner who'd shill herself for twenty lousy bucks.

I was so eager to get out of there I nearly tripped over the battered box at the foot of the stairs. I picked it up and glanced at the address label. Fair Fortune LLC, attn: Lydia Vallecillo. As much as I wanted to be anywhere but there, I could hardly leave Lydia's stuff in the vestibule for someone to steal. I tried her door. It was open. And weirdly enough, I felt myself calm down a few notches in the atmosphere of that tacky waiting room with its black-hung walls and dusty shrine.

I leaned over the Buddha and waved at his jeweled belly button. The inside door opened, and Lydia greeted me with, "Hello, neighbor."

I held up the dented package. "Personally folded, spindled and mutilated by your friendly local mail carrier."

"C'mon back. Let's see if there's a damage report in my future."

"I really should head home."

"Truth be told, I'm dying for a smoke. C'mon, kiddo, don't abandon me in the throes of a nicotine fit."

She headed toward the back stairwell and I followed. Another piece of furniture had joined the barstool on the landing: an old wooden school desk with a chipped saucer to use as an ash tray. She perched on the stool and I crammed myself onto the desk's attached chair. I barely fit. Even so, I was touched by the sudden urge to launch a spitball. Amused, but slightly saddened.

When had all the playfulness drained from my existence?

Lydia took a deep drag to stave off her withdrawal, then tore into the side of the box. She dumped out a clear plastic bag full of hemp and beads. "Looks like they made it intact," she said.

"What's with those bracelets, anyway? Even my mother has one."

"Some study they did in Denmark last year—I don't bother trying to puzzle through the dry research, but I know a good profit margin when I see one."

"What kind of study?"

"Figuring out whether gemstones affect mood."

"Puh-lease. That's so subjective." I made a *may I?* gesture at the plastic bag and Lydia motioned for me to go ahead. I plucked out one of the bracelets. String, a couple knots and a few pinkish beads. "How much are people willing to pay for one of these?"

"That depends...mostly on how you present them. Thrown in a pile like this, they look as cheap as they are. But in a glass case, or maybe a fabric pouch, I've seen them go for fifteen, maybe twenty." She tugged a bracelet out of the pile and one of the knots unraveled, sending beads pinging to the cracked cement. "Of course, they'd need to hold together long enough for the customer to try them on." She sighed and picked up a bead, which she rubbed against the crumbly brick wall a few times, then ran her thumb over the bead's surface. "And to top it off, these aren't even gemstone, they're glass."

Big whoop, it was all a placebo anyway.... But I was curious. I traded Lydia a few cigarettes for one of her ugly beaded bracelets.

"And you picked a black bracelet," she said. "Why?"

"It...matches my wardrobe?"

"Black is the color of grounding. You're a skeptic, you don't strike me as someone who needs more grounding."

"And you don't strike me as someone who'd think I'm gullible enough to care. Besides, you said they're only glass."

"Good, you're paying attention. But if they were actual stones, what would you be looking for?"

"You're the 'psychic'. You tell me."

"Prosperity? Money drawing? No, more than that. Money comes and goes, but a good customer, that's a lot more valuable than a one-time Charlie. Citrine, the merchant's stone, that's what you want." She held up a bracelet with beads the color of urine.

"And again, I'm compelled to point out that it's not even citrine, it's glass."

"True. But it can't hurt to keep your eye out for the real deal."

Carolyn didn't call me right away, but given that she'd gone through so much effort to track me down at CUTTERZ, I had no doubt I'd hear from her just as soon as she was ready. And in the meantime, I could stay home, save the money I'd normally spend at the bar, and bone up on the various psychic "talents" so I didn't seem completely ignorant.

The Internet being what it was, legitimate sources were few and far between, and before I knew it I got looped into taking a "How Psychic are You?" personality quiz. And once I was done, it could tell me which Backstreet Boy would be my best romantic match.

In my defense, it hadn't *looked* like a random Internet meme. The site was plain and utilitarian, there weren't any ads flashing in the sidebar, and whoever had written the thing took great care to make it seem legit. But then there were the questions.

Check the statements that best describe you:

_ When part of a song sticks in my head, I hear the song played the same day

_ I often mention songs that other people are thinking about

_ I've found myself singing along with an old song I've never heard before

_ I can guess what a friend is listening to while we're texting

_ I find different meanings in song lyrics when other people are present

Obviously, it was excruciatingly scientific. I didn't agonize over any of my choices, but I did pick the obvious ones to see what brand of mental telepathy it was trying to make people think they possessed. There were some real doozies. I think Pilar would've gotten a kick out of the statement, "I sense when someone is attracted to me." Too bad I couldn't click that one extra-hard.

My end result should have been "Congratulations, you have common sense!" But no, according to the fourteen-year-old who put together the quiz....

You are an EMPATH

People were once said to have empathy when they put themselves in others' shoes and tried to picture how they felt. Now it's been proven that true psychic empaths can actually register the emotions of others. Relationships come easy for you as an empath, and you're seldom lonely. Empaths excel in psychological fields, though you must take care to shield yourself from negative emotions. You may prefer to work with animals instead. You would also make an excellent salesperson.

Ridiculous quiz aside, I'd managed to bone up on enough current Psych research to seem passingly knowledgeable. The more I read, the more I wondered. While I didn't know Carolyn all that well, she didn't strike me as the sort of gullible rube who'd buy into all the hype. And yet she was working with the PsyCops—a program that had surprisingly little documentation online, unless you count angry, misspelled rants in the comment sections of news stories.

She called before the week was up and offered to treat me to dinner. "I've been feeling bad about not paying for my initial haircolor," she said. "And since Red's not around, and your old salon wasn't really involved...." It would've been fun see her try paying Luscious anyway, if only to elicit another volley of tears.

I picked a Mexican joint with margaritas to die for and met her there on a hoppin' Friday night. She showed up in jeans and a clingy black top. And despite the perma bitchface—or now with the blonde, *because* of it—she turned heads.

Once we'd made ourselves cozy with the chips and salsa, Carolyn said, "Red bought a plane ticket to San Francisco but his last residential address is his old apartment in Chicago."

I rolled my eyes.

"Whatever happened is none of my business, I know that. But I care about him. And you."

"It was a sordid love triangle with tears all around—me, the boss, and the boss' pet. We're lucky it didn't end with a murder-suicide." Her face clouded, and I added, "Uh, sorry. I don't know many people who actually deal with things like that other than getting sucked into melodramatic reenactments on TV."

She nodded and stabbed a few holes in her frozen margarita. "I'm concerned you figured out as much about my job as you did based on two fairly vague conversations."

"You high-tailed it out of there while your hair was a lovely shade of tangerine and I put two and two together. Or, technically, Red did. He's *so* observant." Observant enough to spot Carolyn off in the distance on the breaking news, but too oblivious to notice Ralph fucking anything that moved. I tapped my salty rim against hers and said, "Here's to Red. Best of luck in San Francisco. May we never speak of him again."

We turned back to our drinks and sucked on the straws while the icy whip in the glasses got smaller and smaller. I suspected Carolyn was no stranger to awkward pauses. She gazed into her drink, licked her fingertip and captured some of the salt from the rim and touched it to her tongue. And when she was good and ready, she said, "Please don't tell anyone I'm a PsyCop."

Who would I tell? As soon as the thought occurred to me, I

realized my mother would be profoundly impressed, and the tid-bit would definitely wow her friends at Pilates. The Juniors would've emitted some high-pitched squeals. Hell, even my new smoking buddy would probably have a few choice words.

"I'm not in the habit of spreading other people's secrets," I said.

"That's a relief. People act like Psychs are all out to get them. There aren't many I can really talk to."

And there weren't many customers who could be bothered to follow me to a different salon. Then again, I didn't dip from the com-munal salsa with customers, so I supposed I should recognize the relationship for what it was: a budding friendship.

"People seriously find 'Psychs' threatening?"

"All the time. All. The. Time."

"Huh. Good thing you're there to keep it all in check."

"I don't follow."

"Well, no matter what kind of crazy predictions your psychic partner pulls out of his butt, you're there to process it through the filter of rationality."

She finished off her drink, motioned to the waitress for another round, then leaned in close and said, "Crash, my partner's not the Psych. I am."

CHAPTER 17

I'd always thought I understood human nature, but maybe I'd been overestimating my abilities. First I find out Red was in a committed relationship with Ralph. Then Carolyn turns out to be a card-carrying Psych. It was starting to look like I was nowhere near as perceptive as I'd presumed.

Working at a salon gave me lots of opportunities for people-watching. Saturday had better foot traffic than the weekdays, and all of us stylists concurred that Gail shouldn't be the only one offering the walk-in deal. If we had gaps in our bookings, it made more sense for one of us to take the customer than to have them sit around waiting for Gail.

She didn't like it. I knew this not because I'm an empath, of course, but because her facial expression, body language and tone of voice couldn't possibly point to anything else. But she also had four stylists who were seriously annoyed with her, and if enough of us decided not to renew our contracts, it would take a hell of a lot of $20 walk-ins to replace the income we provided.

It was a busy enough day. I scoped out the customers and I watched the stylists interact with them, and I played a little game where I pretended, briefly, that each of them had a psychic talent. Could a telepathic stylist mind-read their way into a more solid rapport, a better haircut, a bigger tip? Or was it all simply a matter of paying attention? All I had to do was notice when someone looked particularly pleased with their cut to make sure they took my business card and promised to ask for me next time. All but two were totally down for it. Even at a higher rate.

Saturday was a booming day for Lydia's business, too. Flush enough that she sent me out to get her a carton of smokes of her very own while she finished up her last few clients. Once we'd enjoyed that delicious after-work cigarette in the back stairwell, we adjourned to the closet-sized office to dissect my current situation.

"So I'm playing this game," I said. "I keep my eye on Gail, on all the stylists, and I pretend I know what everybody's thinking."

"What about that owner lady—what's the script you imagine running in her head?"

"I catch her looking at me and I realize, ha, I'm a threat. I'm younger, I've got better training, and people like me. She's trying too hard. And it shows."

Lydia pulled out her fortune telling deck. She handled it the way I handled my shears, like they were extensions of herself. She shuffled through, cut it in the middle and glanced at the card. She turned it toward me: The High Priestess. "Inner knowing. I love it when this pops up in a reading for someone as cynical as you."

"It doesn't take magic powers—I mean, psychic talent—to read people. It's all a matter of paying attention."

She dragged her thumb across the edges of the worn cards and cut again. Ace of Pentacles. "Usually this one is some kind of windfall, an opportunity, a sum of money that comes out of nowhere. But in your case...see that arbor in the background? Looks a heck of a lot like those bracelets I showed you. I think you can incorporate gemstones into your business strategy."

"You know what I think? That you just want to unload that bag of ugly bracelets."

"Nah, I got rid of those already. A client mentioned his kid was having a birthday party, teenage girls. They're crazy for those things. I even made a few bucks." She gave the cards a fond shuffle then tucked them back into her pocket. "Psychic talent aside, gemstones have a lot going for them. Crystals oscillate at their own frequencies.

So do the cells in your body. Bring them both together and something's gotta shift. They're cheap, too. Really good markup value. Here's what I'd do in your situation. Offer a base haircut that's competitive with that cheapo. But for only five dollars more, you'll do a gemstone profile, tell your customers which stones resonate with them. And then upsell again: another ten will buy them a gemstone totem to carry around and enhance their aura."

As if I could say the word "aura" with a straight face. The specifics of Lydia's plan were preposterous, but the thought of showing up Gail left me giddy with anticipation and delight. Bar time came and went while I was at home on my couch with my laptop, browser tabs filled with a dozen gemstone sites, from folklore to scientific research to wholesalers to crafts. I'd even taken apart one of my old necklaces to try my hand at knotting one of those beaded bracelets, a macrame type thing. It took maybe half an hour. But once I knew how to do it, I'd get faster. And my brain was already working on how much cooler they'd look with more interesting stones woven in.

I managed to rein myself in from hitting that buy button, but only because I wouldn't be home to accept a package before one of the neighbor kids stole it and threw it in the courtyard birdbath. Besides, pictures can be deceiving. If I planned on augmenting my services with trinkets and doodads, I'd need to get a look at them in person.

Naturally, Maxine was delighted when I suggested we scope out a bead store before lunch.

"Isn't this a-dor-a-ble?" she crooned over a necklace kit. Even in the photo on the hangtag, it looked like something you'd see on a middle schooler. The focal point was a chunky, stubby stone heart, pale pink. Rose quartz. And while my initial impulse was to tell my mother exactly how cheeseball I thought it was, I realized that by impugning her middle-aged suburban taste, I'd be passing up a golden opportunity at market research.

"What appeals to you about it?"

"I don't know. It's cute."

"You never wear pink," I pointed out.

"Well, no. I'm an Autumn." She dropped it in her basket anyway.

"It's not like picking out a diamond or anything—it's just a cheap, fun treat. I like it, so why not?"

Why not, indeed? An impulse buy could definitely give my business a boost. I didn't want to end up selling macrame jewelry, though. Over breakfast I'd unraveled my initial bracelet attempt to see if I could shave off some time from their making, but frankly, the five-year-olds in the Hong Kong sweatshop who'd put together Lydia's samples did a better job than me.

Lack of craftiness aside, there was definitely something about the gemstones that got my wheels turning. Not the pseudo-science about their "vibrational fields," but the perceived value.

When people think gems, they picture an engagement diamond and two months' salary (which is just another clever marketing ploy). But the bead store sold bags of gemstone chips for a mere couple of bucks. I even recognized several of their names from my research. Quartz, turquoise, hematite and garnet. I held up a tiny plastic bag of tourmaline and watched the light play through the colors. They weren't unlike a good semi-permanent glaze, bold colors that didn't wash down the drain like the pastel toners that kept blondes from looking brassy. On the surface, it might not seem like hair and gemstones had anything to do with each other. And yet, if I found that connection, I could exploit a unique angle that none of the other stylists had even considered.

If Maxine was connected to rose quartz, I found I was curious about the citrine, despite the fact that I really wasn't a big fan of yellow. No doubt the power of suggestion at work. Lydia had managed to sell me on them, even though I knew they were only so much bunk.

The chips were cheapest. I bought ten varieties of stone chips and a few dozen tiny glass bottles with cork tops. Total expenditure on each potential impulse buy, maybe a couple of bucks apiece, and a lot easier than braiding bracelets for my psychic friends. Unfortunately, they were fussier to put together than I anticipated. Without a tiny funnel, those damn bottles were surprisingly difficult to fill—so yet again I found myself working into the wee hours without so much as a nightcap.

But come showtime, I was ready. Even if I was still picking chips of agate from between my toes.

I scavenged the spice rack from my kitchen—which I never used anyway, since I live on takeout—and set it up at my styling station. My cunning plan was to play it cool, let the little bottles of rocks sell themselves. Unfortunately, maybe I played it a little too cool. Only a couple of customers asked about them, and those who did weren't keen on taking one home.

Another night of studying stretched out in front of me. If my customers were going to be enticed to "treat themselves," I'd need to be able to tell them what the darn things were for. Or at least what the Internet claimed they were for, since no doubt they'd go home and debunk me if they thought I was shilling bullshit. Turns out I'd created some pretty interesting metaphysical vibrational combos based purely on my aesthetic decision to add one color to another.

My printer ran out of ink in the middle of the first printout and it was too late to go hunting for a refill, so I ended up labeling everything by hand. I suspect it didn't take much longer, and it gave me a good reason to tie a business card on each bottle. Plus it gave my rock jars a certain artsy-craftsy appeal.

Unfortunately, customers were sparse the next day. And they seemed more intimidated by my rocks than intrigued.

"Don't give up yet," Lydia told me. "You're the salesman. Sell them."

And so I kept my eyes peeled for the methods other businesses used to bundle their services, from the car wash that charged double for an extra spray of wax, to the meal deals at restaurants that pimped fries and drinks no one needed in their stomach or on their waistline.

Between clients, I turned a dye box inside out and created a "Specials" table tent of my own. The basic was still $35, but for $50 I'd add in a Therapeutic Touch session—basically, a luxuriously lengthy scalp massage. And for $75, they could have the Full Crash Experience and extend their energetic bliss with my custom mineral blends.

Was it ethical to take advantage of people's gullibility by peddling vagaries and nonsense about "energy"? I dunno. I was careful not to make any actual claims. And I made sure my scalp massages kicked some serious ass.

And when my customers talked, I listened. They wanted essential oil? I dabbed it on their temples. They wanted herbs? I packed them in drawstring bags and wrote affirmations on the muslin in fabric markers. Pretty soon the old ladies at the craft store knew me by name. Each new offering required an excruciating amount of research and a hefty outlay of cash, but I couldn't argue with the results. My metaphysical accessories not only paid for themselves, but they allowed me to nudge my basic price closer to what it used to be in a fancy salon—a salon with a parking lot, a receptionist, and a distinct lack of roaches.

Gail was green with envy. She lowered her walk-ins to $15 and turned up the volume on her annoying CDs in an attempt to harsh my customers' vibes, but my clientele wasn't bothered by the pretentiously underground production values. They were the disaffected ex-art-school-punks who listened to that shit themselves. They were hipsters and millennials and even the occasional gangbanger. And the louder the music got, the more my secrets stayed with me. I sank my fingers deep into the clients' hair, leaned over their shoulders, and murmured whatever new agey reassurances occurred to me. No one else could hear. It was just my customer, and me.

I seduced them. I pampered them. I satisfied them.

And then, like a sated lover basking in the afterglow, they'd pick up their phone and brag about it to all their friends.

Time flies when you're having fun...or at least the self-satisfaction of knowing you're worth more than twenty bucks. Between customers, I found a message from Carolyn on my voicemail, and a shiver ran through me that was the opposite of deja vu. More like the feeling that since we'd last spoken, everything had changed.

"Is it too soon to do my roots? It's my anniversary, I've got this dinner coming up...." A short sigh. "I need help."

I booked an appointment. Of course I did. But the rest of the day I felt like an upwardly mobile bride caught in last year's gown. Psychic talent was serious business for Carolyn. She believed it gave her a crimefighting edge. Me, I'd been mentored by a palm reader with a big neon sign, and it showed.

I didn't leave my gear at CUTTERZ where Gail could paw through it at her leisure. I brought it downstairs and stowed it in one of Lydia's tiny back rooms. The next morning I left half of it there in hopes of toning things down and making it less obvious I'd been trading on the popularity of all things psychic.

But knowing Carolyn would be there, I saw my station with fresh eyes. Even without my spinner rack of gemstones and my incense bundles, it still looked as if my haircutting was a flimsy excuse to hawk potions and charms.

And to make matters worse, when Carolyn strode through that door, she dragged the ghost of Red along with her. No, he hadn't perished in some dramatic streetcar accident, he was just dead to me. But seeing her again brought that night in his apartment flooding right back. It wasn't just Carolyn who'd be judging my mortifying song and dance. It was the paragon of integrity, Red.

My voice sounded edgy to me when I greeted her with, "My favorite detective," and caped her with a flourish. She didn't seem to notice. Her scowl was turned inward and the line between her eyes was deep. My shtick had been honed so carefully over the course of the month that muscle memory took over. I sank my fingers into her hair. Not in the cursory way most stylists check length, but in the more intimate way I'd taken to touching my clients while I watched their body language and considered how I might lift not only their hair color, but their spirits.

Something was definitely up. I could see it in the set of her shoulders and feel it in the way her eyes avoided mine in the mirror. I wasn't going to pry it out. When she was ready, she'd talk. I just blocked everything out—the music, Gail's glares, my own embarrassment—and focused on the scalp massage. *Relax, relax, relax. Everything will work out. It's all good.* Obviously I couldn't psychically shoot the ideas through my fingertips. I needed to get myself centered. Thoughts like that are reflected in your stance and your touch, and whether or not people realize it, we're reading body language all day long. Panic is contagious, but so is calm.

Carolyn's eyes had drifted shut, and they opened with a snap.

She blurted out, "My husband isn't attracted to me."

Well...that sucked.

Maybe the change was too much for the guy. Maybe he just wasn't into blondes. (Baffling, I know.) While I could probably come up with a bunch of reasons, I didn't immediately begin flinging them out. I paused, absorbed what she said, and then went back to the massage with my mantra. Relax, relax, relax.

When the hitch between her eyebrows unhitched, I leaned in so as not to scream over the music and said in her ear, "I dug out my old mannequin practice head last night and practiced an updo that's sassy as all getout. Maybe it'll blow him away, maybe not. What matters is that *you* know you're smokin' hot."

We spent two hours together, my icy blonde PsyCop and me, and nary a word was said about my silly novelties—or anything else. It was probably for the best that it was too loud to talk. I'm hardly one to give relationship advice. I might know how to land 'em, but I've got no clue how to keep 'em.

And while I generally don't do makeup—the wedding and prom circuit is really not my forte—I begged a tube of lipstick off one of the other stylists and finished off Carolyn's look by painting her lips a bold, neutral red.

She scowled at herself in the mirror. Even the scowl was sultry. Whatever the husband's deal was, I hoped Carolyn knew her perfect look when she saw it. If a man wasn't into the real you, then what good was he?

Since I didn't have any more appointments lined up, I suggested we swing by our restaurant for a quick pre-husband nip. When our margaritas came, I slid into the same side of the booth with her and said, "Give me your phone." I snapped a picture of the two of us together so she could see herself like I saw her, fun and vibrant, then handed back her phone. "Your husband's a lucky man. Don't you forget it."

CHAPTER 18

Tips at CUTTERZ were nowhere near as good as Luscious, plus I didn't get an hourly rate, but between my special treatments and my marked-up party favors, I was bringing in something like my old income. I didn't have to tolerate Ralph's slimy groping to earn it, either.

Sure, what I offered was mostly window dressing. But the funny thing was, I got off on it. I spent my evenings checking out all the so-called psychic services people offered. Most weren't old-school like Lydia's fortune telling business. Nowadays they were more likely to combine themselves with pseudo-medical "therapies" or semi-psychological coaching.

Bureaucracy being what it is, the city tried to take its cut by limiting and licensing. Being certified as a psych was a four-figure proposition, and that's just a single test. It doesn't take into account the actual coursework you'd need as any kind of real therapist. But if the New Age practitioners were sufficiently vague in their claims, they could make do without an expensive certification—psychic, medical or otherwise.

It's all verbiage. I couldn't call myself a therapist, but I could say my services were therapeutic. Maybe I should have felt "inauthentic" for exploiting loopholes. I didn't. I saw it as my duty to work the system that was trying to validate a bunch mumbo-jumbo firmly rooted in the placebo effect.

I'd put through for a wholesale license, not because I relished doing complicated taxes, but because it allowed me to shop where I could get bigger quantities of my best selling items at better prices. It meant buying in bulk, but so what? I wasn't home enough to be bothered by the growing mountain of boxes dominating my living room.

I'd just scored half a pallet of incense, got it locked and loaded, and only realized once I was merging onto the Eisenhower that my car smelled an awful lot like Red Turner. No way was I going to store it next to the empty fish tank and have my whole house stink in a parody of domestic bliss. If I stuck it out on the balcony, it would get rained on, nearly three hundred bucks down the drain. Hopefully Lydia wouldn't mind the smell. If anything, it might augment her business.

I shot her a quick text asking if she'd mind babysitting a few cartons of stinky incense and got an immediate reply: *Outlook not so good.*

While I'm a strong believer that clairvoyance is a bunch of hooey, several aspects of the reply pinged my radar. First, Lydia is such a heavy smoker, her nose probably hasn't worked right in thirty years. Second, she had the space—I'd just moved two boxes of herbal hacky-sacks out of her closet. And third, she was being suspiciously cutesy by quoting the Magic 8 Ball...and the last adjective I'd use to describe Lydia is *cute.*

By the time I got to Wicker Park, I started telling myself I was overreacting. The building looked the same. No dramatic explosions or rioting mobs. Maybe I just didn't know Lydia as well as I thought I did. I left the incense in the car and hurried in. Everything was hunky dory. The vestibule was its unlovely self and the stairs were still standing. Nothing out of place. Nothing but a single sheet of paper stuck to CUTTERZ front door...a love note from the Board of Health shutting it down for unsanitary conditions.

Numbly, I went downstairs, parked myself within view of the Buddha's belly button and thumbed through an old magazine that extolled Ten Ways to Make Yourself Lucky. I'd go for just one, if there'd be any guarantee it wasn't utter horseshit. After an excruciating stretch, Lydia's client emerged, a twenty-something chick practically aglow from her reading, and I realized with no little disgust that I was jealous. What was waiting in her purported future? Love, money, fame? Whatever it might be, I doubted it was signed by the Board of Health.

Lydia slouched against the doorframe and crossed her arms. A sateen caftan decorated with astrology symbols covered whatever she had on underneath, most likely jeans and a T-shirt. "Tough break, kid. I'm booked up today, but if you want to hang out here..." she cocked her head toward her tiny back rooms. "Feel free."

I realized I wanted to be anywhere *but* there. Ridiculous as it was, I felt betrayed. As a certified precog, the logic went, Lydia should have warned me something like this could happen. Yes, I was fully aware psychic ability was all a trumped up scam. And yet there was a wounded flutter of disappointment deep in my gut anyhow.

I was supposed to meet my mother for a craft fair and an early Sunday dinner, but I needed time to think. Never mind that I now had all the time in the world, since there was nowhere to report for work come morning. I couldn't deal with the thought of fending off Maxine's strained inquiries into my wellbeing, so I texted a vague line about not feeling so hot. She'd presume I was hungover. I didn't bother to correct that presumption.

Back at my apartment, my late optimism surrounded me in the form of great, teetering stacks of boxes. Thousands of dollars, sunk. Herbs and tinctures, rocks and beads. Utter crap. Hours ago, I was positive I'd sell it all, and more. Now it loomed around the edges of the apartment, mocking me.

My Luscious customers were a loss. Even if I hung my shingle right next door, they'd find some excuse to not switch salons. But in all likelihood, I'd keep the clientele I'd started building up at CUTTERZ if I stayed in that neighborhood and worked similar hours. I could count the number of salons in a mile radius on one hand. The fancy ones were all owned by stylists too besotted with or too terrified of Ralph Maldonado to give me the time of day. The small ones were one-woman operations in someone's home or basement. Plus a Mexican barber shop that probably wouldn't appreciate my unique accessory scheme.

Even as I broadened my search, it was all more of the same. Gail had been my one shot. And it couldn't have crashed and burned any more spectacularly.

I was staring at the same online map, clicking through the same few red salon dots hoping maybe I'd missed one that would fit, when my cell phone rang. I could not deal with Maxine. Not now. She'd insist on giving me a spirited pep talk—bad enough—and even worse, I'd undoubtedly hear the threads of relief and self-satisfaction as she not-so-secretly reveled in my failure. Because clearly, I wouldn't be in this predicament if only I'd been something more respectable, like a senator.

I almost sent the call to voicemail before I realized it wasn't my mother, it was Pilar.

My pall lifted. "Long time no hear, girlfriend," I said. "I sure as hell hope you're not looking for a chair over at Gail's place."

"Why, what happened?"

"Condemned by the Board of Health, that's what."

"Wow. That's a drag. But once she fixes the violations...."

"I highly doubt it." In the course of my research, I happened upon some of the fines she would have racked up. Beaucoup bucks. She could do fifteen-dollar cuts round the clock and not even put a dent in them. "To be honest with you, I really won't miss working with Gail. I always felt like I had to keep one eye on her or else she'd undercut me...and I'm not talking about a high fade, either.

"But you—I really miss working with you. You know how to treat people, and you take the time with them to make them feel special. Your cuts are right on the money, every time, and your clientele keeps coming back.

"I'll bet if you flew the nest, enough of them would follow. Think about it: me, you, a little shop of our own. We run it like we want. No stupid Square Days or meltdowns at the reception desk. Charge what we want and keep every last cent, plus the tips. And best of all, no *Ralph* to deal with."

"Since you left," she piped in, "he's been kind of a non-issue."

"You'll have to help me out. I can't even begin to picture that."

"He's laying low. Stays in his office, mostly, and just focuses on the business end."

Maybe for now. But Ralph was too old of a dog to learn new tricks; he'd start focusing on an end much fleshier than the *business* end just as soon as he recruited another stylist who got under his skin in all the right ways. "Obviously I won't wish his wrath on anyone, especially you. But you know it's just a matter of time. Nothing will ever really change there, he's too married to the power. Tell me you don't sense it every time he hands out the tip envelopes."

There was a pause. Three years of sounding off at me about Ralph, and suddenly she needs to be diplomatic in her choice of words? With me? "Funny you should say...that's one of my duties, now."

"Handing out the tips?"

"Anything to do with the Junior Stylists. He put me in charge."

She'd spoken gingerly, as if she was scared of pissing me off. Which pissed me off even more. "Senior Stylist. I see. I suppose I should take you out for a celebratory drink."

"Totally. Next week, maybe? Not right now—things are crazy busy right now." Right. So if Pilar wasn't calling to bitch about Ralph, which I now realized was the basis of our relationship, and if she wasn't calling to gloat about her promotion.... "Actually, I was hoping you could put me in touch with Red."

Oh, girlfriend. You did not just say that.

"Because Julia was in for a touch-up and I'm starting to see some green peeking through—box color is such a mess, and I don't want to make it worse. If he could tell me what he used to counteract it in the first place—"

"No." I said it calmly. I think. Pilar waited for me to elaborate. I didn't.

"No, you don't have his number? Or no, you won't help me out because you hate Julia?"

I took a deep breath, let it out slowly, and said, "*All* the no."

"Fine. And not that you asked for my advice, but maybe if you acted more like a professional, people would start treating you like one."

CUTTERZ closing when it did was the perfect storm. I'd just paid a fat stack of bills including rent on both my apartment and my booth.

Yes, Gail owed me that money back, but I wasn't counting on her forking it over anytime soon. So that left me with a bank account running on fumes, a living room full of gimmicky rocks, and absolutely zero income in the foreseeable future.

I thought being free from both Ralph and Gail would feel liberating, but instead their absence just made me aware of the nagging feeling I should *do* something. If only I knew what.

One good thing came out of all that time off. I got so sick of looking at my empty aquarium I finally put it on Craigslist. People are funny, though. Despite the quality of my tank, no one was willing to pay even a quarter what it was worth. The local FancyFish had a tank that size on sale, and even though that model was a cheap piece of crap, the prevailing argument was that mine should be even cheaper because it was used. So I told them if they felt that way, they were welcome to shop at FancyFish.

Maybe I told one or two to fuck off, too.

The thing about Craigslist is that it's so easy to wander over into the personals and end up wasting time on a bunch of lame nooners. On the plus side, I met several hot guys over the course of the month. Too bad none of them were paying clients. And none of them knew the value of an aquarium, either.

Meanwhile, all my daily expenses went on the plastic. Every time I tried to stick to an allowance, I'd realize my gas tank was empty, my stomach was rumbling, or I was distressingly sober. Eventually I decided the daily allowance was an abstraction anyhow. What good was it to try and balance income with expense if my income was always zero?

My job search broadened. If it came down to it, I was willing to babysit a cubicle or wait tables to get my feet back under me. But looking like I look, I didn't endear myself to the corporate types—and restaurants weren't willing to take someone without foodservice experience, even when I did argue that I loved people and I was used to being on my feet all day. I suspected the arguing part hadn't scored me any points. Then again, I wouldn't have had to argue if they'd just kept an open mind and given me half a freakin' chance.

I was closing in on the first of the month again, and with that, all the bills and payments I'd so cleverly engineered to come due at once. At the time, it was a matter of convenience. Now I was well and truly worried.

Once the first of the scary bills hit my inbox, I fled down to Wicker Park to see if Lydia might have any ideas. She managed to support herself without an unbearable boss or a shitty dayjob. She'd help me come up with something.

"I figured you'd come around sometime soon," she said. "The Page of Wands has been hopping out of the deck all morning. C'mon in back and help me get these hangings to the laundromat."

If I'd felt even remotely guilty for doing all the taking in the relationship, I rid myself of that notion ten minutes in. Those old ceilings are high, and unhooking the dusty curtains was nasty, precarious, eye-watering work. It took almost an hour for us to bundle them into some hampers—how had she planned to do all this herself?—and then three trips up and down the block to stuff them into the huge industrial front-loaders.

We parked ourselves in the plastic chairs to watch the curtains begin their journey to cleanliness. It was comforting. Who knows if it was the hypnotic motion of the sudsy water churning through the fabric, the camaraderie, or the fact that I was somewhere other than my stifling apartment. Even though I was still coughing up dust bunnies, for the first time since CUTTERZ went bye-bye, I could actually breathe.

Lydia said nothing, just sat in silence in the chair beside mine, absently drumming the heels of her sneakers on the linoleum. Her mere presence was a comfort. So much so that my guard dropped, and I blurted out the words, "I think I'm fucked."

She turned to me with a look that was part wiseass grin, part affection. "It ain't over till it's over. I'm sure you'll bounce back."

"Right. Is that your professional opinion?"

"You can't afford my professional opinion." While she said it with a smile, I could tell she was utterly serious...and I realized that anytime she'd exchanged a cut of the deck for a cigarette, she could have just as easily gone across the street and bought her own pack. "But I'll take a look just to satisfy my own curiosity."

She pulled her deck from the pocket of her hooded sweatshirt and began to shuffle. I put my elbows on my knees, parked my chin on my fist, and watched the laundry spin. "See if your cards know where my rent is coming from."

Lydia cut the deck. I was doing my damnedest to act like I wasn't looking, but my curiosity got the best of me. She was smiling to herself. "Looks like your best bet is to move."

"If I knew the Mother's Basement card was lurking in your deck, I wouldn't have asked."

"Oh no, nothing like that." She turned the image toward me. A blond guy in armor stood in a chariot pulled by two dog-sized sphinxes, one black, one white. "This move would be more of a victory. Not a retreat."

There were several more months left on my lease, and signing a new one with no job and no money for a security deposit was about as likely as me sprouting a pair of wings and learning to fly, but I kept that opinion to myself. I knew going in that Lydia at least claimed to believe psychic powers were real—if the big neon sign wasn't a clue, I don't know what was—so I kept my mouth shut. Lately, I needed a friend a hell of a lot more than I needed the satisfaction of being right.

"Your old salon will be back on the market just as soon as they're done ripping out the plumbing they auctioned off," Lydia observed.

"The place that was shut down by the Board of Health...if living *there* didn't make me a badass, nothing would."

"It's zoned both business and residential."

"I'm not even remotely optimistic enough to launch my own salon. I just watched someone fail spectacularly, and I'm a pretty quick learner."

"Who says it's gotta be a salon? That inspector cites the manicure joint down the block every few weeks, but he's never once come through my place. The Board of Health won't bother you if you're not doing anything that can transfer communicable diseases."

"Well, that's no fun at all," I said listlessly.

The washer spun fast for a few seconds, paused, spun the opposite way a few times, then settled to a stop. Lydia carted her hangings to the massive wall of dryers, then came and sat back down. "How much is your rent now?"

Too much. I shrugged.

"The place upstairs was going for seven-fifty."

My ears perked up. Surely I'd misheard. "Dollars? Are you sure you've got the decimal point in the right place?" Good luck renting so much as a closet for anything less than a grand.

"They're not the most hands-on landlords, but you can't beat the price. I'd put in a good word for you."

I closed my eyes and allowed the soothing whoosh and tumble of the dryers to wash over me. "Thanks, but no thanks. One thing at a time. What I need right now is a source of income."

CHAPTER 19

Lydia ended up agreeing to try and sell off some of my herb bags for a 25% cut. She might be a friend, but she was a businesswoman first. Since anything was better than nothing, I'd agreed, but it was tough to hide my disappointment. A ping on my Craigslist aquarium ad was as good an excuse as any to head home.

I had little hope of actually selling the thing—hell, I had little hope for much of anything these days—but I was relieved the guy who showed up to look at it didn't mention the FancyFish sale. He was kind of adorable in an understated way, too. A saddish sincere look about the eyes. A wistfulness to his smile, albeit somewhat passive in the sack. Not that he didn't ooh and ah in all the right places, but for the most part he just laid back and enjoyed it while I did all the heavy lifting. The shower afterward was actually more fun than the main event. He gave shameless utterance to the world's worst puns. I laughed at them just as shamelessly.

Afterward, I watched as he circled the tank, wet-haired and barefoot, shirt untucked and pants a little rumpled, running his fingers along the wooden base. "This is just what I'm looking for. But how *firm* are you...on the price?" He winked.

I rolled my eyes.

"Sorry, gotta ask. I'm told it's weird if you don't barter."

"I guess I could come down a hundred bucks." It wasn't as if anyone else was hounding me for it. Besides, we'd just enjoyed some quality time together that really lifted my spirits.

It must've been the way the daylight streaming through the windows glanced across the sheen of his damp hair that stirred up my tender domestic feelings. I wanted to card my fingers through the wet strands, and not just to check the angles of his most recent cut. Guys look more wholesome in the light of day than they do in the bleary wee hours after last call. I can picture them doing things other than dropping trou, like maybe watching TV. Or grocery shopping. Or joining me for Sunday brunch with Maxine.

"And you're selling it because you're moving?" he asked.

I cut my eyes to the stacks of boxes piled up against the living room walls. Moving would've been an ideal reason to sell, but I wasn't about to lie. Now I'd have to get into the whole faulty heater incident and hope he didn't think I was trying to unload a leaky tank on him by distracting him with my charms.

"This is such a great neighborhood," he went on. "Restaurants, bars, shopping, all of it right here. And the layout is fantastic. Mind if I take a look at your kitchen?"

"Be my guest."

He strode through, caressing everything. Countertops, cabinets, even the high-arched faucet. Was this the sort of guy who knew how to cook? I could see it. The type who'd make me dinner—or even breakfast in bed. Framed by the cabinetry, he turned to me with his melancholy smile and said, "My boyfriend would absolutely love it."

What?

I didn't say that aloud, of course. I was too stunned to make a sound.

Oblivious to my utter lack of response, he went back to his fondling—now his greedy fingers were all over my stove—while I reminded myself we'd never actually discussed whether or not we were single.

Normally I wouldn't have presumed. My mistake. Clearly he'd happened upon me in an aberrant state of vulnerability.

If I didn't have a bunch of payments coming due, no income to pay them with and no job prospects either, I might have told him to keep his hands to himself, put on his shoes and get the hell out. Funnily enough, though, I was suddenly so sick of my life, I found myself saying, "Well then, maybe I can interest *the two of you* in a sublet."

The legalese of moving went smoothly enough, and even though I was jobless, my new lease got approved. I put the cost of the movers on one of my credit cards, piggybacked off Lydia's wi-fi, and set up my bedroom in the middle of the vast gutted space that used to be a salon. Living room, dining room, everything else, too.

The open plan setup looked edgily chic, at least if you weren't facing the wall where the CUTTERZ shampoo station used to be. I supposed the hole-riddled plasterboard and capped off plumbing served as a cautionary reminder: it might be tempting to set up a salon here, but don't do it. You'll never get away with it.

Cos the roaches? They were persistent little fucks.

I hired a pest control service. They came out and sprayed once a week. "I'd be careful around all that hazardous stuff," Lydia cautioned—through a haze of cigarette smoke—but it wasn't like I could just sit back and do nothing. Unfortunately, a few days after the exterminator did his thing, I'd invariably find an interloper wriggling its antennae at me from the kitchen counter or the bathroom sink. Unless we sprayed the entire building from top to bottom, and then our neighbors on either side, and then the rest of the block too, my six-legged friends would keep on coming back.

Eventually I switched to glue traps. They were a lot cheaper and no less effective. Plus I didn't have to worry about poisoning myself.

Or my guests. Because while I had no desire to open a salon while the watchful eyes of the Board of Health were on my building, who was gonna stop me from throwing parties? It was a tradition as old as Tupperware. Painting parties, beading parties, candle parties—I've suffered through many a retelling during my Sunday visits with Maxine. I had inventory to unload, and I had a phone full of people who'd be willing to come visit me on a Friday night, share a few cocktails before bar time, and take some charm bags off my hands.

I dubbed the parties Sticks and Stones Soirees. The booze flowed freely on its inaugural night, so my first party only netted me about a hundred bucks once I factored in the cost of the liquor. Still, that was a hundred bucks toward my car payment I didn't have before. I tried some different times. People still expected wine, even on a weekday right after work, and even boxed wine adds up. Daytime Saturday, though, I could get away with serving coffee and cookies. Initial attendance was sparse, but I couldn't argue with the profit margin. I scored a hulking, old-school percolator at a thrift store and offered my party-goers a 25% discount on my psychic tchotchkes if they brought a friend.

They brought friends. And I've always been a people-person. Especially when that person is Vibing.

My Saturday was winding down and it was just a couple of pierced and pastel-haired girls on the couch exclaiming over the latest racist dumbassery on Twitter, and a guy who wanted to adopt a pet rock but couldn't decide which one was "perfect."

A stone was a stone. But the thing I was actually selling people went beyond hunks of tumbled mineral. I sold them an idea. A story...a hope.

I'd scavenged several long, thin folding tables from the alley. Enough black spray paint will make anything look new again, as long as you don't brush up against it and scuff off the enamel. The tumbled rocks and crystals sat on velveteen cushions that were an ottoman in another life. I might not know which end of a needle to thread, but I can wield a hot glue gun with the best of them. Beside each stone stood a simple piece of cardstock, folded in an inverted V and hand-lettered with the purported properties of each stone.

I sidled up to the guy and said, "Was there anything in particular you were looking for?" He turned the full weight of his Vibe toward me. He wasn't what I'd call conventionally attractive, but there was something endearingly boyish about him. "Maybe I can help you... find it."

"I hope so." He stared at my mouth as I talked, and he blushed a little. He'd never felt a tongue stud flicking against the underside of his dick. And he wanted to. Badly. "The other day at the gas station

I saw air fresheners that are supposed to enhance psychic powers. Clairvoyant Mindset. Telepathy Trance. And as far as I could tell, they just smelled like vanilla and pine. It's hard to know what to think anymore."

I eased closer. "Totally hard."

His blush deepened.

"So," I said, "have you gone through the whole rigmarole of having your ESP tested?"

"No. Not yet. I want to. At least, I think I want to. It's expensive. My company's HR department has some preliminaries, and if you do well enough on those screenings, they'll foot the bill. But I'd want to practice first so I don't blow my chance."

"I don't blame you." I assessed the level of his Vibe—body stance, eye contact, tone of voice—and decided to go in for the kill. I put my lips to his ear and said, "Besides, I can think of far more interesting things to blow."

Normally I don't encourage people to stray into the series of phenomenally small rooms beyond the far doorway unless they've *really* gotta use the john. And even then, I'd prefer they hit the taqueria down the block. But all signals were go. If I didn't strike while the iron was hot, this guy would slip through my fingers. Maybe he'd buy a rock or two, but unless I really sold him on my personal wares, I'd probably never see him again.

I cranked up the tunes to cover any untoward noises we might coax out of one another, caught him by the sleeve, and led him deeper into my web, through a cramped office filled with boxes and into the world's narrowest galley kitchen. I backed him into the countertop, and soon it was all a blur of roving hands and hungry mouths.

The music cover turned out to be unnecessary. He wasn't a moaner, though his face did contort into the most exquisite mask of strained disbelief. He held my head while I sucked him off, and stared down at me like he couldn't quite fathom what was happening while he prayed that it didn't end anytime soon.

Sure, I did treat him to a few barbell flutters, but it wasn't the hardware he found titillating, it was the idea. The dirtiness. Never mind that it was just a piercing and a tiny ball of surgical steel. He got off. Hard.

Twice.

And I was straining against my fly waiting for my turn to come around, rock hard from all the squirming and gasping. Once he'd recovered from his bonus round, I stood, shoved down my jeans, and held myself ready for his forthcoming reciprocation. Except...there was no forthcoming. Not even a third, for that matter.

He didn't quite meet my eye when he said, "Do you have a condom?"

"For a blowjob."

"Since we don't really know each other...."

"After you shot in my mouth. Twice."

His blush went scarlet. "You could have asked. I would have worn one."

The thought of getting my dick sucked was quickly losing its appeal. I yanked up my jeans and shimmied my ebbing erection into its usual position. "Never mind. I've got a party to see to."

I headed back out to check if I should put on another pot of coffee. The couch was empty and the women were gone—in fact, other than me (and the hookup who really needed to leave) no one was in my apartment at all. I noticed that. Then I noticed the front door was slightly open. So were random drawers in my dressers and desk.

My heart sank.

I checked my desk first. That's where I kept the cash. It's best to have lots of small bills around so you don't end up losing a sale because you can't make change. And I'd had more than just small bills. I'd sold well that day, and there'd been a fat stack of twenties I'd earmarked for my car insurance, with enough left over for groceries. Gone now. All gone.

Not only that, but my tablet and laptop, too. And my wallet? Fucking hell, my wallet too. Only one piece of plastic was in there—I'd stashed the rest in my freezer on the advice of some crackpot money management website—but there was my drivers license, my photos...sonofabitch, my only picture of Miss Mattie. Every time I'd thought about tacking it up at my station, it felt too private to put on display. But now I regretted keeping it to myself. All the other pictures I'd rescued once CUTTERZ closed were in a pile on my desk, but the most important photo I owned was gone.

I stared in dismay at a pile of books splayed across the floor. Red's book was among them...as if it mattered. But somehow I was relieved it hadn't been taken from me too.

I turned off my stereo. The guy whose dick I'd just sucked piped up. "Aren't you going to help me pick out a crystal?"

Without even looking at him, I closed my eyes, shook my head, and said, "Get out of here. Go."

While I had precious little to be grateful for, at least I still had my phone. I cancelled the charge card, pulled up an app and disabled my tablet and laptop so no one could hack into my bank accounts. Not that they'd find any money there, but it would add insult to injury.

I'd never been robbed before. And while initially I wanted to hunt down those two women, hold them upside down and shake them until my money fell out, it occurred to me it was doubtful they were the ones who'd ripped me off. I had their contact info. We ran in the same social circles. It was just as likely someone had wandered in off the street and cleaned me out. I even called one of them to see if she'd make up some shifty story, but she answered my call right away and sounded genuinely unconcerned when I asked her when they'd left, and whether there'd been anyone else in my apartment when they did. But no. She didn't say anything incriminating. And she didn't know anything helpful.

I called Lydia. She came upstairs and joined me, and even canceled the rest of her appointments to sit with me in my sorry apartment, which no longer felt particularly safe. "Tough break, kiddo." She helped herself to what was left of the cheap cookies. "So what's your next move?"

"I have no idea. What should I do now?"

"You could call it in, file a police report. You'll need that for your insurance claim. But since you say they made off with mostly cash, and you earned that cash doing something under the table...how useful would it really be to report it? You're not paying taxes, you don't have any retail paperwork filed—and even if you did, you'd never see that money again. Five years ago a kid with a handgun came in and grabbed my cashbox, and the pigs didn't do squat to catch him. Since it was cash and I didn't have receipts, my insurance weaseled out of the claim too. And that was business insurance. Do you even *have* business insurance?"

I sighed.

"And let's say they catch the guy, and miraculously, he hasn't sold off all your stuff. You think you're getting it back? Ha! Think again. It sits there in some evidence locker, and it rots."

Fuck. "Then what? I just do nothing?"

"Live and learn." She crunched through a stale chocolate wafer. "And think about installing a nanny-cam."

What I needed to install was some good, old-fashioned common sense. I'd let myself get so carried away peddling stupid twigs and rocks that I'd started to believe it was all real, and that my life would be buoyed by my good vibrations and the purity of my intent. That I understood how people ticked, and that somehow I'd figured out a way to escape the rat race each and every one of us is forced to run from cradle to grave.

I'd left myself open and vulnerable. And look where it got me.

At least I still had a phone. That's what I kept telling myself. But it's hard to feel grateful when you don't have the cash for groceries. Trying to force gratitude down my own throat was only making me angrier, and no less hungry. Thankfully, it was Sunday. And that meant a raft of food would be ripe for the taking.

"I don't see why we couldn't meet at the Italian restaurant." Maxine took in the steakhouse's wood-on-wood decor with an overdone pout. I absently perused the menu. If I remembered correctly, this joint's portions were big enough to feed a family of four. Which meant I could take home a doggie bag and fend off starvation, at least for a couple of days. "I thought the carbonara was good."

"Something I ate there didn't sit right."

"And I'm sure it had nothing to do with whatever you drank the night before."

"Go easy on the sarcasm. It's not your color."

As thoroughly convinced as I was that psychic powers were a huge scam perpetuated on a gullible public—by whom? Some lobby group that represents a greedy corporation making money off it, no doubt—I often wondered if there was some grain of truth in *a mother's intuition*. Because whenever I was riding high, Maxine made sure to ask if I needed anything, insistently, like three, four times. And whenever I did need something, she cinched her purse strings tight.

I attempted to steer the conversation away from her disappointment in my restaurant choice and toward the housewarming gift she hadn't offered. "So, my new place...."

"Ronnie tells me that whole area is one of the most up-and-coming neighborhoods to be in." My cousin Ron sells real estate. Maxine has always thought this would be a perfectly respectable job for a college dropout like me.

"You know Ronnie ate paste until he was like, nine." Maybe even ten. Yeah, that was about right. I was two years older, and by then I was already kissing boys.

Maxine prattled on about various businesses that were opening branches in Wicker Park, and how a factory that used to make light bulb filaments was now being converted to lofts that went for five grand a month.

"It's a colorful neighborhood," I said. "That's for sure."

"Ronnie says it's an interesting job. Always new things to learn."

"I'll bet."

We stared at our menus for a long moment, and she said, "Ronnie says he could get you a job interview."

I let the corner of my menu dip and glared at her over the top of it.

"Don't give me that look. You could make good money on commissions."

"Except when I don't, and then I'm taking home minimum wage. Plus I'd be a *realtor*."

"That smart mouth is why you have such a hard time holding down a job."

"My last salon closed. What does that have to do with my 'smart' mouth?"

"Lorraine Baker hired someone else to do her lawn after you sassed off to her."

"That again? For fuck's sake, I was in middle school." I snapped up the menu-barrier between us and glared at the photos of rib eyes and filets and strip steaks with their perfectly diamond-shaped grill marks. "Look, there's politics involved in my dry spell."

Maxine sighed heavily. "Which is why you should really think about talking to Ronnie."

"Whatever. In the meantime, could any of your friends be persuaded to let a big-city stylist take a whack at their hair?"

My mother isn't what you'd call subtle. When she's nervous, she flutters like a sparrow in a birdbath. At the suggestion that her cronies might be enticed into a haircut, she started plucking at her cuffs, smoothing her napkin and wriggling around in her seat.

Why?

"I do know how to cut hair," I reminded her.

"Of course you do."

"I wouldn't talk them into anything outrageous. I've got more common sense than that."

"People have their routines, that's all. If they saw you, it would be like they were cheating on their own hairdressers."

Maybe. Or maybe it was more than that. If anything, she seemed... embarrassed. "They already know I'm gay." The PFLAG bumper sticker so proudly displayed on her Beamer made that abundantly clear. "So what're you so ashamed of?"

She laughed. It was stunningly forced. "Now you're being dramatic. Pick out an appetizer and we'll talk about something else."

"But why? The subject of you being unwilling to approach your friends about me cutting their hair has so many rich and unexplored depths to plumb."

"If you're that desperate for something to do, come over and trim Dumpling's bangs."

I stared at her uncomprehendingly.

She helpfully added, "They're getting in his eyes."

I'm not sure what was more insulting—that she sincerely saw no difference between a groomer and a stylist, or that she thought she was actually being constructive.

CHAPTER 20

Maybe I should have been a groomer. It's nowhere near as glamorous as the life of a stylist, but at least my mother's Shih Tzu has never given me a look that conveyed he saw me as an utter failure. Although maybe he would, actually, if he got a load of me in the orange and yellow checkered ClipLand smock.

It occurred to me, when I read and initialed page after page of the stunningly detailed and casually insulting employee handbook, that I was far too old for a minimum wage job. And that's what ClipLand paid. Minimum wage. Plus tips...which we were supposed to report, according to the section on Wages and Tips I'd initialed. I tried to tally in my head what I might make. Even though we were expected to turn around a dizzying four cuts per hour, I couldn't imagine anyone who'd only spring twelve bucks for a haircut would tip more than a buck or two. And on top of that, ClipLand would withhold taxes from the tips.

Plying hand-jobs under the viaduct was looking more and more appealing.

Still, as the weeks rolled by, it was a relief to have a job—even if, after all the deductions, I was lucky to clear three hundred bucks a week. I'd sold off most of my electronics to make rent. I was tempted to sell my car, but I kept it so I wouldn't have to admit to Maxine how desperate I was. Plus I wasn't entirely sure I wouldn't be living out of it soon.

It didn't help that I was only working thirty hours. I'd make more if I could pick up additional shifts, but I hadn't exactly endeared myself to management. Sure, I abided by the dress code. I took out my nose ring, kept a clear acrylic stud in my tongue, and made sure my "slacks" didn't fit too provocatively—as if I'd bother wearing anything decent under that appalling smock anyway. But apparently my "smart mouth" refused to be dumbed down.

I'd met the shop's owner all of once. I've heard he has no actual interest in hair, that he was just looking for a franchise where he could funnel his money. Judging by his cut, I'd wager that statement was entirely accurate. The store's managers rotated through, depending on whether it was a weekday, weekend or evening, and whether or not they needed to sub for each other. Everything was distilled down to a formula so precise, theoretically a monkey could run the place. A very bitchy monkey.

I received multiple warnings for socializing and lingering too long over my cuts. And I hadn't even given my phone number to the cute guy with the snakebite piercing and the scrollwork inked on his fingers. Soliciting business outside the shop was grounds for immediate dismissal; no booty call was worth losing my horrendous job.

Which was why I damn near had a heart attack when I looked up from sweeping hair and saw Carolyn Brinkman giving her name to the receptionist. "You do haircolor here, right? I would only want Mr. Ash to do it."

Oh hell, ix-nay on the olor-cay. Even if I had the two hours it would take me to do it, they didn't stock the right product. No, I wouldn't fry her regrowth...but I could never achieve the subtlety and dimension she was used to. Not in the miserly time slot they'd allot for me.

"Carolyn," I called out—a mark on my permanent record for being too loud—"time for a trim?"

"No, the ends aren't bad. But look at the roots."

I hustled up to the receptionist and said, "Put her down for a cut." I hadn't yet determined which receptionists simply do their jobs and go home and which ones report back to the managers in hopes of catching one of us violating an obscure franchise rule, so I hoped we weren't dealing with a tattle-tale. I didn't think so. She just looked down the chart, glanced at the group of people waiting, and said, "I can get her in to see you at three-thirty." My faithful client. After all the walk-ins. Right.

I turned around each customer in record time, and even still, hitting the fifteen-minute goal was a struggle. That amount of time might have been adequate for the actual cutting, but it didn't leave me any mental space to think my angles through. Luckily I'd cut Carolyn's hair before, and I could still feel the angles in my fingers and wrists.

She sat and watched me intently in the mirror as I dampened her hair with a spray bottle and quickly sectioned it off. "I was surprised to find you here," she said. *You and me both, sister.* I could've asked how she'd managed, but she was a detective, after all. I imagine they have their ways. "What's wrong with your phone? I get a weird automated message about your account being suspended."

"The joys of my new pay-as-you-go plan. If I don't keep putting money on it, they cut me off quicker than a bartender at last call. But that's a whole story in itself. I'd never do it justice here."

She kept on watching me like a hawk as I combed and cut, reacquainting myself with the side that tended to flip the wrong way if you didn't finesse it just so. Was she reading my mind with her "psychic powers"? Who knows?

I gave her a soft zig-zag part so the regrowth looked less stripey and finished with a tousled blow dry, then leaned in close and whispered, "You don't want your hair colored here."

"I'm worried about you," she said, even lower.

"I'm fantastic," I said brightly. There might not be any Buddhas around, but according to my lengthy employee handbook, I was still under the gaze of a mechanical eye.

Her brow furrowed. "Do you have dinner plans? We really need to catch up."

CHAPTER 21

We met at "our" Mexican joint, where I filled up on chips while I waited. Heads turned when Carolyn showed up. She'd found herself a tube of neutral red lipstick just like the one I'd picked out for her back at CUTTERZ, and a top to match. If life was a cartoon, every horny man in the place would have sprouted a wolf head with projectile eyeballs.

"Dang, girl," I said when she slid into the booth across from me.

She gave me a sheepish eye-roll. "You were right. About Doug. My husband. He's fine. We're fine."

"Glad to be of service."

"We can be vague with each other sometimes. You know, because of my T3." Gotta love how she referred to her "telepathy" as if it was some kind of genetic disease. "When I asked him how I looked and he said, 'That's some dress,' I read something into it that I shouldn't have. I thought he was avoiding commenting on my looks, when actually, he just liked that dress. A lot."

"Listen, you don't need to keep trying to convince me you can read people's minds. As far as I'm concerned, you've got zero to prove."

"When you said you were fantastic, I knew you were miserable."

"Congratulations. You speak sarcasm."

She gestured for the waiter, then said, "What's with the water?

Did you give up drinking?"

"I'm broke," I said simply. No use in lying to a certified Psych, after all.

She gave me an "oh, please" look and ordered a pitcher. "Okay, first things first, just to get it out of the way. This guy is way too old for you, right?" She held up her phone briefly, like a flashcard, then shoved it back in her purse.

"Wait, whoa, time out." I grabbed her wrist and said, "Show me that for real."

She complied. Grudgingly.

"Holy Stiffness, Batman. That PsyCop guy? He's gay?"

"You couldn't tell?"

I arched my fingers in a parody of a gang sign and said, "He wasn't flashing the secret rainbow symbol when I saw him on the news."

"But usually you know, right? That's what you said last time when you were checking out the waiter, that you can always tell."

"My level-10 gaydar only works in person. You think the two of us would hit it off?"

"Not like you and Red."

"Newsflash—Red has gone the way of soul patches and neon windbreakers. And the more I consider this partner of yours, the better he's looking. But since you're clearly not down with the idea, why bring it up at all?"

"I didn't want to. Jacob saw that picture of us together and he's hounding me for your number. But what could you possibly have in common? He's in his forties."

"So? That's why they make Viagra." Besides, I'd be looking at thirty soon enough. I pinch-zoomed in on his face. Even at the awkward angle, he was clearly hot. And a lot more interesting now that I knew he liked dick. "I'll be gentle—I promise, I won't break him."

"It's not him I'm worried about."

"You're adorable."

"I'm serious. Listen." She fixed me with a look. "Can you promise that what I say here stays between us?"

"Absolutely."

Her "psychic powers" must have confirmed I don't blab. She

hunkered down close and said in all seriousness, "Jacob is not a nice guy."

The poor thing was so damn sincere. So help me, I laughed. "Like, how? He's on the take, or...?"

"Nothing like that. He's ethical. He's good. Morally, he's a good person. He's just not...how do I put this? He isn't someone who'd make you happy."

The more she warned me away, the more intrigued I grew. "You'd be surprised what makes me happy."

"I'm not talking about in bed. Generally. His personality. It's intense."

I took another look at the photo.

"He's selfish," she added.

I pictured him naked.

She sighed. "And you'll go right ahead and do what you want to do anyway. Just don't say I didn't warn you."

I almost didn't pick up when Carolyn's PsyCop partner called. I was on the bus. More specifically, I was on the bus because I'd finally sold my car—not for the meager thousand bucks left over once my loan was paid, but for relief from both the car and insurance payments, not to mention the disgust of finding a new ding or scratch every time I looked. As much as I appreciated my freedom from that massive liability, it was still a huge blow to my ego to find myself relying on public transportation not for my own convenience, but because I had no other choice. It wasn't the ideal place to make contact. But I didn't recognize the number, and since I'd seen a few clients under the table lately, lack of proper insurance notwithstanding, I couldn't afford to let a potential customer go to voicemail.

"Sorry if this sounds incredibly forward." Actually, he didn't sound sorry whatsoever. "But I was hoping you'd want to get together for coffee."

Hooking up with a complete stranger, I would have preferred something with more alcohol involved. But since I was scheduled for a half shift at ClipLand later that afternoon, coffee would have to do. I picked a place within walking distance of my apartment, not because I thought I'd get lucky...but because I had no fucking car. Turned out I should have vetted the place first. I thought the name *Magic Brew* was a reference to coffee beans. Instead, the walls were decked out in more New Age Psychic crap than Lydia's waiting room.

Great. Now Jacob would think I was a gullible flake.

He stood as I came into the packed shop. I'd only seen him in a suit and tie before, and now he was in jeans and a very mainstream leather jacket, but there was no mistaking him. Most people you see on TV feel smaller in person, but not this guy. He was tall. And broad. Everything about him seemed larger than life. I was about to lead in with, *we can go somewhere else—and make of that what you will*, when he said, "This place is great. I'm glad you suggested it. Judging by the outside I never would have thought to stop in."

"It's something, all right." Handsome, yes. Steady eye contact, too. Unfortunately, if the distinct lack of Vibe he exuded was anything to go by, he was only being polite, and he was finding me a lot less intriguing in person than he'd hoped. Good thing we'd only have to limp through a coffee's worth of awkward chatting. How disappointing. Carolyn's warning had built up all kinds of intriguing notions in my head, but honestly, maybe her first assessment was right, and her partner and I actually didn't have much in common. It would be harsh to blurt out, *Y'know what? Never mind*, and turn around and leave, so I plunked into the seat opposite him and said, "So you're really a PsyCop, huh? You don't just play one on TV?"

"Five years now. And you? How long have you been a stylist?"

"About that long."

"Carolyn's looking fantastic, by the way."

Which was more Red's doing than mine, and it galled me to take any credit for it. But before I could figure out how to exorcise Red's intrusion on the stilted date I was so valiantly attempting to have, a squeal of feedback sounded from the corner of the room, and a chick with a neo-bohemian jewelry fetish and rainbow tinsel glinting from her graying hair hoisted a microphone and said, "Thanks for coming out to the Psych-Out Poetry Slam, the most cutting-edge LGBTQIA psychic poetry event in Chicagoland."

Oh God.

I must've been doing my deer in headlights impression when Jacob leaned across the table and said, "Coffee?" I nodded dumbly. He went up to the counter while I scanned the crowd and noted how many people were clutching Moleskine notebooks to their chests. Too many.

Hippy Sparkle introduced the first reader—someone shameless enough to bill herself as a "clairvoyant life coach"—and the date's awkwardness devolved rapidly to torture. The poet was a plain woman in Birkenstocks and wool socks who looked like she'd just been abducted from a feminist bookstore. She took in the room, centered herself with a deep breath, and said, "Third eye."

I glanced toward the door. A cluster of earnest lesbians was blocking my exit. Damn.

"Third eye. Third eye. Only sense that doesn't lie. People be trippin, they trippin, they never stop skippin the money they slippin...."

Aaand there it was. White-lady ebonics. Maybe I was dreaming. If so, someone needed to pinch me. Hard.

Jacob set a huge black coffee in front of me, a veritable cauldron of java in a hand-thrown mug. He followed it up with a handful of creamers and sugars, then slipped back into his seat and put his full attention on the "poem."

"You say I don't know but I know, oh I know, I know how this will go and it's gonna sink low...."

I dumped every creamer into my coffee with the intention of downing the thing in one huge gulp and inventing a sudden urgent excuse to bail, but it must've been a fresh pot. Even with all the creams, it was too hot to chug. As I blew and sipped, I scoped out my date from behind the protective barrier of the gigantic mug. His style could use an update—grow out that goatee into more of a beard and take down the sides of his taper fade, and he'd literally stop traffic. But despite the conservative hair, the way he carried himself like he owned the damn place definitely held a certain appeal.

Too bad he wasn't into me. So not-into me that he was pretending to find the Birkenstock rapper utterly fascinating. He watched her while I watched him and convinced myself it was really all for the best, I could text Carolyn those three little words everyone loves to hear: *you were right*. And then go put on my checkered smock and earn myself a whopping fifty bucks...minus taxes.

Birkenstock was on quite a roll when Jacob gave a little start, pulled out his vibrating phone and scowled down at whatever it said. He thumbed in something, then turned the screen toward me so I could read it.

Work, sorry. Rain check?

Honestly, the easy letdown was unnecessary. If we were anywhere we could actually speak aloud, I'd tell him so. Nothing I took personally, just a stunning lack of chemistry. I gave him a sorta head-shake-shrug combo, like whatever, don't worry about it, it's fine.

He stood and rounded the table, then bent to say his final goodbye in my ear—or so I thought. Before I fully grasped what was what, he'd taken me by the chin and steered me into a full-on kiss. On the mouth. In broad daylight. In a goofy poetry slamming coffee shop.

Deer in headlights? Hell, the collision was so unexpected, I felt more like roadkill. This guy was so cocky he even stood there afterward to gloat that extra moment, eye to eye, and dare me to challenge him.

I think I blinked. Maybe.

Actually, it was a bit of a blur, at least until I watched him turn and make his way through the scattering of telepathic poetry queers and head out into the bald light of day.

What was up with that kiss? It was too deliberate, too lingering, to be anything less than a clear message of *yes, you oblivious man, you're hot*. And once I received that message, my own libido perked right up to match his Vibe. Still, it was nothing short of baffling. If he'd been into me all along, how could I possibly have sat there with him all that time—half a freaking coffee—and not picked up on a single cue?

I texted Carolyn, *Tell me what he says*.

She replied first with a simple *No*. And then a minute later, *I'm not letting you two pump me for information about each other*.

I ignored that and replied, *I can't tell if he's into me*.

Really?

I'd thought that was the end of it since Carolyn said no, and she

means what she says and says what she means. The evening rolled
on while I did my time in the checkered smock. Strict ClipLand policy prohibits stylists from even carrying their phones in the salon,
but all of us did anyway. We were just careful about shutting off the
ringtones.

I was on the bus back home when I finally realized Carolyn had
replied. *He won't shut up about you. Happy?*

I was. Confused, but happy.

CHAPTER 22

"It makes no sense. I always know when I'm tripping someone's trigger," I told Carolyn.

"And despite your perceived lack of attraction, you agreed to another date."

I got why she didn't want to be the go-between, but how could I help myself? I was curious. Plus I had her on the hotseat for as long as it would take to touch up her color, and since we were at my place and not ClipLand, I was determined to take my sweet time and squeeze out every last juicy drop of info. "Seriously, I thought he was faking a call yesterday just to get out of there."

"It's the nature of our job. We're not going to tell an assault victim to hang tight so we can take her statement at our convenience Monday morning—not only would that be completely insensitive, but memories degrade quicker than you'd think. If you weren't working last night, once we had our statements, he probably would've tried to take right back up wherever you left off."

"He could have. I'll bet the chick with the lame rhymes was still going strong. Maybe even beatboxing."

"I still think you're making a big mistake."

"And are you able to see the future?"

"No," she admitted.

"Then don't you worry your pretty little head."

It was Jacob who picked the spot for our next date. He called and gushed about a lecture at the Sulzer library on supposedly precognitive cave art. My initial impulse was to say, "Good one—but where did you want to go, really?" But I quelled it when he was gentlemanly enough to offer to pick me up, and decided to go with the flow and see what the evening had in store. Because as much action as I usually saw, I might've been a little rusty at "dating."

In fact, I tried and failed to recall a single actual date I'd ever gone on, one that involved doing an activity as a means of getting to know someone before we climbed into bed together. Not since, what...a high school social? And even that was a thinly veiled attempt to duck into an empty classroom and squeeze my hand down David Garcia's pants. He totally chickened out. But then I hooked up with another kid from Art Club I'd had my eye on, so it was all good.

In the end, I suppose I was curious. I gave Jacob my address and we made our plans.

He showed up right on the money and called me from the car. "Normally I'd come up, but I'm double-parked."

"Not a problem, be right down." How hokey—both the picking me up, and the thought that he needed to do anything more than pull up and beep to impress me. Even so, a flutter of anticipation settled in somewhere behind my sternum and I second-guessed my choice in wardrobe as I locked my sturdy new deadbolt tight. I'd gone heavy on the jewelry, with ripped jeans, combat boots, studded belt and a retro ringer tee. Thought about toning it down, but in the end decided my best bet was to be transparent about what he could ultimately expect.

I found him out front leaning against a black sedan, looking both masculine and polished. He rounded the car—and, get this—opened the door for me. The gesture was so adorably sincere, not a single smart remark sprang to mind. As I attempted to slide in, he smoothly maneuvered himself into a hello-kiss, again square on the mouth, and said, "You look amazing."

I took him in—conservative, sure, but all big and hard-bodied—and said, "You're not so bad yourself."

And again, there was that eye contact. Brief, since the right lane was getting pretty pissed off at the two of us, but exceedingly deliberate. Vibe...right? Even though I had a trace of his spit evaporating from my lower lip, weirdly enough, no.

The black sedan was obscenely roomy. Every time Jacob hit the gas, I felt dinosaurs weep over the squandering of their remains. I sprawled sideways in the passenger seat as much as the seatbelt would allow, and watched him as we crawled our way up Damen. He made some apology about ditching me Saturday, though it was fairly perfunctory. Not that it was insincere, but he clearly thought the importance of his job was self-evident.

Hard to say if the reason I couldn't read his Vibe was because he was used to schooling his expression. Because in his line of work, he'd need to clamp down on all his normal tells. One thing I did read from his body language was an unquestionable arrogance, which was probably an asset at his job, too.

Also hard to say if that arrogance ticked me off or turned me on.

Maybe I did have a weakness for a man with a good, solid pair of cajones. There must've been some reason I let Ralph lure me behind the closed door of his office time and time again. And if Red hadn't been the epitome of self-congratulatory pride, letting him slip through my fingers wouldn't have done such a number on my ego.

I stuffed all thoughts of Red back into the mental lockbox where I normally kept them. If I was to survive an official adult date, I couldn't afford to waste time wondering what I should've done differently. I'd sifted through the reruns a million times before. Even if I managed to figure out where I went wrong, what did it matter now? The battle was lost, the war was over, and the troops had fled to the West Coast.

At the library, I got out of the car before Jacob could open the door for me, but he insisted on being courtly at the building's front door. As I stepped across the threshold, I made a quick attempt to cool his jets by saying, "Full disclosure—I'm not entirely convinced psychic powers aren't anything more than a bunch of hype."

"Really?" He didn't sound threatened at all. More like he found my skepticism intriguing. Or even a bit of a challenge.

The talk was being held in an auditorium that could seat maybe a hundred people, though only a couple dozen intrepid souls had turned up. I'd been hoping to spend my time people-watching to get a handle on what sorts of folks put stock in extrasensory perception, but with the lights off and a slideshow playing, it was hard to tell. The lecture didn't hold my interest. The University of Chicago professor droned on, trying to make the case that a Paleolithic rock painted with red dots foretold everything from the Thirty Years War to the rise of Hitler. Her voice rose and fell in the darkened room while boring pictures of Bavarian caves blinked past, and I considered how much to read into the steady pressure of Jacob's knee against mine. He wasn't clingy, which was good. I'd get sick of someone continually pawing at me. But I assumed he was trying to send a message with all the mouth-kissing and door-opening and knee-pressing...since after spending a good hour and a half right beside him, I had no sense whatsoever as to whether he dug me or not.

After an interminable history lesson, the lights finally came up and the professor opened the floor to questions. I leaned in and whispered, "Can we get out of here?"

The look he flashed me as we walked out might or might not have been a Vibe. I paused to light a smoke, and Jacob turned to block the wind. Hell, he was probably put out he hadn't picked up a lighter so he could light it for me. I took a drag, thought through how diplomatic I should probably be, and then decided, fuck it. "So what's the plan here?"

"You mean, dinner?"

"Dinner. Post-dinner...and beyond. Fill me in, Jacob, 'cos I can't tell if we're on the same page or not."

His shoulders slumped. "It's the lecture, isn't it? I had no idea it would be so dry. Give me another chance to make a good impression." This, said with the confidence of someone who was clearly accustomed to making an impression with the velocity of a wrecking ball. "Dinner..." he eased in close. "Maybe takeout?"

"*Takeout*, huh?" Well, hell. Whether or not I had a handle on his Vibe just yet, if that wasn't an engraved invitation, then I was a blushing virgin. "Sounds...tasty."

I named a killer Thai restaurant nearby, and we scored some food and headed back to his place.

Judging by the condo with the underground parking and lake view, Jacob made good money and wasn't afraid to spend it. His tastes ran hypermasculine, big furniture pieces with lots of dark colors and wood. The only area that didn't feel like a Leathercraft Furniture showroom was the kitchen, where there were still dishes in the sink, and a few too many gizmos and gadgets crowded onto the countertops.

He served us on big ceramic plates (black, of course) but at least we ate on the couch, and not at that giant, formal slab of a dining room table. There were all of four beers in the fridge, which he split with me. Not nearly enough for a buzz, but enough to make us chatty. Safe topics. Where we'd grown up. Places we'd lived. Siblings (his) and cousins (mine). And eventually, lovers.

"My last relationship was with another cop," he told me. "It didn't end well."

"Do they ever?" I suppose I meant it philosophically, because really, what did I know? He gave an uncomfortable shrug—possibly the first chink I'd seen in his armor all night—and I took pity on the big lug. "Look, I've got zero expectations here. You don't need to impress me."

"Maybe I want to."

"You sure about that?"

"I thought I was being pretty obvious."

And I'd learned the hard way that people will fuck you for all kinds of reasons—some of which had nothing to do with lust. "Not exactly."

"Then allow me to clarify." With a sultry bedroom-eyed expression that would've been right at home on any afternoon soap, he leaned in for a kiss.

CHAPTER 23

So the sex was adequate. Actually, that's not quite right. It was good. Really...pretty good. All things considered, it seemed like I'd enjoyed myself. Jacob went at me like a man with something to prove, and in the throes of the naked, sweaty action, he displayed some solid bedroom skills. Afterward, he even invited me to stay. I probably should have taken him up on the offer. It was late. His bed was comfy. Plus, no doubt he'd do justice to the saying "rise and shine."

But my heart wasn't in it, and in the end, I dropped a cab fare I really couldn't afford and headed home.

I wouldn't have given the encounter much more thought, if not for the text waiting for me come morning.

Can't wait to see you again.

My thumbs itched to text back that I couldn't fathom why, since he really didn't seem all that into me. But when I thought back on the night, there wasn't any particular part that proved otherwise. Jacob had showered me with niceties. He'd held the door at the library, bought dinner, and treated me to a bonus round in bed.

So maybe the problem was me. Maybe I just wasn't into him. Which made no sense, since all in all, he'd be a really sweet catch. Smart. Buff. And no Viagra necessary.

I pondered my reply—on the bus, through a dozen hasty cuts, over a sorry brown-bag lunch, and well into my afternoon slog. I puzzled so long over how I should respond that I must've looked like I was playing hard to get. And that only spurred him on. Once my shift was done, I found several hang-ups and one voicemail. "I had such an incredible time last night. Not...the library. You definitely get to pick the place next time." Next time? What next time? "But after we finally got out of there...I can't stop thinking about it. About you."

Huh. I'll be damned. For all that I'd convinced myself I wasn't really Jacob's type, he sounded pretty hot n' bothered. I supposed I wouldn't mind a replay of the previous night's finale, but treating each other to dinner would start getting old, fast. Frankly put, I couldn't afford to reciprocate. I'd been living off sandwiches made of 99¢ turkey baloney that was crunchy with beaks and feet, and wouldn't dream of offering that atrocity to a guest.

How terrible would it be to invite this guy over for a hookup and nothing more? Give up this pretense of "dating," a ridiculous and outmoded social convention perpetuated by people's need to pair off two by two, and really get down to brass tacks. He was hung, I was limber, and both of us had plenty of fuel in the tank.

But then there were the boxes to consider. When I finally called him back, I said, "I'd invite you over, but I'm in the middle of a project and my place is a wreck."

"What kind of project?"

"Sorting through a bunch of old merchandise, taking inventory, snapping pictures."

"I can help you," he said, without missing a beat. "Let me help."

"Fair warning. There will be spreadsheets involved."

"I'd love to help."

The thought of keying in all that info on my phone was pretty daunting. "Can you bring a laptop?"

"Sure. I'll grab dinner too."

Whoever had trained this guy to display such an elaborate mating ritual really should be commended. I pushed through the bus's stubborn back door and made my way up the block, wondering the whole while if I should've just come clean and told Jacob he really didn't need to impress me if he wanted to get laid. I guess I was curious. Since I'd been specifically warned he was a selfish dick, I wondered how far he'd go to get on my good side. And why.

I hadn't been exaggerating about the state of my apartment. It looked like it had been ransacked by a band of roving hippies. Charm bags, stone jars, all the oddball things I'd put together from my various craft store excursions were arrayed on every available surface as I tried to figure out what I could charge for them and where they might sell. With any luck, I could unload it all online. Craftacular. com only took a 15% commission, so I had nothing to lose by giving it a try.

Jacob showed up maybe an hour later with a laptop bag slung over his shoulder and his hands full of Korean barbecue. While we took inventory of my collection to get an idea of what I had in stock, I did my best to explain about all the new age crap without sounding apologetic. Funny thing was, I didn't really understand why I'd gravitated toward it myself. "People are drawn to things," I said. "Sentiment, psychology, who really knows why. But my customers were happy with their souvenirs."

If Jacob thought I was making excuses, he didn't show it. He held up a bottle of gemstone chips to the light, turned it this way and that, then read the hand-lettered card attached with twine.

"It's a shame to have it all going to waste," I added.

He picked up a charm bag. "May I?"

"Knock yourself out."

He unknotted the tie and tipped the contents into his palm. What had been kitschy and fun at my CUTTERZ station seemed pathetic now as he scrutinized it. Iron filings. Quartz flakes. Myrrh nuggets. Burdock twigs.

I said, "It might look like a jumble of sticks and stones, but it's more than just floor sweepings. Everything's got a traditional meaning associated with it."

He scrutinized it harder.

"I mean...actual thought and effort went into these things."

He looked up from the bag. "Obviously."

Did he mean that, or was he just humoring me so I'd stop defending the charms he'd never actually impugned? I didn't know him well enough to say.

"You can sell these from a website?" he asked.

"That's the plan."

He tipped the mojo back into the muslin bag. "Well...I'll buy this one."

"Oh, please." I rolled my eyes. "You brought takeout. That's all the sympathy I can stomach."

"But I've handled it. You can't sell it now."

"I doubt anyone but you has the wherewithal to dust it for prints."

"My energy's all over it."

Guess I kept forgetting true believers didn't all wear dreamcatcher pendants and organic cotton underpants. "Look, I can't charge you for it. You don't see anyone else helping me set up my online storefront, do you? Consider it a token of my appreciation."

"You worked these into a haircut? How?"

"Simple." I rounded the couch and grabbed him by the head. "Sit back. Relax. And enjoy the ride." Mostly I was itching to fix that frumpy angle on his sides, but I quelled that impulse and pretended we were back in my rented station, and I'd just given him a wash and an ultra flattering cut. I mapped the plates of his skull. The brainpan isn't round, like most folks imagine. It's full of planes and ridges and curves. I mapped the topography with my fingertips and learned the lay of the land, and said, "Okay, suppose I just picked out that charm for you. Which one is it?"

He checked the bag. "Grounding."

"Right. So let's say you told me you're having crazy dreams, and you feel spaced out all the time, and you're having trouble focusing." I walked my fingers to the hairline and began massaging tiny circles at his temple. His body shifted—*relax, relax, relax*—and he eased into my sofa. "So think about the burdock. The way it smells, the way it feels. Imagine you're falling into it, getting smaller and smaller while the herb looks like it's growing. Think about the iron filings getting bigger and bigger, forming themselves into a strong, protective gate, keeping out all the freaky vibes you want to deflect. The quartz and the myrrh, they're boulder-sized now, grounded, vibrating with the energy from the earth. You get even smaller. Pretty soon you can see the cells and molecules, you're in a forest of burdock, great big thistles, and all the vibrations coming at you bounce off the fence. Whatever's left inside, anything boiling under your skin that's making you edgy and weird, all of it gets vibrated away by the circle of boulders, carried down into the earth, where it breaks up and dissipates until it's nothing but harmless, neutral energy."

My hands trailed down to his shoulders and I quelled an embarrassed laugh. "Anyway. That's the type of spiel I would do."

"That was amazing." He caught me by the wrist and turned to face me, and lo and behold, the Vibe couldn't possibly have been more obvious. "I'm tingling all over."

"Is that so?"

He turned and grappled me across the sofa back, and dragged me into a sloppy, needy kiss. We tumbled through various pieces of furniture as we shed our clothes, knocked over an end table and nearly destroyed my favorite lamp, but thankfully my bed was only a few steps away.

We were both dewy and panting by the time he mashed his sticky forehead to mine and gasped, "Can you tell me those things again? Inside me?"

Just when I thought I'd heard every fantasy under the sun. I pawed another condom out of the nightstand. "Prepare to have your mind blown."

And so we got down to business. We weren't swinging from the chandeliers; there were no silicone aids or vibrating toys. In fact, I didn't even say anything provocative. Even so, Jacob wasn't the only one to end up with a blown mind.

I've ad-libbed some crazy sex fantasies in my time—just ask the guy from the car wash who insisted he wanted to be cannibalized, then ended up getting sick in my wastebasket when I told him exactly what I was gonna do to him. This was different. Not because it was any more realistic, since I was waxing eloquent about chakras and vibrational fields, but because this persona Jacob wanted me to wear while I plowed him? It wasn't some construct he'd been carrying around in the dirtiest folds of his brain, a role in which any warm body would suffice. It was me. Or at least some version of me, a rendition I'd trooped out and introduced to him while we were playing with some charm bags.

Suggestion is a powerful thing. Despite the fact that I knew we were just a couple of rutting animals, I got caught up in the fantasy that we were made of stardust and magic, and it wasn't just Jacob's prostate I was bumping up against, but his soul. I came so hard my head spun. When I rolled off, I left him splayed out on the bed like every last bit of his juice was wrung dry. We lay there together, staring up at the cracks on the ceiling and re-learning how to breathe. Normally, after such a spectacular performance, I'd give props where props were due. But it would've been a shame to mar the occasion with something as common as words.

Eventually, though, our flesh could no longer be transcended by the bliss of our minds. My arm fell asleep, and when I rolled away, Jacob pried himself off the mattress to visit the bathroom. He came back with a towel to throw over the wet spot he'd been stewing in, then settled on his side with his head propped on his fist, facing me. Ever the gentleman, he asked, "Can I stay over?" Then he cemented the deal by adding, "I don't want the night to end."

By that point, even though my post-coital endorphin rush was technically history, I teetered on the brink of saying, "Sure, baby." Since I couldn't trust myself not to reply with anything schmaltzy, I nodded instead.

Usually after I shoot my load, I can't wait to jump up and have a smoke, but this time a heavy lassitude kept me in bed. Not unpleasant, not by any means. It wasn't all that late, though, and I was stone cold sober. Jacob traced the mehndi inked up the side of my thigh like he found every last inch of me fascinating. And as naive as it might be, I ate the attention right up.

He mapped all the tattoos he could reach—without insulting the Mattie, thank you very much—ending with the thorny swirl up the side of my neck. His fingertips then lit on my cheek. With utter sincerity, he said, "I hope you know how special you are."

Even though I was firmly in bed, with those words, everything dropped right out from under me, and I realized what it truly meant to fall for someone.

CHAPTER 24

So lightning didn't strike me dead when I decided that, yes, I was willing to own the b-word. You know the one: *boyfriend*. Unfortunately, the real world had this annoying habit of intruding on my love life. Even without the expense of owning a car, there were more bills to pay than reserves to pay them with. And Jacob's not an idiot. No matter how cool I tried to play it, he could tell the contents of my mailbox were causing me undue distress.

"It's the plastic," I groaned. "I'm paying more in interest now than I make in a week."

"Let me help."

"I'm not taking your money." Bad enough he insisted on "treating" for dinner, drinks, or any other incidental expenses that cropped up while we were together.

"I know a way you could eliminate a major monthly expense," he said, only half-teasingly.

"While the sordidness of shacking up with someone I've only been seeing for a few weeks does appeal to me, I think not." Plenty of guys joke about needing a sugar daddy, but the prospect of actually having one left me cold. Swapping fluids was one thing. Without equal footing, I'd never dream of mingling our households. "Besides, where would all my boxes live?"

While I changed out of my appalling checkered smock, Jacob

settled himself on the couch, cracked open the laptop and checked up on our Craftacular store. Customers get snippy if you don't ship their order the nanosecond they hit the buy button, I learned that the hard way. And a single one-star review carries a hell of a lot of weight when it's the only review you have.

"Anything?" I asked.

"One." He jotted down two items, a bottle of pink rocks and magnet filings, and a love mojo bag, then handed the note to me. While I poked through boxes and gathered up the stuff, he addressed the padded mailer. I wrote up a thank-you by hand, slipped it into the envelope, and leaned it against the door so he'd remember to drop it at the post office in the morning. As second jobs went, not too demanding.

Unfortunately, I suspected it wasn't particularly lucrative, either.

I poured myself onto the couch and he slung an arm around me. "How's the store doing, anyway?" I asked. Jacob brought up the account page. I scanned it, and scanned it again, trying to make sense of what I was seeing. "Wait a sec, that's the profit for the month?"

He moused to the date range field and held it down. Yep. We were looking at the month.

"Fifty bucks? We've been babysitting this thing every night for a measly fifty bucks—and we pay out half of that in shipping." By that point I wasn't snuggling anymore, I was sitting up ramrod straight. I commandeered the laptop and scrolled down to the reviews.

** (2) Smells nice but I thought it would be bigger.

* (1) Worthless crap!!! Returning!!!

*** (3) as ordered

* (1) package arrived beat up and dirty

"My *average* star rating is 1.75?" I snapped. "What the fuck is wrong with people?"

Jacob made a dismissive gesture. "Don't take it personally. It's the internet."

"Yeah, well...fuck the internet." I shoved the laptop onto the coffee table, jumped up and started pacing, then planted my hands on my hips and huffed out a sigh. "I've seen people react to this stuff, Jacob. In person, they fucking love it."

"In person," he echoed.

"In person." I spotted my old percolator over in the corner, looking all dry and forlorn. Next Saturday I wasn't scheduled at ClipLand until six. There was time enough to take down that thankless online store and put together another Sticks and Stones Soiree. The whole robbery experience had soured me on the thought of having strangers in my home. But I was on to that asshole who ripped me off, so if he had any more funny ideas, I was ready for him.

While he didn't come right out and say it, Jacob obviously got off on the idea of throwing a party for all my psychic-wannabe friends. Once I sent out the invite, he came up with all kinds of useful odds and ends to contribute, from a stereo to replace the one I'd sold, to a scrap of drywall to patch the gaping hole where the shampoo station used to be. Bright and early Saturday morning, he helped me rearrange the furniture. We took apart my bed and stashed the mattress in a dinky back room where a tower of boxes used to live, upright against the wall. Amazing how commercial the apartment looked without a queen sized mattress smack dab in the middle.

I texted Lydia to come up and see what she thought—and really, I was trolling for her opinion of the party setup, and not Jacob. She ogled him shamelessly anyway. In fact, she was all over him. At least until she asked him what he did for a living and he said he was a detective.

"Like the Rockford Files?" Lydia suggested.

"Not exactly. Rockford was more of a P.I."

Lydia's eyes narrowed. "So...you're a cop." And with that, an appointment for a tarot reading suddenly materialized, and she fled downstairs to her curtain-draped warren.

My old clientele hadn't forgotten about me while I was earning minimum wage in my checkered smock. Foot traffic was steady, and some folks even brought along a friend or two. With tunes going in the background and the goods so generously arrayed, sales were surprisingly vigorous. Especially once Jacob figured out that we could accept credit cards on his laptop.

I was sorely tempted to call ClipLand and tell whichever manager was on duty that something had come up. Not only would I make more money hawking charm bags, but it was way more fun. Send Jacob out for a few boxes of wine, extend the party.... But no one wanted to work Saturday night at ClipLand, and if I bailed, someone else would need to fill that spot. Damn my overdeveloped sense of fair play—I couldn't bring myself to blow off the obligation.

Still, I was in the midst of trying to convince myself that my ClipLand coworkers wouldn't hesitate to saddle me with a crappy shift when one of my party guests caught my eye. I'd just finished setting out a fresh array of incense: pungent, oily, slightly misshapen hand-made cones that smoldered fitfully and left an exotic pall behind if you felt brave enough to actually burn one. My fingertips came away stained chartreuse, and reeking of something that smelled like a mixture of pine needles, weed, and cheap mango ice cream. The guy wasn't staring at me, like the two chicks who giggled and looked away every time I noticed them. He wasn't making a spectacle of himself, like the overcompensating guy who couldn't stop showing off the new tattoo on his ass. He wasn't really doing much of anything, just sitting quietly on the couch and flipping through one of the psychic pseudo-science periodicals Jacob had fanned across the coffee table.

Flipping through, I immediately saw, but not reading.

His body language screamed discomfort. Not any one particular detail, but a combination of things: the angle of his knees, his distance from the arm rest, and the way his eyes sort-of tracked across the page. He was young, maybe eighteen, smallish and kind of dumpy. White. Ghetto. And judging by the state of his lank, greasy hair, none too clean.

There was something wrong with him. Something very wrong.

Jacob was on the other side of the room, engaged in an earnest conversation about crystals with a dreadlocked, braless neo-hippy in toe shoes and hemp cargo shorts.

"Hey, babe," I murmured. "C'mere a second." I walked him over to an unoccupied corner, one that afforded a really good view of the back of the kid's head, and said, "Something's up with that guy on the couch."

One of the things I dug about Jacob was the way he treated

whatever I said like gospel, and this was no exception. While, like Lydia, I had no great love of cops, it was a thing of beauty to see him deploy and scope out the scumbag who thought he was hiding in plain sight. Jacob circled the room, took him in from a few different angles, then eased his way back around to me. Lips against my ear, he said, "Do you want me to get rid of him?"

What I wanted was my stolen stuff. "Remember how I said my laptop got swiped? I don't have shit for proof, but I know that's the creep who took it. I'm positive."

And then I braced myself, because at that point any sane person would have told me I didn't have a leg to stand on, and to stop being such a drama queen. But not Jacob. He just pulled out his phone, hit a number, and said, "Carolyn? I need your help."

I knew Carolyn well enough to know she wouldn't be comfortable around the two of us as a couple. And I knew Jacob well enough to know he didn't care. But it's a free country, at least on paper, and apparently she'd chosen to get involved.

"Heads up." Jacob nudged me with his elbow. My robber was on his feet with his eye on the door, ready to make a break for it. "Can you stall him?"

By "stall," I was guessing he didn't mean knocking the guy down and wrapping him in a clothesline, preferably while I called him a few choice names. But I had years of experience making small talk with miserable folks I'd just as soon slap upside the head. Smooth as can be, I insinuated myself between the kid and the door, and exclaimed, "Say, don't I know you?"

The guy flinched and cowered. "No. I...no, I don't think so."

"Sure I do. You hang out at Magic Brew, right?"

He tried to step around me but I matched the move before it got him anywhere. "Never been there."

"Oh, I know. You're a cashier at the gas station."

"No."

"I'll bet you get that all the time, people who know you from somewhere but can't quite put their finger on it."

"Look, I gotta go."

"Hold on, hold on, it'll come to me." I looped my arm through his and walked him toward the snack table and away from the door. Tension sang through his body like an electrical current. "Why don't you try a pecan sandy while I figure out how I know you. Crumbly, but surprisingly good."

Eager to appease me so I'd back off and allow him to make his escape, he grabbed a cookie and shoved it in his mouth. Chewed. Didn't quite manage to swallow, though his Adam's apple bobbed up and down in a gratifying display of nervousness. Even fear.

"Now I know where I've seen you before," I said while his throat convulsed. "You were at my last party."

Maybe I should've put a damper on my satisfaction, because the jig was up. I knew. And he knew I knew. And so he did what any guilty-assed tweaker would do in that situation—he threw a platter of cookies on the floor between us, and he ran.

The outburst was as unexpected as a nineties guitar solo in an acoustic art house navel-gazing three-piece. The milling crowd froze, which made the creep's escape seem all the more imminent...until Jacob blocked the door. Not with arms crossed, like a bouncer making a big show of himself in hopes of avoiding a fight with a drunk, but with his hands loose at his sides, like someone who knew how to handle himself.

The kid stopped, cowered, then spun around, searching desperately for another way out. But unless he was prepared to swan dive out the window, he was trapped. "Sorry to break up the party," Jacob told the gaggle of stupefied coffee drinkers who couldn't quite process what was happening, "but you'd best get going."

His tone was clear—*obey me*—and everyone set down their mugs and trooped out the door. The thief desperately wanted to slip into that line, but even he wasn't that stupid. Jacob motioned for him to sit back down on the couch, and so he sat.

"There's no reason to run," Jacob said soothingly. "No one's going to hurt you."

Actually, I sorely wanted to clock that jackass, but I refrained from saying so.

Jacob said, "Let's all just take a few deep breaths. That's right."

While we gathered ourselves for a nice, civil discussion, someone jackhammered the other side of the door and sent the kid flying out of his seat. "In here," Jacob called, and Carolyn whammed the door open. Fuckin-A, who taught her to knock, the Incredible Hulk? Up until then, I didn't think she looked very cop-like when she wasn't wearing a suit with a heavy badge hanging from the waistband. But now, even in jeans and T-shirt, her stance marked her as law enforcement. That, and the gun on her hip.

"Everything's fine," Jacob insisted, stunningly calm. "We're just going to chat."

I'd thought Carolyn's body language was aggressive when she was making the weepy receptionist let loose the waterworks. I now realized I hadn't seen nothin' yet.

Jacob said, "Your name, sir?"

"Reggie?" the guy squeaked out.

Jacob looked to Carolyn. Carolyn nodded yes.

"Do you have any identification on you?" Jacob asked.

Reggie shook his head "no." Jacob looked to Carolyn, and she mirrored Reggie's headshake, negating his "no."

"It really is in your best interest to show your I.D." Jacob told him. "Unless there's something you're trying to hide."

Reggie shook his head again. So did Carolyn.

The questioning went on like that. Jacob calmly asking. Reggie answering, scared out of his gourd. And Carolyn, also calm, confirming or denying his answers.

When you see psychics on TV, they're pretty dramatic, like the ship's captain on Clairvoyage who's always announcing the upcoming storm with a dire, booming voice—and, no, I don't watch it myself unless I'm at Maxine's. She'll go into a tiz if she doesn't catch the end of the show. What chilled me to the bone about these two was how they came off as placid as a customer on the receiving end of a full-body massage...though a hell of a lot more intense. And it was obvious that Jacob treated Carolyn's psychic impressions as if they'd rolled right off a polygraph machine.

The thing about Clairvoyage is that, duh, of course the crew is going to make it through alive to the next episode. Reggie, though, I wasn't really banking on. If he had a weak heart, he might very well expire right there on my couch.

In his calm and entirely reasonable way, Jacob proceeded to extract all kinds of information from Reggie. Where he lived, where he worked, names of family members and associates. The guy had a shit job and he drove a shit car. And he also had a hard-on for H, which can put a real ding in a part-time fast food cashier's paycheck.

When Jacob then asked me how many people had been at the party, Carolyn turned her attention to me, even though I wasn't the one under the microscope. At least, I think I wasn't. I conjured up a mental guest list. "Maybe thirty, give or take."

Jacob looked to Carolyn, and she nodded.

A sickening chill raced down my spine.

The questions continued but I tuned them out. Mostly I was marveling at how I was suddenly so spooked by both of them—my margarita buddy, and the guy who'd tossed my salad the night before.

I'm not sure if they were pushing too hard, or if there's a natural point in interrogations where resistance overshadows fear. They reached an impasse at which Reggie's answers started earning more headshakes than nods, and at that point, Carolyn stepped into the captain's position.

When she started questioning the guy who'd robbed me, I wondered if I should've arranged for him be sitting on a towel. Under her terrifying scrutiny, he admitted to everything I knew was missing, even the cash. Obviously the money was gone. My laptop and tablet too. He hadn't ditched my wallet, though.

Carolyn looked to me again. Still my same old friend, I told myself...but I'd be lying if I said the hair on the back of my neck wasn't standing at attention. She cocked her head toward my kitchen and said, "Let's talk."

I followed her back, chafing gooseflesh off my arms.

"While Jacob's keeping an eye on this guy," she said, "I need to know how you want to proceed. You never told me about this robbery so I take it you didn't report it. Was there something involved you didn't want to end up on a police statement?"

"Like what, drugs?" I half-laughed. "Nah, I can't be bothered with that scene. Just cash, and I figured it was long-gone anyway."

She nodded, as if to herself, and I realized she wasn't just asking me friend to friend...she was doing that thing, the thing she did with Jacob.

I lowered my voice and said, "So this is how it works, huh? You can seriously read that guy—not only that, you're reading me?"

She looked at the floor. "I'm always reading you. I always have."

I shivered.

"It's not just you, I'm always reading everyone. And most people talk a big smokescreen of half-truths and outright lies. Weaving words and stories out of lies is so prevalent it's just a matter of course. It's refreshing to be with someone brave enough to say what they mean." She met my eyes again, and now she was the one who looked spooked. "And I suppose this changes everything."

"Why?"

"Because it always does."

I almost blurted out, *No it wouldn't,* but then I caught myself. "Maybe. But not in the way you think."

The potential of her catching me with my pants on fire was not the issue. The thing that turned my world around was the indisputable evidence that she could sniff out an untruth as easily as I could spot a counterfeit cologne.

"If drugs aren't involved, there's no reason not to press charges," Carolyn said.

"What's the point? It won't recover my stuff. Call me sentimental—I just want my wallet back."

CHAPTER 25

Evidently, even though Jacob was off-duty and outside his precinct, he was still within his jurisdiction. A few phone calls later and a pair of actual cops showed up, decked out in checkered hatbands and bulletproof vests. They cuffed Reggie and stowed him in the back of the baconmobile while Jacob filled them in on the situation. The uniformed cops jotted a few notes, then hauled off my "guest,"

Since our adventure had eaten up the time I'd normally use inching toward ClipLand on the Damen bus, Jacob gave me a lift to work. It was silent in the car. Not a companionable silence, but a stunned and awkward space where words would have been welcome, but felt too damn elusive to grasp.

We pulled up in front and idled. The orange striped awning felt surreal. "Are you okay?" Jacob asked.

"I don't know *how* I am."

He unbuckled his seatbelt so he could lean into me, and caressed my cheek with his knuckle. "I'm here for you, okay? If you need anything, just let me know."

I had no idea what I needed.

The shift was a blur. Visions of Reggie's interrogation played and replayed with every comb through, every snip. It wasn't Reggie who spooked me, though, it was my friend and my lover, who were now cast in entirely new roles. Human truth serum. I felt a little queasy. It was like I'd been acting out an edgy sex fantasy, then discovered the toy gun was not only real, but loaded.

I found Jacob waiting for me when the shop closed at nine. He was still him—the guy who made good marinara and bad jokes, who hogged the bed and then accused me of throwing the pillows on the floor. And yet he was something more. Something scary. Something... thrilling?

He leaned into a brief hello-kiss, and though I returned it, I couldn't help but feel like it was a stranger's mouth on mine. As we all know, I've got no problem with that. But, still.

"We should eat," he said. "Do you have anything at your place?"

I gave a short, humorless laugh. He scoped out a nearby a drive-through, then ordered two grilled chicken sandwiches with enough sides to feed a small army. It had been a few hours since I'd witnessed Reggie's interrogation, enough time for the adrenaline rush to calm back down. But my stomach was still doing queasy flips, part fear, part titillation, over the sight of Jacob.

We climbed the narrow stairs, same as always, and I turned the key in my lock, same as always. Except my hand shook a little, and that was new.

"It's okay," he murmured, and the hair on the back of my neck prickled.

I opened the door, flipped on the lights, and scanned the room. It was still set up for the party, so it looked more like a shabby commercial showroom than a place where someone lived. I was disoriented. My boyfriend, my home, everything felt entirely surreal, and me without a lick of intoxicant to blame.

Jacob busied himself unbagging the food and setting it out on the coffee table. I stood and watched. When dinner was served, he turned to me.

"Tell me something," I said.

"What is it?"

"Levels and talents, mind reading and spoon bending, all of it is really real?"

"Well, the spoon bending turned out to be a hoax." A valiant attempt at humor, but I was so not in the mood. Jacob rounded the sofa and eased me out of my leather jacket. "Eat something. You'll feel better."

I allowed him to lead me to the couch and sit me down. I put food in my mouth, chewed and swallowed, and didn't taste a damn thing.

"Are you up for talking about it?" Jacob asked.

I shrugged.

"Officers recovered your wallet, but not your laptop or tablet, and no cash to speak of. They'll need a statement from you for the criminal suit. The guy's only other record was juvenile, and since there was no violence involved, no forced entry, it's unlikely he'll get anything more than community service."

I waved the explanation away. Not only was it my own fault for leaving my front door open for strangers to traipse in and out with my stuff, but Reggie was a little weasel I could pound with one hand tied behind my back. It wasn't thoughts of him that had me spooked. "Who was reading minds, then? Carolyn or you?"

"I thought you understood the basics of how PsyCop teams work."

Evidently, I didn't understand the basics of jack squat. I made a "go on" motion, looping my fingers through the air.

"Carolyn is a telepath. I'm an NP. We question the subject as a team. She uses her telepathy, I use observation and common sense... plus I do the paperwork."

"So, it's true. The whole time you guys were grilling Reggie, she was reading his mind?"

Jacob stirred his coleslaw for a long while before he answered. "Lying is her trigger, and nothing else, just the lie itself. That doesn't mean she sees the truth, necessarily. Only that she can always sense when something's false."

"Even, y'know, a diplomatic fib?"

"Even that."

Wow. The weepy receptionist never stood a chance.

We ate. Despite the queasiness, my body must've needed the fuel, because I didn't hork anything back up. Jacob was especially attentive—the perfect boyfriend. He refilled my iced tea three times and cleared the table when we were done, while I sat and stared at the carpet, and wondered what it all meant.

If someone can see the future, does that mean everything is predestined?

If someone can speak to the dead, there must be an afterlife.

And if someone I knew could always spot a lie, what the hell had I said to her over the course of umpteen conversations that I really might need to revoke, or at least qualify?

Jacob interrupted my deep thoughts by suggesting, "If you're not up for putting your apartment back together, I can pull out your mattress and lay it on the floor."

Right. My bedroom was still crammed against the wall in the closet that called itself an office. It was tempting to take him up on that offer, but it seemed like it would be easier for *la cucarachas* to crawl up and join us in the sack with the mattress on the floor, despite the fact that they could undoubtedly climb up the bed frame without breaking a sweat.

We moved a couch, dragged out the headboard and started screwing everything back together. By the time the mattress was stacked, the sheets smoothed and the pillows fluffed, the clock struck midnight and my adrenaline shakes had morphed into tremors of exhaustion.

"You're still wired," Jacob said. I nodded. "Do you have anything that might help you sleep? I can run out to the store and grab something." He pressed up against my back and nuzzled the crook of my neck. "Or we can try a more natural approach."

I took his hands and clasped them around my middle, and allowed myself to sag back into him. When I spoke, I was so weary that my voice sounded like it belonged to an older, dustier version of me. "Never thought I'd hear myself say this...but not tonight."

He turned me in his arms and kissed me. Not with insistence, but tenderness. "I won't let anything bad happen to you."

Noble sentiment. But with reality cracked open to reveal a writhing nest of alien tentacles where the logical levers and pulleys were supposed to be running the show, what good were a couple of feeble NPs?

I can't say I slept well, but I did sleep. Jacob is usually a zombie in the morning, but when I woke up, he was still in high chivalry mode, focused and alert. Not only was he already up and at 'em, he had coffee brewed—the good stuff, not the store brand mud I use in the old percolator. He brought me a cup and perched on the edge of the bed while I unglued my mouth with that first bitter sip.

"Are you working today?" he asked.

"Of course I am. It's a weekend and my seniority is squat." And then I was supposed to meet Maxine for our standing Sunday meal. I was daunted by the thought of busing it to a neighborhood that didn't terrify her. I'm sure Jacob would have jumped at the chance to not only drive me, but to join us. But I just couldn't deal with having both of them in the same room.

Not yet, anyway.

He watched me trying to absorb the caffeine by steaming my face with the mug. It was weird, this solicitous show of concern. Maybe somewhat intriguing, but mostly weird, since I'd been a lone wolf ever since I could remember. When finally the pressure of his scrutiny started giving me the heebie-jeebies, I sighed, set my coffee down, and said, "What?"

He flinched like I'd called him out on something he thought he'd gotten away with. "Nothing, really." Some hemming and hawing sounds, and then, "Just a little...it's no big deal."

Sure. I cocked an eyebrow at him and fortified myself with another sip.

He stood and paced around the room a few times, then went and retrieved a small box from his jacket pocket. "After I dealt with Reggie yesterday, I picked up a little something...just to satisfy my curiosity."

Whatever this thing might be, it was no bigger than a pack of smokes. He turned it around a few times as if he didn't know where to begin.

I've had plenty of awkward conversations in my three decades on this earth, but this one didn't seem to have anything to do with a humiliating kink he was struggling to share. Given that he was game to say or do most anything in bed, whatever had him so stumped, it was nothing so pedestrian as a sexual aid. He made a few more stammery attempts to explain, and at that point my impatience got the better of me. "For crying out loud, what is it?"

"A game."

"A game," I repeated, with a tone that projected, *bullshit*.

"Cards. That's all."

Obviously it was more than just "cards," but heck, whatever the catch might be, how could I refuse? After all Jacob had done for me over the past 24 hours, he'd built up his fair share of boyfriend credit. "C'mon." I patted the edge of the bed. "Whatever it is, can't be any weirder than certain hookups I've endured."

He peeled a film of plastic from the box, picked open one end and slid the deck into his palm. "Focusing on me, not the cards, I want you to guess high or low."

"Whatever tingles your jingles."

He held the top card so the back was facing me, and he looked. "Okay, whenever you're ready."

"Low," I said randomly. He flipped another. And another. And another. "Low. High. Low."

"Focusing on me," he repeated.

"I heard you. And I'm doing exactly what you said. I'm guessing high or low."

"Focusing on *me*."

"Yes, Jacob. Focusing on you."

Here's the thing about people like Jacob: overachievers, do-gooders—people who think they're perfect. They tend to presume you're basically a knucklehead. In my case, not because I'm inherently stupid, but because I'm willfully thwarting his wishes. Focusing on Jacob, what I could see was that he was annoyed. "Just" a simple game, maybe...but as he drew card after card, it was obvious I was managing to play it wrong.

I grabbed one of the discard piles, the "high" pile, and turned it over, expecting to see a bunch of twos, threes and fours. Except there were no numbers. Or suits. Or the mystical mish-mash of symbology from Lydia's deck.

Instead, there was a puppy. A vapid, fluffy, big-eyed puppy sitting in a field of daisies. I fanned out the pile. More dogs, but that's not all. Interspersed with the puppies, bugs. Not interesting bugs, either, but the type of pointy, squirmy, venomous-looking things that make you chafe your forearms and shake out the bath towels.

Jacob picked up the other pile and shoved it back into the box. "Never mind."

"So what's the deal? You seriously thought I'd psychically sort the puppies from the bugs? Wait, don't answer, that's exactly what was going on, according to my mystical powers." That and the look on his face. "And now you're pissed."

"I'm not angry."

"Look, I never claimed to be a mind reader. If you cooked up some fantasy where I was, that's your own damn recipe. Not mine."

I re-reminded myself how much he'd done for me and headed for the bathroom to put my hair up before I said anything I'd regret. Boyfriend cred only stretches so far. We'd gone from warm and fuzzy to cool and distant in the span of a single card game. It was pretty obvious where I wasn't meeting his expectations. For some reason, he thought I had talent—aside from my skill at hair design, or copyediting, or fellatio.

Unfortunately, the disappointment was mutual. I'd thought Jacob was into me for who I was, and not who he imagined me to be. Maybe he'd done a great job of playing the white knight, but once the dust settled, it turned out Mr. Perfect wasn't so keen on scratching around in the dirt with plebes like me.

CHAPTER 26

My shift sucked ass, definitely not in a good way. I got called off the floor by the manager not once, not twice, but three times. Apparently my pants were too tight. And saying "dick cheese" wasn't professional. And making a jerk-off motion, complete with spurting noises, offended some customer's tender sensibilities. I would've told management to peel open my tight pants, kneel down and eat my dick cheese—accompanied by jerk-off motions and a few juicy spurting sounds—had I not been within half an hour of ending my shift. I suppressed the urge. I couldn't afford to jeopardize my puny paycheck and even punier tips.

In the face of so much rampant disapproval, I could hardly be expected to deal with Maxine. Sure, calling her to cancel would only invite more recrimination, but better to endure it for the course of a phone call than the stretch of an entire evening.

Luckily, when I got home, Lydia was leaning up against the building enjoying a cigarette outside on a mild spring evening, so I wouldn't need to spend the entirety of my tips on a nicotine fix. I parked myself beside her and said, "Got enough to share?"

She shook out a cancer stick and passed it over. "Rough day?"

Rough day? Week? Year? Fuck, I couldn't even remember the last time something had gone my way. Even back when I made good money and lived in a human abode, how could I count any of that as good fortune when eventually it all went to shit?

I shrugged.

"Whatever it is," she said, "people always say you should talk it out. But I think talking's overrated. It's what you do that really counts."

I suspected she was trying to make me feel better, but it backfired. All I could think about was how everyone seemed so disillusioned with me that I was beginning to suspect I was inherently flawed. I finished my cigarette, flicked the butt into the gutter, then said, "This guy I've been seeing, the cop...I thought he was in it for the hot sex, maybe the free haircuts. But it turns out he had the crazy notion I was psychic."

She slid me a look through her smudgy fortune-teller eyeliner that said, "What's so crazy about that?" as clearly as if she'd spoken it aloud.

"He had this ridiculous deck of cards...."

"Colors? Shapes?"

"Poodles and centipedes."

"Ah...I've heard of those. That's based on new research—and I gotta admit, I'm more than a little curious." She cocked her head toward her palm reader sign, now dark. "C'mon inside and tell me all about it."

We parked ourselves at her kitchen table, a burn-scarred slab of plastic veneer that was peeling at the edges. She set out a couple of shot glasses, then set a bottle of birthday cake flavored vodka beside them.

I slammed my shot, shuddered, then described the card game as best I could. "I felt like I'd let him down," I said, and tossed back another sickeningly sweet shot.

"Maybe it's a decent litmus test. If the two of you aren't compatible, you'll want to know sooner, not later."

"Compatibility's not the problem."

"So he has a big dick," she said. I may have snorted some caustic vanilla into my sinuses over her ability to read between the lines. "So do plenty of guys. Just because someone's good in bed doesn't mean they're your soulmate."

"Is this advice of a general nature...or is it telepathic?"

"Get your terminology straight, bucko, I'm a precog. And no, I haven't looked."

"Why not?"

"Matters of the heart are touchy. How much time something lasts is beside the point. It's what you get out of the experience that counts."

I did a third shot, thinking I'd be used to the cloying sweetness already. I wasn't.

Lydia pulled a pad of sticky notes from her junk drawer, then dredged up a chewed pencil. "Do you think you'll be better off in the long run for having met this fella?"

"Who knows?"

"Exactly. So tell me more about this test." She scribbled herself a note. "What did he say when he gave it to you?"

"He told me to focus on him." About a million times. "And to guess high or low."

"Nothing about the puppies?"

"No, I didn't see the pictures until later."

"So you thought you were guessing numbers. Not feelings."

"I didn't think much of anything. I was just doing it to humor him."

The syrupy vodka churned in my empty stomach. I wandered into the bathroom, waited for a few minutes to see if it was gonna revisit me, then came back out and topped it off with a glass of tap water in hopes of keeping down the alcohol.

"I want to make sure I've got this straight," she said when I parked my ass back at the table. She held up a note, sticky side facing me. "So this is a card. And you're supposed to guess high or low, right?" I gave a *whatever* hand flick. "Wouldn't it make more sense if you guessed happy or sad?"

"It's adorable that you think logic applies in this situation."

"C'mon, kid. Let's try it my way."

"Happy," I said. She put the note face down on the table. "Happy. Happy. Sad. Sad...." I wasn't being entirely random—I did consider her for a moment before each guess. Jacob and my mother were both profoundly disappointed in me. I couldn't afford to alienate anyone else that day.

Once I guessed through all the notes, Lydia said, "Huh." Then she stuck the two piles together and stuffed them in her pocket.

"You're baiting me. Is that it?"

"Not at all."

"Were they blank?"

"Nope."

I crooked a finger. "Then give it up. I played fair—so I get to see the score."

With an overdone eye-roll of resignation, Lydia handed over the stack of yellow squares. I expected the top note to have a word on it. Instead, she'd jotted a dollar sign. I peeled them apart. Dollar, dollar, dollar, heart. What the heck? Dollar, dollar, heart, heart heart....

"I don't get it," I finally admitted.

"Love and money. I guess I'm a true romantic, and you picked up on it. Probably doesn't hurt that you've got the same predilections."

I peeled through the notes again. The top half was mostly money, the bottom mostly love. "I'm still not sure what I'm looking at."

"Money—*sad*, love—*happy*. I could've just written the two words, I guess, but that wasn't how the puppy deck worked, was it? Pictures are more conceptual, more visceral. I'll bet a successful stockbroker going through a divorce would've had the opposite result...if he was sensitive enough to pick up on it, anyhow."

I stared at the notes without grasping the point, awash in that maddening tip-of-the-tongue feeling that comes with forgetting a word you've known your whole life. I'd watched her sort the two piles as I guessed, and I'd seen her stack one on top of the other. The preponderance of dollar signs up top and hearts beneath went way beyond mere chance. "So you tapped into your precognitive talent and guessed which way I would pick?"

"Do those things *look* like my tarot? Sorry, kid, I'm off the clock. If anyone tapped into anything, it was you."

I'd left Lydia's apartment with the intention of looking up anything I could find on psychic empaths, but soon discovered her wi-fi was acting up and my crappy, overpriced data plan was tapped out. Since internet research was a bust, I ended up swinging by the grocery store and grabbing a bottle of plain vodka to dilute the fake birthday cake I'd already imbibed. Besides, mid-priced vodka was a heck of a lot cheaper than limoncello, or another gig of data.

This notion that I might actually be an empath was, of course, ridiculous. And yet so many people I knew and trusted—Lydia, Carolyn, and even Jacob—were convinced I'd picked up on more than body language when I spotted the loser who'd robbed me.

On the way to ClipLand the next morning, I pondered my fellow bus riders. How many of them thought they were some flavor of Psych? And, of those folks, who among them actually were?

I felt subdued during my shift. Pensive. The other stylists decided I was hungover, and teased me ruthlessly whenever the manager snuck out back to talk on her phone. I didn't play along, exactly, but I didn't correct them either. Sure, the two different cheap vodkas hadn't mingled in my gut very well, but mostly I was just wrapped up in my own thoughts, at least until the guy in my chair exploded.

"What the fuck, man, you can see my scalp! I look like I'm getting drafted into the fucking army."

He'd told me to take it down close—what was I supposed to do, read his mind? Like...Red?

Red fucking Turner. I tried to push him out of my head, but it was too late. I was already awash in the memory of losing myself in his big, dark eyes. He'd always struck me as self-contained, even cagey, and now it made a lot more sense. Red kept himself to himself because he knew secrets. Not because anyone blabbed about them in his presence, but because he soaked them up through the pores of his being. He hadn't just imagined the wind in Olga's hair. He'd seen it, or felt it. Maybe even *lived* it for that fraction of a second in which she'd been on the receiving end of his whammy.

Going home, I was happy enough to ride the bus for once, because I was so lost in thought, who knows where I might have ended up if I'd driven myself. I didn't know what to make of anything anymore. Sorting my way through a stack of hearts and dollars should have been the big wakeup call that made me a believer after all these years of clinging so passionately to my carefully cultivated mantle of skepticism. It wasn't, though. It was the memory of Red saying, "Tell me a story," and gazing deep into a customer's soul.

Not only that, it was the certainty that in the storage closet, when he'd grabbed me by the head and asked about Ralph, he'd subjected me to that same psychic scrutiny.

How I felt about that, I didn't know. Equal parts violated and vindicated. He didn't blame the fiasco on me, but that hadn't actually mattered. In the end, I supposed the purity of my intent didn't amount to a hill of shit. It hadn't kept Red in Chicago, had it?

What good was being psychic if it didn't help you satisfy a ClipLand customer...or figure out your boyfriend was screwing all your co-workers? I was struggling with both my philosophical conundrum and my mailbox key when the outside door opened and a big, backlit figure filled the doorway.

Jacob.

Interesting. Despite my feeble mind-reading performance yesterday, he hadn't given up on me after all...unless he'd come sniffing around for an argument. What his antagonism might look like to my inner eye, I had no idea—and besides, he wasn't lighting up. I wouldn't know what was on his agenda unless I could get a better look at his physical tells—body language, facial expression—so I cocked my head toward my door and said, "Come on in."

As he mounted the stairs behind me, I reached for a sense of how he was feeling. I got a whole load of nothing.

I let us in, and locked the door behind him. He had on a dark suit that made him look like an extra from a generic cop show, and his expression was serious. My "smart mouth" was itching to offer up a snarky apology for not adequately sorting his puppies, but I stopped short when he pulled a wallet from his coat pocket. My wallet.

"The cash is gone," he said apologetically. "But the DA isn't prosecuting, so I pulled a few strings and had it released from evidence."

Okay, so maybe it was a bit of a brag, but it was touching anyway. Lydia'd had me convinced I'd never get back so much as a scrap of lint. And here was my wallet. Just a stupid piece of cowhide. But maybe....

"Your license is there," Jacob said.

"Sweet. I'm sick of pointing out my emerging crow's feet every time someone cards me." I flipped it open, and there it was. Along with a Lincoln Square coffee shop loyalty card, various business cards, and....

"Oh my God," I breathed. And then I immediately felt guilty as I snagged a dog-eared corner and tugged out the old photo, because the only thing Miss Mattie ever scolded me for was taking the Lord's name in vain.

The print was faded. It looked like I was seeing it through an Instagram filter, but that was all age, not special effects. Dad shot on film until I was well into high school, and in this picture, I couldn't have been more than eight. That's how old I was when Mattie's heart gave out. And there she was with her arm around me, smiling at the camera, very much alive.

Maxine was in the background, talking, mid-sentence. Informing my dad that he was doing something wrong, no doubt. She was always criticizing him. And he'd always say, "Yes, dear," then go about doing his thing without even pretending to alter his course.

In contrast to my parents, Mattie just felt so...present. Everyone else had their scripts they'd parrot, a predetermined list of observations and responses they'd choose from. But not Mattie. When we talked, she wasn't busy sorting through her response list for the pithiest reply. She actually listened.

Maybe Jacob was ready to listen, too. It just took him a bit longer. He shuffled his feet and said, "I know the wallet doesn't make up for me springing that empath deck on you yesterday...."

"Like hell it doesn't." I propped the photo on my bookshelf, tossed the wallet on my coffee table, slung my arms around his neck and thanked him with a big, wet kiss. "You want to play cards, we'll play cards. Just be upfront about it, okay?"

One kiss led to another, which then inspired a delightful round of make-up sex. While obviously the first thing on my mind was getting my rocks off, simmering beneath that basic urge was the concern that maybe, at heart, I wasn't as much of a lone wolf as I'd always presumed. I'd figured Jacob was history because I couldn't deliver on a pile of puppies, but here he was, not just apologizing, but smoothing things over by recovering my one and only photo of Mattie. Was it possible I'd never bothered with relationships simply because I was too quick to bail? Scary thought.

I was stunned at how relieved I felt over patching things up with Jacob. If the depth of that feeling was any indication of how far gone I was, I'd need to consider the possibility that I was officially smitten.

CHAPTER 27

Though Jacob and I were both on our best behavior, attempting to be all lovey-dovey and contrite, the next morning saw our usual disagreements rearing their unwelcome heads. For Jacob's excuse, I supposed he was just tired. He was no morning person, and sleeping at my place meant he had to get up at least half an hour early to go home and gear up for his PsyCop gig, freshly coiffed and suited. My bathroom did have ample hot-running water, but it was so narrow it could fit in his shower stall. And while I could have invited him to bring along a fresh suit the next time he dropped by, I was mortified by the thought of a stowaway insect dropping out of his sleeve while he was grilling a confession out of some perv.

So of course it was more logical for me to stay at his place, but for whatever reason, it was the last thing I wanted to do. It might've been the fact that there were only 24 hours in a day, and I wanted to spend as few of those hours as possible on the bus. When you're really into someone, you'll do whatever it takes to be with them, so I'm guessing the bus-aversion was just an excuse. More likely my stubbornness was a gut reaction to the way he'd started dropping comments, yet again, that there was "plenty of room" in his condo for me.

"Seriously, do I strike you as the type of guy who could deal with being your kept boytoy?" I blurted out. After which, he worked his jaw a few times, shook his head, and left. And then I felt like a massive jerk for driving off the guy who'd gone through great lengths to rescue my wallet from an evidence locker.

I gazed into Mattie's smiling face on the faded, dog-eared photograph, and wondered what sort of advice she'd have for me. People who state things as if they're incontrovertible tend to bring out the contrarian in me, and leave me grasping for every disagreement I can think of. But not Mattie. When she made a pronouncement, my gut reaction was always yes, of course, that makes *total* sense.

"Is his biological clock ticking or something?" I asked the photo. "I shouldn't be expected to move in with the guy to prove I'm committed."

I was committed, I realized. Random men hadn't stopped showering me with the Vibes that would draw me into all kinds of questionable liaisons, but I'd totally stopped acting on the impulse to pursue them. Initially, Jacob's perseverance hadn't left any room for me to hook up with anyone new. He'd show up, and before anyone else even got a chance to catch my eye, we'd have dinner in our bellies and a spent condom or two in the wastebasket. There was no "now we are a couple" conversation. After a few actual dates, though, I'd sensed a tacit agreement that it would be seriously uncool to score with anybody else.

I sighed and stroked Mattie's face. "I wish you'd still been around... back when the news hit. Y'know how Dad tortured us all by watching at least two hours of news every night? That night, it was just the one story, over and over and over. The Federal government released a 20-year study involving something called a ganzfeld experiment that purported to definitively prove psychic powers were real. It was like someone discovered Atlantis, then plugged the coordinates into a GPS for everyone else to come and gawk.

"Dad kept flipping channels because he thought it was all a big load of crap. Maxine, though, she wasn't so fast to pooh-pooh everything. I remember how I kept catching her looking at me, and then she'd look away real quick, like she wondered if I understood what was going on. Dad finally found a BBC broadcast and declared the Brits wouldn't dream of jumping on the psychic bandwagon. But all they did was haul out more complicated numbers from the same damn reports."

I picked up the photo and cradled it in the palm of my hand. There were a few times when I was really young that my father got downright hostile when he overheard Mattie telling me I had *the gift*. "Would you have been vindicated, hearing everyone on the national news going on about talents and levels? Dragging out scientists for the talking heads to interview and plastering the screen with info-graphics? Probably not. You always knew the score, and I never once heard you say *I told you so*."

Since I had a few hours before my shift started, I stepped outside with Mattie for some air. In certain neighborhoods, it's not uncom-mon to see guys loitering in parking lots or leaning against build-ings—and not all of them are out to panhandle your spare change. So no one gave me a second glance as I propped up the building's façade and watched foot traffic roll by.

Most folks were heading for work, either walking to the train, or trying to figure out where they'd parked the night before. At least, that's what I presumed they were doing. But that was my logical mind piecing together hints like their wardrobe and facial expression and gait. When I tried to ignore that information and focus instead on how they might have felt, I wasn't so sure of myself. I couldn't help but notice the way a person was scowling and deduce that they weren't exactly thrilled.

"This is getting me nowhere fast," I told Mattie's photo. "It's com-pletely unscientific. What I'd need to do is blindfold myself and...."

I trailed off as an older guy in a suit strode past, talking very se-riously on his cell. He glanced at me—no more than a fraction of a second—with his frown firmly in place. And yet, the slap of the Vibe was so obvious, he might as well have ground to a stop, dropped his pants and pummeled me with his businessman dick.

He didn't break stride, even when our eyes met, and before I could convince myself there must be dozens of subtle non-verbal cues at play, he was halfway down the block. I craned my neck to watch him walk away until he turned a corner and was gone. And I told myself not to get carried away. Not until I knew for sure.

I picked another random person out of the crowd, and another, and another. I was out there for at least an hour by the time I registered another dozen Vibes. Searching for that particular vibe without actually wanting to hook up was a major eye-opener. A few of the hits came from women. Some of them were pretty conservative, too. Age didn't seem to matter. But only the people who actually looked at me stood any chance of registering on my emotional Geiger counter.

In the end, I reminded myself, I could've been making it all up... but I strongly suspected I wasn't. No, Gaydar wasn't one of the six official psychic talents, but there must be a reason I was uncannily good at spotting Vibes.

I took Mattie's photo upstairs and parked it back on the book-shelf for safekeeping. "What would you make of my 'gift' nowadays?" I asked her. I supposed I would never know.

Irrationally worried that I'd let this photo, this last memento, slip through my fingers again, I angled the glossy surface away from the glare of the overhead light, pulled out my phone, and snapped a picture of the picture. Not bad, though it needed cropping. I pulled up the photo editor and picked out the edge of a book to use as a guide for straightening the shot. I'd been fiddling with the angle for nearly a minute before I noticed the title: Mindfulness Methods.

Red's book.

Whether or not I had talent, I'd never believe the universe was guiding me through a series of obscure omens and signs. Miss Mattie was not reaching out from beyond the grave to tell me to read the damn book already. The spot where I shoved Red's book was within easy reach, and therefore it was the easiest place to prop up her photo. That's all.

Still, it was good to know I still had the darn thing. Not because it was Red's, but because I needed more information, and Lydia's wi-fi was being especially patchy again. I flipped the book open to the contents and scanned, and just like I figured, there were a few obligatory general chapters about psychic ability before the meat of the book began. History, terminology. I'd been schooled in that lately, and plenty. But the section on drugs? That was an eye-opener. The side effects of antipsyactives included dizziness, nausea, and a splitting headache. And psyactives were no better; while they might cause psychs to test higher on their scoring scale, they also had the unfortunate propensity for neurological damage.

The languaging in that particular section made me leery. It was a funny combination of specificity and vagueness, a bunch of hyperbole peppered with carefully curated statistics. As far as I could tell, the main purpose was to try and convince the reader that meditation was just as powerful as drugs, and a hell of a lot less risky.

I'd always figured meditation was just another way for middle-aged women with too much money to one-up each other. After all, who can afford to sit and do nothing unless a crew of underpaid Mexicans handles the lawn's perfect manicure? (Plus, there were so many cushions and beads and other meaningful accessories to consider.)

But according to the book, meditation was critical to harnessing one's psychic abilities, and the only thing it need cost is your time. It even pointed me to a page where I could download some guided meditations for free.

I picked one, popped in my earbuds and sat down cross-legged on the floor. The music began. Annoying music. Like a dog walking across a keyboard. But once the narrator began, the music faded to the background, and I felt my annoyance ebb.

Her voice was pleasant, even soothing. I closed my eyes and settled in as she instructed me to find a comfortable position and ensure I would not be disturbed. Inhale. Exhale. Relax. Not bad. I could do that. Exhale completely this time, making a whoosh sound. Silly, though it wasn't as if anyone but the roaches would hear me. Inhale through the nose for four counts. Okay. Hold for seven...which, for me, topped out at around five. And exhaling for eight? Forget it. The only way my lungs would abide such deep and lengthy breaths would be sucking the goodness out of a Camel Light.

She counted. I breathed. And just when I thought I might get the hang of it, she stopped counting breaths and started telling me to imagine things. A shoreline. The ocean. Glittering waters and azure sky, with sand between my toes, palm trees swaying on the breeze, and—get this—the scent of coconut in the air.

I did breathe deep, then, when I sighed a vigorous and gusty sigh.

Because, come on. Could this meditational fantasy I was supposed to buy into possibly get any more cliche? Blue sky, sandy beach, blah blah blah. How was that supposed to help me relax? All I could think about was the way it didn't match a single beach experience I'd ever had. Finding coins and bottle caps on the rocky shore, checking out the manflesh, staring off into the horizon and wondering how far away Michigan might be, getting pounded by bracingly cold waves and coming home waterlogged and sated. That's how I remembered the beach.

Why presume everyone's idea of a good time involved some kind of kitschy island tourist trap? It only reinforced my belief that all of this namby pamby meditation B.S. was designed for bored housewives.

I clicked through a few more meditations, but each one was more irritating than the last. Once annoyance took hold in me, it festered and grew. Pretty soon the pseudo-soothing voices took a mental cheese grater to my brain, and I seethed with the urge to give the speaker a good, solid smack.

I opened my eyes yet again and glanced at the meditating guy on the book cover. He didn't seem to be struggling with the urge to whack someone upside the head. But now that I got a closer look at him, I noticed the small half-smile on his face looked less like contentment, and more like mockery.

Red Turner can do this. Why can't you?

"Fuck you," I told him. And he kept right on smiling.

I showed up for my shift so ticked off and frustrated that I didn't even remember to be dismayed by the ridonkulous uniform. According to the smug book left behind by smug Red to remind me of his smugness, sense number six wasn't anywhere near as reliable as the other five. Its sensitivity varied, both from person to person, and situation to situation. Imagine if you could only see when you were well-rested and emotionally primed, and the rest of the time you had to flounder around in the dark.

On one hand, that explanation seemed like a convenient way to excuse perfectly mundane random results. Bad day? Must be meta-physical interference. Good day? Key the fanfare, you're psychic. But on the other...I'd seen that stack of hearts and dollars in Lydia's kitch-en. Not random. Not at all.

Yes, randomness was something the researchers considered, but supposedly the key element in the ganzfeld experiment was some formula that controlled for it. However the government crunched their complicated numbers, they somehow used that formula to compute the levels of most skills...most, but not all. Telekinesis and mediumship didn't have enough baseline scoring to accurately measure, while precognition might not pan out until some point in the distant future. For talents like that, researchers used other met-rics—basically, I think, they winged it. But empaths, telepaths and clairvoyants were a lot easier to score. And controlling for things like emotional upsets, lack of sleep, or even simple distraction, studies all pointed to an increase in psychic ability among those who meditated. Sometimes as much as two full levels.

Once I cooled off, I decided it was silly to be angry at the med-itation. The cover model on the book, too. (Red? I was still pissed at him.) During my next stint at ClipLand, I worked my way through one 15-minute cut after another, sending out tentative feelers to every client who sat in my chair, and getting nothing in return. Was the issue on the sending end, or the receiving? No idea. I'd have to put on my big boy panties and do more actual research.

Considering my lack of funds, the library might be a good place to start, at least until I had a chance to talk Maxine into taking me bookstore shopping. I finished my shift, grabbed myself a Big Double from the Burger Barn next door, and hopped on their wi-fi to check out the library's offerings while I waited on my ride. Would the sig-nal extend to the bus stop? Why, yes, it would. I was engrossed in my burger and phone when a pair of voices rose over the general noise of traffic and snagged my attention. I glanced up and found a guy getting chewed out by a woman half his size. The older woman looked like she could've been in Maxine's Pilates class. The guy was a big, balding hulk of a man in mechanic's overalls, someone you wouldn't notice unless he happened to be following you down a dark alley.

And then there was the dog on the end of the leash he held. A pug.

The dog didn't strain against the leash. More like he was doing a weird little dance. Not an anxious dance like the one Dumpling did whenever I stopped over, but a dance of triumph. Head high, the pug kicked one back leg, then another, as if he was trying to bury the shiny black convertible beside them. Since he was on a sidewalk, other than a few stray pebbles, there wasn't much to kick up. But he'd settle for going through the motions.

That dog is pleased with himself. I knew it. In fact, I knew it as definitely as I'd known the dude in the suit that morning wished I would rub my ballsack on his face.

A cluster of braying car horns obliterated the majority of their argument, but when the big mechanic pulled a rag out of his pocket and went down on one knee beside the rear tire, I got the gist of it: the dog had marked his territory, and the woman was no fan of watersports. The guy buffed the tiny pee-mark off the whitewall, apologized profusely, and retreated as quickly as the pug's tiny legs would allow. The angry woman glared at the tire, got in, and made a big show of checking and re-checking all her mirrors.

Me, I stood there, baffled, with a wad of half-chewed burger in my mouth.

I'd just picked up on the dog. *The dog.*

While I could deny my own perceptions of people by rationalizing about social cues all I wanted, no way could I have made up the profound satisfaction that pug was feeling. Yes, feeling.

The dog had emotions.

I was suddenly hyperaware of the wad of meat in my mouth. It gagged me. I rushed over to rid myself of the glob in the trashcan outside the restaurant door, but it wasn't an open-topped model. I had to spit the chewed food into my hand to shove it through the flap. I followed it with the rest of the burger, and while I wasn't exactly heaving as I did so, I'd be lying if I said I hadn't felt some pukey spasms in my esophagus.

I wandered back to the bus shelter, dazed. A pragmatic Mexican woman standing placidly in the shade of a large poster told me, "If you get a bad burger, you should take it back. They'll give you a different one. Sometimes a gift card, too."

Maybe so, but no thanks. I was awash in sympathy for the poor cannibal guy who'd yakked in my wastebasket. The thought of shoving a sentient creature down my gullet was so abhorrent, I knew my burger days were over.

CHAPTER 28

I had a lot to think about, and a long, solitary night in which to think it. If I was psychically empathic—sensitive enough to read a freakin' pug—then how was it that I'd managed to let Ralph manipulate me? Knowing what someone's feeling should have given me some kind of edge, right? Evidently not. Either I was too busy trying to talk myself out of what my gut was telling me, or Ralph was a psychopath speaking an entirely different emotional language than the rest of the world.

Another possibility, according to the good ol' internet, was that Ralph had been taking steps to ground himself. Apparently anyone can do it with enough mental training—and unless you want three percent of the population to be picking stray thoughts out of your mind, it behooved you to make the effort. Made sense. Unfortunately, that's where the information superhighway took a decidedly weird turn, blaming everything from fluoride to vaccines to bluetooth signals for causing psychic ability, and also for squelching it.

Purportedly, the other way to build up the grounding muscle was through something just as absurd: meditation. Before I could rile myself up over the stupidity of that claim, I stuck my phone in its charger, pulled my covers up over my head, and allowed myself to slip into a disgruntled slumber.

I woke the next morning to a text from Jacob. *Dinner tonight?*

Aww. The bed had felt conspicuously spacious without him in it. I texted back *9pm*. Sent it. Thought about the pug. Then followed up with *vegetarian*.

If Jacob thought my request was weird, he didn't remark on it. And as I showered and shaved and put up my hair, I considered that if anyone had reliable information on the field of psychic research, it would be the professional PsyCop. I shot him one more missive: *Bring info on Psych research.*

I spent my day attempting to cut hair and read minds, and found that overthinking the process was definitely not conducive to good results. I couldn't tell if everyone was twisted up in knots or if it was just me. Plus I got reprimanded by the manager for working too slowly, on three separate occasions.

I was relieved to finally head home. Jacob was a sight for sore eyes, waiting there for me in front of Lydia's darkened palm reader sign with a stack of books and a sack of falafel.

I'm not really one for idle chatter—I endure enough of it throughout my workday that by the time I'm off the clock, I'm happy enough to give the talking a rest. Jacob seemed to be wrestling with something, though. Halfway through the meal, I took pity on him and said, "What is it?"

He sighed and set his messy pita on the coffee table. "I didn't mean to back you into a corner about moving in together."

"I know." I nudged his knee with mine. "I'm flattered you're so into me—and the feeling's mutual."

"I just wanted to put the possibility out there."

"And you've been very persistent. Can we both agree that the offer's on the table and you don't need to nag? Living together is a big step, and I'm not gonna do it on a whim."

He cut his eyes to me, and I caught a little twinkle—one that telegraphed, *Aha, but you would theoretically do it. I'll just bide my time and eventually I'll wear you down.* This was not a psychic transmission of any sort. Still, it was crystal clear.

Once we'd cleaned up the tzatziki sauce from the various places it had managed to drip, we spread the reading material across the tabletop and dug in. At first, I was excited. No cheesy New Age cover art in sight. These books didn't need to market themselves to a fickle public. They were intended for professionals, so they didn't pretty themselves up with stock photos that featured meditating douchebags blissing out on the beach. They were plain text, with scintillating titles like *Understanding Telepathy* and *A Practical Guide to Clairvoyance*. But while it seemed like they'd offer me some actionable, no-nonsense advice, once I'd picked my way through a few dense pages, I realized they were mainly lingo and statistics. Bone dry. And if they applied to my current predicament at all, I'd have a heck of a time figuring out how.

I dug through the stack in hopes of spotting a less mind-numbing text, and uncovered a DVD on the bottom—a DVD with a title that was decidedly un-psychic. *Glazed.* With three guys leering at one another on the cover, wearing baker's aprons and nothing else.

Jacob hadn't noticed. He was deep in a chart, or possibly a graph. Without comment, I went to the entertainment center, popped in the disc, and set the volume to a level that wouldn't scandalize the entire building. At the sound of the cheesy background music running behind the title, Jacob's head snapped up. I caught his eye, opened the fly on my regulation-fit ClipLand slacks, and announced, "Study break."

Porn actually doesn't do much for me. Jacob, however, was raring to go. He practically fought me for the right to yank my pants down, and he had my dick in his mouth before the opening credits were done. I'd always chalked up my porn non-reaction to personal preference, but in light of everything I was learning about myself lately, I suspected there was more to it.

Porn was a one-way street. I couldn't connect to the models emotionally.

No wonder I could never find a good example of a Vibe for Pilar. It was like searching for a color photo in a pile of black and white snapshots. The key information simply wasn't there.

I trailed my fingertips over Jacob's scalp and he made a happy sound. He was obviously enjoying himself. Yet, when I searched for the Vibe (or whatever its might technically be called) I wasn't so sure. I'd gotten a clearer hit off the guy on the sidewalk that morning than

I was currently feeling from the guy between my legs.

"Do you meditate?" I asked.

He switched over to jacking me with a wet hand, and sat back on his heels. "Not regularly."

"But you have."

"It's been a while. Maybe I should try again. It's supposed to be... helpful." He stood and led me to the bed, and we peeled out of the rest of our clothes while the DVD guys exchanged a few lines then started stripping, too.

"Helpful how?" I asked. "For grounding?"

"Psychs test higher when they meditate regularly, but NPs? I'm not convinced there's any real benefit. I guess that's why I haven't made it much of a priority."

Over on the bakery set, one of the naked guys pulled out a piping bag and laid a strip of frosting across the other guy's chest, then the third guy licked it off. I considered the scenario. Was I witnessing something other than a random act of porn-osity? Maybe Jacob was trying to tell me something—and maybe that something was the kink that would unlock his Vibe. A food fetish wouldn't be so bad. It was a heck of a lot tamer than cannibalism, anyhow.

"Should I go grab the rest of the tzatziki?" I offered.

"Why?"

I replied by flicking my eyes toward the screen.

"We'd make a huge mess," he said. "Unless...you really want to."

I shrugged and nudged him back downtown. Again, he started going at me with all the enthusiasm I could possibly hope for. And again I felt as much of a charge from him as I did from the inanimate TV set.

Frosting spurted. Two-on-one tonguing...and maybe that's what Jacob was hinting at. Group action. Totally doable—the busboy with the dick pics would jump at the chance for a threesome. Especially once he got a load of Jacob's generous endowment. I put on my naughty-voice and said, "I could call a friend."

He looked up at me like I'd lost my mind.

"No?" I laughed and rolled my eyes. "Okay, then, I'm stumped. What's the point of this educational filmreel?"

"No point. It's just porn."

Just porn. Right. If I've learned anything about sex, it's that those little off-the-cuff hints are usually the culmination of years of thwarted longing too shameful to admit.

Jacob got back to business while I hit fast-forward. He didn't complain, so it was unlikely I'd skipped his favorite part. Two-on-one blowjob. Dick frosting. Dick sucking daisy chain. Butt close-up. I slowed to normal speed. Baker #1 spread the cheeks while baker #2 piped a lopsided ring around the third guy's rosy. Then they both ate it off. Nothing all that risqué—in fact, nothing we hadn't done together before, albeit without the frosting.

There was more piping action, more licking, and then the scenario progressed to penetration. First with fingers, then the piping tip. I checked in on Jacob to see if he was trying to inspire me to shove a random household object up his butt. Didn't seem to be. What a relief. Not that I had any problem with that, but you hear too many stories that start with playful experimentation and end up in the emergency room.

Maybe the porno really was just a porno, a little background noise to entertain us, keep us company while we got it on. I let the lip-smacking and frosting-fucking sounds serenade me through the appetizer and into the meal itself. Jacob rolled onto his back and encouraged me to ride his dick, which was interesting in lots of ways. Not just the feeling of his hugeness jammed all up in me, or the power to run the show however I damn well pleased. The eye contact, especially with all the lights on, was intense. Still, there was something nagging at me, something just out of reach, that I felt I didn't quite grasp. At least until Jacob's attention snapped to the TV. Just briefly. A second, maybe less. But not only had I definitely caught him checking in with the bakers—I'd *felt* the lust surging through his veins.

I resettled myself and glanced over at the screen. The bakers were done fucking, and now they all whacked off into the piping bag. There couldn't have been all that much jiz in real life, so the crew must've filled it with something else, too. There was no lack of icing when the bakers held down their love cupcake and started piping him with the combined spunk.

I was just about to make a smart remark when I glanced back at Jacob and saw the Vibe was gushing out of him faster than fake semen from a piping bag. Seriously? *That* was what churned his butter—taking a load? Apparently so. When I offered him a facial, he got so amped up he nearly finished without me.

In the grand scheme of things, phenomenally tame. Dare I even say...vanilla?

Afterward, while Jacob slept the sleep of the truly sated, I lay there staring at the ceiling, wondering if I'd really had a psychic connection with a random dog. It seemed unlikely now, considering that I couldn't tell if my own boyfriend was enjoying himself until he spurted all over. But the mind is a mysterious thing. Maybe it was acting the part of the surgeon who refuses to treat a family member. Because I'd lumped Jacob in the scary and untested "boyfriend" category, the empathy wasn't willing to bloody its hands.

Not that anything I'd read supported a theory like that, but it was better than nothing. Enough of a reason, anyhow, to decide that practicing mind reading on Jacob was a one-way ticket to Frustrationville. Just look at Carolyn and her hubster. Poor guy didn't only need to watch what he said—he had to control his very thoughts.

Relationships were hard enough to navigate without one party having access to an unfair advantage, and there was a whole world of people (and pugs) out there for me to violate with my empathic feelers.

I didn't need to practice on Jacob.

CHAPTER 29

The next morning, once Jacob headed off to fight the good fight, I hit the books again. While I tried to make heads or tails of all those psychic studies, I started doubting them when I realized they contradicted each other. One claimed lack of sleep was a psyactive, for instance, while another said well-rested subjects tested higher. I would have been inclined to chalk the whole thing up to a bunch of nonsense, a stack of random books from someone's garage sale, were it not for the thick black marks that peppered the oldest text. Redacted names. Once I realized what I was looking at, I set the tattered little tome on the edge of my coffee table and carefully avoided going anywhere near it.

I shoved aside a book that threatened to put me right back to sleep and knuckled my eyes vigorously with both hands. I just wanted to know how psychic empathy worked. Was that too much to ask?

I headed downstairs and found Lydia de-cobwebbing her shrine with a tiny hand-held vacuum that generated more noise than suction. She was glad enough for the interruption. "Let's say for the sake of argument I'm empathic," I said.

"Gotta love how you still qualify it with all that preamble."

I ignored the remark. "How do I do it? What can I use it for? What good does it do me if I can't tell whether or not I'm just making up a bunch of bullshit?"

"Are you asking for a reading, or were you just hoping for some general advice?"

"I can't afford one of your readings."

She perched on the arm of her almost-matching sofa, considered me, then said, "You need to relax. You might act like a party boy, what with the leather jacket and the hair, but underneath that getup, you're driven. Relax a little. Stop trying to figure out how to get it right, and focus on exploring what you can do." She gestured to the certification that hung on her wall like a diploma in a doctor's office. "For instance, take *that* pricy bit of necessary evil. It's not like a piece of paper made a damn bit of difference in my talent, but so many Psychs swear by their numbers. Don't be like them, hung up on external validation. It ain't worth it."

She went on about how it was a gift to understand people and added some rah-rah talk about trusting in myself, but my mind kept wandering back to that certificate. I rankled at the thought that I required external validation. And yet, if one of those agencies were to hand me a slip of paper that said I was unequivocally psychic?

Then I'd know for sure.

Unfortunately, those tests required a significant outlay of cash. While I was well versed in the art of comparison shopping, I quickly discovered that official psychic screenings were so closely regulated by the government that whether you tested in a rundown Englewood office or a glitzy Michigan Avenue high rise, the exorbitant fee was the same.

I could have afforded it, back when I worked at Luscious. Not easily, but I had disposable income to save. Now, though, there was no way I could fund the screening myself. I did have one good resource, though. I'll accept gifts from Maxine, but cash is tricky. Hopefully getting me tested was something we could both get behind.

Asking her over the phone would've been easier, but given the price tag, I decided to wait until Sunday and spring it on her over dinner. We met down in Greektown over crisp white tablecloths, flickering tea lights, and bowls of exotic olives. She ordered a salad and I gorged myself on a flaming cheese. I tuned out the waiter trying to catch my eye and did my best to ignore the aroma of sizzling lamb flesh while Maxine regaled me with a tedious story about her neighbor and his car lot.

Something about his deadbeat son embezzling from the family business, and did I go to school with the kid? No? Well, good. Because it's such a shame when children take advantage of their parents.

Not what I was hoping to hear on a money-finding mission. I attempted to steer the conversation away from the embezzler. "Too bad there wasn't a telepath on staff. Y'know, someone who could've pointed out that the kid was shady before he made off with too much cash."

"That's not the point." She was confused. Who's to say if I felt it in my gut, or simply inferred it by the look on her face. Or maybe we just know each other well enough that it's obvious when one of us says something the other doesn't know what to do with. "It's not about how he got caught, it's that he shouldn't have done it at all."

"You've got to admit, though, having a psychic around would be pretty handy."

"I guess," she replied halfheartedly.

I forged ahead. "Lately they're saying the three percent estimate was low. One in twenty people could be psychic. Some of them don't even know it."

"You should see the commissions he was making. And a company car, too."

"Maybe people are getting extrasensory impressions all the time."

"A company car," she repeated firmly.

It didn't take a psychic to figure out that neither one of us wanted to hear what the other was trying to say. Graciously, I decided to hear her out. "Okay, Maxine, go ahead. Make your point."

"The dealership needs help now. It's good money."

"And you think I'd make a good car salesman?"

"Why not? You've always been outgoing. And if you had a company car, you wouldn't need to use public transportation."

Me, selling cars? Kill me now. "Fine. Job offer heard. And since we're on the subject of broadening my horizons...I'm looking into the Psych Certification—"

She paled. Before I even got all the words out, the conversation fizzled. I felt it like a suckerpunch, like the room had dropped out from under me, and I was hanging there in mid-air just waiting to fall.

I stopped cold.

"Most people aren't psychic," she said. "And that's okay. But no matter how you scored on a test like that, it wouldn't mean you're not special."

My stomach clenched—did Carolyn's do the same whenever someone fed her an obvious lie? Maxine was attempting encouragement, but the feeling behind it was less than encouraging. She was embarrassed, for me. And not only embarrassed, but ashamed.

The cheese congealed in my gut. So much for getting help from my own damn mother. I might as well try to bum a smoke off a panhandler. I stood up, threw down a twenty I couldn't afford to cover my half of the meal, and said, "Gotta go—I have a train to catch."

An angry walk and a cigarette later, I parked myself on the Blue Line, slipped in my earbuds and congratulated myself for not telling my own mother to go to hell. Five grand, give or take. She'd drop that kind of dough to have perfectly good shrubs ripped out along the driveway and slightly different shrubs planted in their place. But I couldn't bring myself to ask her for it, even a loan. Not if she didn't believe in me. The train rumbled along the Eisenhower median then descended into the subway tunnels, and the lights did their flick-flick, and I allowed my anger to be lulled to a simmer by the rocking of the train car.

Special, my ass. I'd show her.

As I spun out a fantasy where I'd socked away thousands of dollars for a rainy day (although, obviously, this was not my style whatsoever) a text came in from Pilar.

You got robbed?

Like, ages ago. Why bring it up now? I thought back along the gossip chain. I'd run into Trevor at the beauty supply store maybe a week ago and mentioned something to him about it, probably in reaction to his assertion that Wicker Park wasn't cool anymore now that it was all gentrified. He'd only just told her now? Ouch.

Yeah - got my wallet back but that's about it.

I'm replacing Nick's computer. Want it?

While it was certainly no five grand, a used computer was a lot better than the big fat nothing I currently had. Maybe my day wasn't completely shot to hell after all.

I hadn't been to Pilar's in a while, but other than a different pile of laundry on the sofa, it hadn't changed. She and her teenage son lived in a brick post-war box where the bedrooms were too close for comfort—as in, she couldn't have an overnight visitor without giving her kid an earful—but she always said she was saving for tuition and he'd be gone before she knew it. And now that time had come.

"I know it's probably nothing as nice as what you're used to," she said, "but it's built for gaming. Nick says it's fast."

"It's plenty nice," I said. A desktop would make my life a hell of a lot easier.

"And the printer. You can take that too if you want. I never print anything."

"Sweet. Don't mind if I do."

"How about the printer stand? I won't really need it either."

It occurred to me that with Nick gone, it would be the perfect time for Pilar to escape from Luscious and strike out on her own—either in Chicago, or anywhere else she might care to put down roots. "Is there something you're not telling me?"

"Like what?"

"Come on, girlie, why else do people ditch furniture?"

She sighed. "Okay...but don't tell anyone. You know how the Juniors gossip."

A cascade of fantasies unfurled, each one more exotic than the last. Pilar moving to Hollywood and primping the stars on a movie set. Pilar in Hawaii reigning as the premiere bridal expert. Pilar jetting around the world as the personal stylist of Scarlett Johansson or Winona Ryder or Angelina Jolie. "I won't breathe a word."

She hunkered in close as if she was worried her own walls might overhear, and said, "I'm hiring an interior designer and redoing Nick's room."

"As a home salon?"

"No." She was scandalized by the mere thought. "A home theater."

"But why should you care if Juniors know or not?"

"You know how catty people can be. My salary is none of their business."

It was when I found myself wishing I could be happy for Pilar that I realized I was disappointed. While working at ClipLand was certainly nothing I'd ever aspired to, at least there was the sense that I could leave whenever something better came along. Not Pilar. She'd never been entirely comfortable at Luscious, but it was clear she planned on digging in her heels.

For the first time since I'd ditched all that melodrama, I finally appreciated the magnitude of my relief.

CHAPTER 30

I wasn't exactly sure what I was planning to do with Nick's old stuff when I grabbed it, other than cursing myself out for having to haul it up those narrow stairs. The bedroom set was old and battered, covered in manga stickers and gouged with random graffiti. Kid furniture. If I tried to sell it, I'd be lucky to recoup the cost of the U-Haul.

But if I put it to use, and sold my good stuff instead....

The computer might not be the latest and greatest, but I was tickled to have it. Putting together a Craigslist ad was so much easier with a keyboard.

Maxine and I may disagree about many things, but she was right about this: I was a good salesman. Not only did I liquidate my bedroom set within a couple of days, but once I had cash in hand, I went a little overboard and sold off all my other big pieces, too. I hadn't anticipated coming so close to funding my Psych certification, and once I was closing in on that goal, I started adding price tags wherever they would stick. I may have gotten carried away playing empath, too. When I detected a certain warm fuzzy from someone, a Vibe minus all the screwed up power plays and need for validation, I laid on the charm. They were happy to take the furniture off my hands.

The scarred floors and rough plaster had looked edgy and chic as a backdrop for all my nice stuff, but now that the place was empty, it was just shabby. I had only the one day a week off, and I spent it rearranging my worldly possessions. First I pulled out the soiree gear from the office, the display tables and folding chairs, just to make the room feel less abandoned. Then I shifted some boxes and tucked away the twin bed in the dinky bedroom, where it wouldn't feel so dwarfed by the vastness of the huge empty space.

The apartment was transformed yet again, though what I could do with the current configuration, I didn't know. Without the conversation pit in the center, the display tables weren't enough to support a party. Not unless I planned on hosting a ballroom dancing class or a roller derby. I was attempting to come up with more creative uses for folding tables when a text came in from Jacob.

Dinner?

Dinner. While I did have a surplus of tables, we normally ate on my couch, which was gone. Maybe watched some TV, also gone. Then retired to my big bed. Ditto.

Your place? I texted back.

Sure. Vegetarian?

Awesomesauce. (Auto-correct had a field day with that.)

I stood in the middle of my big empty room with my hands on my hips. A wave of perfectly non-psychic empathy washed over me and I saw the room through Jacob's eyes. Vacant. Abandoned. Barely habitable. As if I was planning to move.

Or planning to move *in*. With him.

Some small part of me was thinking, *Would that really be so bad?* And then the rest of me rolled its eyes and said, *Duh!* Cohabiting would be one thing, but I refused to show up at his place with nothing to my name but an old computer, a checkered smock and a bag of hair product. I couldn't stand the thought of being a man's charity case. Call me old-fashioned, but I refused to live together out of financial necessity.

I refused to cab it to his place, too. In fact, I took all the cash I'd amassed selling off my stuff and ran it over to the bank before I was tempted to piss it away on minor conveniences like transportation or food.

It took two buses and a three-block walk to put me at Jacob's condo. Talk radio was playing in the background when I got there, and the whole place smelled like garlic and basil. "You're making me an actual meal?" I wasn't sure my stomach would know what hit it, but I was flattered nonetheless. I perched myself on the granite countertop and observed the proceedings with mild interest.

"Is cheese okay?" he asked.

"More than okay. Lay it on me."

"I wasn't clear if vegetarian meant lacto-ovo, or vegan."

"Cheese is fair game." Unless I caught it feeling sorry for itself, anyway. "Eggs...I haven't exactly decided."

"So you're not watching your cholesterol."

"Nah, I'm hale and hearty. I've just developed a philosophical aversion to the consumption of animals."

"Does it bother you if I still eat meat?"

"Not at all."

I watched him lug a huge cauldron of pasta to the sink and dump it through a strainer. Steam billowed around him, and the light on the range hood threw some yellow backlight. His features should have been softened, but instead they were thrown into starker relief, more dramatic, more intense. It was a weird effect, practically cinematic. And he looked like some kind of action hero...making me noodles.

My heart gave a little palpitation—not sparked by cholesterol, but emotion. I couldn't recall the last time anyone had done something so nice for me. He hadn't questioned my motivation, hadn't cajoled or insulted or teased, only asked what I needed from him. I slid down from the counter and pressed myself into his back. My lips fit themselves perfectly to the nape of his neck, and he sighed and leaned back into the embrace. "I love you," I whispered against the heat of his skin. "And don't you dare even think about parroting the words back to me because it's socially acceptable and you think I expect you to."

He dropped the pot and turned to face me. I did my best to mash him into the sink so he couldn't do it, but I was fighting a losing battle since the guy's built like a tank. I thought he was about to ignore my directive and lob the phrase back at me—maybe with the vocabulary slightly modified so he was technically not disregarding my request—but instead he gathered me in his arms, squeezed the breath right out of me, and cut off any potential protests by crushing his mouth against mine.

Pasta congealed as we anointed his place from one end to the other, first with me doing a backbend over the butcherblock, then Jacob splayed across the coffee table, and eventually both of us tangled in fitted sheets that popped off the corners from the exertions we placed on the poor, beleaguered mattress. Sweat cooled on my limbs and across my chest as my heart rate slowed to normal and I caught my breath. I was hungry, I realized vaguely. But I felt so gloriously wrung out and sated, a little thing like an empty stomach hardly mattered.

We'd been so busy working up to our grand finale, we hadn't even bothered turning on the bedroom lights. Jacob uncoiled an elasticized sheet corner that was wrapped around his leg like a boa constrictor, then rolled over to pin my shoulder to the bed and give me big, dark doe eyes by the hallway light. I supposed if he insisted on relaunching that L-bomb I'd dropped, I was braced for it.

So, of course, what he said was, "Move in with me."

I closed my eyes and did my best not to make a face.

"I've hardly seen you all week," he pressed on. "You work nights and weekends. My schedule's all over the place. I want to fall asleep listening to the sound of you breathing. I want to wake up with your hair poking me in the shoulder."

Damn if he wasn't eroding my resolve. But since my little head was satisfied, my big head was thinking clearly—and what it told me was that any partnership I entered into without being able to carry my own weight would be a sham. Once we'd exhausted our repertoires of sexual positions, the inequalities would be more noticeable, and then resentment would start creeping in.

I opened my eyes. He was still giving me that damn doe-eyed look. I sighed, looped my arm around his head and hugged his face to my chest. "I'll think about it someday, but not right now. And I need you to listen when I say, it's not you, it's me. There's too much I've gotta figure out. I told you how I feel, right?" I felt him nod in the crook of my elbow. "So ease up on the thumbscrews and let's enjoy our time together."

I peeled off a spent condom that was stuck to my thigh, dropped it over the side of the bed, and said, "Look, finding someone to hook up with is easy. The way you don't second-guess my every last decision, the fact that you actually believe in me? That quality is exceedingly rare. I'm not interested in a sugar daddy, but I'm sunk without your moral support."

"I'm doing what anyone would do."

"Bullshit. You helped me build my Craftacular storefront. You were amazing at the Soiree. Hell, you're supportive all the way down to the pesto we didn't get around to eating."

"It's probably separated by now," he murmured.

The thing about giving someone your trust is that it's even lousier when they let you down. I took a deep breath, steeled myself, and said, "I'm trying for the certification." I realized he might think it had something to do with hair, and added, "Psych certification."

I'd been worried he would scoff, or laugh, or anything that would ruin the night, and worse, throw me off my trajectory. But no. He squeezed me tight and said, "I was hoping you would."

Obviously Carolyn didn't know Jacob half as well as she thought she did—either that, or I'd been dating some real losers—because for such a reprehensible cad, Jacob was turning out to be pretty great.

"And don't make a big fuss over it," I told him, "but I may be willing to leave a toothbrush here."

In a voice logy with impending sleep, Jacob said, "I'll be sure to treat it with the respect it deserves." He rolled off me and wound the duvet around his midsection. I curled onto my side, nestled against his broad back, and considered rinsing the texture paste out of my hair. But nah. Let it poke him in the shoulder blade—if that's what he was into, who was I to judge?

CHAPTER 31

Jacob's condo might not be exactly my style, but there was something to be said for furniture. A single night at his place made me regret my decision to sell everything off. I turned to Craigslist. Stuff there could be had for free or cheap, but I soon realized it was all stained, tattered or just plain ugly. A crooked entertainment center wouldn't class up the place, and a beige microfiber sectional that bore the worn impressions of a thousand ass-rubs would never make my cavernous living room look full. Just shabby. And the room was doing that well enough itself without help from anyone's sorry castoffs.

I was standing in the middle of the wide-open room, wheels spinning, when there was a rap on my door.

"You home, kiddo?" Lydia called.

I let her in and gave a sweep of my hand to encompass the depressing emptiness. "If you could call it that."

I dragged a pair of ancient metal folding chairs to the center of the room, kicked them both open, and situated them in a conversational angle to one another. She circled the room, took a good look around, then parked herself in a chair. "Is this some kind of fashion statement?"

"I needed cash. I liquidated."

"Good. I was worried you were moving out."

"Where would I go?" Other than Jacob's place, obviously. "You can't beat the rent."

"No. But you can't really live like this. Can you?"

"I set up the bedroom," I said, though spending time in the teen-ager bed wasn't anything I looked forward to.

"What about these boxes?

I sighed. "They'd probably be just about as comfortable."

"That's not what I mean—I'm asking what's inside."

"Crystals. Doo-dads. All the stuff from my Sticks and Stones Soirees that I haven't gotten around to selling."

"And you chose to sell off the furniture you were actually using rather than moving the metaphysical gear because...?"

Good question. "Because...I suppose I knew I'd take a big loss if I tried to offload this crap in bulk. To turn a profit, I need to hand-sell it piece by piece." I sighed. "And now I have nowhere to sell it. Don't worry, the irony is crystal clear."

"Chin up, kid. Where there's a will, there's a way."

"Is there? At what point do I concede that my innate stubbornness isn't doing me any favors? If only *someone* could look into the future and tell me whether all this effort is even worth it."

She cocked an eyebrow. "And now you believe in precogs? Whaddaya know. My cards are downstairs—but bum me a smoke, and I'll see if I can pick up any quick impressions."

I lit one for each of us, handed one to her, and re-planted myself in the creaky chair. Lydia took a deep drag, eyes focused softly. I watched. I won't lie—it felt a little funny seeing her in action without my barrier of cynicism protecting me. She looked around, focusing mostly on the doorways: front door, far door, and the broom closet I never used because the slop sink inside gave me the willies. Lydia pointed to the creepy door and said, "That's important." Then she cocked her chin toward the front door and said, "More boxes come through there. And after that, more people."

"So I should start throwing parties again."

"You'll note I didn't claim you *should* do anything whatsoever."

I stretched my legs out in front of me, straining the dubious chair, and let my head sag back. With nothing more than a coffee pot and a pile of folding chairs, the only thing I was qualified to host was an AA meeting. "What's the use of inviting people over for Sticks and Stones if there's no furniture for them to hang out on?"

"You think people come for the furniture?"

"Not exactly." I gestured toward the cavernous room. "But the setup is part of the whole experience. Without anything in it, this whole space just feels *off*."

"Ah." She nodded sagely. "And there you have it. Without all your stuff to ground it, what kind of vibes does this place give out? The failure of the last five business that couldn't make it."

Five? Shit. Like the fallout from CUTTERZ wasn't bad enough.

Lydia said, "I don't throw the s-word around lightly, but in this case I'll make an exception. What you *should* do is cleanse the space."

"I take it you're not talking about the roaches."

"Nothing you can do about those, they'll just come back. I'm referring to the vibration." She must've caught me giving her a look, because she added, "I do my own place at the start of every fiscal quarter. And you already have all the gear, so what have you got to lose?"

We poked through my boxes and located some incense and a few bags of herbs that she claimed would do the trick, but she had bookings to attend to, so she couldn't babysit my faltering attempt at clearing my space. Maybe that was for the best. I felt like an idiot waving incense smoke at all the nooks and crannies while I attempted to visualize positive vibes clearing out all the bad juju.

Even with no one watching, I felt like a dumbass.

I adjourned to the web to see if there were any actual techniques I could be putting to use. But it was the internet, after all—teeming with so many amateur attempts at proficiency and flat-out scams that I couldn't trust a damn thing I pulled up. Finally one site seemed promising, with its detailed lists of emotions and their thorough definitions, until I realized the "psych" wasn't extrasensory, but psychological. Frustration. Yep. There it was.

I dragged over a box of books and started flipping through some of Jacob's PsyCop material. The dry stuff—the more tedious, the better. Not because I thought I'd find something as pragmatic as metaphysical cleanup techniques inside. More like I was hoping to find a reference to a legitimate, searchable website. But no dice. Either the books predated the modern web, or the items they cited were buried deep in subscription-based metaphysical research journals.

I was wishing the universe could throw me some kind of bone when I picked up the last of Jacob's stuffy textbooks and revealed a paperback at the bottom of the pile that had definitely not come from him. *Mindfulness Methods*, my ass. The only thing I was mindful of was how inexplicably pissed off I got every time I saw the cover model's self-satisfied grin.

No doubt I was experiencing displaced anger at Red for blowing out of town without so much as a goodbye. But it sure as hell felt like it would be amazing to kick up some sand and wipe that smirk off the model's face. Maybe the book needed to be exorcised. Or penanced. Or whatever the terminology was. More likely, though, the book was a shining bastion of high vibration, and I was just too spiritually inept to handle it.

Even so...maybe it had an index.

I flipped to the back and a business card fluttered onto my lap. Rainbow Dharma: Chicago's LGBTQIA Meditation Gathering. I felt a pang. This was the non-date Red had invited me to share. How might things have turned out differently if I'd been less of an ass?

I picked up the card and scrutinized it. Tacky printing, lotuses and rainbows. No phone number, no website, not even an email. Just a Facebook group. No doubt it was all as dumb as the rest of the internet, but you never know where links will eventually lead.

The group's page opened to a quote: *"Radiate boundless love towards the entire world — above, below, and across — unhindered, without ill will, without enmity." – The Buddha.*

Below that, some pics of a potluck. The attendees looked pretty normal. Not just the sort of folks who'd come to a Sticks and Stones Soiree, but people you'd see on the bus or the checkout line of the grocery store, too. Some of them I knew by sight. Some may have even spent time in my chair, back when my apartment was CUTTERZ.

I clicked to the members list to see if any of their names rang a bell, scrolled down a few taps...then froze in my tracks. There in the far back of the crowd was one guy I knew, all right. Red Turner. Even as I clicked the photo to take a better look at him, I wondered what I was getting so worked up over. Because the way I reacted to that tiny glimpse—heart pounding, mouth suddenly dry—you'd swear I actually gave a shit. I moused over the tags to click through to his profile, and found I was actually nervous as it loaded. I told myself to stop being stupid. Everyone stalks everyone on Facebook. And it didn't mean squat.

Maybe I had a touch of the precog. Because the page loaded, and I realized it really *hadn't* meant squat. It wasn't Red at all, but a totally different guy who only looked like him from a certain angle when he was rocking a snazzy fedora. Obviously not Red, given the preponderance of duckfaced selfies on his wall.

And the crushing pangs of disappointment I couldn't deny.

I clicked the back button so many times, the browser brought me to all the way back to the home page, then refreshed it four more times. What business did I have getting whipped into a frenzy about seeing Red, anyway? I'd just rolled out the L-word.

I'd moved on.

...and what was I doing again? Finding out how to clear the energy. Right.

Fuck the internet. I hadn't found a single thing that would help me psychically fumigate my apartment, and to make matters worse, I couldn't get that image of Red out of my mind. I'd never even boffed the guy, so I could hardly think of him as *the one that got away*. But, damn it, there was no denying that's exactly how it felt.

I was not pining for Red. No way. I'd just proclaimed my *love* for Jacob—and that had not been done lightly.

Throughout my teenage years, I'd gone through a phase of puppy love in which I fell hard for anyone curious enough to fondle my junk. But in college I figured out the difference between love and lust, and realized that loving someone wasn't a prerequisite for screwing them, and in fact, *liking* them was not even a necessity. Since then, I'd had all kinds of practice hooking up with people that only connected with me via the friction points on our bodies, so nowadays I didn't take love for granted.

And I was totally into Jacob. One hundred percent. To prove just how unshakable my devotion was, I opened that goddamn smug-faced mindfulness book Red left me, and I read.

Once I thumbed past the first chapter, it wasn't all about meditation. In fact, there were more breathing type exercises than anything. While too much deep breathing only made me conscious of the fact that I could stand to cut down on my smoking, it didn't piss me off like the eye-rolling visualizations of fluffy clouds or tourist trap beaches.

Be in the present.

My ClipLand shift went more quickly than normal that night. Not because anything inherently interesting was going on—the customer who stiffed my coworker and gleefully darted out the door without paying his twelve bucks notwithstanding—but because I'd challenged myself to stop worrying about the past and anticipating the future. Clock-punching jobs like ClipLand couldn't have been more perfectly designed to encourage people to watch the clock count down, but I let go of the anticipation and nudged myself back to what I was doing, and only that.

Angle, texture, style—I concentrated solely on the hair. Customers expect chatter. It's part of the whole shtick. But at minimum wage and nobody tipping worth shit, what did it really matter? Maybe I was a good salesman, but with effort, I could be an even better stylist—an artisan. That night, a few of my customers did linger an extra moment to admire their cuts, and I couldn't help but let my attention wander to the vibes they were giving off. They were pleasantly surprised.

It was tempting to bask in the external validation, for sure. But since I was on a mission, rather than getting all full of myself, I simply acknowledged my pleasure in a job well done, and then re-focused on the next task at hand, task after task, until the manager reminded me that my shift was over, and if I wanted overtime, I'd need to clear it with the scheduler first. She acted huffy, irritated. Usually I'd ramp up my own emotional charge to match, but tonight, I decided I had better things to do, and I let it drop.

When I un-silenced my phone, I found Jacob had texted that he was working late, so I headed home to seek out my own dinner and my own bed. I opened my front door, and the smell of incense hit me. It's a totally different fragrance once it burns, obviously smokier, and not as cloying as the raw product. It wasn't terrible. In fact, I didn't feel the urge to turn around, walk away, and be anywhere *but* my apartment. A vibrational shift, or wishful thinking? Hard to say.

I spent the next morning on the computer. House blessings were one of the most common types of ritual, right behind love charms and prosperity spells. Apparently they were called smudgings.

And apparently, practitioners offered these so-called smudgings as a paid service.

Interesting. I'd been hoping to repopulate the furniture so I could draw some customers to my soirees, but in the meanwhile, maybe I could bring my sticks and stones to them.

Paid smudgings started at a hundred bucks for maybe an hour of work. Credentials varied. Some folks advertised their years of experience, while others used lots of big, esoteric words to make themselves seem knowledgable. But the priciest sellers only needed two words to really jack up their rates: *certified psychic.*

Someday I might be able to claim that title without resorting to elaborate card trick demonstrations, but for the moment, I'd need to make do with what I had—a customer base. I sent out a text to my party list: *New! Sticks and Stones comes to you with house smudging rituals. Raise your vibe. By appointment only.*

I'll admit, I was excited, since I'm always down for trying something new. And with the hundred-dollar price tag, I wouldn't need many nibbles. I watched my phone, and I waited. Usually when I sent out a party invite, a few texts pinged me back right away, short replies like "cool" and "see you there." Unfortunately, my new idea was met with utter silence.

Being fully present at work that afternoon wasn't difficult. It was better than second-guessing the actions of the past, though I'll admit, during break time when I checked my inbox and still had zero replies, it was tempting to admit defeat. Had I worded my offer badly? Maybe no one knew what smudging meant. Maybe I should've used the word *blessing*, whether I had a philosophical aversion to it or not. Or maybe these folks knew damn well what a smudging was, and they wanted nothing to do with it.

To add insult to injury, the manager on duty asked me to stop by her office before I left. What I was being called out on this time, I had no idea. One thing was for sure. Mindfulness practice or not, my patience could only stretch so far, and one of these days I'd snap and say something I'd regret. In fact, I was chanting a mantra to myself when the showdown finally came. *Don't react. Do. Not. React.*

I was chanting it so hard, I almost neglected to hear what the manager actually told me.

"I noticed your probation period is up." She clicked through a few computer screens. "And you got a few really nice customer feedback cards this week. Most people don't bother filling those out unless they're complaining. So I'm putting in a recommendation for a raise. It's only twenty-five cents an hour, but it's better than nothing."

I thanked her. Sincerely, even. Not for the stupid quarter, but for the lesson she'd just delivered. I'd spent my shift worrying about my failed text message (the past) and preparing for a confrontation (the future) that turned out to be nothing. I shifted my attention to the present and felt the linoleum under my feet, smelled the product-and-flat-iron salon scent.

Everything was fine. I just needed to stay out of my own way.

I did my best to stay present, all the way home. It wasn't easy. But I did it. And once I got there, a call came in. Not from one of my customers. From Pilar.

"This text you sent," she said cautiously. "Is it for real?"

"If it's an offer for me to come clear your space, then yes. But before you say anything, I have two caveats. One, it's a *psychic* cleansing. Cleaning out your garage or steaming your carpets is not part of the deal. And two, I didn't mean to tap you—you're not on the list. So feel free to ignore it."

She could have dropped the whole thing, left the conversation at that. But she didn't. "I've always thought spaces had certain energies to them, but I never brought it up with you. I figured you would just tease me."

"And at the time, you were probably right. I guess I've had a change of heart."

I studied harder for my first smudging than I had for my State Board Cosmetology Exam. If it was just some random customer who liked my head massages and bottles of rocks, maybe I could've winged it. But not with Pilar. I cared about her too much to just take her money without giving her my best effort in return.

Our session was scheduled the next morning at the ungodly hour of nine, to give us a good couple of hours before we'd need to head out to our respective salons. Pilar picked me up at quarter till so we could hit a botanica on our way over and stock up on some sage—not the kind that comes in the little jar in the supermarket spice aisle, but bundles of dried leaves meant for arcane uses, not culinary.

"Are you sure this is the place?" Pilar asked as we pulled up. "It looks...spooky."

"It looks abandoned," I added, though I hoped it wasn't. As far as I could tell, sage was the main ingredient in a smudging recipe, and I didn't want to try any substitutions on my first official ritual.

The store's website had seemed normal...as normal as you could hope for with an esoteric type establishment, anyhow. But to call the physical location a hole in the wall would be putting it kindly. It might even be an insult to wall holes.

An eye-level sign on the door in English, Spanish and Polish informed us that photography was not allowed inside the shop. I hadn't been planning on taking any pictures, but now that the sign said I couldn't, I was tempted. We stepped inside, where we were the only two customers. The aisles were narrow, so closely packed that Pilar looked like she was worried she might not fit between them. Or maybe it wasn't her body language I was picking up on, but a thread of emotional discomfort.

I was also getting something from the frowning woman behind the desk, though to be fair, her facial expression alone spoke volumes. Her stiff hair was a box-dye black that sucked the light out of the room, and she had a pair of reading glasses perched on the tip of her nose—all the better to scowl at us over. I would have been glad to simply grab what I came for and leave, but her hostility prompted me to stick around long enough to prove a point. While I strolled up and down the few narrow aisles, I took a mental inventory of what was stocked and how it was arranged. What was priced to move and what was covered in dust. Basically, whatever piqued my interest or tickled my fancy.

Only once I'd conveyed that glaring at me would only ensure I lingered did I meander up to the counter. Small items that could be easily pocketed were displayed there beneath a scuffed plexi surface. I was struck by the selection of crystals and tumbled stones—mainly I was surprised I already owned so many of them myself. The incense on top of the counter, though, was another story. Inside tall glass apothecary jars, nuggets of resin glowed amber, crimson and gold. The names were exotic: Dragon's Blood, Three Kings, Mayan Copal. They were pricy, but they intrigued me. Plus it was satisfying to put that sour woman through the effort of scooping out just a tiny bit of each one into tiny wax paper bags.

All told, we only spent about ten minutes in the store. It felt a heck of a lot longer, though, and Pilar seemed even more distressed than she had when she first picked me up. "That woman was horrible," she said. "Maybe she was psychic. Maybe she sensed the darkness around me."

"Or maybe she's pissed off at the world, and it had nothing to do with you at all. There's no 'darkness' around you, girlfriend. You work for a sonofabitch, your kid left for college, and you're stressing. That's all."

Pilar gripped the steering wheel hard, blinked rapidly, took a few deep breaths, and sighed. When she spoke, she was all choked up. "Things just aren't the same at Luscious without you. I miss you so much. It feels like I chose Ralph over you, and I hate it."

Despite all her job interviews and talk of leaving, she was still at Luscious. Considering the bullshit Ralph must put her though on a daily basis, I wasn't necessarily sure the vibration of her house had much to do with her distress. Even so, I'd try my best to help.

Inside, I consulted the instructions I'd saved to my phone, lit up the smudge stick, and began filling the house with sacred smoke.

We determined that burning sage reeks. And also, her smoke

detectors were fully functional.

If it were only my own happiness on the line, I would have given up sooner, like I did back at my own place where I called it quits once my incense stick burned down and I was sick of sandalwood. But not only was Pilar paying me—she needed to know she had an ally. Each of us took the other seriously, and that made a huge difference in how much of myself I poured into the smudging.

By the time we'd smoked out the entire place, I felt as if I'd just finished a brutal session of interval training. I rolled my shoulders and wondered if I could count the house smudging as my Wednesday workout. 'Cos, man…I felt like I needed a Gatorade. Afterward, we sat together on the porch in silence. I'd tried—but come on. House clearing? The whole thing was ridiculous. I'd blundered through the place like a moron, waving around a bundle of smoldering twigs and trying to "push" my energy around. I'd made a fool of myself, but at least I'd done it in front of a sympathetic audience.

Maybe it was a farfetched idea to think I could do esoteric rituals as some kind of sideline, but the day hadn't been a total loss. I'd seen firsthand what sort of ulcer I'd be nursing if I was still working at Luscious—plus I'd spent time reconnecting with my friend, and I'd been able to act supportive. That had to count for something.

"I think the house feels different," she said tentatively.

"You don't need to stroke my ego."

"Gracious as ever about taking a compliment." Pilar heaved herself out of the wicker chair. "It's later than I thought—I'd better take you home."

When I pushed open my front door, it seemed to me the place wasn't quite as dauntingly empty as before. The scent of incense lingered, and all my boxes were still there, pushed up against the walls along the perimeter. But mainly, the space was filled with a calm silence, a patient potential. I didn't mind being there, I realized. Even by myself.

As I stood in my big open room and considered the possibility that the smudgings had actually done something, I felt the buzz of an incoming text. One of the Soiree folks had replied to my offer.

And they couldn't *wait* to have me smudge their apartment.

CHAPTER 32

Compared to what I would have earned for a couple hours' work at a high-end salon, the fee from house smudgings wasn't all that remarkable. Given that I was no longer working at a high-end salon, however, but at ClipLand (where a five-dollar tip was a big deal), the money was fantastic.

I'd done nearly a dozen sessions throughout the city and my confidence was growing. I felt less self-conscious about the proceedings, and more tuned in to the smoke, the Vibe, even the client. For the customers with more money than they knew what to do with, I managed to upsell a few gemstone bottles. For the ones who needed their hundred dollars a lot more than I did, I worked out "mini" sessions and cut them discounts. And for the guy with a sleek new camcorder sitting untouched in its box, I negotiated a barter and scored a decent birthday present for my man. Jacob really dug it, too. No more futzing with the buggy app on his phone.

Win-win-win.

Still, despite the fact that I was now able to pay both my rent and my minimum credit card payment in addition to the whopping test fee, signing up for the psychic screening was daunting.

"You'll do great." Jacob murmured the words against my bare belly. He'd insisted on me spending the night at his place so I was alert and rested the morning of the big test. Instead I was borderline woozy.

We'd gone so many rounds, I suspected I might black out if I didn't replenish my electrolytes. The mattress pummeling did provide a distraction—at least until the big-O headrush abated, my heart rate slowed to normal, and I remembered I'd sold all my worldly possessions to prove I was empathic...a notion I wasn't 100 percent sold on, myself.

I was so nervous I'd even considered breaking out my suit, which I only wear at weddings and funerals. But no. I felt like enough of a poser in my presentable job interview slacks and button down shirt. I was hoping to make a good impression, not psych myself out to the point of panicked failure.

The screening was downtown in the heart of the Loop. El tracks blocked the midmorning sun, pedestrians streamed in and out of skyscrapers that housed hotels, offices and department stores. Jacob wove through the El track girders and parked in the bus lane with a cop's flagrant disregard to laws. He turned on his hazards, leaned across the seat, and pulled me into a kiss. "Call me if you need anything."

"I'll be fine."

"You'll be amazing."

"What I'll be...is relieved when it's all over."

"You're sure I can't pick you up later?"

"Nah. Train's right here." I bumped foreheads with him. "See ya on the flip side."

I checked my directions and rode the elevator to the fifteenth floor. There was a table set up outside the suite where a man and a woman were waiting to sign folks in. She had on a silky blouse that showed off her cleavage while he wore a hardcore no-nonsense suit, but both of them were rocking a nametag. Beatriz and Jack.

Although I was currently their only customer, neither of them jumped to attention to greet me. They were too busy bickering with each other.

"It's fine," Jack said.

"It's not fine," Beatriz shot back, with an accent that gave her proclamation twice the oomph. "*Your* name isn't the only one on that report. If you turn it in late, you make *me* look just as bad."

I toyed with the idea of turning around and leaving—I was hardly on their radar. And yet, if I did run off with my tail between my legs, what then? Go back to my empty apartment, call my boyfriend who was as emotionally invested in the process as I was, and tell him I'd changed my mind?

No. I was committed to this thing, and I'd damn well follow through. I stood there in front of the bickering testers and waited for them to stop their kvetching. Finally, Jack turned to me and said, "Sorry—what was your name?"

"Curtis Ash."

He turned to a list and began paging through, while his cohort Beatriz looked me up and down. "Do you work with other people?" she asked me playfully. Perhaps even flirtatiously. Except when I thought about it, I didn't pick up any tug of sexual chemistry. The flirting didn't feel manipulative, exactly, more like business as usual. Most men probably went out of their way to steal lingering glances at her chest, and she'd figured out how to use her looks to her advantage. Who was I to judge? When I cut hair, I did my own rendition of the low-cut blouse and the fluttering lashes.

"Sure, I work with people."

"How do you stop yourself from strangling them?"

She might've been trying to distract me from my jitters, or it might've been an attempt at building rapport. Either way, she wasn't particularly invested in my opinion, and the question had less depth to it than, *Got any kids?*

"You do what you gotta do," I sighed. Seriously, how hard was it to find a surname that starts with *A* on an alphabetical list?

After three passes, Jack finally found my registration (at the top of page 1, go figure) and took possession of my big check. I thought I was in the home stretch, until Beatriz spent a baffling amount of time poring over my driver's license. While she scrutinized the plastic, Jack turned his attention toward me. He was a muscular guy with a shaved head and a thick bodybuilder's neck, but his most striking feature was his unsettling pale eyes. I could only hold eye contact for a couple of seconds before I had to look away.

After what seemed like an eternity, Beatriz handed my license back and wished me good luck. I suspected I'd need it.

"Follow me," Jack said, and we headed off down a nondescript hallway. Once we were out of his colleague's earshot, he muttered, "Women...always flying off the handle."

"It's no big thing," I said. "She's just venting."

"You think so?"

"Piss her off for real and you'll see the difference."

I was beyond bored with their halfhearted melodrama by the time Jack divested me of my cell phone and parked me in a small meeting room. Blessedly alone. Just me and some bottled water, a tray of fruit and bagels, and a stack of paperwork heavy enough to brain someone. It was like high school all over again, except instead of math and English aptitude, these answers had no empirical right or wrong.

I spent nearly an hour trying to describe my baseline attitudes about myself and the world. On a scale of one to five, one being not at all and five extremely, how much did I agree with the following statements?

I have meaningful relationships. Red popped into my head, despite the fact that it hadn't even been his Facebook page I'd recently stumbled across. There was meaning in that relationship, all right, and that meaning was disappointment. I colored in the circle beside the five.

My career is satisfying. Five—extremely. I love hair. And after all, it didn't say job, it said career.

I had a happy childhood. Five, obviously. I grew up in the burbs, went to the best schools, no one bullied me and I never wanted for anything. Except when Miss Mattie died...and I began "acting out." And Maxine started shipping me from therapist to therapist. And my father retreated into his incessant news-watching. Other than that, five.

I'm sure there was no right or wrong answer, they were just typing me for whatever stats they had to collect. Even so, it was grueling. It was like the silly online quiz...on steroids. There were pages of the questions. *Pages.* It so was exhausting I was beginning to think I should've slept in my own bed and pursued more hours of actual sleep. I was about to start filling in circles randomly just to get it over with when I turned over a sheet and found the multiple choice had given way to essay questions.

I supposed that required some actual thought. I cracked open one of the tepid bottled waters, and read.

What, for you, is typical psychic experience?

Describe a particularly strong psychic episode you've had within the past thirty days.

Do certain circumstances trigger your psychic impressions?

Well, shit. Either I'd need to make a big deal out of the smug pug, which not only was an isolated incident, but a ridiculous one—or I'd have to tell a bunch of faceless statisticians, in writing, about the Vibe.

Again, I wrestled with the impulse to skulk out to the lobby, beg them to return my cashier's check, and run back home. But I didn't. Because, damn it, working at ClipLand was not the pinnacle of my experience. I would make something of myself. I had to.

I can typically read people and determine if they are favorably inclined toward me.

I recently received a particularly vivid emotional impression from a dog.

Hard to say what triggers the connection, though I am hopeful a more disciplined regime of meditation and mindfulness would be helpful.

I finished all the questions as best I could, then followed the printed instructions to flip over the sign on my door letting the proctors know I was finished.

And then I waited. No telling how long, since my phone was being held hostage. But a while. The whole time, I thought about going home and slipping that checkered smock over my head. I'd figured my current circumstances for a dry spell, but now I considered the possibility that the upturn would never come. What if Luscious had been the apex of my success, and everything after was just part of my relentless decline?

I was just about ready to scrawl *failure* across my own paperwork and head back home when a tap on the door startled me out of my reverie. Beatriz sashayed in and gathered up my test. "All filled out?" She flipped through the pages without really checking. "Time for the fun part."

"Fun. Right."

Once we were so deep in the warren of identical office doors I wouldn't be able to navigate without a road map and a homing beacon, she asked, "Did Jack say anything about me?"

"What difference does it...? Oh."

She slid me a sidelong glance. "Oh?" she repeated playfully. Except the breezy tone was a total put-on. She seriously wanted to know what I knew.

"You and him. Office romance. Impossible to resist, I know. Been there, done that. And believe you me, it's way more trouble than it's worth."

Maybe it wasn't the smartest thing in the world to share what I'd so cunningly deduced, but at least it shut her up. She didn't say another word until we got where we were going, and when she did speak again, it was all business. "You'll be paired with ten different subjects over the course of the match test." With a swipe of a keycard, she unlocked the room. No fruit platter to be seen, though there was bottled water and a box of tissues at hand. A single office chair, so new it still had tags on it, was positioned dead center. The far end of the room was blocked with an acoustic half-wall, the type of modular piece that made up a cubicle farm.

"Take a seat," she said, "and do not cross the tape line on the floor until you have permission." I glanced down at the floor. There it was. Tape. Very low tech. Nothing to be afraid of. "For the duration of the study, in order to control for distracting name associations, the subjects will be referred to by a randomly-assigned city. For your first session, you will work with Subject Cairo."

Subject Cairo? Shit. Tape or no tape, this whole thing had me spooked. I'm a hair stylist, I thought, not James fucking Bond. Maybe I should've worn my funeral suit after all. I'd figured I would be filling in blanks and maybe playing a few hands of spider chihuahua, but this test flew so far over my head it wasn't even funny.

"Your subject is behind this wall. He or she has been instructed not to speak to you, only to focus on an assigned image with strong visual and emotional content. Subjects have been chosen from a large pool of applicants by high-level certified psychics as being capable of clear and sustained focus. Your highest and lowest sessions will not count toward your final scores to eliminate random lows and highs. You will have five minutes to give any impressions you receive. If you're more comfortable writing things down, you can, but since you're being recorded, you can speak your impressions aloud. Sketching is also acceptable. Your time begins when I leave the room. Do you have any questions?"

I liked it better when she was pumping me for information about her boyfriend. I gave the acoustic divider a dubious look. "So I just write something down? Anything?"

"Or speak or draw. Are you ready?"

As ready as I'd ever be. Meaning, not at all. I shook my head and said, "Let's get this over with."

Beatriz nodded and left the room. And there I was. Me, and the acoustic divider.

"So," I said. "Come here often?" The urge to insult the person behind the wall panel was overwhelming—Maxine always said my mouthiness would be my undoing. "I thought I had no expectations coming into this screening, but apparently I did. Because this...whatever it is...I've got no idea what to make of it."

Impressions. I was supposed to give some impressions. But without having a conversation, how could I? "Coming in here and listening to people spout off about random shit—that's some kind of crazy job. You must hear a lot of weird stuff." I stood and paced, noticed the tape line, and backed up a few steps. "So you're looking at pictures? I hope for your sake it's nothing too heinous. Though I guess there's a 50/50 chance it might be something ugly."

In fact, it was quite possible someone on the other side of that divider was looking at crime scene photos with bloody, nasty images they couldn't un-see. But if they were, I wasn't picking up on it.

I wasn't picking up on anything.

"Maybe it's something neutral. A baseball, a train, a park bench, a rock?" I guess even stuff like that would have an emotional charge. But if it did, I couldn't feel it. I named a bunch of random items, colors too, but then I realized it was all just stuff I'd seen that morning, from the pale green grapes on the fruit platter to the navy flecks in the office carpeting. I spouted off random words until there was a tap on my door, and Beatriz breezed in with a clipboard in hand.

"That's five minutes," she said. "Any questions before we move on?"

"Just one. Is there anyone in this room other than you and me?"

She approached the divider wall and said, "Cairo, can you turn to the window?"

The acoustic divider wall was on wheels. Beatriz gave it a tug, and it angled out to reveal a woman with a ponytail facing the window. From what I could see from the back, just a normal looking person in a sweatshirt and jeans. So I was definitely not alone. But for all the "empathic" impressions I'd received, I might as well have been.

"You're doing it right." Beatriz swung the panel back into place. "Just try to relax."

Easy for her to say. She had nothing at stake here, not like me.

She led me into the hall, then paused to check her clipboard.

"Certification isn't cheap," she said. "What makes it so important to you?"

"At this point...I have no idea." I sighed. "It's no state secret. I'm just experiencing some hardcore buyer's remorse."

"Because you think you're not doing well."

"Ha. I *know* I'm not."

"And if you did? If you walked out of here with a big certificate that said you are psychic, and this thing, it says this is your talent? This is your level? What then?"

Then...I would be vindicated.

Which was a bizarre notion. So Maxine had scoffed at the suggestion that I was an empath, so what? I couldn't recall the last thing I'd done that had garnered her unconditional approval. But I had to admit, if I did walk out the door with a shiny piece of paperwork I could rub in her face, I'd take great pleasure in telling her all about it.

Showing up my mother wasn't my only motivation. Lydia would no doubt have some intriguing suggestions on how I might exploit my official psychic status. And if Jacob showed me a good time just for taking the test, imagine how stoked he'd be if I aced it.

As for me? Maybe I'd finally be able to quell that lingering voice that periodically crept in and taunted, *Wouldn't you feel like a huge ass if you were just making this whole thing up?*

Beatriz parked me in a series of small offices identical to the first, with the same instructions. I did my best to focus on the subject behind the divider—Bristol, Auckland, Miami and so on—and I said whatever came to mind. I even tried to sketch, though my misshapen circle seemed even sillier than the random words I was blurting out. After several hours of guessing at nothing, worn out and demoralized, I was finally put out of my misery. My wrangler read through some statement where I promised not to divulge the contents of the psych screening to anyone, then led me to a lounge where I could await the preliminary scoring from the day's farce, then left me there reeking of disappointment and dried flop sweat.

With a heavy sigh, I headed for the bathroom to freshen up, but instead of the safe haven I'd been expecting, I discovered I wasn't alone. Not only were there two other guys in the john, but they were arguing. One of them was, anyway, a skinny guy in a Cubs jersey. The other one, Jack, zipped up at the urinal with a shrug and said, "Look, Freddie, I don't know what to tell you."

The Freddie guy waved a paper at Jack and said, "It's so vague. An irregularity? What does that even mean?"

"You'll have to take that up with the coordinator, not me. My job is to make sure the right people are in the right room. That's all."

"But I've seen you at these things before. You must know something."

Jack gave a humorless sniff and shook the water from his hands. "Only to expect the unexpected."

"Come on, man. There's gotta be something you can do to help me out. If I don't get paid for today, I'm screwed."

"Think about it this way. You've had a good run and you made a few bucks. Maybe you should just be happy with that."

"I got alimony due, buddy. Mouths to feed."

Jack stuck his hands in the automatic drier, which roared like a jet engine and nearly drowned out Freddie's pleas, at least until he complained even louder. "I did my job, I put in my hours. This isn't fair!"

I edged around them both and grabbed a handful paper towels.

He turned to me as I ran them under cold water and said, "It's not fair."

I blotted my face, then looked over the towel wad and met his eye in the mirror. "Tough break, man." Unlike the proctors, who were just bitching for the sake of bitching, this guy was pretty damn upset.

"A whole day's pay. I did exactly like I always do. I looked at the pictures and I thought about them. I swear, my mind didn't wander. The whole time."

The drier powered down, and Jack said, "Remember the non-disclosure you signed, Freddie."

"Screw that. If they're not gonna pay me over some fucking *irregularity*, why should I care?"

"Because you're not doing yourself any favors by freaking out. Try to calm down while I find someone for you talk to, so you don't come off like a lunatic and blow it. Salvage today, maybe even salvage your place in the program. But if you come at management yelling and swearing and making a big stink, who do you think they're gonna call for the next screening? You, or the next guy on the list?"

As Freddie considered that notion, Jack the government drone made his getaway. Freddie's shoulders slumped, and he looked hard at the floor like he was fighting back tears. "And now I'm replaceable—that's what I just heard. Am I right?"

I untucked my shirt and swabbed my pits. "That's the gist."

"Fuck." He paced in a tight circle between the sinks and the stalls, shook his head, and repeated, "Fuck."

Fuck was right. No one cared about the subjects or testers. It was all just a job, or a number, or statistic to these people. Whether they were bleeding every last cent from the poor dupes who'd come to talk to the acoustic dividers, or stiffing the people behind those dividers out of their pay, it was business as usual. As long as more ignorant hopefuls kept lining up to test and be tested, we were nothing more than cannon fodder. Totally expendable.

"Fuck," he reiterated, weakly now.

There wasn't much more to say, was there? I put myself back together and went out to face my verdict.

CHAPTER 33

So, I failed. And I suck at failure.

My senior year of college, after my father dropped dead from a massive heart attack, I kept re-living our last phone call, where he said I'd "grow out of" my rebellion and just be "normal." And how I told him that he should stop harboring fantasies about me going to bed some night and waking up straight. I played through that conversation my every waking moment. Sleeping, too. Although in my dreams we'd been face to face, so I could see the look of disappointment—even disgust—in his eyes.

Once he died, between the assignments I'd missed and the tests I'd bombed, I would have needed to score straight A's through the end of the semester to merely pass. So I did what anyone with a scrap of pride would have done, and I withdrew.

Too bad I hadn't had the balls to do the smart thing with the psychic screening and pull the plug before we started. The impulse I'd ignored, when I'd stepped off the elevator and fought off the urge to turn back around with my cashier's check and go home? I really should have listened to my gut.

The guy who explained my test results was a jocular old Russian with a wide gap between his front teeth. "These things can be very subjective," he explained to me in his thick accent. "Test you on a better day, you might score a two. Today...well, today was not a good day."

"So I was *almost* a two? How is that not good?"

"For certification, you need a solid level-two. You scored a high level-one."

"But if most people score zero and the numbers only go to six, a high one's gotta mean something. It's practically a two."

"It's not a proportional scale. On a good day, you might score a low two. Maybe. But not today."

Failure was not an option. I hadn't sold all my worldly possessions to be scored a high level-one and go home with nothing. I looked hard at the Russian and did my best to read him. No Vibe. Pity, maybe. Sympathy, tolerance...although I was gleaning all that from his body language and tone of voice. Anybody would draw the same conclusions from his demeanor. And if I rolled out a divider wall and hid him behind it? I'd probably get nothing.

Well, fuck.

Apparently I'd bought in to everyone's confidence that I was some hotshot empath, including my own, because I had no plan B. The Russian gave me some info about where I could download more specific results once the final tabulation was done, but it was nothing I couldn't have figured out myself from reading the paperwork. He even suggested that if I wanted to amplify my talent, I could try meditation.

I laughed. It was an ugly sound.

"I'm sorry," he said simply, and left the room.

I sat and stared at the carpet, numb. What would I tell Lydia? What would I tell Jacob? I'd banked everything on the presumption I'd show up on the supernatural scoreboard and propel myself into a lucrative career in the psychic realm. Now I had nothing but a horrible job, an empty apartment and a pile of credit card debt.

I collected my phone, signed another raft of forms, and headed back out into the cold, cruel world. I walked past the subway that led to Jacob's place, and kept going till I reached the line that would take me home. As I rode, I read and re-read the preliminary analysis. Inconclusive. Inconclusive. Inconclusive.

The lack of conclusion might have led me to have hope that maybe someone would find something in the scoring process to

push me up into a level-two, solidly enough to enjoy official certification. But given the sympathy the Russian had been exuding, I
knew that wouldn't happen.

I was just a couple stops from home when instead of the usual
text, Jacob called. The urge was strong to let it go to voicemail, but I
figured it was better to come clean with him sooner rather than later.
I answered with, "If you've ordered a celebratory strip-o-gram, you
should probably cancel it."

"What do you mean?"

"To say I bombed would be putting it mildly."

He was quiet for a long moment. On the subway, it was hard to
tell if the quality of silence on the other end was dead air or a deliberate pause. But eventually he said, "Are you okay?"

"Dandy."

He grunted, considered my news some more, then said, "Where
are you now? It sounds like the train."

"Yeah. About that. I'm gonna just head home tonight."

"If that's what you want. Let me know if you need anything."

I told him I would and said goodbye, but I had no intention of
accepting his charity, or his pity. Maybe he was a PsyCop, and maybe
he could throw his weight around and pull some strings. But even if
he could, I'd blown it fair and square. The only thing left to do was
wallow in my failure.

On the way home from the subway, I stopped at the big grocery chain catty corner from my place and grabbed a dusty bottle of
vodka from the lowest shelf. Serious rotgut, but the price was right.
My front door was only a few dozen yards away, and even so...fuck
it. I tossed the bag, cracked the plastic seal and took a big swig right
there on the sidewalk.

Warm. Repulsive. And perfectly fitting.

Once I was across the street, I stopped every few steps and took
another slug. Lydia's neon sign was on, but I wasn't in the mood to
talk things through. I wanted to drink, wallow, and hopefully pass out
without puking. That was the extent of my ambition.

I opened the vestibule door and paused at the threshold, took a
long drink to fortify my impending walk up the stairs, then nearly

did a spit take when my mother's voice rang through the stairwell. "Curtis?"

I lowered the bottle.

She stood at the top of the stairs in front of my door. God only knew how long she'd been waiting there.

The shabbiness of the stairwell hit hard. Dingy plaster, worn carpet, the stink of cigarettes and sandalwood threaded through with piss. And there was Maxine, framed by the squalor, with her lacquered hair and coral lipstick, forcing a smile she thought looked cheerful. It wasn't even Sunday and she was completely out of context.

"Since when do you just drop by?" I demanded.

"I called to let you know I was downtown but you didn't answer."

I whipped out my phone and checked, and there they were, three missed calls I'd swiped right past on the subway. And then the vodka hit my system, part buzz, part stomach churn.

My options were limited. I could manufacture an argument right there on the stairs and get Maxine to leave. I could lure her out the door under the pretense of being hungry and broke. Or I could face the music.

The warm vodka in my belly prickled my stomach lining, and exhaustion surged through my veins. I was too tired, too empty to keep on pretending everything was normal, everything was fine. Without a word, I walked up the stairs, handed the vodka to my mother, and unlocked my front door.

I stepped in and flipped on the lights. Maxine followed. I steeled myself, but the accusations didn't come. She simply stood there clutching the cheap vodka to her chest, turning a slow circle, scanning the room in confusion.

"Well?" I finally asked.

"I don't understand. Where's your apartment?"

"You're standing in it."

She blinked. "You...live? Here?"

"Be it ever so humble." I grabbed a metal folding chair from up against the wall and kicked it open. It obliged with a squall of metal on metal. "Make yourself at home. Can I get you something to drink? A glass of tap water? A shot of warm vodka? I can even mix the two if you're in the mood for a cocktail. No ice, but since the freezer door's frozen open, maybe I can scrape off some of the frost if you don't mind a little Pad Thai flavor in your beverage."

"You...live here."

"Don't want a drink?" I grabbed the vodka from her unresisting hand. "Fine, more for me."

While I tipped the bottle back and forced down a few more swallows, Maxine did a slow circuit of the place. She checked out the broom closet, then the miniature roomlets behind the office, and then rejoined me in the middle of the big, empty space that had been the site of a half-dozen failed business attempts. "Where are all your things?"

I gestured toward a bank of cardboard boxes shoved against the far wall. "You're looking at 'em."

"Whose bed is that? Where's your TV? And your beautiful maple dinette...where do you eat?"

If she wasn't going to make use of that damn chair, then I was. I dropped onto it and put my head in my hands. "I sold it. Everything."

"Why? Are you on drugs?"

I could hardly snip at her over that assumption, given the fifth in my hand. I took another slug. "There are no 'drugs.' A run of bad luck, and the decision to try to invest in myself, fat lot of good it'll do me. I had a screening."

"A *psychic* screening?"

She said it like it was the most ludicrous thing in the world, and her tone would've been enough to piss me off. But the accompanying burst of dismay that came with it sent me into defensive mode. "Why is that so farfetched?"

Silence hung there for a moment while Maxine scanned the room as if some real furniture might appear. When it didn't, she retrieved a folding chair, set it up next to mine, and sat. "Do you remember in junior high when you were part of that focus group for the toy company?"

"Random. But yes."

"It wasn't a focus group."

The memory wasn't particularly vivid, though I could dredge up a detail or two. We were in the Loop. I never had a reason to be there unless I was visiting the Art Institute or checking out the Christmas windows at Marshall Field's. That day, Maxine had driven me all the way down to play with the world's most boring building sets while a bunch of frowning guys with clipboards took notes.

"It was a screening," she said. "And your scores were average."

"Hold on...you had me tested and you never told me?"

"None of the children knew. It would have caused performance anxiety and skewed the test results, that's what they told us."

I tried harder to remember exactly what went down in that stuffy high rise office, but the details were hazy. I was more interested in the gourmet popcorn store afterward. No doubt there were parts of the test I didn't quite recall—how easy would it have been for a researcher to say, "How does this toy make you feel?" with me none the wiser? But overall, I didn't see how they could have been testing for empathy specifically.

"The tests are fucked," I said weakly.

"Your father was against it, but Mattie used to have this way of putting things. When you were little, she convinced me you had some 'gift.' Once they could actually test for it, I got all carried away with proving it to your dad."

An image of him came to mind, coiled in his chair and glaring at the news. "It wouldn't have helped. He never liked me."

"Curtis! Don't say that. He loved you."

Maybe. But he didn't *like* me, at least not since...when? Since I started taking interest in the "wrong" gender? The timing would've been about right. I'd been hung up on boys since I got a load of my babysitter Terry Keller, all suburban grunge and manufactured ennui.

I was eight.

The big coming-out wouldn't happen until high school. But what if I wasn't the only one sensitive enough to pick up on things? Imagine feeling your son shooting a ravenous Vibe to his dramatically disaffected male sitter, and...well, it would explain a thing or two. Yes it would.

Maxine swung her chair around so we were facing each other and demanded plaintively, "Why didn't you tell me all this was going on?"

"Because you've never once supported a career decision I've made and I wasn't in the mood to be second-guessed."

"I'm your mother. All I want is for you to be happy."

"In a way that's acceptable to your neighbors."

"That has nothing to do with it."

"As a car salesman. Or a realtor."

"Stop attacking me. I was just pointing out that you shouldn't limit yourself. You're young, you don't have the same perspective I do. Yes, you went to cosmetology school, and yes, you like cutting hair. But if all the good jobs in that field dry up, you need to try something new. It doesn't mean you never do hair again, but why suffer in the meantime?"

I forced down another warm swallow and gave serious consideration to concocting a vodka-and-freezerburn shave ice.

Maxine wrung her hands. "I hate seeing you like this. Working at that awful place just to prove a point, coming home to this dilapidated empty room. Sitting here drinking. Alone."

Useless level-one or not, I could tell my mother was genuinely upset, and not just because she was worried what her Pilates friends might think. I capped the vodka, let the plastic bottle bounce to the floor and roll a few feet away, and said, "I'm not alone."

She gave me a look brimming with pity.

"I'm not," I insisted, slightly nauseated now, thanks to the booze—not to mention overly loud, and hell bent on making my point. "I have a boyfriend and it's serious."

Her cloying sympathy spiked.

"What? You think I'm inventing him to make you feel better? His name is Jacob."

"Why haven't you mentioned this 'Jacob' before?"

"Because I knew you'd be so fucking supportive." I considered how far the bottle had rolled, and the fact that if I attempted to retrieve it, I probably wouldn't want to get back up off the floor. It pissed me off whenever she referred to someone in my life as "this" or "that," as if they're fictional, or dubious, or unsavory, and I felt compelled to defend him. I couldn't do him justice, though, not in my current state of queasy inebriation. Hell, probably not even sober. Jacob was a suburban mother's wet dream, everything she could want for her wayward gay son: polite, thoughtful and financially secure. Basically, everything I wasn't.

Although I was in no state to eat dinner, I let Maxine take me to a trendy Asian fusion joint up the block just to get her the hell out of my shitty apartment. I endured a half-dozen stories about various remodels she or her friends had commissioned, and waved away the offer of a consultation with the interior designer who was the darling of Chicagoland's middle-aged lady population. My problems ran too deep for a facelift to fix. A coat of designer paint would only serve to highlight the cracks and the roaches.

Conversation was rough. Normally, I would have been able to dredge up something to say. I'd get her to talk about what her neighbors were up to, or maybe tell a story about her dog. But I was prickling with dried sweat and nauseated from the day-long onslaught of adrenaline I'd topped off with cheap vodka.

"So you have a boyfriend," Maxine said. "How long have you been seeing each other?"

I shrugged, and thought back. "Since...February." I forced myself to meet her eyes. Just as I suspected, she was hurt. Not mentioning it until now, at the height of August? Not only was I a shitty psychic, but a shitty son, too. "Look, how 'bout this—I bring him to dinner Sunday, and you can meet him." The hurt in her expression softened, and I whipped my phone out on the spot and started thumbing in a text. "We'll hit that bistro on Irving you like."

Maxine didn't know what to make of my sudden rush of purpose, but since I was tipsy, and since she didn't vigorously object, I finished my invitation and launched it.

Dinner Sunday 6pm at The Lantern?

I stared at my phone until I received the single word reply.

Sure.

CHAPTER 34

I burned the couple of days between the invitation and the dinner plowing through twelve-dollar haircuts and dreaming up ridiculous things to be nervous about. Maybe Maxine would call me Little Peanut in front of Jacob and undermine all my dirty bed-cred. Maybe Jacob would be embarrassed by her painful attempts at humor. Hell, maybe the sky would open up and rain dildos. Life is seriously random, and prepping for its surprises is an exercise in futility, so I told myself to stop rehearsing scenarios where everything tanked...and I took a few minutes to consider why the hell I was so nervous.

Seven months—shit, more than half a year—of course it was time for Jacob to meet my mother. In fact, it was long overdue. And once we got that out of the way, I could forget about my big psychic plans, buckle down and find a decent place to work, somewhere Ralph had drunkenly burned his bridges, somewhere I could land on Pilar's reference alone. And once I had a grownup's income, move-in negotiations could begin.

The Lantern was crowded, but Maxine and I both showed up so precisely on time that I suspected she'd been sitting in her car twiddling her thumbs, not unlike the way I'd hopped off the bus four stops early and walked a quarter mile so as not to be absurdly early myself. I'd dressed deliberately casual. Ripped jeans, scuffed boots, a black T-shirt with an orange constellation across the flank from of a

wayward splash of bleach. She'd dressed like Maxine, painfully coor-
dinated and nebulously uncomfortable. She pecked me on the cheek
and said, "What am I supposed to call you in front of him? Does he
know your name?"

After seven months? I spared her the eye-roll. "He does. Either
Crash or Curtis is fine."

The hostess checked our reservation and tried to seat us, but we
decided to give Jacob a few more minutes. Maxine probably didn't
want to look too ensconced when he got there. Me, I just felt the need
to be on my feet.

"I wish I'd thought about the initials," Maxine said.

"What?"

"Curtis Raymond Ash. If we'd put my grandfather's name in front
of your dad's father's, it wouldn't have spelled anything," she said. I
scanned the street for the big black gas-guzzling sedan. "Or maybe
just Rash."

Which was equally as punk rock, though it might've hampered
my love life. I checked my phone. My mother fidgeted under the
impatient eye of the hostess.

"Your hair looks nice." She said. "But your roots are due for a
touch-up."

When there's any regrowth to be seen on me, it's deliberate.
I'd told her as much I dunno how many times. "Thanks," I said
distractedly.

"I'm sure your Jacob is just looking for a spot," she added.

Well. I was equally as sure something wasn't right. I texted, *I'm at
the restaurant*, then sat with my elbows on my knees and my phone
in my hands, waiting.

A minute later, he replied, *Sorry, working. Reschedule?*

I stared down at those three little words. I may not be a certified
psychic, but I had a queasy certainty that he wasn't working, he was
avoiding me. And he wasn't sorry, either.

And if I was correct about those two things, I wasn't planning to
reschedule. Not just the outing with my mom, either, but all future
engagements.

I wasn't angry, I was livid. But I sounded pretty calm, I think, when I gave Carolyn a quick ring and said, "Hey, girly, where are you right now?"

"At home. Why?"

Hah. Working, my ass. "No reason...gotta go. Talk soon."

I'm not sure whether my curt reply registered on her mental polygraph over the phone, or if she could tell how I felt from my fake tone of voice. She called back, and I sent it to voicemail and turned off the ringer. After a few more attempts, she texted, *Talk to me.* And then, *I knew this would happen.* And then, *I don't know what's going on, but it better not affect our friendship.*

We're good, I sent back, and pocketed my phone. I stood and told my mother briskly, "Jacob's not coming tonight after all." Not between *my* legs, at least. "Might as well eat."

It was like every other Sunday Mom-Dinner, just Maxine and me, rife with subtext and pity, all of it buried under an inane wall of chatter. My mother could tell I was upset so she cranked her wattage extra-bright, filled me in on the minutiae of her numerous random acquaintances, and ordered enough appetizers to host a soiree. "You know, I was talking to my dermatologist about psychic screening," she said lightly. I'd picked up my patently false "nothing serious" tone from her, so I knew it when I heard it. "She read that some people score higher on their second attempt because they know what to expect, so the anxiety is much lower."

"I could see that," I allowed.

"Was it stressful?"

Her genuine concern caught me off guard. I looked up sharply and met her eyes. She stared at me across the table so earnestly I hardly knew what to do with her authenticity. "Yeah. It was."

"And do you think you'd do better if it wasn't all such a shock?"

"Maybe." I thought about my inability to read though a room divider, the way it felt like there could very well be nobody behind it, and the fact that I needed to see and hear people to gather my impressions. Who knows, if I'd ever worked in a cube farm for more than a few weeks at a time during an odd summer job, maybe I would've picked up the ability organically. Although.... Nothing stopping me from practicing now. "Yeah, maybe."

"If you really think it would affect your score," my mother said, "maybe you should try again."

"Even though I bombed the kiddie-test too?"

She waved the concern away like it was nothing. "That was ages ago. You were just a child. Mattie always said you had a feel for people, but you told me they made you play with blocks. How could anyone possibly test for empathy with blocks?"

True. Unless someone had a pretty hardcore block fetish, I'd have no reason to notice.

"I'm sure those old-fashioned screenings were nowhere near as good as they are today," Maxine added.

My mind reeled. She wouldn't bring up the subject of re-testing unless she was willing to support it. Financially. I'd been so sure the door to psychic certification was closed for good, I hardly knew what to make of another chance. I was scrambling to make heads or tails of my own feelings on the topic when a Vibe nailed me right between the eyes...one I hadn't even needed to see to pick up on.

I pinpointed the source from halfway across the room, a clean-cut, middle-aged gay guy with expensive clothes and thinning hair. He was staring at me like he'd just had an epiphany, though he looked away just as soon as I met his eyes. But not before I knew exactly what he wanted to do with me...or, more precisely, what he wanted me to do to him.

"Testing standards change all the time," Maxine said. "Like they found all kinds of bias in IQ testing and they're scoring that differently these days too."

"Hold that thought," I murmured, as I set my napkin on the table and stood. The guy who'd twanged my radar was looking fastidiously at his plate now, but I knew he could feel my eyes on him. I was sure of it. Like me, he was having a Sunday dinner out with the family. A sister. Her teenage kids. I crossed the room and marched right up to his table, and he looked up with a hunched, sheepish eagerness.

The wanting spiked. I embraced it, and more details flooded me. His fascination with cleanliness warred with the desire to be utterly debased. Somehow, somewhere, he'd taken a shine to musky astringency of urine, and he wanted it now. Desperately. To see it? Smell it? Or feel it splashing across his bared chest? Yes, yes, and absolutely, yes.

I leaned in and casually said, "You look like you've been here before. A guy who knows the lay of the land. So tell me...." I leaned in farther. "Where's the bathroom?"

His pupils dilated. While his family looked at me a bit strangely for choosing him in particular as the one to answer my perfectly generic question, they had no idea that in his mind, I was baptizing him with my piss. He stammered something about going past the bar and behind the kitchen door, and I thanked him and rejoined my mother, who was looking at me just as strangely as the guy's surly teenage nephew. I re-settled my napkin and said, "Thought I knew him."

And if the impression I'd just received was correct, in a way, I did.

"I want you to take that test again," Maxine said. "And don't worry about the cost. Anything I can help you do to get ready for it, just let me know."

My phone buzzed and I snuck a quick look at it under the table. Another text from Jacob. *We need to talk.*

Says the guy who couldn't even bother speaking to me to stand me up. In fact, I hadn't heard a peep from him since the screening.... the one I bombed. If I had an official certificate to wave under his nose, I bet he would've had plenty to say. In fact, I *knew* he would. Working or not, he would have at least fucking called instead of just texting his nonexistent regrets.

I supposed I was psychic enough to know all along he wasn't much into me—not without that piece of paper. I just hadn't yet been forced to confront the knowledge so bluntly.

"Once you're certified," my mother said, "all kinds of opportunities will open up for you."

Sure. And Jacob would come running right back to me, too. The thought of which pissed me off to no end.

Our server started clearing the appetizer plates to make room for our main course, and the sight of the half-eaten canapes made me feel nostalgic for my soirees. I didn't need a certificate, I realized, to recapture that feeling. And maybe I was just being contrary, but if Jacob's approval hinged on me being certified, then the official piece of paper was the last thing I wanted.

"You know how much the screening costs?" I asked. Maxine nodded. "Well, if that money's on the table...what would you say if I used it to start a business instead?"

CHAPTER 35

Maxine and I hoarded our table by lingering over our meal long after the dessert plates were cleared. Normally I'd be more sympathetic to the hovering waitstaff, but fuck 'em. It wasn't every day you got stood up and lied to, then rounded out the evening by planning your own business. Every decision branched into a dozen more details that needed to be sorted out, and when Maxine dropped me off in front of my apartment, I had a list of stuff as long as my arm that needed research and planning. But as I headed for the stairs, I spotted a handful of flyers on the vestibule floor—an ad for one of the trendier nearby bars. Sunday night was two-for-one well drinks and no cover charge. And since I'd been drinking bottom shelf liquor so long I hardly noticed the vile aftertaste, it would be a shame for all that conditioning to go to waste.

Hitting a bar isn't just about the drinking. I was perfectly capable of making a watered down screwdriver myself. Barhopping is about seeing and being seen. Brushing up against other people. An attempt at socialization, connection.

Even with the drink special, the Sunday night crowd was lackluster and thin. I was considering finishing my drink and heading on home when I recognized my old friend Matthew peeling out of the bathroom and doing a quick scan of the crowd. I raised my glass to him and his face brightened at the promise of juicy gossip and a

satisfying bitch session. "Look who decided to grace us with his presence," Matthew exclaimed. "Haven't seen you in any of your usual
haunts lately."

Too true. "I've been keeping myself busy."

He must've known I was at ClipLand these days, but he didn't
seem eager to prod that particular wound. "Well, you got out of
Luscious while the getting was good. Red's gone, Trevor's gone, It's
just me and Pilar and a bunch of annoying little babies fresh out of
school."

And Matthew thought he was oh-so-experienced. Well, maybe
he was. He'd endured a lot over the past year to keep his prestigious
job. Maybe he wasn't quite as naive as I'd always suspected.

Poor Pilar, though. I would've thought she'd have figured out
how to move on by now. All her planning, all her hopes and dreams.
I might never thank Ralph for the way he treated me, but at least I
wasn't stuck at Luscious.

Matthew trailed a lingering glance over my body. "Look at you,
all angular and pissed off." Yeah, a diet of ramen and disappointment
will do that to you. "You're a sight for sore eyes. Everyone else here is
so phenomenally boring."

The minute Matthew deems the situation *boring*, someone's
about to get their rocks off. And I supposed it would be easiest to
suck each other off in his car. I'm not sure why I didn't suggest we
adjourn to the backseat. After all, it would've been more comfortable
than my shitty apartment.

Maybe I wanted him to see it. Maybe I wanted everyone to know
I'd really scraped bottom, so that when I rose from the ashes, they'd
know what hardships I'd had to overcome.

Maybe I wanted to make sure Jacob knew.

It wasn't extrasensory perception that told me Mr. Perfect would
put in an appearance, it was good, old-fashioned common sense.
Carolyn wasn't able to resist letting him know about our conversation. Not from any desire to stir the pot, but her compulsion to ex-
pose the truth. And Jacob, well, he'd need to set the record straight.

We weren't exactly dawdling on the way back to my place, but we
weren't in any hurry, either. We were within a block of my building

when the black sedan idled up and started pacing us. I felt it, felt *him*, lurking there in my peripheral vision long before Matthew did; he was still chattering away about the latest blowup at Luscious when I stopped and turned toward the street, and the tinted passenger window powered down.

"We need to talk," Jacob said.

I crossed my arms and gave a one-shoulder shrug.

He put the car in park right where it was and strode out onto the sidewalk. He can do shit like that because he's a cop. He can do whatever he damn well pleases and never has to answer for any of it. Well, not anymore. I was done.

"Who's your friend?" Matthew asked. His overly casual tone dripped with eagerness to witness some drama unfolding, and I had the feeling he was about to get a pretty good show.

Jacob gave him half a glance, then said to me, "What are you playing at?"

I slipped my hand into Matthew's back pocket so there was no doubt as to my intention. "Getting reacquainted with an old colleague. Care to join us?"

He didn't dignify that with a response. "I miss one date and that's it, you move on to the next guy?"

"And there you go, spinning the situation to make me sound like a tool. Not that I had any doubt you would, seeing as how you're so perfect."

"You called Carolyn to check up on me. That's a huge violation of my trust."

"Is it? Or are you just embarrassed you got caught?"

"Do you seriously think—?" He planted his hands on his hips. "I can't believe you're so phenomenally immature."

He worked his jaw so hard that sinews leapt in his neck. But while he looked pretty pissed, I wasn't getting an angry vibe off him, just an icy chill. "Look," I said, "you don't need to pull the age card, or to play up the melodrama like you're oh so hurt. We've got nothing in common, and I'll never live up to your standards."

"That's bullshit. And we have plenty in common."

"What, we like to eat and fuck? So do sponges and cockroaches.

Here's the deal, we had some fun and now we're done. As simple as that. I'll put it in a way even you can understand." I disengaged from Matthew, pulled out my phone, thumbed in a single word and texted it to Jacob.

Goodbye.

PART THREE

Sticks and Stones

CHAPTER 36

It was just as well Jacob and I called it quits when we did. Since I overlapped my ClipLand job with the brick and mortar version of Sticks and Stones until the last possible moment, I had zero time for deep dinner conversation and naked desert. For weeks on end, I stayed up until the wee hours, not between the sheets, but parked in front of the computer. I had to grind through a mind-numbing array of forms and fees required to open a retail shop in Cook County. And then there was my inventory software to set up. And my website. And advertising. And...well, you get the idea.

Not that I'm complaining. Admin work is dull as dirt when you're doing it for someone else, but seeing as it was *my* baby being patched together? I got a charge out of it. Even if I was only clocking four hours of sleep a night.

I hadn't realized exactly how sleep-deprived and crabby I was until Maxine showed up to "help" me paint...with one gallon of semi-gloss acrylic. I sized up the can and said, "What, pray tell, is that?"

"Sultry Amethyst." She looked at me expectantly, then said, "Don't you like it?"

Sure, the color was great. But... "Where's the rest of it? I gave you forty bucks."

"And I spent it." She handed me the receipt. Thirty six dollars. Plus tax. Shee-yit. "One gallon of paint? One gallon?" I gestured at the disgusting stairwell. The ceilings were nine feet in the shortest part, taller than that as they came up the stairs. And the whole thing was covered in graffiti and filth. "We'll run out before we even hit the first step."

"I talked them into free samples of Sun-Kissed and Cerulean Dream, too."

"Samples? Wow, that changes everything!"

"Don't yell at me. I'm trying to help."

"This isn't your suburban breakfast nook, Maxine, it's a public hallway. I'll be painting it over and over again. I don't need a designer color—a bucket of thick white generic paint will do."

She gave petulant pout. "Fine. I'll take it back."

"Don't bother. It wouldn't be right after you had it custom mixed." I crossed my arms and took in the wall in all its ugly squalor. "Even if I could afford to paint the whole thing purple, what difference would it make? It'll be covered in gang tags before the week is out."

"In that case...use this paint for your focal point. Your front door."

Grudgingly, I let myself warm up to the idea of dropping such a big chunk of change on the color of my door. After all, folks pay all that and more to color their hair, and that grows out. "I suppose it couldn't hurt to have a focal point."

We had the bright idea to paint the front door yellow, but partway in, realized the sample wouldn't stretch to cover. No problem. We added blue stripes. The doorframe, we did in purple. And as it came together, I had to admit, it looked pretty sharp.

While Maxine had a great eye for color—you've gotta figure I inherited my own good taste from somewhere—manual labor wasn't her forte. Despite my best efforts to tape everything off and contain the spillage, she somehow managed to wear more paint than she applied. When a whopper of a spider squeezed out from the behind the molding and startled her, she tottered back and stuck her hand to the wet can lid. And while a normal person might've wiped it off, Maxine somehow flailed against the wall instead and left an arc of Sultry Amethyst fingerprints behind.

"I'm so sorry." She grabbed for the paper towels and sent them rolling down the stairs. They unfurled to the halfway point, and then the paper core detached from the end and bounced the rest of the way down.

She made a grab for the roll, and I caught her by the shoulder before she went tumbling down the stairs behind it. Only then did I realize something was seriously wrong. "Hey." I tugged her around and made her look at me. "What is it?"

She smiled brightly, but I saw right through it, even more than usual. Not just because she was blinking away tears.

"Is someone sick? Are you okay?"

With me unwilling to play the *everything's fantastic* game, her façade slipped. "No one's sick, honey. I'm just worried."

"About who?"

She laughed then, a genuine laugh that was really kind of a sob, and the dam broke, and a tear rolled down her cheek. "All I ever wanted was for you to be happy."

"I am," I said. And then I checked myself.... Was I? "Sure, I'm stressed out, and no matter how careful I try to be, I hemorrhage money. But the whole experience of setting up this business was amazing, even the boring parts. I can't deal with working for some power-hungry boss. I won't. Cruising along and playing by someone else's rules was killing me. And if that means living on the cheap and putting in long hours, so be it. Stuff is just stuff. Now that I'm tasting what it means to live on my own terms, I wouldn't trade it for all the material possessions in the world."

I reeled in the paper towels, mashed them into an unwieldy bunch, tore off a random hunk and handed it to her. But instead of wiping off her own hand, she attempted to scrub off the purple fingerprints she'd left behind on the wall.

Too late. The prints were already drying, and all they did was smudge.

I didn't *see* Maxine's precarious optimism plummet...I felt it.

"I've got an idea," I announced briskly, and stuck my hand in the paint can. If I know anything, it's confidence. And the best way to bluff your way through a mistake is to make it look deliberate. I daubed a dozen more fingerprints next to hers.

Maxine chided me with a stern, "Curtis," but her mood stopped tanking.

I was only half listening anyhow, because I was in the midst of an idea—a way to draw customers up the stairs. "I think I've got an easier way to camouflage this graffiti." And an interesting way to stretch out that single gallon of Sultry Amethyst, and the dregs of Cerulean and Sun-Kissed.

I owned plenty of colors. They were meant for hair, not walls, but as anyone who's tried to tint their own hair knows, they'll stain anything they touch. Flame Red, Fuchsia, Indigo and Green Apple—I let my potential clientele know I was a gay-owned business by leading them to my door with a pointillism rainbow. And once Maxine saw it start coming together, she was absolutely delighted. So much so that when she whipped out the hot glue gun and stuck a bunch of twigs and rocks to a salvaged hunk of wood to spell out the store's name, I didn't have the heart to tell her there was no need to be so literal. I guess part of being an entrepreneur was knowing when to accept collaboration.

By the time the paint fumes dissipated, I was ready to spring my venture on the world.

My grand opening event wasn't terribly eventful—I hung flyers on neon colored paper and cranked up the huge coffee urn. But soiree folks came. And if they were surprised to see my mother in the helper role rather than Jacob, they kept their comments to themselves. People didn't linger quite as much as they had when a big cozy conversation pit dominated the room, but there was a decent stream of customers. Lydia was in and out several times, and Pilar put in an appearance. Carolyn, too. She didn't mention Mr. Perfect. Neither did I. Still, it wasn't lost on me that Jacob would've really got off on setting up the store together. Hell, maybe it would've even fulfilled his burning need to set up house.

Oh well, I thought. What's done is done.

It was a long, grueling day. There was a lot left to do after the doors closed, but Maxine looked like she'd been through a marathon. I took the broom out her hands and said, "It's okay, Mom. I got this."

She looked at me oddly for a moment. Her expression was ambiguous, but the love and pride rolling off her nearly bowled me over. "What?" I asked.

"You called me *Mom*."

I groaned. "Don't get used to it. It's not like you ceased to be yourself and became this generic *Mom* person just because you pushed me out of your vag. You're an individual, not a concept."

She gave my shoulder an awkward squeeze. "But I like being your mom."

"Go home," I said with over-emoted tolerance. "You're getting loopy."

I herded her out to her car, kissed her on the forehead and shoved her behind the wheel. It wasn't late-late by most people's standards, but I felt like I'd been drinking all night, hooked up in the bathroom and then shot the shit till last call. But no. It was a quarter after eight.

I walked back toward the building and tapped out a smoke. As a new player in the retail game, I was painfully aware of the glut of Back to School ads coming at me from every angle. It was the first week of September. Heat radiated off the sidewalk but the nighttime air was cool now, and sunset came a little sooner each night. I lit up, leaned against the building, and wondered how it was possible to be so tired and so buzzed, all at once.

At my elbow, the door opened. Lydia, in jeans and a hoodie. "Heard lots of traffic on the stairs. Good day?"

"Haven't counted out the drawer yet. But yeah. I think so."

She pulled out her own smoke, propped herself against the wall beside me and glanced down at my hand. "You making some yoga gesture?"

I glanced down and noted that I'd been pressing my fingers into a mudra without giving it a moment's thought. "Guess I'll take my energy wherever I can get it."

We stared out at traffic and we smoked together. While I lit a second cigarette, Lydia said, "You've changed. In a good way. Meditation, contemplation, maybe it's not as exciting as nightclubs—"

"Nah, I'm more of a dive bar aficionado."

"Anyway, I like it on you. It feels mature."

"Heaven forbid." I smiled to myself, vindicated. I hadn't told her about Jacob's parting remark, but hell, she was a precog. Maybe she'd heard it long before we finally parted ways. The weeks between then and now had flown by in the face of all the work I'd done—transitioning jobs, setting up the shop, and yeah, figuring out the whole meditation deal. I'd gone to Rainbow Dharma in hopes of drumming up business and ended up with a sitting practice. It cut into my precious drinking time, but I figured it was a price I'd have to pay if I wanted to run a metaphysical retail establishment. After all, I didn't want to be like the sour old broad who'd sold me the smudge sticks. People turned to magic to improve their lives. No doubt they'd rather buy it from someone who could actually walk the walk.

"You haven't asked my professional opinion about whether or not your shop will be successful, either."

"Huh. That's true."

Lydia cut her eyes to me. "And you're not going to."

"Nope. I've made up my mind to do this thing, and I'm gonna do it. If you tell me I'll be a wild success, I might get lazy and sabotage myself. And if it's a huge flop, I'd rather not spend my time between now and then waiting to crash and burn."

CHAPTER 37

Eventually, I settled into a groove. Setup was complete and I could run the show without Maxine's help. It meant dealing with the public—and long days on my feet—but that was nothing new. Dare I say, I even enjoyed it.

Reviews began to trickle in. Four-star average on Yelp, and I'm guessing the one-star review dragging me down was just my competition trying to put me in my place. Even the wimp who freaked out over an intrepid daytime roach gave me a three for my scintillating customer service.

There wasn't much rhyme or reason to the ebb and flow of customers. Some days, folks would be elbowing each other out of the way to get at the prayer candles or the incense burners, while others were just me and my lonesome watching the incense smoke dance in a sunbeam. Since I'm a people-person at heart, I used social media to fill the hole on those days when my customers ran thin. Why not? It was good exposure for the store. And if anyone gets off on filibustering a troll, it's me.

The thing about naysayers is that I tend to see where they're coming from. I was going back and forth with a guy on Twitter named BornSkeptic who claimed broadcast news was run by lobbyists, and found some of his points were actually valid, although the idealist in me refused to believe every last journalist is for sale. We

were tweeting faster than my thumbs could keep up, and I'd retired
to the old behemoth of a desktop in my office to out-type him. I was
so deep in conversation that I almost missed the sway of the beaded curtain at my elbow that told me when the front door had been
opened. A quick glance at my very own Buddha-cam image in the
upper corner of my monitor showed Carolyn's familiar blonde head
as I finished my tweet.

"Crash?" she called out.

I added TTYL so my online buddy didn't think he was getting in
the last word, and stepped out into my store—*my* store—and razzed
her for not having visited me since the opening. Except mostly I was
taking in the surly guy who'd followed her in. His Vibe didn't only
scream out "Do me," but "Do something nasty to me...I probably deserve it."

He'd be tons of fun.

"This is my friend, Victor," she told me. "We came to see you
about healing."

I'd been dabbling in energy work since I put my chakras in order.
Still, I couldn't *legally* call myself a healer, and she damn well knew
it. But if mister tall, sulky and complicated was looking for a healer,
I wasn't about to correct her. His hair was black (natural, not bottle)
and his eyes were a pale, cold blue. I've known plenty of posers in my
time who put lots of effort into acting pouty and disaffected, but this
guy wasn't acting. Scared, angry, belligerent and sullen, and doing
his best to look anywhere but at me. Because apparently he was pretty keen on what he saw...and he couldn't afford the vulnerability of
wanting anything.

I fired up a smoke and considered him. What a delightfully pungent melange of angst and need. If the subjects behind the acoustic
dividers had been more like him, I would've scored that solid two.
Hell, even a three or a four. I gestured for him to come closer and
took stock of him. What would most non-empaths see, a guy with
a frown line etched between his brows, which they'd interpret as
anger? It was clear the feelings were nowhere near that simple.

Although there was a countertop between us, I held my hand
up and stopped him before our energies mingled, and did my best

to untangle the snarls as emotions rolled off him in great, churning clouds. It was like a home dye-job gone berserk, with neon oranges that wanted to be blond, and greens where the subtle brown low-lights should be. And I was the expert alchemist attempting to nor-malize the whole thing without leaving him a fried, broken mess.

"What is it?" Carolyn asked. "Do you see something?"

"Don't get your panties in a twist, Little Miss PsyCop. I'm not in high gear all the time like you are."

"Vic is psychic."

Big newsflash. "Do you mind? I can do it myself."

"I'm just trying to help."

And *I* was trying to figure out where the hell to begin. I can't see chakras, exactly. I'm not sure anyone actually *sees* a rainbow of spinning energy balls like they show in all the books. It's just a visual representation of some other, less tangible sense. But clearing and balancing those energies would be the guy's best start.

"He's a medium," Carolyn added.

I'd never met one in person, not that I knew of. But I'd read about them. "A big overblown TV antenna. Yeah. I get it." Maybe that's why I was feeling his feels so hard. You'd need a strong signal to breach the barrier of death itself. This Victor's complexity went deeper than that, though. Carolyn took my silences as hesitation, but that wasn't it. I couldn't wait to jump in...just as soon as I figured out the lay of the land. "Okay, c'mere." I grabbed him by the sleeve. His Vibe begged me to do more, to keep on pulling until I'd dragged him across the countertop and shoved my tongue in his mouth—but there'd be time for that later, once I figured out why he was practically spewing freakout. "Hold still. It's not like I can see the problem written on your forehead." Not exactly, anyway. His crown chakra was blazing. He squirmed in my grasp, and images blossomed in my mind's eye: me holding him down, shoving his wrists into the narrow mattress while I had my wicked way with him. He'd struggle just like that. And he'd relish every second of it.

Carolyn would skin me alive for getting involved with another one of her friends, but even so, I couldn't stop myself from flirting. "You're not right," I said, and was rewarded with a ramping up of his delicious discomfort as he pictured my tongue stud slithering down the side of his neck. How refreshing. The first thing most guys think about is their dick. I slid my fingers up the sleeve of his jacket, over the boniness of his wrist and the whisper of the hairs on his forearm. I was gearing up to make him an offer he couldn't possibly refuse when I felt it: genuine distress. Something that went way beyond the delicate push-and-pull of seduction.

Well, fuck. I could hardly keep mashing on a guy who was truly upset. Not until I helped him get himself together, at least. His energies were as jumbled as a string of old Christmas tree lights. We'd have to deal with that before I could delve any deeper. "I'd do a gemstone cleanse first. And once that's done, take a look at fine-tuning."

He snorted, and an energetic wall slammed down between us. "That's it?"

"I'm serious about the gemstone cleanse. If you really are a medium and not just a bullshit artist, it might even help you shield. Unless you live beneath high tension wires, in which case there's nothing to do but move. It's all energy: particles and electrons."

"How can crystals help me shield?"

There were so many fun ways I could educate him—from the traditional uses of crystals in native ritual to the more recent findings on crystal structure in water responding to emotions—when the door banged open, and a certain unwelcome someone strode through in all his self-righteous glory.

And here my day had been going so well.

At the sight of Jacob, the playfulness inside me shriveled up and died. His jaw was grinding and he held himself so taut I could see a vein pulsing at his temple from across the fucking room. But was he angry or hurt? Did he miss me at all? Even a little? I took a jab at him to see what bled out. "Are you here to tell me you're sorry, or are you just tagging along with Carolyn today?"

"I'm only the chauffeur," he said dryly.

"How ridiculous, thinking an apology might come out of you, seeing as how you're always right."

"So can you help Victor, or is this just *another* waste of time?"

Oh, as if he was the only one who'd pissed away months of his life and had nothing to show for it. And the maddening part was, he didn't really care. Carolyn was emanating waves of dread, while Victor seethed with discomfort. But Jacob? He was as still as the plaster effigy of Saint Anthony beside my front door, and just as cold.

Who knows why I thought he might have changed. I ignored his nasty looks as best I could, got the medium set up with a bag of rocks, and cleared them all out of the shop as quickly as humanly possible. Just as soon as the three of them were gone, I lit up a smudge stick. I walked up and down each aisle and aimed my sacred smoke at the four corners, and followed it up with a spritz from a house blessing aerosol can. It didn't feel much different when I was done. Maybe the ritual would dispel nasty psychic juju. But the pall of seeing Jacob again? It would take a lot more than a smoldering twig to dispel.

Between the sage, the incense and a few Camels, the store was brimming with smoke, but maybe the rank energies reached a lot farther than its four walls. I was attempting to pry open a window that had been painted shut for at least as long as I'd been alive when my phone rang. Jacob. And I must've been in the mood to twist the knife, because I picked up. "What now?"

"You'd think that kid I found you with would be the worst part, but you know what I can't wrap my head around? After everything we'd been through together, you still didn't trust me."

"Do I seem like an idiot to you? It doesn't take a fifth-level empath to figure out you were all over me until I tanked in that fucking screening, and then suddenly you're texting me flimsy excuses. You went from begging me to move in with you to blowing me off in the space of a weekend, and you know why? 'Cos you were never into me as a person to begin with. You had a hard-on for some *idea* of me you'd fabricated in your head."

"Go check your empathy score before you start telling me how I feel."

"Y'know what? I'm glad you texted your regrets that night instead of actually calling. Because over the phone, you do a plausible imitation of someone who actually gives a damn."

He huffed at me like a bull pawing the ground, and hung up without another word. I took my frustration out on the window frame with a screwdriver. It looked like an axe murderer had gone at it, but eventually I gouged the fucking thing open. I sucked in a deep, cleansing breath. A gust of cooking grease filled my lungs, so rancid I literally gagged—and my gag reflex is minimal. As I dragged the window back down, I couldn't help but ponder that maybe some things are better off left alone.

How disturbing that my wounds were still so fresh. It pissed me off, so I did what I always do when I need serious distraction, but I can't go anywhere and I can't start drinking yet: I poured myself into my work. Paperwork for Sticks and Stones multiplied faster than the vermin behind my medicine cabinet, so I parked myself in front of the desktop, regretfully closed my Twitter app, and set about determining why an elaborate claim form on a mangled delivery had been rejected.

I was deep into a mind-numbing field of checkboxes when I spied movement in my Buddha-cam. The walking ouija board was back, standing there at the counter staring at the crystals. And talking. I listened for a reply, hoping for Carolyn's voice but dreading I'd hear Jacob's. If either of them answered, I didn't catch it. I enlarged the Buddha-cam window and checked all my aisles, but didn't see anyone other than Victor. I waited a few moments more, then steeled myself against a surprise ambush from my pissy ex, and swept out to see what was what.

"Back for more?" I said.

Victor flinched and looked around. He appeared to be alone. He shuffled his feet, swallowed a few times, then said, "This crystal thing is new to me."

Was he shitting me? "Carolyn said you were a Psych."

"I'm certified, yeah."

"And you can't do a simple crystal cleanse?"

"They didn't teach it where I trained."

That was so implausible I would've figured he was just looking for an excuse to stop by for a quickie, except now his Vibe was reined in to a dull simmer. No doubt Jacob was cock blocking me, talking shit behind my back. Not blatantly, of course, that's not his style. But a smooth insinuation that I was some kind of fraud would hardly show me in the best light. "Okay, fine. I'll go through it with you step by step."

"That's all right." He backed up and put some space between us. "Your assistant helped me figure it out."

"Assistant?"

"The lady who works here," he said. "I didn't catch her name."

Oh. I got it. This was all a test to see whether I was legit. "Don't fuck around. I'm the only one who works here."

"Whoever the woman in the flowered scarf is—her."

Prior to that afternoon, I hadn't met a real life psychic medium in the flesh, but I'd seen plenty of folks on TV talk shows playing up their ability to commune with the "other side." They were no different from any other fake fortune-teller; they knew how to read people. *I sense a female energy*, they'd proclaim, and watch as their gullible subject got all choked up. From there on, it was all guesswork. *It feels like a mother, a grandmother, a sister, a friend.* Casting the bait and waiting to reel the suckers in.

He ducked his head and said something under his breath. Maybe I hadn't walked away with one of those coveted certificates like he had. But honestly. I wasn't born yesterday.

He stopped muttering to himself and said, "Who's Curtis?"

He had a flair for the dramatic. I'd give him that. "So Carolyn told you what my driver's license says. Big fucking deal."

"Who's Miss Mattie, then?"

Mining info on me was one thing, but bringing Mattie into his ridiculous charade bordered on sacrilege. His recon was good—he'd figured out whose death to throw in my face. A less crafty charlatan would've trumped up an urgent message from my father, but this guy dredged up someone I actually missed. Acutely. Maybe Jacob wasn't talking shit about me after all. Maybe he was setting me up to play the dupe. "Who told you that name?"

"The...um...full-figured African American woman told me. The one in the flowered scarf."

Sure. "What color is her scarf?"

"I don't know. Lots of colors." He fumbled out an ancient flip-phone and pretended to get a text. "She went into your closet and I can't see it anymore."

I didn't know which betrayal would sting worse, my ex's or my friend's. "Someone told you about her—who, Carolyn? Jacob? You're all in this PsyCop bullshit together, aren't you?"

"You could say that." He turned and headed toward the door in response to his "urgent" missive.

"Where are you going?"

"Police business. Gotta go."

"Oh, shit, you're a cop, too?" My heart sank. "You don't act like a cop—I thought you were just a consultant or something. Get the hell out here and leave me alone. I've had enough bacon to last me a lifetime. And tell Carolyn I don't want to meet any more of her pig friends."

CHAPTER 38

I thumbed in, *Are you avoiding me?* and hit send. And waited. And before I could threaten to show up at Carolyn's house and embarrass her by shooting the moon on her front lawn for all her neighbors to see, she texted back a single word.

Yes.

Not fair. She started this whole thing by bringing Surly Guy into my shop. She owed me an explanation as to where she'd found him, and what his deal was, and who the hell had told him about Miss Mattie. Most people ask about her the first time they see my ink, at least if their mouth isn't busy on my dick. But I don't go into detail. I'll say it's a memorial tattoo, and that's all anyone needs to know.

Detectives being what they are, though, I'm sure it was possible either Carolyn or Jacob could've dug up dirt on Miss Mattie. Though when I plugged in her name and scoured the internet myself, my own searches brought up nothing. And they wouldn't even have the advantage of knowing her surname was Hicks, and she spent umpteen hours a week in church praying the rosary, and when she laughed it was this big, deep booming sound, and she brought me homemade oatmeal cookies in the pocket of her apron, wrapped in paper towels with flowers printed on them. They would only know the name Mattie. And that shouldn't tell them squat.

I glanced at the old photo tacked to the wall behind my monitor.

There she was in her groovy seventies multicolored scarf.

Hmph. Psychic medium, my ass. The only thing the PsyPig had actually mentioned was her weight and her head wrap. And I'd been so startled, he almost had me going for a minute there. Almost. But not quite.

When I looked at that picture, I'd try to remember the specific moment it was captured, as if dredging up the somatic feeling of the scene would reconnect me to Mattie herself. Why? I suppose she was the only one who made my childhood self feel like I wasn't in dire need of improvement. Everyone else qualified their affection with "if only." If only I could sit still for half a second. If only I would focus on my grades. If only I'd be like all the other Stepford children up and down the block. But not Miss Mattie. When I was with Mattie, I was enough. Just the way I was.

Victor wouldn't have been able to glean any of that. Not from a photo.

I often wonder if most mediums are really telepaths tuning in on people's minds and parroting back snatches of remembered conversation and glimpses of memory. I knew mind reading was real—I'd seen Carolyn in action. But ghost talking? It would take more than the description of a photograph to convince me that mediumship was legit. It bothered me, the notion that someone might be privy to knowledge that transcended life itself. Some things aren't meant to be known, at least it seemed that way to me. And how did they test for it, anyway? Hold seances on the other side of the acoustic dividers?

The world wide web had no answers for me. If only I could think of some better terminology to search with. The search term *psychic medium* brought up a bunch of ads, and *REAL psychic medium* was no better. *Psychic medium PsyCop Victor Chicago* was a bust too, just a bunch of Chicago PD propaganda for their block parties and after school programs, some astrologers and a ghost tour.

I didn't really expect to find much when I navigated to the psychic wiki in search of more info on the PsyCop program. Jacob's smug picture was all over the place, but Carolyn's wasn't. So the lack of anyone named Victor—the lack of any psychic medium at all— didn't tell me anything conclusive.

The ads in the sidebar seemed psychic themselves. The books I'd scoped out, the clubs I'd perused in hopes of a decent drink special, the leopard Doc Martens I couldn't possibly afford. With each click of the wiki, the ad refreshed, and a new and tantalizing glimpse of something I thought I wanted was presented for my scrutiny in hopes that repeated exposure would wear me down, and I might change my mind, surrender, and hit the buy button.

I ignored the ad and focused on my search. What other search terms could I use? Spiritual? Occult? Metaphysical? How about...ethical? That last one seemed promising, at least until I got a load of what they did to my sidebar...with Red Turner's face gazing out at me from the electronic ether, all heavy-lidded bedroom eyes that knew way more than they should, and a supercilious tilt to his slightly raised eyebrow.

Inner Beauty Salon Services. Right.

Well, Red could stare at me all he wanted to. I wasn't about to be sucked in by that knowing look. Because he might have acted as if he knew everything, but he didn't see Ralph for what he was, did he? Sure, really enlightened. And so I refused to click. No way.

Nope.

Not...gonna....

I clicked.

Of course I fucking did. And I hoped it cost him a big hunk of his pay-per-click ad budget, too. As if it was as disappointed in my lack of self-control as I was, my connection chose that moment to lag. And lag. And lag. I stood up, sat back down, stood again, and was on the verge of inventing a new swear word when the browser symbol stopped spinning and a page began to load.

My heart skipped a beat, but then I realized it wasn't taking me to Red's site after all, just a generic landing page telling me the domain was for sale.

I hit the back button, but whatever hoodoo had served up Red's photo decided I needed to see an organic shampoo alternative in that ad slot instead. Searching for his business only brought up old history, mentions from before his move to Chicago. Red Turner had dropped off the map. And no amount of coaxing would convince my pixels to yield him up again.

It took the jingle of a customer at the shop's door to draw me out of the office and stop me from lobbing various search terms at the cold, cruel internet. An aging hipster in a parka meandered up the herb aisle with the browse of someone who knew his stuff, but wasn't after anything in particular. While he shopped, I carried on my fruitless search for Red on my phone. Because surely it was just a matter of using the right terms. People don't just disappear.

I got so deep into the search that I forgot the guy was there until he stepped up to the counter. "Did you find everything you were looking for?" I asked him.

He gave a jaded laugh. "I always do."

"Guess that makes one of us." I considered his stuff as I rang it up. Sometimes I can read a person by their shopping choices, whether they follow a certain path or they're tackling a particular problem, but not this guy. Some of his items were utilitarian, like herbs and incense, and some was decorative, like the hand-dyed prayer shawl. A little bit of everything, but nothing that added up. "Crisis of faith?"

"That would require having faith to begin with. It's not all for me—I have lots of interesting friends who could stand to broaden their horizons. You'd be surprised how many Psychs are averse to using props." He hefted a polished gazing crystal off the counter, then added it to his pile. "Me, I'm a fan of working smarter, not harder."

"So, you're a Psych."

"I'm lots of things—an art collector, a secular humanist, a hopeless romantic, and a phenomenally bad cook. Some things are safer topics of conversation than others."

"A Psych who's not shoving his talent and level down my throat? How refreshing."

"It's not worth the bragging rights. The thing about the psychic ranking system is that it comes with a cost."

"No shit. I could pay down an awful lot of bills with the wad I blew on that asinine test."

"I'm not talking about the money. As long as you're still up and kicking, you can always make more." He leaned in and dropped his voice. "Psychics make convenient scapegoats. And with the internet, we're so connected nowadays, it's practically impossible to lay low."

Sure. Tell that to Red.

"Funny thing about the internet," the customer said as I bagged up his purchase. "Some people are bright enough to keep photos of their drunken indiscretions from ending up on Facebook for their proud parents to behold, but they don't realize it takes more than clearing your cookies to wipe out a search."

No doubt when I was a teenager, Maxine had gotten an eyeful of plenty of stuff she couldn't unsee. Porn might not trip my trigger like good, old-fashioned flirting, but I had to pick up my bedroom techniques somewhere.

And I could think of a certain someone who would really appreciate that education.

Once I closed up shop for the night, I gave Carolyn a ring. I told her I'd been too hard on her pal the medium, which was true, and asked if I could get his number to smooth things over. She didn't question whether that was the only reason. Guess she didn't want to know.

I called him. "I acted like a dick before," I told him. "You know? But it just blew my mind when you said you were talking to Miss Mattie." Even if mediumship was nothing more than telepathy-meets-therapy, it might be interesting to explore my connection with Mattie from an adult perspective. "So is she, like, watching me all the time?"

"No. She comes and goes."

"That's a relief. 'Cos I know a few moves that'd probably kill her all over again if she saw 'em. I can show you some, if you wanna come over."

"I don't think so."

He was playing hard to get. How cute. "C'mon, man. I know you want to."

"I'm in a relationship right now," he said. And as I tried to finagle a workaround, he added, "With Jacob."

CHAPTER 39

There's plenty of fish in the sea—and plenty of guys on Tanngo. So I wasn't wallowing in too much annoyance that Jacob had discovered a taller, broodier, more psychically tweaked replacement for me. Who needed a boyfriend, anyway? It would've been a distraction. All the dinner and conversation and lengthy, drawn out bedroom antics were fine and dandy. But my priority was combing eBay for good deals on odd lots and balancing my books. I was busy, so once the hookup du jour left, I was perfectly content to spend my evening time alone. Although, when Carolyn called and asked if I wanted to help her find something to wear, I realized it was Valentine's Day... and I did notice a little pang that felt suspiciously like loneliness.

We hit a boutique in a gentrified part of Bucktown where artsy met commercial. The jewelry was chunky, the woolens were hand-spun, and the clerks all smiled at me as they made sure I wasn't stuffing my pockets with their soy candles or sea glass.

I considered buying my mother an early birthday present, but nixed the idea. I could find the same stuff online at half the price. No, I wouldn't be supporting my local art community by outsourcing, but so what? Borders are arbitrary. I'd support the global community.

Carolyn turned and held a silk scarf to her throat. The tints were subtle. Pale celadon and a hint of slate. "What do you think?"

"Go bolder. You can totally carry it off."

She reached for a slightly darker version of the same. I hustled over and grabbed the reddest red I could find. It looked like someone had used it to staunch a nosebleed. And it was perfect. "Stop trying to pretend you think you're mousy."

"I'm not pretending."

Funny, now that the shock of knowing she was telepathic had worn off, it was so easy to forget her curse of truthfulness. "Fine. Then allow me to reiterate the same damn thing I always tell you. You're gorgeous. Get used to it."

She scowled into the mirror as she arranged the scarf, gave it a critical once-over, and said, "I probably can't. But maybe that's better than being arrogant."

When we were done shopping, we decided to evaluate the margaritas at the bar across the street. It was a pretentious joint and the prices were outrageous, but the music was low enough that we could tuck ourselves away in a secluded corner and talk, and actually hear one another's replies. Carolyn was frowning into her drink as she said, "I don't suppose you'd consider giving Jacob another chance."

"The sociopath with the emotional resonance of sawdust? I don't suppose I would." I refilled our glasses. "Why, was the other PsyCop too much work for him?"

"I wish." Her shoulders sagged. "I'd love to think Jacob can handle himself. But this guy he's involved with...damn it, this guy is a disaster waiting to happen."

That probably shouldn't have intrigued me as much as it did. I leaned in and said, "Go on."

"First there was this *thing*, this predatory...forget it. I don't even know what it was. It's gone now. But then this splinter group kidnapped him to test some kind of psych-enhancement equipment on him."

"They kidnapped Jacob?"

"No, Detective Bayne."

Oh sure. Even the guy's last name was cool.

"Not just random people, either. A PsyCop and a doctor. They'd infiltrated the police department *and* our private medical clinic. How is that possible?"

Where there's a bribe, there's a way. "What about you, they didn't do anything to you, did they?"

"No. Different precinct." She shuddered. "Thank God. But this is why we need to be careful. It's not safe for psychics. There are just too many ways we can be exploited. And since Jacob's a Stiff, he's totally cavalier about the whole thing."

I had a sneaking suspicion Jacob wouldn't be circumspect even if he was a fifth-level whatever. Hiding his light under a bushel basket would never occur to him. No matter what kind of deadly moths were drawn to that flame.

Not only was I disinclined to try and woo Jacob away from this Victor Bayne—deep in my gut, I knew I couldn't. Maybe if I hadn't flaunted Matthew in Jacob's face...no, even still. When things were good between Jacob and me, they were pretty good. But when they weren't, they tanked fast and hard.

The thing that did surprise me? I was actually worried about the big lug.

At two o'clock in the morning I gave up all pretense of trying to sleep and decided to see about this kidnapping myself. I opened up a private browser, typed the letters V - I - C...and then stopped myself. Maybe a private browser would keep your porn history from popping up on your mother's computer, but would it really stop Big Brother's prying eyes? I checked in with my buddy BornSkeptic and he gave me the lowdown on some open source software that would shield me by bouncing my data through a warren of random nodes. But once I read the accompanying documentation about all the entities who regularly track everything we do, I decided I didn't know enough about Spy vs. Spy-level computing to risk searching any deeper than I already had.

I was running on fumes the next day when my door opened and the man himself walked in. Victor Bayne. Cop. Medium. Kidnapping victim. I'd been gearing up to stick him full of barbs ever since I found out he was Jacob's new psychic bedwarmer. His atrocious suit, for instance, was just begging for an insult. But in the grand scheme of things, taking pot-shots at him would be petty, and instead all I could come up with was, "What now?"

He rubbed the back of his neck as if he'd slept wrong and said, "Um...I was thinking...since you know about things." Great. He'd led with flattery, of the unintentional sort. Which is the worst kind of all, when you're doing your best not to get involved. "A big, overblown antenna. That's what you called me."

"Sometimes words are just words. Don't read into every little turn of phrase that comes out of my mouth—that's bound to piss you off."

"I'm not pissed off. I want to know more."

I'd been trying to cut back the in-store smoking since I read the review that said shopping at Sticks and Stones was like wallowing in an ashtray, but if any occasion called for a cigarette, this was it. I stuck a "back in 15" sign to the door, locked up, and invited the distraught medium into my office. I was so cordial I even let him sit in the office chair while I perched on a box of prayer candles. I lit up, took a deep drag, and said, "Okay. Let's say for the sake of argument that psychic energy exists—"

"Can we skip to the part where electricity screws up the signal?"

"I never said that."

"Sure you did. High tension wires." Well, maybe I did, right after BornSkeptic had spent nearly an hour trying to convince me that tin foil hats served an actual purpose. "Look," he said, "I know you think I'm full of shit, but suspend your disbelief for a few seconds and tell me this—what part of an old tube TV might hum in the same frequency as psychic ability?"

"Electronics aren't my forte—I was on the college prep track in high school, and shop class wasn't part of the curriculum. But I have a friend who might know." I reached across him and jiggled my mouse, and the screen lit up. The private message tab was still up, right where I'd left it, with a string of messages between Skeptic and me about which Netflix show we should binge watch next. "Go ahead, type in your question."

He began hunting and pecking his way across my keyboard. His two-fingered typing was like something out of a cheesy police procedural. I studied his profile. Cute enough, but I knew Jacob would be on board even if he was a dumpy little troll. Whoever said beauty is only skin deep wasn't accounting for fetishes.

Vic started pummeling my d-key and said, "It's not working."

"You only get 140 characters."

"Why?"

"Why?" Was he seriously that oblivious? "Because it's Twitter, that's why." I hit the return key. "There. Keep going."

He started clicking on the hunk of message I'd just sent. "How do I fix a typo?"

"For crying out loud." I pulled the keyboard away from him and read what he put down so far.

AshMan_Namaste: @BornSkeptic67 lets say if you cuold see ghosts & a TV set could make teh ghosts disappear-and this is totally hypatheticle- which part of the TV set woul

"Gimme that before you break the internet." I typed in, *That wasn't me, let's try this from the top.* And once I got over the atrocity that was his typing, I said, "You came across a TV set that tuned in ghosts?"

He swallowed. His Adam's apple bobbed. A chill ran through me. I couldn't tell if I was the one who was spooked, or if the unease was bleeding over from him. "Not...on the screen. Not like I was watching a show. You wouldn't have been able to see it." He flinched. "Which I totally don't mean as any kind of insult."

"None taken," I said softly, and I realized what a grade-A dickwad I was for letting my impatience run rampant. He'd been freaking kidnapped. I mean...kidnapped. Fucking hell. "Was this some kind of equipment you were testing? Maybe...against your will?"

"You heard." He stared hard at a dog-eared sticky note gathering coffee rings on my desk. "It was kinda messed up."

I let my breath out slowly and we both sat there feeling awkward, until the conversation on the screen scrolled up.

BornSkeptic67: You'd need a strong medium to figure that out. A real medium, not some scam artist. Good luck finding one.

Vic might not be a stellar typist, but he could read. He barked out a humorless laugh and said, "Never mind."

He tried to roll back from the desk, but I stomped my foot down and blocked the chair's wheels. "Hold up, cowboy. How do you expect to find anything if you fold at the first sign of resistance?"

I typed.

AshMan_Namaste: Hypothesize, @BornSkeptic67.

BornSkeptic67: Depends on the TV. LCD/LED or plasma.

"Not a flatscreen," Vic said. "An old one. With a tube."

AshMan_Namaste: CRT

BornSkeptic67: Electrons boiling off a tube can be directed either to amplify an electrical signal or to make phosphors glow. Why not a ghost?

I read that a few times. Vic stood up and said, "I guess it was stupid of me to think I could make my own GhosTV."

I planted myself so he had nowhere to go but right back into the chair he'd just vacated. He sat down hard. "Not so fast—first you come in telling me the other side is driving you crazy, and now you want to crank up the volume?"

"Fuck, no. The volume goes both ways. I don't want to amp them up, I'm trying to pull the plug." As he spoke, a quiet and easy sort of anxiety emanated from him. It felt so right, I suspected it was his baseline vibe. And behind that, a gut-coiling embarrassment. He didn't talk about this shit, I realized. And while it was scary for him to lay his cards on the table, it was also a relief. Vic's back was to the monitor now. BornSkeptic expounded on waves and particles, and the feed scrolled along. Meanwhile, Vic's eyes defocused as he stared at something, my earring maybe, and said, "I hardly ever come across someone like Miss Mattie. Most of the dead are tethered here with vengeance and spite. They wanna make sure whoever was responsible for offing them gets their just desserts. Either that, or they're some kind of fucked up film loop that keeps on dying, over and over and over."

His eyes locked onto mine, and widened as if he hadn't intended to reveal quite so much, especially not to someone like me—someone unwilling to *ooh* and *ah* over his big-time psychic ability. I might not be impressed by his credentials, but heck. I couldn't deny that he was genuinely distressed. I crouched between his knees and gripped the chair's armrests. "Listen, if it's that important to you, I'll see what I can find out about this cathode ray tube. But let me do it in a way that's not so traceable."

"Okay. Cool."

We stared at each other for a longish pause, and I enjoyed the feeling of his relief as it licked at the corners of my awareness...and I enjoyed the Vibe creeping in, too. The sight of me on my knees made his heart go pit-a-pat. And me, well, I must've dug the idea of toying with something I couldn't have. Would he be nasty in bed, I wondered, or utilitarian? I had a feeling with all the neuroses swirling around behind those baby blues, he'd be into something freaky, whether he would admit it or not. I dropped a hand to his knee, and he stood so fast he nearly knocked me on my ass. And not in a playful way. He muttered something disjointed about not taking up any more of my time, and before I knew it, the only indication that he'd been there at all was the beaded curtain swaying in his wake, and a string of nonsensical crap in my Twitter.

CHAPTER 40

Ultimately, I played it safe. Not by easing up the pressure on Vic when he popped by the store—I got too much satisfaction from watching him squirm. No, it was the *research* I was handling with kid gloves. I didn't know enough about computers to fully trust the cloaking software to cover my trail, so I hauled myself down to the library instead, and earned all kinds of dirty looks from people waiting in line to rip CDs and download porn. Tough luck. I had data of my own to collect.

Over multiple sessions on the private browser of a public computer, I discovered that Victor Bayne might've emitted plenty of psychic particles and waves, but his electronic trail was nonexistent. Since he was so clueless about Twitter, I wasn't surprised he was absent from social media, but other things? Articles, news bites, all the crap that popped up when I searched Jacob? Nonexistent.

I could've searched Carolyn too, but decided I'd better not. One day the topic might come up, and if I found out anything about her I wasn't supposed to know, I wouldn't be able to deny it.

No matter how creative I got with my search terms, there was no "GhosTV" either. And the kidnapping? Never happened—even though I'd watched Carolyn's involvement in it unfold, so I knew damn well it was true. I have serious chops on Google. I can Boolean search with the best of 'em. So if I couldn't find anything, there was nothing to be found. And that absence of information made Jacob's new squeeze a heck of a lot more intriguing. Possibly scary...nah, intriguing. I think.

I didn't have a clear idea of Vic's schedule. He stopped by with random concerns at various times of the day, in various states of dress-up or dress-down. Sometimes a couple weeks would go by without me seeing him. Other times, he'd be in every half hour making me re-explain centering techniques he could learn from any armchair meditator. Some concepts he got right away. Others slipped through his fingers time and time again. And if I ever felt annoyed by his periodic question, "So when you say counter-clockwise, which way is the clock facing?" I'd recall a time when my only definition of *sitting* involved styling chairs or barstools.

I also remembered how gentle Red had been when he suggested I might benefit from quieting my mind.

And then I felt abandoned.

Fall had turned to winter, and while I did occasionally attempt to dredge up some evidence of the GhosTVs, I no longer expected to find anything. But while I was incognito online, I also boned up on mediumship. If Vic was the real deal, I'd hate to screw him up any worse than the world already had. Plus, even though he resisted every advance I slid his way, I knew if our stars ever aligned, we could do some seriously naughty things together, him and me.

That winter had come early and hard, and one fine, brisk morning, after sweating me out of the place for nearly a month, the boiler up and died and left my radiators cold and silent. The temperature in my store plummeted, thanks to the windows I'd chipped free of their insulating layer of old paint. Lydia advised covering my windows with plastic. The concept baffled me. I'd been raised in a home with immaculate tuckpointing and double-paned glass. Maxine wouldn't have taped plastic over her windows any more than she'd stick a flamingo on the lawn. But, hey, a few sheets of plastic were way more affordable than a new space heater and the electricity to run the damn thing. The store wasn't open yet and I was up to my ears in plastic sheeting and tape when someone rapped on my front door, then followed it up with a call.

Must've been my lucky day. That was Victor Bayne's M.O., my windows were tall, and he had himself some phenomenal reach. Luckily I like to razz him about showing up early before I let him in, because when I went to pick up the call, I saw it wasn't Vic after all.

It was Jacob.

I answered with, "To what do I owe the pleasure?" in a commendably neutral tone. He hadn't taken any pot-shots at me lately, so I wasn't about to give him any ammo to claim I'm being immature.

"Are you home? I was hoping...we could talk."

His voice was dripping remorse. When someone's as full of themselves as Jacob is, I've got a real soft spot for hearing them eat crow. I opened the door and found him standing there in his casual gear—jeans and designer leather jacket, black on black, with a dusting of snowflakes melting at the tips of his too short buzz-cut. "Why aren't you playing cops and robbers?" I asked.

He shook his head. "I've got a million and one errands to take care of. Can I come in?"

I stepped aside and indicated my store with an outstretched arm. He walked in. Humbly, if such a word could possibly apply to Jacob. Judging by his facial expression and body language, at least. In terms of emotional resonance, he might as well have been weatherproofing his windows.

"We haven't really talked since you opened the store."

"No. We haven't."

He strolled around the register and took a look around. "Vic spends an awful lot of time here."

I was already regretting my decision to let him in. "And?"

"And nothing," he claimed.

"Sure."

"Come on, I'm trying to smooth things over. He doesn't have many friends. I'm glad he's found one in you."

"It's such a relief to have your blessing." I cocked my head toward the window. "C'mere a minute. I need a hand."

He assessed the window situation and said, "You need a stepladder, too."

"Be that as it may, I don't have one. What I do have is this chair, this roll of tape, and a monstrous sheet of plastic that keeps trying to stick to itself."

True to form, Jacob loved nothing more than a problem waiting to be solved. He waded in with me to wrangle plastic. It slithered between us, and we moved in synch to contain it. Funny. I thought we'd surely be out of step after so long. But no. Apparently not.

The shielding power of plastic shouldn't be underestimated. Even though Jacob and I could see one another through it—even though the two of us were touching as closely as we would through a condom—the barrier allowed him to speak to me without dredging up our old wounds and rubbing my face in them. And it allowed me to listen. "What you've done with the store is fantastic."

"It beats working at the chop shop."

"Hold that corner." He pinned the side in place with his elbow, grabbed the tape roll from my wrist, and tore off a small piece with his teeth. "Now tack it in place so we can do some longer strips."

We fell into a rhythm so easily. Maybe it shouldn't have come as any big surprise, given how much time we'd spent learning one another's moves.

A corner drooped, and our fingertips brushed as we both made a grab for it. He didn't shy away—neither did I. It occurred to me that I might be presented with an opportunity to discover what all the ex-sex buzz was about. That'd be a new one for me, since I hadn't really dated anyone other than Jacob long enough to consider them an ex. When I scoped out the level of Vibe, though, there was none. And maybe that was a relief. "So what's it like trying to hook up with another PsyCop? Between both of your important police schedules, you probably never see each other."

He focused hard on tacking down plastic. He wasn't looking at me when he said, "We're moving in together."

Big shock. Most people bring flowers or champagne or a vibrating tongue stud to their second date. He brings a U-Haul. "Your place or his?"

"Ours. There's a property we've been after for a while now and our realtor finally waded through all the red tape."

That stung. I wasn't quite sure why. If playing house was what I'd wanted, a white picket fence with my name on the mortgage, all I would've had to do was ask. I hopped down from the chair, plucked my tape out of his hand, and said, "Thanks, I got it from here."

"Don't be that way."

"And what way am I being, Jacob? You found someone as needy as you are—congratulations."

Anger seethed off him and raised goosebumps on my forearms. "So this is how it is? We have mutual friends, but when I'm around you, I'm supposed to walk on eggshells?"

"Gee, sorry, how *immature* of me to act like being with you actually meant something to me. I'll just stuff it all down deep and congratulate the two of you. What did you want for a housewarming gift, a pair of handcuffs to make sure this one can't get away? Oh, wait, you've already got a pair on your belt."

"Are you through yet?"

"That about covers it."

Jacob sighed. "Being with Vic, having him come home at all hours of the night, watching him go quiet and vacant when he's been on a crime scene all day, it made me realize what it must've been like for you. Especially since you don't have any idea what we actually deal with on the job. Theoretically, maybe. But you don't see what we see—you're not taking the statement of someone who's just been raped or beaten. You don't get to feel that rush when you catch the scum who did it."

"No. You didn't really talk about it."

"I didn't want to bring the ugliness home with me. All day long, the thing I'd look forward to most was leaving it behind so I could be with you. What little time we spent together, I didn't want to contaminate it with the things I'd seen."

He took the tape from me. The roll squalled as he pulled off a long strip, and I let the taping of the plastic fill the void where I didn't know what to say. He seemed matter of fact about the whole thing, but why wouldn't he? Where I hadn't managed to measure up, he'd found someone who did. And now they were making it official.

ॐ

Once Jacob took off and went back to his big, important job, the one where he saved the world each and every day while I stood around peddling incense, his little visit continued to weigh on my mind. So we weren't seeing each other anymore. It didn't mean I wanted him to be alone. I was happy for him. For *them*. Really. For real...even if I did nearly bite off Carolyn's head when she called a few days later and asked me to help unload their moving truck.

"Why should I spend my precious free time hauling boxes?" I said. "Let 'em hire movers for the grunt work."

"Apparently you need to book these things farther in advance," she said. "Look, it's either you or Doug. And I have serious doubts as to whether my husband's back can take it. Besides, it's no easier to find a sitter on the spur of the moment than it is to get movers on the first of the month."

I supposed if I was looking for an opportunity to prove just how magnanimous I was feeling about the big move-in, I couldn't do much better than unloading the damn truck with my bare hands. "Whatever. Fine. But if I break a nail, it's all on you." I ended the call and got to work ringing up a customer. A few more people wandered through, most of them sightseeing rather than shopping. And just when I'd resigned myself to an underwhelming end to a mediocre day, my friend in the parka, the undocumented Psych, hoisted a massive armload of reading material onto the counter.

I turn a good profit on books, but nowadays, between the steep online discounts and the two-day shipping, books are typically impulse buys. I'll only sell one or two at a time. But this stack was so fat, it made my counter groan.

As I rang up the sale, I almost felt guilty enough to tell the guy he'd pay half as much online—and then I did my best to strike the thought from my mind, just in case he was reading it. After all, if he wanted to nudge my ledgers into the black for the day, who was I to complain?

"Nothing like the printed page to lull you to sleep," he remarked.

"I suppose it's healthier than a stiff drink."

"So true. And a lot safer if you need to jump up and drive off in a hurry."

And here I thought he just wanted to support local business. Funny, though, he didn't strike me as delusional, only cautious. Either numerous discussions with Vic had inured me to paranoia, or the notion that psychics were monitored and tested, tracked and silenced, was actually starting to seem plausible. Because my customer wasn't setting off any of my internal alarms. He felt calm, well-adjusted, and entirely rational.

Then again, crazy folks don't know when they're hallucinating, do they?

The books were so heavy, I had to divvy them up to keep the bags from splitting. The customer hefted one of the bags and said, "I suppose ebooks would be the way to go."

"But then you couldn't sniff the pages."

"Oh no, I'm not sentimental. E-readers...you're not the only one who knows what's on 'em. I'm perfectly fine with whoever monitors the servers knowing I've actually read *50 Shades of Gray*." He held up a book to display the title: *Activating Latent Psychic Talents*. "But this one is our little secret."

"So I'm guessing I can't convince you to sign up for my mailing list." I gave my signup sheet a nod. I went through glue sticks like crazy, changing out the display every few weeks, and customers still managed to ignore it. The current image was a field of sunflowers with cut-out llama heads in the centers.

The guy considered it, then shrugged and picked up the pen. "If anyone's watching me, they already know I'm here. It's not as if I can turn invisible...though that *would* be a good trick."

Under "First Name" he scrawled *Con*, and under "Email," *BornSkeptic67@Q-mail.com*. He watched me with a twinkle in his eye while I read. And comprehended. And then wadded up a sale flyer and lobbed it off his head.

"You dick!" I said. "When the fuck were you planning on telling me it was you?" I squinted at the form, then said, "And what kind of name is Con—are you out on parole?"

"It's short for Constantine. That's what you get when your parents are history buffs."

"Sonofabitch. How many times have you skulked through here

without letting me know it was you?"

He held up his hands in surrender. "Just the once. Cross my heart."

"Fuckin-A."

"Aw, c'mon, we both know I had to check you out before I made contact."

"Made contact? What the hell do you call our 2 a.m. philosophical debate about the obsolescence of religion, or the new Clairvoyage season we buddy-watched last week? Check me out? You know me better than the last guy who sucked my balls."

"Glad to hear I've managed to leapfrog over that particular right of passage."

Now that I knew I actually *knew* the guy—seriously, much more intimately than the last dozen guys I'd bonked—I couldn't help but wonder, "You really think your Amazon account is being watched?"

"I don't just think so, AshMan. I know so." He pulled a money clip out of his faded hoodie and peeled off a few hundred-dollar bills like they were singles. I'd had no idea my online crony was so flush. "The credit card companies...they can access all kinds of data too." He held up the last hundred and worked it between his fingers. "Believe me when I say, this is the only kind of paper trail you want to leave. And if ebooks are potentially damning, you can imagine what a goldmine your web history can be if it falls into the wrong hands. Sad but true, you can burn a book. But like I've told you a million times, digital echoes are a heck of a lot harder to silence."

I double-checked his emotional barometer. Still normal. Disturbingly so, given the implications of what he was telling me. "Don't you think that's a little extreme?"

"I wish it was, my friend. I wish it was."

Once Con hauled half my reading section out the door, I had to wonder. Did he know I'd stumbled across Red's banner ad, or was he talking about my PsyCop research? Or had he just been making a general observation, and my own niggling suspicions filled in the details?

I shouldn't have anything to worry about. Thanks to his online coaching, I only researched PsyCops and GhosTVs where the trail wouldn't lead back to me.

But I couldn't be so sure about Vic. And if I told him not to look up any of that stuff himself, he'd go and do it just because I told him not to. So what if I'd blown the empath test—I could read him like an unencrypted web page. It would be easy enough to put him off researching GhosTVs and make it seem like his idea. Get technical. Start talking particles and waves, and he'd glaze over and change the subject. Then a web search would be the farthest thing in the world from his mind.

That's what I thought. So, of course, the very next moment the two of us were alone, the first thing out of his mouth was, "Hey, you know about computers, right?"

CHAPTER 41

It was after the move-in, which had been awkward as hell, though not for the reason I'd thought. Instead of feeling pissy over the fact that Jacob and Vic got to live in a gorgeous loft together while I squatted in my crappy hovel alone, I was busy strategizing how I could introduce the subject of cyber safety without freaking everyone out. Jacob and Carolyn were both called in by their precinct. Alone with me, Vic was his usual sweaty, awkward self. Likely he was so busy figuring out how to stop Vibing that he didn't notice I was preoccupied.

We'd emptied the truck, then he asked me to help him hop online. I attempted to get a wireless network going, gave up, and plugged his laptop directly into the modem. He breathed down my neck for the first ten minutes, but pretty soon he got bored and wandered off to start dragging boxes around.

If my clandestine searches for the GhosTV earned me a cautionary warning, I could only imagine how much info Vic leaked out for all and sundry to see. To my massive relief, his operating system was ten years out of date, and the location services that could broadcast his whereabouts didn't even exist. And not only had it been more than a month since he'd even been online, but his browsing history was innocuous. Weird, but innocuous. Sites about police bullshit and natural sleep remedies, and searches on questions like, *Why so many traffic lights?* and *How do you spell burocracy?* and *What is soy milk?*

I locked down all his permissions tighter and set his browser so its default mode was private. I considered clearing his cookies, but figured it was possible he'd lose his every last password and blame it (correctly) on me. Then I set up a little peer-to-peer chat so that in the future he could come to me for answers, rather than flinging out anything hazardous on the shockingly traceable World Wide Web. And in an effort to get him to navigate somewhere safe and normal, I planted a little seed of a suggestion. "So. Why couldn't you wait for Mister Perfect to help you hook it up? Gonna download some porn to keep yourself occupied?"

"No."

"Jacob doesn't get jealous of porn, does he?"

"None of your business."

"Probably not with you. You're such a good, faithful boyfriend, you don't give him any reason to doubt your loyalty."

"Yeah. I'm a saint." Laboriously, he navigated to a browser, pulled it up, and hunt-and-pecked the words *find person*.

Fantastic. I stifled a sigh.

His laptop gagged on the request for a good few seconds, and as it did, I wondered if the machine was really that geriatric, or if Big Brother's spyware was slowing it down. The lag resolved, and then a list of potential people-finder sites appeared. Mostly clickbait, so obviously lame that even the flip-phone aficionado didn't bite. He said, "I want to look up an old friend of mine from Heliotrope Station, see how he's doing."

"Camp Hell's classified," I said. "You won't find anything about it online." He ignored me and typed it in anyway. A bunch of nothing came up. And since the can of worms was now officially open for business, I figured the best bet would be for him to get the damn search out of his system. "Pop your buddy's name in there. I'll bet you don't get anything."

I watched his profile while he typed to see if he was bullshitting me. I didn't think so. Any hesitation he showed in typing in the name looked less like subterfuge and more like a basic inability to read the keyboard.

He huffed and typed in *Cook County Mental Health Center*, and was annoyed when it popped up. He tried a series of names—some scored hits, some didn't. Either result only served to piss him off. I recognized his brand of stubbornness. It takes one to know one. Maybe, I figured, some acknowledgement would be enough to satisfy him. At least for the moment. "Some evil shit went down at Camp Hell. I'll bet you've got a story or two to tell, Victor Bayne."

"No." He closed the laptop and it let out a long, shrill beep.

I angled it toward myself and opened it again. "You want me to change the preferences so that it goes into standby mode when you close it?"

"I don't care."

He sauntered off and started beating up some cardboard boxes, while I stared at the screen and wondered how to look out for someone who clearly didn't want to be protected. If he was bound and determined to search himself, there wasn't much I could do to stop him. I went out to watch him shove furniture around for a minute or two, then said, "I know I give you a hard time, but seriously. If you wanna talk, it won't get any farther than me."

"Okay, great." Discombobulated and pissy—baseline normal. For him, anyhow. He snatched up his keys. "Let's go. It's late."

He stewed all the way back to my place while I decided if he wasn't going to bring it up, I might as well. "Ever do a web search on yourself?"

"No. Why would I?"

"Idle curiosity. People search their own names all the time."

"Why do you ask?" He refused to look at me. "Have you?"

"Maybe. According to the World Wide Web, you don't exist. But you and I know differently."

"Don't search me on the web."

I could ask the same of him, but if I did, he'd go straight home and key in his own damn name. Instead I pointed out the hickey he'd been angling away from me all night. "Sure thing, tiger. I snagged a picture of that pulsing love bite on my cell phone. What more do I need?"

I left him fuming in the car and emerged from the heady cloud of confusion and need with half a chub. I was debating whether to check Tanngo, take matters into my own hands, or skip the pyrotechnics and go right to bed when I stepped into my stairwell and was struck by the smell of urine. Not just a lingering trace, either, but a fresh pong of rankness. And I saw the mail carrier had disgorged a pile of packages up against the wall in his usual haphazard way. And they were all soggy.

And the top one was addressed to Sticks and Stones.

What compelled people to be such fucking assholes?

I would've loved to pitch the goddamn box out onto the street, but given that it was full of merch, I couldn't afford to indulge my frustration. Instead, I sliced it open with my keys, determined that the resin inside was all wrapped in plastic and the plastic hadn't been breached. I picked up the cardboard—it was moist—removed the contents, and tossed the saturated box out the door.

I tried to tell myself it wasn't as if I'd never touched someone else's urine. Watersports aren't my bag, but as long as no one gets hurt, I'll give anything a good shot. This was different, though. An insult. A violation.

My place felt like a hovel. Fuck staying in. My hair was a glorious shade of Envy Green, plus my arms looked all pumped from hauling furniture. Someone would be willing to buy me a few drinks, take me home—to a place that *didn't* smell like piss—and make me forget my troubles.

I was struggling into a pair of overly elaborate boots when hickey boy called. "Changed your mind?" I teased. "I was just getting dressed to go out for a drink. You're welcome to come upstairs and undo all these buckles."

He pointedly ignored my flirting. "You said you found out online that I was fifth-level."

"Oh. So you do pay attention when I talk." I gave up on the boots and lit a smoke. "I thought you were too busy picturing me bending over the nearest horizontal surface to hear my conversation."

"So which time were you lying—when you said I'm nowhere on the Internet, or when you bragged about finding out my test scores?"

"I'm probably lots of things, but I'm no liar. Ask Carolyn."

"Either I'm online, or I'm not."

So. I hadn't been particularly successful in dissuading him from Googling himself. "The actual words—in a password-protected Usenet group, I might add—were 'a certain Chicago medium tested out at fifth level.'"

"A certain Chicago medium."

"That's right."

"What makes you even think that means me?"

"Do you know any other certified mediums in Chicago? Let alone Class Five?"

"I'm going."

He hung up. I considered calling him back to propose a trip to the library in the morning to show him what was what, but chose to let the matter rest. My muscles were sore, my temper was short, and my boots were just not cooperating. I kicked off the boot, stripped down, had myself a good, hot shower, and climbed into bed.

Just as soon as my eyes drifted shut, my phone rang again.

I was under no illusions that Vic would actually break down and join me for a quickie. No doubt he wanted to keep arguing about what was, or wasn't, online. Although I knew it would be summarily rejected, I was formulating my invitation to rendezvous anyhow when I blearily noted it wasn't Vic's name on my screen, it was Jacob's. And he wouldn't be calling me at half past one unless something was wrong.

"What's up?" I said cautiously.

He sat quietly for a long moment—I could hear him breathing— and eventually he said, "I'm outside. Can I come up?"

Funny, how much easier he was to read over the phone. A more suspicious person might have thought he was coming to make trouble. But immediately, I could tell something had him worried.

If I felt tired and sore from the day's activities, I could only imagine how burned out Jacob must be. He stood in the doorway in his suit and tie, shoulders slumped. I stepped aside and gestured for him to come in.

An echo of the times we'd curled together on my sofa made me nostalgic for the furniture I'd sold off. I led him into the office, made him sit in the rolling chair, and perched on a two-drawer file cabinet that was even less comfortable than it looked. Eventually, he took a few deep breaths, and said, "In all the years I've worked sex crimes, nothing's hit me as hard as this."

I made a murmur of encouragement, and he went on.

"This poor old woman was assaulted in her bed. She's so vulnerable, Crash. So...so completely vulnerable. She can't even walk. She can't get up and leave. Can't do anything but just lay there and...." He stopped, gulped air, and said, "He raped her. Multiple times. And then ejaculated...on her...face."

He stood up so quickly it startled me, darted through the kitchen in five good strides, and ducked into the bathroom where he folded to his knees and retched into the toilet.

Damn. Not much fun when porn actors in bakers' costumes aren't involved. I refrained from making the connection aloud. Whether or not I was still bedding the guy, I didn't want to be the one to ruin his favorite nude pastime. I stood in the doorway and watched him for a few minutes. He was mostly bringing up spit and bile.

I turned back to the kitchen, put a big mug of water in the microwave, then ducked out into the shop to raid my bulk herbs. I didn't bother firing up the lights. Instead, I lifted the lids of the old apothecary jars and picked out the flowers and roots I was looking for by scent. Chamomile, peppermint, ginger root. That would do. I grabbed a hefty pinch of each, mixed it in my palm as I walked back to the kitchen, then tossed it into the hot water and carried the whole stew back to Jacob.

He was no longer actively spewing, but he sat up against the tub with his knees bent, arm draped over them, and his head down on his forearm. I tweaked his cowlick and said, "Come on, big guy. Don't sit on the floor. You're only giving the six-legged houseguests an opportunity to migrate over to your new place."

I gave him a hand up and swung him over to my bed. It was unmade, and rumpled, and it looked even narrower than usual with his bulk denting it. But, so what. We didn't need to sleep there, or even try to fuck. Just sit.

If Jacob felt sorry for me, with my twin-sized mattress in its closet-sized bedroom, he didn't show it. He just sat on the edge of the
bed and put his head in his hands. I set the tea on the nightstand,
then squeezed in beside him, propped myself against the wall, and
considered him.

He dealt with this sort of atrocity on a regular basis, and where
did he turn to sort it all out? He didn't think I could handle this side
of his personality, back when we were intimate. *Physically* intimate.
He'd only wanted me to see the strong parts, not the vulnerable ones.

What a shame.

Suffering is an annoying little ditty, and according to the folks
at the meditation center, our own resistance to "what is" only turns
up the volume. Jacob wouldn't alleviate the old woman's suffering by
adding his own to it. But I could hardly fault him for trying, since
seeing him agonize made my heart ache.

I planted my foot on his thigh and kneaded his quads with my
toes. Nothing's permanent. Not even suffering. While no one's ever
told me they found me particularly consoling, I couldn't help but
offer the encouragement, "You'll figure out who did it."

He slid me a look in return that I had no idea how to interpret.

"What?" I said.

"Maybe. Maybe not. Cameras, security...none of it saw a damn
thing. And maybe a year ago I would've chalked it up to a delusion
of her aging mind. But now, knowing what I know and seeing what
I've seen—not as a PsyCop, but as a human being? Now, I'm worried
that maybe I will figure it out. And whatever did this, I won't be able
to stop it."

I wasn't sure whether or not our little chat did him any good, so
I was surprised when he showed up the next day at closing time with
a heaping helping of pasta primavera from the deli up the block and
a burning need to tell me about his day. I had duties to tend to—
money that needed counting and shelves that looked like someone
had suffered a seizure against them—but Jacob and me, we'd spent
too damn much time together to require that squirmy, dewy-eyed
attention you'd lavish on someone you actually needed to impress.
He got dinner plated without any help from me, and I absorbed the

horror of his day without comment. It was just like old times, every-thing but the part where we'd go back to his place and roll around naked when we were done. And I didn't really miss that part as much as I might have expected.

Apparently, the seal of our moratorium was broken. Jacob start-ed texting me again, and showing up at oddball times of the day to vent his concerns and talk through his frustrations. And me, well, I started looking forward to his visits. It beat the tedium of reorga-nizing a rack of books that would just be shuffled back around the minute anyone browsed it.

We'd fallen into such an easy rapport that I nearly forgot about his impressively tall and intensely awkward boyfriend—the one he now *lived with*—until Vic showed up on my doorstep with a cheap suit on his back, an irritated look on his face, and a young Hispanic chick at his side.

"Lisa," he said, "this is Crash. He owns the store."

"I'm Carolyn's best friend in the whole world," I clarified. "You must be the infamous Lisa Gutierrez, secret psychic."

I'd imagined Lisa Gutierrez would be taller. Hell, the way Jacob had made her out, I thought she'd be rocking a Wonder Woman getup and spouting off ominous predictions. But, no. Like every other PsyCop I knew, Lisa looked like a regular person in a suit. An off-the-rack polyester blend, at that.

Burning with curiosity, I led both Psychs into the shop and put on some coffee. Lisa glanced at the makeshift shrine I kept behind the counter where a plug of incense was smoldering, and asked, "You burn copal?"

"Yeah, I dig the vibe. It works for me." I supposed it would be too forward of me to see if she had any sage advice to offer, kind of like the guys who thought they were entitled to a lifetime of free haircuts after a quick tumble in the sack.

Vic, meanwhile, ranged up one aisle and down another. Before I could ask what he was looking for, he snapped, "She isn't here."

"Would you chill out? You just got here." Gooseflesh prickled my forearms. I still had trouble wrapping my head around him talking to Mattie. "And why are you both wearing cheap suits? You on duty? I thought your sergeant made you ride with that Ziggy-whatsisface."

"Zigler," he said. "I took the day off."

"We're helping Jacob," Lisa told me.

Good to hear, though according to Jacob, they were playing some sort of power game to stop him from abusing her talent. But I know better than to take anything Jacob says at face value. "That's some evil shit going down at Rosewood."

Lisa turned to the counter and started browsing my audio collection. Maybe her appearance didn't mark her as a high-level Psych, but the way she didn't think it was weird for Vic to talk to thin air definitely spoke volumes. I pulled out a CD and handed it over for her inspection.

"Chant! How'd you know?"

"I'm good at reading people." Her, for instance. She felt solid to me. Sincere. I liked her already. I handed her another disc.

"Oh, I have that one. It's my favorite."

As we compared the merits of my various recordings, about a million and one yes-or-no questions occurred to me. Would Sticks and Stones ever turn a profit? Should I invest in better shelving? Expand my hours? Would I do better to focus on my online presence, or was my second-floor location dooming me to failure regardless?

And had I blown my one and only chance at happiness when I walked away from Jacob?

Obviously, I couldn't ask her that. Hell, I wasn't really entitled to ask her anything. Unless.... I considered the CD she was turning around in her hands. "If you wanna save yourself twenty-five bucks, maybe we can do a little barter."

I cocked my head toward the beaded curtain and she followed me in back. "I'll load this whole folder of chant onto your phone if you just avail me of your particular talent."

She sighed.

"I know, I know," I said. "Jacob's been putting you through the wringer and treating you like a psychic ticker tape. But this isn't the same thing. I don't even have a question, not right now. It's a safety net, that's all. And I won't cash out unless it's really important. Heck, maybe I just want the security of knowing that I can."

"Having you pay for a sí-no doesn't feel right."

"Then don't think of it as a payment. Think of it as a favor. Between friends." Which really amounted to the same thing, but I could tell by the look in her eye—she wanted that music.

Or maybe she mostly wanted a friend.

"If you really need a sí-no someday," she said, "you can have it. But there's no room on my phone for all that music."

I turned and pawed through my box of random cables and connectors until I found an old off-brand MP3 player I wouldn't mind giving up, and brandished it triumphantly. "There's a solution to every problem," I said. "It's all just a matter of not giving up too soon."

CHAPTER 42

Eventually, Jacob solved his case and his after-hours visits to Sticks and Stones dwindled, but he must've figured out how to transfer his apprehensiveness and frustration to Vic. Looking at it that way, I didn't really envy the two of them their idyllic relationship, active sex life and supercool loft. Not as much, anyway.

"So, how do you stop remote viewers from looking at you?"

If I had a quarter for every time Victor Bayne barged into my shop and asked me something weird…I'd be able to do my laundry with impunity.

With Lisa back in California, Vic was turning to me again. Not as if I had any answers, I supposed, but with the hope that at the very least, I wouldn't mock him for fielding the questions. "Is this just a vague idea you've got, or is someone watching you?"

"That's what I've heard."

"You could start with the chakra cleanse—"

"That didn't work."

"Hey. You asked me for advice. Don't bite my head off." For all that Vic has the self-esteem of a teenage girl at fat camp, the minute he wants something, he becomes the center of the universe. It was a busy afternoon and I had half a dozen customers browsing my wares, and there he was expecting me to drop everything and explain to him, yet again, how the world worked. As if I even knew, myself. "How am I supposed to know what would keep the invisible eyes off you?"

"I need to back off my talent."

"No—you're thinking about it all wrong. You want to strengthen your own mojo so that you can bounce their energy back at them."

"Great. So that means if I'm on antipsyactives, I'm a sitting duck."

"You mean to say you think someone's watching you right now? All the time?"

"I'm pretty sure of it."

"Look, this place isn't a fortress or anything, but I do take precautions to make sure the less ethical botanicas don't curse me out of business. I'd be surprised if your Remote Pen Pal could reach you here."

Vic closed his eyes and drummed his fingers on the countertop as he attempted to get centered, but he was a bundle of nervous energy with nowhere to spend itself. You didn't need to be an empath to pick up the waves of anxiety rolling off this guy. The customers felt it too. The one who wanted to buy something paid up and split. The one with a habit of stealing small items she was too embarrassed to purchase left empty-handed. And the one who was on the fence about a shrine statue—a sale I really needed to make—was looking like she might choose to take her business elsewhere.

Vic spun around and started combing through a shelf of divination tools. "What have you got that's a psyactive?"

"I don't stock prescription drugs. Too risky. If I was raided...."

"No, not a prescription psyactive. I mean something like the High John the Conqueror bath salt. Do you have any more of that?"

It was obvious he had no intention of going home to use it—in fact, that cannery of his didn't even have a bathtub. I stepped around him, pulled a bar of High John soap off the shelf, and handed it to him. He made a "may I?" gesture toward the beaded curtain and I waved him through.

Once he was out of site, the energy shifted. There was a couple shopping for tarot cards. The woman reminded me of Maxine, though her husband was nothing like my father. Dad wouldn't have crossed the threshold of Sticks and Stones without a gun to his head.

"Don't take the cards out of the box," I called over. "You'll get your energy all over them." Not to mention the fact that I couldn't sell something that looked shop-worn. "If you need to see what they look like, I've got a chart right here."

A series of thumps sounded from beyond the beaded curtain. Followed by swearing. My current customers were unlikely to make off with anything big, so I ducked in back to make sure Vic hadn't somehow managed to maim himself with a bar of soap. I found him in the middle of the galley kitchen—shirtless, covered in hickeys, soapy and soaking wet—groping blindly for who-knows-what. Seriously, you can't leave the guy alone for even a minute. I grabbed a towel from the bathroom, shoved it into his hands, and went back to my post.

The sour woman over by the statues was now pawing things, too. She wouldn't leave a trail of bent boxes behind, but her energy was a downer. I'd have to smudge that whole area. "Are these from China?" she asked, though the vibration behind the words was more like an accusation.

"I don't do Chinese imports—the energy sucks. Those crystal balls are from Brazil, the Ganesh is from India, and the laughing Buddha is from Thailand."

"I saw something on the Shopping Channel that said all the supposed jade out of China was really green-dyed marble."

People are so fun to argue with when they think they know what they're talking about. "It says it's from Thailand, right there."

As I attempted to prove my point, Vic burst through the curtain with his shirt buttoned wrong and his hair sticking out sideways, grabbed me by the arm, and blurted out, "Where's your mugwort?"

"In a second," I said, but when I didn't immediately halt my conversation to appease him, he stomped off down the Wiccan aisle. The couple by the tarot cards looked uneasy—the fake jade woman too. And then to add creepiness to the discomfort, Vic announced, "I don't have my gun."

For fuck's sake. "Go lay down or something, okay? I'll close the store."

"It's got to be here somewhere."

"What, your gun? I doubt it. Seriously, chill out. I've got some Stoli in the freezer. Have a shot, or five."

That got his attention. He fled back to my apartment while my customers looked at me like they wondered if they should offer to call the cops. Fat lot of good it would do me. "Don't worry about him," I said to the room at large. "He's...special."

People do what they do for all kinds of cryptic, deep-seated reasons. Whether it was fascination, sympathy, or the appreciation of a good melodrama, the customers all trooped up to the register with something to buy just as soon as I said I was closing. And then a few more came in, to boot. By the time I bundled everyone out the door with their cards and their Buddhas and their other esoteric supplies, my till was fat.

And my apartment? It was suspiciously quiet.

I expected to find Vic sulking in the kitchen because I hadn't rushed in to placate him...and instead he was in my bed, curled into the fetal position around the vodka bottle, which was mostly empty. He'd been flying high on antipsyactives, and now this. How dangerous of a combo was alcohol and Auracel? I pulled out my phone and did a quick search to see if I should call an ambulance, but no. According to the web, operation of heavy machinery was contraindicated since drowsiness was likely. Given that Vic was unlikely to climb out of my bed, let alone get behind a wheel, I supposed he didn't have much to worry about. Medically speaking, anyway.

I plucked the bottle from his inebriated grasp, considered what percentage was probably backwash now, and finished it off. I needed as much fortitude as I could muster to call Jacob, since he'd probably find a way to blame me for whatever had just taken place. Right when the scars from our war wounds had started fading, too.

I went back to my phone, and considered it. Miss Mattie smiled up at me from her photo on the lock screen. "If ever there was a day he could've used your advice, it's today." I glanced over at Vic. He even scowled in his sleep. "For someone who's got it all, he's pretty damn miserable. And now, whatever I do, no doubt I'll screw things up even worse. Let him sleep it off here, they'll impugn my virtue. Call in the cavalry and I'll look like a snitch."

I shoved Vic's feet over—he didn't so much as stir—and sat cross-legged at the foot of my bed with the phone face-up in my lap. "Can something as simple as a pill really keep you from talking him down in his moment of need?" I asked Mattie. "Maybe, in a way, that's a comfort. Makes it feel less personal that you show up for him, and not me.

"And Jacob...he'll have a field day with this." I took another look at Vic. "How long do you give the two of them? Because it can't be healthy. Jacob with his savior complex and Vic hanging on by a thread. Do their broken places really fit together all that well? Are they stronger together, or is it a brittle façade that's gonna come crumbling down when something hits it in just the right spot?"

I might not've been on Auracel, but even so, Mattie had no answers for me. I tapped the call button on Jacob's contact and he answered right away. I greeted him with, "Care to come over and collect your drunken boyfriend?"

"What are you talking about? Vic doesn't drink."

"Tell that to my very last bottle of Stoli."

He sighed and said, "I'll be right over."

I've always teased Jacob about his age. How could I help it? He wore his wear a hell of a lot better than he had any right to. But when I found him on my doorstep with a resigned look about him and the lines of concern etched deep, I refrained from mentioning that he looked every last one of his years, and then some. I spared him the need to play twenty questions by giving him a quick rundown. "So Vic showed up tweaking on Auracel. He was convinced that a remote viewer was watching him, and that I needed to help him detox from the antipsyactive. Then he drove off my customers, drank all my vodka and passed out."

Jacob simply shook his head.

"Do you want anything—tea? Uh...water?"

He waved my offer away and headed up the aisle. I followed. When he was no longer looking me in the eye, he was able to say, "I just don't get him. I'm here for him but he never tells me anything." When I scoffed, he shot me a look over his shoulder and said, "No, the shoe doesn't feel any better on the other foot."

"Guess not."

We filed into my bedroom and took a good long look at Vic. He was in the same position in which I'd left him, curled on his side, knees bent, face scrunched in a scowl. "Must be out cold," I said. "He hasn't budged."

"For him, that's saying something. He tosses and turns all night long. In the morning, when I wake up, he's usually up and dressed and on his third cup of coffee. It's like he sleeps with one eye open and flies out of bed at the crack of dawn. I guess I never appreciated the contentment of watching someone sleep those last few minutes before the alarm goes off."

Booze isn't exactly a reliable tranquilizer. Sure, it knocks you out, but not for the duration. No doubt Vic would surface soon enough. "I'll give you two your privacy," I said, and went out to count my drawer and straighten my shelves. It didn't dawn on me until I was armpit deep in jade statuettes that Jacob's pre-alarm Sleeping Beauty had been me.

CHAPTER 43

Disturbing PsyCop visitations aside, my week was a pretty average week. I sold stuff, but not enough to pay my bills. I meditated and chanted and contemplated the meaning of my existence, then bit someone's head off for saying my competitor's charm selection was better than mine. And I hooked up with a guy who seemed intriguing at first, only for him to ruin it all by bragging about how easy it was to steal tips off the table when the waitstaff's back is turned. It was a relief to get a call from Carolyn, even if she was after a touch-up and not a pitcher of margaritas.

I bussed it over to her place and tapped on the door. Her twelve-year-old kid, Lexi, answered. I greeted her with, "What's shaking, Babycakes?"

She scowled. She's the spitting image of her dad, round-faced and pale, but she'd grown up in a household where even the tiniest of fibs didn't quite fly, so her facial expression was 100% Carolyn. And since she'd never been able to pussyfoot around a topic, she didn't bother to mask her disdain. "You're bleaching mom's hair again?"

"Indeed I am. It's important to maintain the blonde. Unless you were hoping I could talk her into something a little racier." I took off my hat and shook out my hair, which had faded to a delicate shade of minty vanilla. Lexi clucked her tongue and sauntered off into the living room. I poked in my head and said, "Hi, Cora," to the younger one. She was busy trying to keep Lexi from prying an iPad from her clutches, so she ignored me.

Carolyn's kids are awesome, a couple of shameless little ids with no superegos to hinder their actions. Heaven help their parents once puberty struck.

Carolyn came downstairs to grab me before I could swing into the kitchen and say hi to the hubster. Unlike the kids, Doug likes me. After all, I'm the reason his wife is so foxy. But interrupt the guy while he's in the midst of making dinner and the results might be toxic.

The Brinkmans' place is a typical Chicago bungalow, brick on the outside and hardwood floors throughout, sturdy and a little bit boring—which, I suspected, suited Carolyn and her Mister to a T. I'm not judging. The lack of pretense under their roof was refreshing.

The bungalow's basement is an odd-smelling, clammy-feeling, partially finished expanse where the family's various DIY projects crawl off to die. Pottery, painting, quilting and scrapbooking supplies languished under a fine sifting of dust. A decrepit 70's bathroom adjoined the laundry room, too ugly to really use and too much trouble to update, but with a rubbery sprayer attachment stuck on to the sink's old faucet, it was a serviceable makeshift salon.

As I sectioned Carolyn's hair and clipped it out of my way, her eyes met mine in the pitted vanity mirror. "This reminds me of the way we met," she said, "with you finishing my hair at home instead of the salon. At Red's place. Which makes me think about how much I miss him."

"Well, that makes one of us."

Our reflections both scowled. Hers, because my reply was patently untrue. Mine, because I was so sick of pining over the ones that got away. I was debating how deep into the Red conversation I really wanted to delve when someone came thundering down the basement stairs—and it sounded a hell of a lot heftier then Doug or the girls. Or even the three of them combined.

Jacob skidded to a halt in the bathroom doorway, flushed and intense. "I want to try again."

"I told you not to get your hopes up," Carolyn said. "Though I can't imagine why I thought you'd listen."

"This sounds juicy already," I said.

"Vic has a theory that there's more to being a Stiff than just a lack of ability," Jacob said, which Carolyn countered with, "And I don't think you should hang your hopes on it until we figure out a more accurate way to measure it. You don't realize what's involved in testing a Psych. A quick game of true or false in the car isn't enough to go by."

"Hold on," I said. Vic's paranoia must've been rubbing off on me. "I'm never keen on admitting it, but I think Jacob's got the right idea. It's smarter to figure out what's what before he goes running off and getting anything noted in his permanent record that he'd rather keep to himself."

Jacob said, "I know it's nowhere near as thorough as official Psych testing, but I don't care about thorough. You're certified. I know you, I've worked with you for nearly two years. Between the both of us, we can figure this out." He pulled something from his pocket—the world's most twisted card game, Puppies and Bugs. "We can even make a spreadsheet."

"Ooh," I said. "Now I know it's serious."

Carolyn's resting bitchface got active as her eyebrows pulled together and the corners of her mouth drew down. "I don't like this. I don't like any of this."

"I know you," Jacob repeated. "And I doubt you're worried about being the only Psych on the team."

"No, of course not. But given the litany of tests the department has put both of us through, I can't imagine that they would have overlooked something as important as a psychic off-switch."

"Not overlooked. Just...forgotten." Before Carolyn could argue, he added, "I've seen certain original documents—"

"What documents?" she demanded. "Now you're just being cryptic. This revolves around Vic, doesn't it? He's walking into something dangerous and you're just following blithely along because you think you're untouchable."

Jacob gave her a *look*. She must've been used to it.

"Originally," he explained, "at the conception of the whole PsyCop partnership, Stiffs weren't just NPs. Yes, they scored negative on all the typical psychic evaluations, but they had ability of their own. They stood up to clairsentients—they could shield against probing. But the documentation of PsyCop training was so lengthy and convoluted, part of it dropped off a degraded photocopy and nobody added it back in. It's not just wishful thinking. I saw the primary source myself."

I ignored the major case of the willies attempting to manifest. Either the bureaucracy was so incompetent they'd lost a key piece of information to a screwy copy, or someone had "helped" them forget. Neither scenario was much comfort. I stirred my developer and said, "You kids do what you need to do. I'm not letting this go to waste."

I was perfectly content to be a fly on the wall, but Carolyn wouldn't let me blend in to the scenery. "Jacob can't test with both of us in the room. It would skew the results."

"Maybe so," Jacob said. "And wouldn't that be worth knowing?"

I dabbed at Carolyn's regrowth and said nothing. She huffed and rolled her eyes, and finally said, "I suppose." I could tell she would've rather said "no." Sucks to be her.

Jacob wedged his way in, perched on the edge of the tub and pulled out a note pad. "Just tell me if I'm lying or not." He flipped a card. "Scorpion."

"True."

"Beetle."

"True."

"Doberman."

"I don't think so. No. That's a lie."

They plodded through the deck, and Jacob made various tick marks and notations as he went. He wouldn't be scoring her. We all knew she could weed out a lie, so he must've been seeing whether or not he could block. I'm glad no one asked me in front of Carolyn if I was intrigued. Because I'd want to deny it, but frankly, I found the whole thing fascinating. And to add even more upheaval to the chaos, every few minutes either Lexi or Cora joined in to accuse her sister of screwing up whatever game they were attempting to play. I finished my application, snapped on the plastic cap and set my timer. Carolyn jumped up and abandoned her current round of cards to go referee her daughters' meltdown, which left the bathroom suddenly calm and strangely empty with only Jacob, and me, remaining.

He turned the cards over in his hands a few times and said, "Want to try?"

"Why bother? I don't see how the deck could possibly work for an empath without the wires getting crossed. Even if my accuracy was off the charts, what if you've got a fetish for bugs? What if I have a puppy phobia? That's bound to skew the results."

"A *puppy* phobia?"

"I just don't see the point. It's not like I'm any good at this stuff even in the best of conditions."

Jacob picked up an old gossip rag that had slid into the narrow gap between tub and toilet, one of those tawdry magazines that suck me in at the grocery store checkout line even though I know it's chock full of alternative facts. "How about this? I look at a photo of a celebrity and you tell me whether or not I like them. I won't say who it is—I won't even be facing you, so you can't read into my facial expression."

"But my logical mind wants to override my gut already. Who's in there anyway—a bunch of vapid actors and washed up reality stars? I'd be shocked if there's anyone on those pages who doesn't annoy you."

"Don't be so sure. Here's a pic of Justin Trudeau waving a pride flag."

Who *didn't* have that image indelibly burned into their brain? Even I drooled a little whenever I saw it.

The lecture about sharing that Carolyn was giving her kids carried through the heating vent. By the sound of it, we wouldn't be interrupted anytime soon. "Fine. Whatever. Lay it on me."

"Got it, go ahead."

How ridiculous, I thought, to even make the attempt. My only claim to fame was picking up the Vibe. With Jacob's back turned, there was no entry point. I might as well have been trying to read the toilet. "I got nothing. So I'll go with dislike."

"And now?"

"Honestly, no clue. Dislike."

Pages flipped. "Now."

I was about to repeat myself, but then I yielded to the niggling impulse to change my read. "Like."

And so it went, him flipping, me guessing, him jotting down my random guesses in hopes of forcing them to make some kind of sense. There couldn't possibly be enough of them to create a pattern. We'd need thousands of guesses to arrive at anything statistical. As it was, we'd be lucky to reach fifty before Carolyn's timer dinged. "Next," he said.

I breathed, I focused...and with only a hint of sarcasm, I said, "You're crazy about this one."

His shoulders hitched as if he'd stifled a laugh.

I told his back, "It's useless, right? Don't say I didn't warn you."

He turned toward me and held out his notepad. The people on the list weren't gleaned from the magazine, they were real people, people he knew. His coworkers, his parents, his friends. And the very last entry was *Crash*.

My heart did a sorry little twist. And while all the ramifications sank in, he told me, "All the ones I was deliberately trying to project, you got right. The others are roughly half and half."

That must've been what all the tick marks and scorings meant. All those months, he hadn't been ambivalent—he'd been blocking my read. "And here I'd always figured you weren't that into me."

We sat with that for a few seconds. Upstairs, Carolyn was threatening to take the iPad away so neither of them could use it—and both kids stopped whining immediately. Their mother didn't make idle threats. She couldn't. Eventually, Jacob said, "We both played our part in what happened. I could have told you I loved you, and I didn't. I thought you'd bite my head off."

And I could've told him the dinner he'd skipped out on wasn't just any dinner. "Supposing you really can switch your psychic access on and off. What's your default position?"

He lowered his voice. "Working with Carolyn all this time? I'd guess I'm shielding more often than not."

If that was true, it would jibe with the fact that I only felt the rarest glimpses of him Vibing, and even when my eyes told me he was ready to burst a blood vessel, my gut told me he wasn't even angry. Hell, that must've been why I could read him better over the phone, going by his tone of voice and not a jumble of mixed signals. Add to that the natural psyactives we periodically handled for the online store, and no wonder we'd never discovered any rhyme or reason to his pattern until now.

"I hope you've both learned something," Carolyn said. Upstairs. To her kids. But the same could be said for Jacob and me. I'm not sure which realization hit harder—the fact that Jacob actually possessed some kind of talent, or the evidence that mine might be more accurate than I realized.

CHAPTER 44

After that conversation in Carolyn's basement, Jacob didn't mention the failed wreck of our relationship, and I was no more eager than he was to prod its putrefying remains. As winter rolled into spring, we saw one another often enough. I did a monthly house smudging for him, he helped me move some stunningly heavy filing cabinets. He didn't seem angry anymore. I supposed I wasn't either. Vaguely sad, maybe. Though whenever I caught Vic standing there in the middle of the cannery with a blank look on his face like he couldn't imagine how on earth he'd ended up there, I often wondered if everything might pan out like it does for a reason. That could never have been me. Even if Jacob and I had been psychically compatible, I still wouldn't have moved in with him, not within a few short months of knowing each other. So there was a damn good chance he simply wasn't the guy for me. Close, as they say, but no cigar.

And I can't say it was any big hardship to keep sampling guys. My latest conquest—very fun, very limber, though not the brightest crayon in the box—must've ducked out sometime during the night, since I had my narrow bed to myself when I woke to my phone's alarm. When I turned it off, a voicemail from my mother was there waiting for me. Of course it was. "I can't believe my Lit-tle Pea-nut is turning thirty!" she gushed. "I'm picking you up at nine o'clock sharp, so make sure you're ready."

Fabulous, I had ten minutes to wash the stank off me and throw on some clothes. But my bedhead didn't look too bad, so after I swabbed off, I could get away with a quick primp and a spritz of finishing spray. Hair managed, I changed my outgoing message, stuck a *closed* sign on my door and skipped down the stairs to go meet Maxine.

Either the break from manning that register or the prospect of a nice infusion of cash had me in a pretty good mood. Thirty was a milestone birthday, right? Maxine only did subtle when it came to upholstery and nail polish. Whatever gift she had in store for me, it was bound to be big.

She was excited. Her energy was always high, but that morning it practically rolled off her in waves. "We'll spend the morning getting massaged and pampered, and then we have a reservation at an authentic tea house."

Good thing I didn't mind standing in for the daughter she'd always wanted. "Awesome."

While it wasn't exactly my cup of tea, I can think of worse ways to start my day than a mani/pedi, a mineral wrap and a massage. But, like so many things in life, the experience came with a lot of baggage. When I noticed my esthetician pulling down her sleeves to cover the tiny yin/yang tattoo on the inside of her wrist, I couldn't help but see things through the staff's eyes. They were polite and deferential...in fact, maybe a little too subdued. And they all emanated a resigned sort of dread. Bitchy manager or monster boss? Or both? Despite my best mindful breathing, my tranquility was sullied by flashbacks of Ralph. Even though the loungers were cozy and the place smelled good, by the time my purple sparkle nail polish had set, I was more than ready to get the hell out of there.

We stuffed ourselves full of petit fours and macaroons and cucumber sandwiches in a three-season porch that overlooked a suburban garden of carefully crafted disarray. The weather was post-Memorial-Day mild, and our waiter was easy on the eyes. And while Maxine rambled on about a show she'd seen on decorating with burlap, it occurred to me that I enjoyed this new dynamic where she no longer steered our every conversation around finding me a new job. But also that she was feeling a little edgy. Or maybe it was just eagerness. On her, it's hard to tell the difference.

We hit the big department stores and shopped until we were hungry again, then had a light dinner at a brewpub where, thankfully, the staff didn't come out and join my mother when she sang to me. And just when I thought maybe I shouldn't have settled for three pairs of jeans, she keyed in another address on her Beamer's GPS.

Another gift was in store. Had to be. Massages, tea rooms and shopping trips were fun and all, but they hardly ranked as birthday material. Especially for the big three-oh. We headed back into the city, back toward my old stomping grounds, when I'd lived in a swanky apartment. With furniture. Like a person.

My gut roiled. While my mother might finally approve of my vocation, she was less than thrilled with my living arrangements. What if she'd done something totally over-the-top, like bought me a condo? It would be just like her, wouldn't it? On one hand, holy shit, a condo. But on the other, the gift would also be a criticism, an implication that I was unable to handle my own living situation. That, in fact, my own preferences mattered so little, she could buy it with zero input on my part as to how many rooms, what style, or heck, even which neighborhood I'd want to call home. I was attempting to dredge up a modicum of sincere gratitude when she pulled up in front of a single family home, a craftsman-style beauty that must've been worth a cool half-mil. Even Maxine's bank account and generosity wouldn't stretch that far.

So if the house wasn't my big present, what were we doing there?

Maxine turned to me, grabbed my manicured hand, and said, "I can't wait for you to meet her!"

"Okay, I'll bite. Meet who?"

"The most respected astrologer in Chicago." Maxine gave a dramatic pause and a mini hand-flourish toward the porch. "Julia Vogel."

I made a grand effort to not roll my eyes. Astrology? No, seriously...*astrology*? Who cared if I sold good luck charms for a living—that didn't mean I thought the Easter Bunny was real. Still, there was Maxine, gazing upon me with her painful smile and her brittle eagerness. It was no condo, that's for sure. But at least I'd only need to live in the ill-fitting experience for the next hour or so.

"You've heard of her?" Maxine asked earnestly.

"The name sounds familiar."

"I'm sure you have. She's on the Windy City Morning Show all the time."

"If that's where I've heard it, then I'm way too familiar with the Menopause Channel." We trooped up the stairs and rang the bell. My mother was a bundle of enthusiasm, while I was hoping I wouldn't nod off from the extra slab of quiche in my belly. But my ennui turned to O-M-G when I realized I did indeed know Chicago's most lauded astrologer. In fact, I'd seen her numerous times in Pilar's chair.

Ms. Vogel was better known to me as "Julia the racist."

I'll give credit where credit's due. Julia was a professional. While we both blanched at the sight of each other, she was courteous and polite. As was I. And the whole while, Maxine babbled heedlessly over the top of our mutual revulsion.

Who knows where my idea of astrology readings came from? I thought there'd be more obscure and arcane props involved, gear to keep the casual observer occupied while the so-called professional spun their B.S. But no. Maxine had supplied my birth data ahead of time, and Julia was armed with nothing but a few printouts.

She began with a spiel about sun signs. When daily horoscopes come to mind, sun signs are what most people are thinking of, but they actually have little to do with much of anything. There were rising signs and moon signs, houses and nodes, transits and returns. According to her, it meant nothing that I was a Gemini, because purportedly, my Saturn was so fucked up.

She didn't say it in so many words, of course. But her melodramatic tone spoke volumes. "Natal Saturn is in your ninth house, which affects your self-esteem and worth. People with this placement tend to have trouble finding success."

No doubt she would point out the turd in the punch bowl with any placement just to watch me squirm. She went on about my inherent skepticism, rigid thinking and lack of depth, and I suspected she'd strayed from her astrological mumbo-jumbo and was now just impugning my character for the fun of it. But then she said, "Saturn can also be a father figure. Sun squared Saturn, especially with your natal Chiron where it is, could indicate a difficult relationship with your father."

Give her nothing. I smiled dismissively.

She pointed at one of the meaningless squiggles on the chart. "Age twenty-two would be a particularly hard time."

The very age I was when he keeled over dead, with zero warning.

"And here, age twenty-eight, this trine would give you an opportunity to heal the difficulty."

Sure. Except for the fact that dear old Dad was no longer among the living. And I didn't have any mediums at my disposal then. Not yet.

I must've let some micro-expression slip, because she hastened to add, "Maybe not with the same person. But an older man."

My wan smile froze as I realized...that was exactly when I'd started seeing Jacob.

"The other Saturn transits might have overshadowed that healing. Age twenty-nine, Saturn return. And a four-month retrograde...."

I did my best to tune her out, but the damage had been done. I'm not sure what was worse, that Julia was spouting all this doom and gloom in front of my mother, or that in some obscure corner of my bullheaded brain, I kinda-sorta believed her.

Thankfully, Julia wasn't eager to extend our session. She hustled us out at one hour on the nose. I still had nothing to say. But true to form, Maxine just got chirpier. I would've been happy to ride home in silence, but she insisted on dissecting the whole reading. "I'm sure Julia could have sugarcoated things, but think about it this way. If the Saturn return was responsible for all of the roadblocks and obstacles you keep coming up against, then you're due for things to turn around any day now."

"I don't need anything to 'turn around.' I'm my own boss. I'm living my life on my own terms. What more could anyone want?"

She pulled into a parking spot down the block from Sticks and Stones and popped the trunk. "I must not've had a Saturn return," she said. "I adored being twenty-eight. That's when I had you."

"And now you're just getting sappy." I grabbed her hand and brushed a kiss across her knuckles. "But I guess that's why I love you."

I loaded myself up with shopping bags, gave Maxine another wave, and headed toward the store. In all the horoscope hubbub, I'd forgotten about the loot I'd scored that day. Jeans and boots and some silky little underthings for when I didn't care to go commando. A decadent cashmere robe. Socks without holes in them. And all the pricy lotions and toners I could ever want to douse myself with. It was a good score. A good day. And even though we'd ended it in Julia's odious presence, fuck her. My life was exactly the way I wanted it. Her suggestion that I was some kind of loser was as ridiculous as her mediocre dye-job.

I was juggling shopping bags as I let myself into the vestibule, and my mind was on my mailbox—specifically, whether I wanted to put all my bags down to unlock it, or make an extra trip up and down the stairs—when I realized I wasn't alone.

On the landing above me, my upstairs neighbor was fumbling at my door, and not for the first time. They don't call him Drunk Tony for nothing. "Wrong door," I called out. "Keep going."

He spun around to face me, and two things occurred to me. One, he was a lot quicker on his feet than usual. And two...it wasn't Tony.

Luckily I was only a few steps up the stairwell when he came bounding down two by two. He gave me a hard shove as he passed, and I managed to pivot so I smacked the railing instead of toppling over backward. Shopping bags dropped and split, and my treasures spilled down the grimy steps. The outer door banged open, and the guy was gone before I even registered what was happening. He'd knocked the wind out of me, but I was more startled than scared.

At least until I got a look at my shop's front door. The paint around the strike plate was so dinged and chipped, I'd bet that asshole must've been hacking away at it for a good long while. What if I'd been home while it happened? What if he'd sunk his rusty screwdriver into more than just my woodwork? As I gathered up my stuff, noting several of my skin care items had ruptured or shattered, I saw my hands were shaking. More from adrenaline than fear, but even so. It hardly seemed fair. Couldn't I catch a break on my own damn birthday?

Thankfully, the inside of the store looked just like I'd left it, and my cashbox was intact. Hadn't bothered making a deposit since there wasn't all that much money on the premises—though it would've really stung to lose what little was there, so I should probably reconsider the frequency of my drop-offs. Once I turned on every last one of my lights and triple-checked that the guy didn't have an accomplice lurking among my shelves, I locked back up and headed downstairs to check on my friend.

"You're worried about me?" Lydia said. "Aww, that's sweet." She hustled me into her tiny kitchen, sat me down, and poured me a shot of birthday cake vodka. How apropos. "You must've been targeted because you were closed on an oddball day, so he figured nobody was home." We downed our vanilla fire water, then she said, "What's with that face, you're surprised someone tried to rob you? Stop clutching your pearls, it comes with the territory."

"It's not that. Not...exactly." I considered refusing the second shot. Lydia poured. I drank. Then I steeled myself and asked, "Is it me? I'm a good person. Fair. Truthful. But then I draw someone like that into my life and I can't help but wonder..."

"Stop dwelling on it. You're fine. Besides, what do I always tell you? It ain't over till it's over. It's useless to take one event in isolation and try to assign it some grand meaning. Everything turns out for the best if you wait long enough to take stock. Everything's evolving."

Maybe so. But as much as I thought Julia the Racist Astrologer was full of shit, her predictions of hardship and failure had left a pall on my mood. "What's your take on astrology?"

"It's more interesting than the advice columns these days, and just about as useful. Why?"

"Apparently my Saturn is fucked."

"And you wish it was Uranus?" Lydia barked out a laugh and slopped some vodka over the side of her glass, and I couldn't help but smile....even if I was annoyed that I hadn't been the one to come up with that remark and throw it in Julia's face. "Look, kiddo, everyone's got a Saturn in their chart. Not just you. So tell me what's really bugging you."

That I was worried the whole father-figure business might hold a grain of truth? Obviously I'd showed up for my special day with one parent, not two. It didn't take a fifth-level fraudster to surmise *something* was up with my dad. "An ugly blast from the past is all, coupled with some asshole fucking up my door."

"And both of them have run their course. Sayonara, good riddance, and here's to a fresh start."

We chatted long into the night, the two of us. While doctors and priests are ethically bound to keep their clients' confidence, psychics have no such moral obligation. Lydia distracted me with juicy stories until the backs of my teeth could no longer stand her cloying vodka, and I headed upstairs to hit the sack. But all the vanilla booze in the world couldn't dull the sight of my door. The Sultry Amethyst might've been a ripoff at forty bucks a gallon, but it always reminded me of painting the stairwell with Maxine. And now the purple doorframe looked like someone had taken an axe to it. A very dull axe.

Was my Saturn to blame?

I pulled up Twitter on my phone and shot a few messages over to Constantine in hopes of him setting me straight, but he must've been busy doing whatever it was he did that earned him those fat wads of cash. The last thing I remembered was snuggling up in my luxurious cashmere robe, swiping idly through Tanngo and enjoying my final smoke of the day...and then bolting awake to the stink of burning hair. How I'd managed to nod off, I'll never know. Either I was worn out from a long day of running around, or Lydia's awful booze packed one hell of a punch. Whatever the reason, I'd fallen asleep with a lit cigarette and christened my new robe with a giant scorch mark, right down the front.

"Fuckin'-A, Saturn. What've I ever done to you?"

CHAPTER 45

It's been suggested that one way of encouraging yourself to stay on the smoke-free bandwagon is to buy yourself a little treat with the money you've saved. A nearby thrift store carried a fascinating array of vintage odds and ends, many of which were in the perfect price range. But I stopped bringing home knick-knacks after I found myself flinging wax fruit against the wall.

According to the various websites I consulted, it would take around three months for my brain to adjust to quitting. By the sultry height of August, I was seriously doubting that one more month could possibly make me feel like a human being again. Then I remembered how I'd nearly marked my three decades on the planet with human fireworks, and I shoved a piece of gum in my mouth and soldiered on.

When customers got on my very last nerve, I was inclined to chalk it up to nicotine withdrawal. Mostly, anyhow. There was a creep who rubbed me seriously wrong—and it had absolutely nothing to do with my shifting brain chemistry. Lately, his visits had become more and more frequent.

He said his name was Nietzsche, though I suspected if I ever got a look at his drivers license, it wouldn't be anything nearly so cool. He paid with cash. And the things he bought formed a pattern that made me uneasy.

In this business, customers expect you to carry goods you might not be too keen on. Spells and charms aimed at changing the behavior of others are coercive, but I stock them. I draw the line at anything that's just plain evil, though. Satanic stuff, curses, hexes, that kind of crap has no place in my store. Unfortunately, many of my herbs, stones and candles are simply tools, and I have no control over what they're used for.

That day, Nietzsche had on his typical outfit of jeans, a stained T-shirt, and a secondhand suit jacket that was stiff, dirty, and frayed around the cuffs. His hair was so neglected it was hanging in mats, and the razor bumps on his neck looked red and inflamed, like he'd shaved dry with a cheap plastic razor. The mere sight of him creeping up and down my aisles made me itch for a cigarette, and I debated whether or not I should offer to help him find anything. I decided against it. He'd scoured every square inch of my retail space umpteen times. He probably knew my inventory better than I did. He'd been lurking around for nearly half an hour by the time he finally ponied up to the register with his typical purchase: charcoal, noxious weeds, and a handful of black candles. He smacked the candles down on the plexi, and said, "Don't you have any more?"

I cut my eyes to the ginormous rack of brightly colored wax five feet away.

"I need black," he said. Which I knew. Nietzsche burned through so many black candles, his shrine must look like a tar pit. And while there was indeed more stock in my office, I had no desire to go fetch it.

I shrugged. "Oh well."

"But I need them. So you should make sure you have enough."

"Is that so?"

"When you claim yourself to be a vendor of ritual goods, you create a social contract where you're obligated to provide what you've advertised."

Oh, please. "Speaking of advertisements," I nodded toward my Lucky Love and Money Mojo display. "Maybe it's time to try another tack. Lose the doom and gloom. There's enough bad juju floating around without you constantly adding to it."

"*Bad* is nothing more than a value judgement, and I don't subscribe to such pedestrian ideas."

I'm not sure what compelled me to be argumentative and finally call him out on what he was buying—nicotine withdrawal, or the fact that I was fed up with pretending that I didn't know he was using things he'd bought from me to feed his ugly delusions. I snatched the black candles off my countertop and dropped them on the floor behind the register. "I'm not nearly as high-brow in my philosophies, but it's true, I am the vendor. It's my store. And I'm perfectly within my rights to tell you to take your black magic somewhere else."

Unfortunately, my verbal smackdown didn't have quite the effect I'd hoped it might. If my gut was anything to go by, Nietzsche was enjoying the conflict. No, even worse...he was *Vibing* on it.

"The Dark Arts are notoriously misunderstood," he said, but I was only listening to his words with a fragment of my attention. Because I felt it before I saw it—he wasn't reaching into his coat for a greasy wad of singles like he had every other time we'd transacted business.

He was going for a knife.

Not only did I feel his intention before the knife even cleared his pocket, but I felt the blade itself. Not cold metal, but warm, from nestling against his heart. And more than that, I felt his sickening anticipation, like the horrible glee Ralph had reveled in when he hammered me with the numbing condom—except this stick-in-the-guts would end with me bleeding out on the floor. There was only one word for it, and I couldn't help but say it out loud. "Evil."

"I don't believe in evil," Nietzsche philosophized, "not like Christians believe in evil. But there's still darkness in the world. The type of actions that cling to your soul like a disease. Like a stain." He turned to my latest newsletter display, where an absurd male underwear model stood with hips thrust forward, and wended the knife's point down the model's chest as if he was doodling on it with a marker. And he was getting aroused from the anticipation of doing the same to me. "It's money—the stuff is corrupted. You shouldn't be handling all that money, you're too pure. I know. I've been watching you." He dragged the blade across the countertop, trailing a delicate scratch behind it, then lifted it to point at my register. "Give it to me and I'll get rid of it for you."

I couldn't pop open that register fast enough. Because if I was lucky, that was all he really wanted—the cash. But even as I handed over every last dollar in my drawer, I felt his energy intensify. "Wait a second," he said, and I knew that no matter how much money I handed over, it wouldn't have been enough. "You're not holding out on me, are you?"

"No." Damn it. My voice sounded so small.

"Don't you know that lying blackens your soul? When you speak an untruth, the one you hurt the most is yourself."

Take the money and go, you fucker. Take the fucking money.

I didn't just think the words, I willed them at him with every fiber of my being. Too bad I wasn't more of an empath—they bounced right off him with no effect at all. In fact, maybe they'd even made it worse, because after I thought them, he looked me right in the eye, smiled, and said, "Do you suck cock? You look like you'd be good at it."

My thoughts ran a million miles an hour. *Just blow him and get it over with, it's not as if you've never had a dick in your mouth.* But even forcing me to my knees would've been too vanilla for him, when what he really wanted was to see me bleed. "You'd hold back on that too," he said, "wouldn't you? You think you're better than me?"

Even as I realized Nietzsche was ramping up to cut me open, I saw we weren't the only ones in the store. Before my life could flash before my eyes, Victor Bayne slipped out neatly from behind a shelf, wrenched Nietzsche's arm behind his back, and shoved him to the ground. He belatedly shouted, "Police—drop your weapon," after the knife went skittering across the floor. It was over in half a second, and even though I'd been treated to a front row view, I could hardly make sense of what I'd seen. Vic was a total badass. He'd smacked down Nietzsche like he knew kung fu—*movie* kung fu. I'd suspect it wasn't really Vic and just some bizarre pre-death hallucination if not for the look on his face, the same petulant scowl he gives me whenever I offer him a hand-job, a gemstone cleanse or a veggie burger.

He trussed up Nietzsche with a plastic tie while I stood there clutching the counter with my vision tunneling, then turned to me and demanded, "Are you okay? Did this asshole hurt you?"

If I wasn't practically pissing myself, I would've made a remark about being surprised he was so incredibly butch. But I could only nod, since I didn't trust my voice not to shake.

Jacob was right downstairs, and Lisa too, and they charged on up to make sure the situation was handled. Which was good, because my knees were so wobbly I was reeling like I'd just raided Lydia's cake vodka stash. Vic was wearing jeans, Lisa was in a sundress and flip flops, and Jacob had on cargo shorts and a summery T-shirt. But the way they spoke, the way they stood—and particularly the way their eyes went flinty—all three of them looked like nothing other than cops.

True fear is a powerful thing. Not sure if I'd ever felt it. Not like I currently did, with a metallic taste at the back of my mouth and my pulse whooshing in my ears. And after the initial spike faded and my thoughts felt more like my thoughts, a cascade of disturbing things occurred to me. What if Vic hadn't been halfway up the stairs already—would Nietzsche have been satisfied with stabbing me dead, or would hunks of my body have ended up in that freak's black candle rituals? Who would find the aftermath, one of my cop friends, or my downstairs neighbor...who was nowhere near as tough as she made herself out to be. And worst of all, if I was murdered, what would it do to Maxine?

I'd known damn well that guy wasn't right in the head. My gut had been pretty emphatic about it long before he perved out. I hadn't listened. Just like I hadn't listened about Ralph.

Whatever that government test said about my lack of empathic ability was bullshit. My days of talking myself out of my feelings were through.

CHAPTER 46

While I might've been single, I certainly wasn't alone. Over the course of the next few days, my cop friends tag-teamed each other to make sure I didn't end up as a statistic on the police blotter. I spent most of my time with Lisa. She was between jobs, between homes, and between men—and even worse, something freaky had happened to her out at PsyTrain that either she couldn't quite articulate or she simply wanted to forget. Looking after me gave her something to do so she didn't have to look too hard at her own affairs, but who was I to judge? Sometimes when your life goes from bad to worse, the only thing left to do is keep busy.

The store was open, but no customers graced the aisles. It wasn't time yet to update my in-house marketing, but the Lucky Love and Money Mojo had gone straight in the trash once I realized how much it reminded me of Nietzsche. Fuck love and money. My next promo would be The Power of Protection.

Lisa was happy to help me put together the next collage. Give her a big stack of work and she'll pick through it for hours. We'd gathered all the abandoned sales flyers from the vestibule and spread them across the countertop. I'd told her to cut out every human body part she could find, and her stack of heads and limbs was growing. My initial idea was to show psychic protection as a circle of arms. But now it just looked like a bloodless dismemberment.

"You don't have to babysit," I told her. "I mean, so long as that creep isn't running around loose."

She checked with her sí-no in a pause so brief I wouldn't have noticed it had I not known the source of her info. "He's still in lock-up. And you'd be fine if I left. But maybe I'm the one who wants the company."

We were two peas in a pod, Lisa and me. I'd ignored the clear psychic message that my assailant was a twisted psycho. She'd known that fondling the shaman's smudge stick was a phenomenally bad idea, and she'd gone ahead and done it anyway.

She sighed. "After everything that happened, sometimes I actually miss him. That's messed up...right?"

"Certain people burrow under your skin and stay there like a stubborn case of scabies. Now and then I still catch myself daydreaming about the one who got away."

"Jacob? No. Then who?"

"An old colleague who never gave me so much as a passing grope. Is forbidden fruit as sweet as it's cracked up to be, or am I just too contrary to take anyone's advice—including my own?"

The front door opened and the two of us snapped to—my attention went to a newly-installed fisheye mirror, Lisa's to her sí-no—but it wasn't another murderer coming to get me, or even a customer interrupting our chat. It was none other than Jacob.

Or, should I say *Detective Marks*? He was all business, from his suit, to his body language, to the psychic barriers at full tilt. This was the side of himself he didn't like me to see, and frankly, shielding me from it hadn't been a bad idea. If this aspect of him had been the one to greet me at the coffee shop, I would've turned around and walked right back out the door. Even if I hadn't yet learned to listen to my gut.

"I'm fine," I called out to him before he could start in on all the security measures he thought I should be taking. "I'm dandy. Between the two of us, we've cleared the cobwebs, restocked the crystals and alphabetized all the herbs. So no need to keep checking in."

Jacob paused to take in the improved lines of sight and additional lighting, then joined us at the counter. "Actually, I'm here for Lisa."

He handed her a plain white envelope. A few choice sí-nos played through her head, but none of them panned out. "What is it?" she asked.

Jacob answered with a single resigned headshake. "I don't know. It's sealed."

"Who's it from?"

"Just...read it."

"Do you need me to leave the room?" I said in annoyance. "It's only my shop and all, but hey, don't let me get in your way."

"Don't be like that," Jacob said. "It's work-related."

Lisa had the envelope open and was already scanning its contents. Whatever it was, she didn't care to elaborate aloud, other than to ask Jacob, "Why are *you* giving me this?"

He considered his answer for a long moment, then said, "Because I'm on the payroll. As of today, I'm officially working for the FPMP."

F-pimp? No shit. I was bursting with questions. Why? In what capacity? And exactly how freaked out was his boyfriend? My gut told me nothing, not with Jacob's aura locked down tight, but experience and logic told me plenty. He might not be happy about this decision, but he was bound and determined to see it through.

"I need to make a phone call," Lisa murmured. I gestured toward the office and she slipped through the beaded curtain.

When we were alone, I said, "Does this mean you're not a PsyCop anymore?"

"Technically, I'm retired."

"So it's Mr. Marks now?"

He sighed. "Agent."

"Seriously? A fed? A real life spy?"

"I'm not a—"

"I know full well what you are—Vic's told me all about it. You're the psychic Big Brother that listens in on his phone calls and tampers with his mail."

"It's not all like that. I'm not in surveillance." He paused and massaged his temples. "Look, it's time to stop pretending everything's status quo and certified psychics are safe. There are dangerous people out there—not just the unstable ones who'd pull a knife on you.

I'm talking organized threats. People who want to turn psychic abilities to their advantage and are willing to vivisect psychics to do it. People who want to round up anyone with talent and eliminate them before they can get organized. You and I both know Vic has some serious ability. That makes him a target. And I'm not willing to just stand around and let some extremist pick him off. Not when I'm in a position to actually do something to prevent it."

He fell silent when Lisa emerged from the office. She waved the folded letter. "They want to meet with me. I'm gonna go."

"Are you sure?" Jacob asked.

"The sí-no says I should."

How handy to have such an unequivocal guidance system. "Be safe," I told her as she headed out the door. Jacob said nothing. I locked the door behind Lisa with the new deadbolt Jacob had helped me install, and rejoined him at the register. "So this new employer of yours...they don't have any idea how good you are at Puppies and Bugs, do they?"

He stared hard at the counter and didn't answer.

Unbelievable. "You *told* them?"

"Just one guy. I had to, back at PsyTrain."

"And this one guy...will he keep it on the downlow?"

"I don't know if it matters. He's the guy in charge."

"And now this guy is passing notes to Lisa. With your help."

I'd only voiced what Jacob had been thinking, but he looked irritated that I'd come out and said it. "Maybe Lisa should have kept her ability secret. Think about the things a criminal could do with her sí-no. Or, for that matter, what an army could do. Or a terrorist. I have no great love for the FPMP, but right now, I don't see a better option."

When it was Carolyn's turn to babysit me, minding the store together was nowhere near as fun as margaritas and nachos. I'd been grinding through real estate listings, hoping to find a storefront I could afford in a neighborhood where I wouldn't be robbed, violated and ritually dismembered. And I was trying to ignore the nagging idea that the Nietzsches of this world were perfectly capable of finding me no matter where I chose to plant my flag. Carolyn, meanwhile, was glued to her phone, volleying emails with her union rep to get out of working. Apparently Jacob hadn't only been shielding himself. Without him by her side at the Twelfth Precinct, she felt vulnerable and exposed.

"My contract stipulates that I'm to be partnered with a specific PsyCop NP."

"Might as well call a Stiff a Stiff," I told her. "Everyone else does."

"Now Sergeant Owens is talking about farming me out to different precincts to forge 'partnerships.' I'm not some show pony he can parade out at whim. I refuse to be part of his politicking. Where does it all end?" She jabbed at her phone and huffed. "And what's wrong with your new wi-fi?"

"The router's got something against me." I was halfway to the office when a customer came in. "Just unplug it and plug it back in so it resets itself. It's on top of the gray filing cabinet." As Carolyn disappeared into the office, I recognized my customer and called out, "Did you get a chance to read that article I sent you about psychic chimps? Or were you worried you'd find your own picture beneath the clickbait?"

I'd expected some banter in return, but Constantine didn't even crack a smile. He strode up to the counter and said, "I heard about the armed robbery. Are you okay?"

I half-shrugged. "Nothing wounded, other than my sense of security."

"Listen, I know you've got your own way of doing things, and far be it from me to elbow in where I'm not wanted, but I can really help you out."

"And this is where you finally let me in on what it is you do."

"If it mattered, I'd tell you." He took in the store with a long glance. "We could beef up your security. Add a panic button."

"That depends. Who's *we*?"

"No one you've ever heard of." Carolyn stepped back out into the store, and Con gave her a lingering once-over, then murmured, "Or have you?"

I cut my eyes to Carolyn. She was scrolling on her phone and paying no attention to us.

"Think about it," Con said. "And if you need anything...you know where to find me."

Knowing the extent to which Jacob and Vic went to make sure no one had eyes inside their building, I opted against pursuing Con's offer of assistance, though every now and then, I found myself sorely tempted to break down and take him up on it. Even between the four of them, my cop friends couldn't manage to babysit me forever. And with summer giving way to fall and the law gone back to their pursuit of putting bad guys behind bars, a week wouldn't pass without some kind of situation going down.

The mailboxes in the stairwell were broken into. Junkies began shooting up on the landing. And of course, the building got egged not only on Halloween, but the next five days running. None of these things were as bad as the knife incident, but I was beginning to understand why Lydia had shown such a non-reaction to the break-in attempt on my birthday.

Vic offered to help me get a gun and teach me how to use it. "Not that my own marksmanship is anything to write home about, but I'll show you how to avoid shooting your own dick off."

After witnessing Vic's takedown of Nietzsche, I was beginning to suspect his "all thumbs" routine was nothing more than an act, and he was perfectly capable of blowing holes in anything he cared to aim at. But me? I did some soul-searching and decided I wasn't willing to point a gun at another human being and pull the trigger. Even in self-defense. I did accept a can of pepper spray. No doubt that would make my mother very happy.

I'd spent my morning scrubbing some brown thumbprints off my stairwell that were most definitely not a result of my decorating party with Maxine, given that neither of us was fond of playing with our own excrement, and I was actually hoping that someone would mouth off to me and give me a reason to put them in their place. As an added bonus, I'd get to feel self-righteous for not macing them. If they were lucky, that is. But the next person through the door threw me for a loop. Because not only was she friend, not foe, but she was bubbling over with such unbridled joy, I thought she'd spark the self-igniting incense if she brushed up against it. "Someone's in a good mood," I called over.

Lisa paused by the hand-dyed wall hangings she'd never once given a second glance, and pulled a gauzy, purply number off the rack with a twirl Stevie Nicks would envy. "I'm okay," she said.

Okay? Sure. And the Shedd Aquarium is slightly damp.

I waited to see if she was about to elaborate on her sublime okay-ness, and eventually she meandered her way up to the counter and draped her purple hanging across the plexi.

"There's definitely something different about you," I said.

"My hair is down?"

"Nope. Not your hair. Something else. Some*one* else." She fluttered her eyelashes like she couldn't possibly know what I meant, and I said, "You've practically got little hearts and cherubs floating around your head. So, dish: how hot is he, how big is his dick, and how many times did he rock your world last night?"

She didn't dignify that with an answer, but judging by the shade of crimson she turned, I'd say the answer to the last question was *several*. But most of my gal-pals didn't go into spurt-by-spurt detail like my male friends did, so I relented and said, "Fine, how'd you meet him?"

And with that, her energy faltered.

"Daaang. He's not married, is he?"

"Nuh uh, no way. No one's taking advantage of me like that ever again. He's free and clear and totally available. But...Vic and Jacob aren't gonna like it."

"Why on earth should they care?" Was she seeing one of their exes? Possible, but unlikely. Maybe one of the other PsyPigs, but again, so what? She wasn't even working for the force anymore. But she was pulling a hefty retainer from.... "F-pimp," I announced. "You're bonking one of those peeping toms." She dropped her gaze and I knew I was right. "So he admitted to watching you shower from the hidden camera in your toilet tank and things just got steamier from there?"

She slugged me in the arm. Playfully, though it still hurt—the girl works out. "He's not in surveillance."

Sure, that's what they all said. "I've been known to date against my friends' wishes. You know Carolyn, she didn't mince any words. They get used to it."

"I guess they will." He eyes tracked back and forth as she verified this notion with her inner guidance system. "Eventually."

"But the chemistry is good?"

"It is. But it's not even the romantic stuff that's so incredible. It's like...it's like he really understands me, you know?"

Did I? Who's to say what anybody made of me. Jacob saw a failed psych. My Junior fuck-buddies saw a failed stylist. In fact, none of the guys I dallied with knew me for who I really was. None of those men made the effort to see the real me.

"And I feel like the world is a safer place with him in it. The very first sí-no he hired me to do, I knew he was different. He cared. Spent a bunch of time and effort making sure an empath—a kindergarten teacher—didn't lose her job just because some parents got freaked out and started weird rumors. He's looking out for real people, certified Psychs with regular jobs. Which is more than I can say for the police up here. The minute they figured out how I scored average on my testing...." Her eyes went distant and her lips moved. "Oh my God. He knew. All the way back then. He knew they locked me up. And he was the reason I got out of holding when I did."

"Sounds like a real peach."

"You don't understand, it's a big deal. I could've been stuck there for days...weeks. He didn't have the jurisdiction—I'm not officially certified. He managed it all under the table. At his own expense."

"I'll admit, that's a spiffy way to try and get in someone's pants."

"We didn't know each other yet. I was just a name on a report. He had no reason to try to make an impression." She consulted her sí-no again, and added, "No, he did it because it was the right thing to do."

Between Lisa and me, she was most definitely not the one you'd expect to end up in a jail cell. Even though she would've never struck me as a damsel in distress, I could imagine being sprung from confinement would be the stuff of some pretty hardcore romantic fantasies. Security might not rank with fluttery notions like intrigue and fascination and good, old-fashioned lust. But in the end, there was definitely something to be said for a man who made you feel secure.

CHAPTER 47

It seemed like everyone I knew found my relationship advice indispensable, though given my personal track record, I had no idea why.

It was a slow, mid-week mid-morning. Drunk Tony hadn't started drinking quite yet, though given how worked up he was getting about his lady problems, I suspected his sobriety wouldn't last long. He'd parked himself beside the counter in one of my various folding chairs, but I'd hardly call what he was doing "sitting." With every emphatic statement he made, he jumped up and ran his fingers through his dishwater brown hair, which was sticking out every which way. He was a paunchy middle-aged guy who couldn't really carry off the punk aesthetic, but even so, it was difficult to keep myself from breaking out the hairspray and giving him a good spritz.

"What did you do now?" I asked him.

"Do you want to drive, or should I pick you up? That's what I said."

I considered the new and interesting silhouette into which he'd tugged his hair. "Uh huh."

"Then she said, *It's up to you.*"

I rolled my eyes. "And you believed her and told her to drive herself. Instead of picking her up. Like a gentleman. And it's been how long since she's returned your calls?"

Tony started counting back. I was about to ask if he needed additional fingers and flip him the bird, when the staccato burst of breaking glass startled me so badly, I jumped right up beside him. I didn't only hear it, I *felt* the reverberation through the soles of my boots. If I were on the bus, I would've figured I'd been rear-ended. But I was safe and sound on the second floor of my walk-up. Unlike... Lydia.

I barreled out of the shop and down the stairs, wrenched at her locked door, and started waling on it. "Lydia? Lydia!" The stairwell looked the same as always and whatever had struck the building was over and done, but I didn't know that for sure with my pulse pounding in my ears. "Lydia!"

I considered flinging myself against the door to break it down, but figured the only thing I'd break was my shoulder. The building might be shabby, but it was made of sturdy stuff. While Tony thundered down the stairs hollering, "What happened?" I charged outside.

Lydia's storefront window looked like it had seen the business end of a wrecking ball. Her neon sign was gone, and one curtain was down, pooled on the sidewalk like a puddle of black window-vomit. It looked so wrong, I could hardly believe it was my building, and I stood there for a second, dumbfounded and reeling. But the sound of stomping and harsh laughter pulled me out of my stunned daze.

Fabric shrieked as the remaining curtain was torn from Lydia's window, and a guy swaddled in black material hopped through, then wadded the curtain and tossed it back inside. Lydia's laptop was in his free hand. Another guy called out to him, and passed the cash box through the broken window, then hopped through himself. He had the Buddha-cam tucked under his arm like a football.

"Lydia!" I yelled—and belatedly, I realized it wasn't a great idea to call attention to myself—but the guys didn't even look, just kept on running. I also realized they'd been using the curtains to shield themselves from broken glass on their way through the window. A long shard of plate glass grazed my cheek as I plunged in, but I barely noticed. I was soaring on adrenaline, tripping on visions of Lydia battered to the floor over a shitty laptop and a few hundred bucks. But as I crunched my way through the wreckage of her shop, I soon realized I was blessedly, thankfully, alone.

Only then did it occur to me that if her door was locked, she must've been out.

"Oh my God!" Tony bellowed from out on the sidewalk. "Is she...? Oh my God!"

I couldn't vouch for God, but someone must've been keeping an eye on Lydia. "It's okay," I called back. "She's not here." I had to pick my way back out the broken window, through all the shattered glass, and backtrack up the stairs to find I'd dropped my phone on the second-floor landing. Luckily it hadn't met the same fate as Lydia's window. My hands were shaking so hard I nearly called half a dozen of my old clients in my attempt to get hold of my neighbor. She answered in a few rings to the ambient noise of a checkout line scanner doing its rhythmic beeps. "What's up?"

As calmly as possible, I said, "Someone broke into your shop." And I really had to hand it to myself, it sounded a hell of a lot better than *We're freaking out because we thought you'd been murdered.*

Lydia processed the information for a few seconds, then sighed, and summed everything up with, "Well, fuck."

While we waited for Lydia, Tony paced in a tight circle between Lydia's couches, which matched even more marginally by the daylight now streaming into the room. "What's the world coming to these days," he ranted. "People used to care about their neighbors, man. They had a sense of compassion. Humanity. Nowadays no one gives a shit about anyone but themselves."

"Calm down. You're more upset about it than she was."

When Lydia got home, she surveyed the damage wearily. "I'm getting too old for this crap," she said. "Look at this—those morons tagged my wall. And for what? I'm outside their stupid territorial pissing contests." She picked up her precog certification, which had fallen from its hanger. The frame was out of whack. She pressed it back into alignment, only somewhat successfully, and sighed. "I thought folks on this side of the tracks had a healthier respect for the mystical. If anything, they should be scared of me."

"Should they?" I wondered. "I don't know if that's necessarily a good thing."

Lydia gathered up a plaster Shakti from the floor. Then she retrieved one of Shakti's six arms. And sighed again.

"Don't worry," I said. Snow and diesel exhaust were wafting in from the street. "We'll figure this out." Lydia continued to stare at the mess as if she hadn't even heard me. I glanced down at the bags she'd dropped inside the doorway and recognized the bottle of a certain cake flavored vodka. I grabbed it and hustled her back to the kitchen to give her something to do besides staring at the wreckage. "Sit." I cracked the seal and poured a shot. "Drink."

I took one for myself, too. It was no better at ten a.m. than at midnight. I poured her another.

"I got this, okay?" I grabbed her phone out of her pocket, pulled up Pinterest, and handed it back to her. "You just sit back, put your feet up, and get some new decorating ideas. First thing in the morning, we'll start hitting the thrift shops to put together your new look."

Back in her waiting room, Drunk Tony was oblivious to my efforts to keep a cool head. "This is bad," he said. "Really bad."

"Dude, chill."

"Next thing you know, it's not just the property that gets hurt."

"Not helping."

"Really bad...." He started pacing through broken glass—crunch, crunch, crunch—mumbling, "This is bad, this is bad, what're we gonna do?"

"Call the landlord," I suggested. Not that I thought he'd be much help, but it kept Tony occupied. Meanwhile, I cycled through all the cop friends in my address book, only to find none of them answering their phones. I supposed they were all too busy dealing with life-and-death-and-afterlife situations to worry about a broken window.

Since the police I personally knew were busy snubbing me, I called the general non-emergency line and was told some officers would be around to take a statement. After that, I figured I could at least call an insurance agent, but Lydia was vague about her carrier. I didn't think she was all that drunk yet, so I let it slide. Tony had no luck tracking down the building's owner, either.

"At the very least," Tony said, "we've gotta get this window boarded up."

It was disturbing how many board-up services there were to choose from. Even more disturbing was how much they charged, and Lydia with no insurance company to reimburse her for the expense. "You've got a truck," I said to Tony, "right? Let's just get some wood and do the damn job ourselves."

Between the three of us, we scraped together the cost of a few sheets of particleboard. Barely.

By the time the law finally showed, Tony was off on his wood-gathering mission, and I'd put on a pot of coffee while Lydia had drunk herself to a spirit-induced facsimile of calm. I tucked the vodka into the cupboard when a uniformed officer took her statement, and my statement too, since I was the only one to actually see the two creeps. I was dismayed by how little physical description I could dredge up. The only thing that stuck with me was how they felt inside, reckless and arrogant, and disturbingly hardened. I didn't suppose most cops would find that observation much to go by. Not the ones assigned to petty crime, anyway.

"Doesn't matter what you saw or didn't see," Lydia told me, once the cop was gone. She articulated very clearly, I noticed, but she was speaking just a bit too loud to be sober. "Pig's gonna write it up, dump it in a file, and that's as far as things will go."

Normally, I'd ask if she actually knew that—as a precog—or if she was just feeling pessimistic. But she was obviously in no mood for banter.

"Ever wonder what it would be like to get a do-over?" she asked wistfully.

Part of me thought my life was nothing if not a series of do-overs, disappointing re-takes that left me sadder, older and deeper in debt.

My knowledge of construction workers doesn't go much beyond hard hats and nudie calendars, but I can drive a nail if someone tells me where to put it. It took us a while, but between Tony and me, we managed to board up the window and clean up the debris. Lydia, meanwhile, worked on her nasty vodka. I can't blame her—it's what I would've done. But by the time we had everything set to rights, she staggered out from the back looking bleary and haggard, and said, "How am I supposed to sleep with all this noise? Get out of here and give me some fucking peace and quiet."

Tony shot back with, "Well, that's the last time I board up your goddamn window," but I steered him out the door before things escalated beyond the griping stage.

That left the two of us alone. I wanted to give Lydia a hug, but I knew she wouldn't abide the pity. So I just said, "You pick out some color schemes by the next time we talk, or I'm picking them out for you."

"You too," she said.

"What's that supposed to mean?"

"Get the hell out of here and go do something fun. I don't want you hovering around, treating me like some pathetic old biddy who needs your babysitting."

Hold on a sec, I was supposed to be the empath, not her. But I put on a brave face and said, "A tough old broad like you? Never."

CHAPTER 48

Normally, I don't get to go to the Saturday afternoon meditation meetups at Rainbow Dharma because I'm too busy trying to keep my store afloat. But no one who came into Sticks and Stones that day was looking for anything other than the juicy gossip of what happened to Lydia's front window. Bad enough living through the experience once. I wasn't about to continue feeding the schadenfreude of a bunch of nosy rubberneckers.

Rainbow Dharma meets in the back room of a dilapidated consignment shop called Still Goods. You'd think the brown-on-brown decor of chipped linoleum and oppressive paneling would get depressing, but no. It was intriguing. The meeting room housed the store's overflow, and it was never the same furniture twice.

The store itself isn't subject to the laws of physics. It's been renovated and added on to so many times over the decades that the rooms sprawl into one another endlessly. I mean that literally. I've never found the back of the building. I suspect it might actually be a wormhole to another dimension—one that's never moved past 1975.

Most of the place smelled of mothballs and old wood. But as I made my way through room after room of vintage clothes and antique furniture, the closer I got to the get-together, the grandma's attic smell gave way to coffee and curry. One good thing about hanging out with Buddhists is that there's always plenty I can eat. Even the omnivores at the potlucks tended to bust out their very best vegetarian efforts. Unfortunately, not all of them are particularly palatable.

For instance, take Red's doppelganger, Latrell—the guy whose Facebook picture nearly gave me a freaking coronary the first time I saw it. In person, he felt nothing like Red. Not only did he have dubious taste in music, but he was also phenomenally easygoing...if somewhat vapid. Plus, he's never once called me *Curtis*.

I spotted him over by a herd of ancient sewing machine cabinets, lovingly stirring the contents of a crockpot, and I'd bet my last five dollars that thing was brimming with mushy lentils. Unlike Red, Latrell wasn't even remotely psychic. If he was, he'd realize that no one actually wanted the recipe he continually tried to give out. I'd personally refused his offer at least half a dozen times.

He glanced up from his soupy legumes and said, "Hey, Crash, how you feel?"

I didn't really want to get into the whole break-in, but I'm averse to pretending I'm fine when I'm not. "I suppose I've had better days."

"Well, you know what they say. Pain is inevitable. Suffering is optional."

I stopped myself, barely, from demanding to know why he bothered asking if he was just going to belittle my experience with an empty platitude. Latrell was harmless. And as much as I love to speak my truth, I sometimes find it's less destructive to walk away.

I joined my cronies in a room with shelves of dusty knick-knacks on the walls and cushions on the floor, and once all the greetings were exchanged and we'd settled into position, the room went quiet, and together, we sat.

It was as soothing a place as I could expect anywhere to be. I was comfortable with the people and the ritual. Even so, bringing my focus back to my breath was damn near impossible. Sensory flashes of my morning kept replaying in my mind. The feel of the brick shattering the glass. The sound of my combat boots crunching through the broken shards. The brutal triumph of the looters as they scampered away.

Dumb idea, to come and sit when I was too wound up to have any chance of calming down. Calling meditation a *practice* seemed all too apt. It should have been soothing. But as endeavors went, my search for enlightenment felt repetitive, grueling, and all-around lame.

Time after time, I nudged my attention back toward my breath. And time after time, I failed. From the sighs of the tattooed chick behind me, to the sound of the store's customers tramping through a distant room, to the smell of Latrell's mushy lentils, my attention focused everywhere but the place I was aiming. If I'd been at home, I would have given up a long time ago, but here, I was trapped in a bevy of earnest, queer Buddhists. And so I kept my ass glued to the damn cushion.

In the scheme of things, forty-five minutes isn't long. Enough time for a simple haircut or a satisfying roll in the hay. But a forty-five minute meditation attempt when you're just not feeling it lasts approximately forever. My nose itched, my ass was asleep, and I was famished enough to knock back a bowl of lentils. But I didn't. I sat.

I'm not sure when, exactly, things shifted, but I do know this: the moment I surrendered, everything changed. The people around me became so much more than hokey sayings and unpalatable vegetarian cuisine—they hadn't changed, but my perception of them had.

The group lit up in my mind's eye like a string of twinkling fairy lights, and their emotions flooded my usual barriers. Not perfect. Here and there, self-consciousness and jealousy and annoyance bled through. But overwhelmingly, the group radiated a sturdy and enveloping calm.

Surrender...I'd always considered it to be a weakness. A lack of determination. A character flaw. As the experience unfolded, though, I understood an entirely new facet of the idea. Surrender wasn't defeat. In fact, I was welcome to keep right on fighting if I really wanted to. But to voluntarily lay down my struggle and be open to goodness all around me was, in my case, an act not only of strength, but, dare I say, maturity.

Tranquility bloomed around me as my anahata chakra balanced. I personally suffered the curse of so many extroverts: too much fire and not enough fuel. If I cared to visualize, I would have seen the chakra as a green pinwheel turning just behind my breastbone—but

I didn't bother. When it eased into alignment, I *felt* it, and I trusted that feeling a heck of a lot more than anything that might translate through the visual brain.

The Psych test I'd bombed so long ago was water under the bridge that's long since dried up. But it was obvious now that I'd expended so much energy pushing against it, there was no possible way I could have scored. And if I took the test again, things would be different. It wasn't a matter of knowing what I knew, but feeling what I felt. And for an empath, that distinction makes all the difference in the world.

It was tempting to start creeping down the path of "what if?" and daydream about all the ways in which psychic certification could turn my life around, but spinning out fantasies, however pleasant, is not the point of mindfulness practice. I acknowledged the thought, nudged it gently aside, and focused once again on my breath.

The forty-five minutes stretched. Suspended, I felt timeless, but not only was I no longer eager to get up and reinstate my circulation, but I felt preemptively disappointed that at some point, the meditation would come to a close.

Everything changes. Yet another dumb saying…but it really is true. Just as I settled in to the sensation of balance, that serene and open place of allowing, the energy in the room spiked as the Vibe to end all Vibes hit me so hard, it nearly knocked me off my cushion.

Even before the meditation's leader gave the all-clear, I opened my eyes. Confusion. From across the room, I found Latrell standing there, stark against a backdrop of antique washboards and battered tin road signs—and he was staring at me, Vibing his heart out like I'd just declared his beans were delicious. For the life of me, I couldn't fathom what was going through his head. We'd never clicked in any meaningful way, so intellectually, we were no great match. And physically? He preferred rugged guys with meat on their bones and hair on their backs. Unless there were lentils involved, it was unlike Latrell to give me more than a passing glance.

Some primitive corner of my brain realized what was going on a heartbeat before what I was really seeing consciously registered. The guy standing there Vibing at me hard enough to rattle the tchotchkes on the wall wasn't Latrell at all.

It was Red.

I didn't just *see* it was him, I felt it. His essence was familiar and foreign all at once, because back when we'd spent forty plus hours per week in one another's gravitational pulls, I'd lacked confidence that my empathic ability was anything more than a shrewd assessment of small tells. But no way was Red projecting anything physically. Outside, it was exquisite posture and a slight widening of the eyes. But inside, he was scoured by a torrent of emotions. Surprise over finding me here. Joy at the sight of me. Regret from being gone so long. Fear that I'd be angry.

I was.

Not just angry, though, but stunned and elated, baffled and chagrined. Emotion roared through my newly balanced chakras, blowing them wide open. So much for alignment. At the sight of Red, I felt raw. Scorched.

And, indeed...angry.

I sprang up from the cushion and practically vaulted over the folks seated between me and the door. Red backed into the next room. I trapped him between an ugly credenza and a bookshelf full of chipped vases, planted my hands on my hips, and said, "Funny seeing you here."

"I needed a few things." He cast around awkwardly as if something useful might appear amidst all the weird tchotchkes. "And I was hoping to see some folks I knew at Rainbow Dharma. I didn't realize you'd started coming."

"A lot can change in two years. I've expanded my horizons. But you? I thought you'd dropped off the face of the earth. Rumor had it you were on the West Coast, but it looked more like you'd gone into witness protection."

"I went somewhere I could think."

"Where? A Siberian bunker?"

He smiled at that, not with amusement, but a hint of sadness. It was a familiar enough expression on him, though I'd never grasped the subtle nuances. Not in any way I was willing to appreciate. When I turned so as not to block the feeble light eking through the glass block windows and got a better look at him, I comprehended several details I'd missed. His mohawk was gone, which was why I'd initial-ly mistaken him for Latrell. Now he wore his hair in a short fade. His cheekbones looked more pronounced, his jawline more chiseled. But the overall bittersweet hint of melancholia was something that I suspected had always been there. I just hadn't had the capacity to see it.

"Things needed figuring out," he said. "How I managed to get where I was. Why my intentions didn't seem to matter. Whether my vocation had any real value."

Every time I suffered another setback, all those things and more went through my head. And the notion that Red and I thought so much alike was baffling.

"I didn't think you'd understand," he told me, "but now, finding you here, maybe I'm wrong. After I left, I joined a sangha."

People tend to think living in community involves putting on funny robes, handing out religious tracts and begging for bread. Not nowadays. I'd never personally had the cash or the time to indulge, but plenty of Rainbow Dharma did. They'd book weekend retreats at ritzy meditation centers, then come back bragging about how they were now so phenomenally in touch with themselves...when obvi-ously they were just in it for the gourmet vegetarian meals and the opportunity to turn off their phones for a day and a half.

"And then what?"

"And then I decided I was ready to leave, and I came here."

"Why, you wore out your welcome?"

He considered his answer for a pause most people would've found uncomfortably long, then said, "I came to a decision."

Two years. Red has always held himself above the level of us mere mortals. Now, with two years of hardcore spiritual practice under his belt, he was bound to be totally insufferable. The potluck buffet I'd been gearing up for was now as appetizing as the dusty knicknacks on the wall, and I came to a decision myself, turned away from him, and walked out the door.

CHAPTER 49

It was a maddening walk home. Part of me wished I'd come up with a scathing parting remark, but part of me was relieved I hadn't. I was leery of that second part, since it was setting its sights on the impossible.

Red Turner had always been just out of reach—and I'm not only talking about those near-miss kisses. All the stolen moments I'd spent gazing at his reflection in the salon mirrors must've added up to a significant chunk of time. But it's phenomenally unsatisfying to fall for a reflection.

My thoughts were a jumble. It was cold outside, but I hardly felt it. I walked around for a couple of hours—until the dinner crowd gave way to the unsavory panhandler crowd—then headed home. Graffiti was already accumulating on Lydia's fresh plywood. If the universe had any mercy, it would spare her the sight of it until the landlord replaced the window, but I wasn't going to tempt fate by checking on her.

I snuck upstairs and made it to my bed without waking her, then climbed under the covers and tossed and turned myself to sleep. Who did Red think he was, traipsing back into my life out of nowhere?

What kind of idiot would I be if I let him slip through my fingers again?

After a fitful night's sleep, I woke up no more rested than I'd gone to bed. I rolled to face Miss Mattie's snapshot, which was currently wedged between my clock radio and a stack of lucid dreaming books. "It's stupid of me to want this guy," I asked her, "isn't it? I should've learned my lesson about falling for arrogant bastards by now. Right?"

Mattie smiled back from the photo and said nothing.

As I rolled out of bed, it occurred to me to have a look at the graffiti by the cold light of day. I threw on last night's clothes and crept down the stairs, marker in hand, to survey the damage.

Gang tags. I couldn't tell you which specific gang, but they all have the same rushed, jagged quality to them. Once the gangbangers marked the turf, other random assholes who just so happened to be carrying around markers decided the plywood was fair game. In addition to the tags, there was some random scribbling and a few choice swear words, but dominating the tableau was a ginormous, erect dick protruding from a cushion of hairy balls.

Just what our customers needed to see.

Or Red. Not that I was hoping he'd come by. But he might.

I got to work scribbling out the graffiti, but it took a fair amount of elbow grease to make it look anything other than dick-shaped. My arm was sore by the time Lydia discovered me on her way home from the overpriced coffee shop down the block. "Isn't that the same shirt you had on yesterday?" she asked.

I shrugged.

"Well, good. You're young. You should be out sowing your oats, not sitting home and worrying about me." The only oats I'd sown lately were stuck to my microwave carousel, but I neither confirmed nor denied her presumption that she'd intercepted my walk of shame.

Did Lydia have any customers booked? Did she need help cleaning up? Would she let me make good on my threat to revamp her digs in thrift store chic? In the past, I would have pressed her on those issues, but I knew her well enough by now to realize that if I got too pushy, I'd only piss her off again.

Yesterday, I'd had to invent a reason to make myself scarce, but today there were people to see and places to smudge. I headed back up to get my stuff together. The cannery is gigantic, and I didn't want to run out of herbs halfway through. I was on my tiptoes, nudging a box of resin off a high shelf, when the shop door opened. My first thought was annoyance that I'd left it unlocked. I never do that, not since my tablet was stolen. But then the Vibe washed over me, and I realized the unlocked door felt like a tiny piece of the grand mosaic. I stared hard at the shelf without seeing it as longing washed over me, hopeless and resigned.

Red spoke. "What I said at Rainbow Dharma about deciding to come back...there's more to it."

"Is that so? I never would have guessed."

"Would you at least look at me, Curtis?"

I turned around and crossed my arms, and imagined a barrier of protective energy springing up between the two of us. "I've got two minutes. So talk."

Before he could, someone else barged through the door, a chunky, windburned guy pushing a stroller—a big one that would never fit down the aisles. "We're closed," I snapped, and he completely ignored me because he was too busy talking to someone named Joey.

"Joey, come here. Joey...Joey, come over here. Joey."

A three-ish kid squeezed past the stroller, darted up to the books, and started plucking them out of the rack and dumping them on the floor.

"Come back during store hours, and leave that monstrosity on wheels at home."

"Joey," the dad pleaded, with utter ineffectiveness. He was too busy trying to disengage the stroller from a soap display to stop the kid.

"You're about to be the proud new owner of several copies of the *I Ching Workbook*," I told the guy.

The stroller screeched free, and the dad lurched after his kid. "Joey! Joey, come here. Right now. I'm gonna count to five."

Joey kicked a book aside and darted toward the prayer candles. "Hey, kid," I yelled. "You really don't want to mess with those."

"Five...four...three...."

I had my doubts that counting down to one had ever resulted in getting the little darling to do anything other than what he damn well pleased. But at the end of the countdown, I'd be itching to slap Mr.

Dad upside the head.

Red was closest to Joey. He hunkered down beside the kid so they were eye to eye, and in those low, soothing tones of his, said, "Hey, you want to look at these? Let's do it carefully and make sure nothing breaks."

They locked eyes. Joey stopped, transfixed by Red's hypnotic gaze, and turned the Fast Luck candle around in his grasp, slowly, deliberately. And then, just as deliberately, he flung it down. There was a thunk of glass on hardwood. Prayer candles don't shatter, the glass is too thick, but they're still breakable. A few heavy shards went spinning off, and Joey's dad scooped him up, looking at me helplessly.

"Just...go," I told him. And he jammed his brat into the oversized stroller and proceeded to squeeze him back out the door, which I promptly locked behind him. Red, meanwhile, crouched down to collect the broken glass. I was worried he'd cut himself. Either that or I was kind of hoping he would. "You too," I told him. "Time's up."

"Not until I say what I need to say." He cupped the broken glass to his solar plexus, shielding it like a hatchling fallen from the nest, and said, "I'm sorry you got caught up in the middle of Ralph and me."

"Gimme a break. That's not yours to apologize for—you didn't know. It's not as if Ralph announced that he had the entire staff pants-down over a barrel. I can't even fault you for not knowing he was a sociopath. It took me longer than it should have to wise up to his twisted mind-games myself. But the way you let me walk out of Luscious alone? That's what still burns."

"It was a mistake. A big mistake."

"And it took you two fucking years to come to that conclusion?"

"I don't blame you for being angry," he said. It's so unsatisfying to argue with someone who keeps insisting they're wrong. I held my hands out for the glass, and he handed it over with exquisite care. What would we have done without that Joey brat? Thanks to him, we could both stare at the broken shards to avoid looking at each other. "I'd be surprised if you weren't upset. But, please, believe me when I say that each and every day I've been regretting the choices I made."

No doubt he had plenty of time for self-reflection while he was meditating with suburban yoga moms and sipping organic green smoothies at his cushy Buddhist va-cay. I turned away and dropped the glass into the nearest wastebasket. "You know what they say about regret. That and fifty cents will buy you a cup of who-gives-a-shit."

"Curtis...."

"No. Just...no. I'm sure you're sorry. I believe you're brimming with enough good intentions to pave a road to Shangri-La. But you dropped off the face of the earth, with zero indication you'd ever be back. So, as sincere as your apology may be, I'm just not up for it. Not today. I'm slated for a house smudging," I glanced at my phone, "right now."

To demonstrate that I actually was busy, I tapped Vic's scowling contact pic, dismissing my conversation with Red before I said anything I couldn't unsay.

Red must've been itching to have the last word, but it was clear I wasn't in any mood to hear it. He gazed at me sadly for a moment, then slipped out the door and shut it quietly behind him. I cradled the phone on my shoulder, turned to my shelves and began jamming things into my bag—charcoal, copal, frankincense, sacred salts and sage bundles. Part of me was very satisfied with itself. But part of me suspected the satisfaction of driving him off again would be cold comfort indeed.

When Vic answered, I said, "I hope you don't expect me to take a bus in this weather."

"Actually, I'm right downstairs."

I found him out on the sidewalk staring at the dick-shaped scribble, and nudged him toward his car. "Let's go," I said. "Jacob wants me to be extra thorough. Says he's worried you're all bringing home FPMP energy. I'm not sure if that's even possible...but why take chances?"

Vic shrugged awkwardly.

I climbed into the car, strapped in, sighed, and said, "I just don't get people. Take this wholesaler I've been dealing with. Part of their order arrives damaged, and when I exchange it, suddenly I'm stuck with a shipping surcharge for not meeting their minimum order. Now customer service says they can't change the computer. Come on, man, I wasn't born yesterday. Add a fucking credit. How hard can it be?"

"Probably not very...uh...."

"But I explain the situation, and all I get for my trouble is some drone parroting back the shipping policy. It's right there on the site. I can read it. I have eyes."

"Sure."

"I'd even take that credit in merchandise on my next order. I'm flexible. And I'm sure as hell not out to take advantage of anybody."

"Yeah. I mean, no."

"But there's flexible, and there's flexible. Someone takes advantage of your good nature, it's up to you to make sure it doesn't happen again. It's naive to expect anyone to change their stripes once they've already proven they're not reliable."

"I wonder where that stripe expression came from," Vic blurted out in a valiant attempt to change the subject. "Maybe a nautical reference? Or the way they repaint a parking lot but you still see the old traffic lines peeking through once the black paint on top of them starts to wear off. Plus they're shinier than the blacktop around them."

Right.

It occurred to me that I didn't feel quite as passionate about Midwest Waxworks as it appeared, and I had my panties in a twist over something else entirely. "I don't know how you can stomach the whole relationship thing. Because it's not like anyone ever does what you expect them to do."

After an awkward pause, Vic said, "That's true."

"Like this guy Red, who waltzes back into town expecting to pick right up where we left off, like I've just been sitting here for the past couple of years, waiting around for him to come to his senses. You don't just leave when things get tough, and then come strutting back. And go around acting like everything's fine and dandy."

Red's leaving was bad enough. But as I walked through the ugly love triangle with Vic—a sordid tale I'd never told anyone—I saw precisely which jagged edge had cut my heart the deepest. "Red could've made a choice: the owner, or me." But instead, he'd chosen no one.

"I'm boyfriend material," I said. "I'm the type of guy you'd consider settling down with. Right? I'm not bad to look at. I can hold up my end of a conversation. I'm actually fairly easygoing on most subjects, and open to negotiation on most others. As for the deal breakers... well, I'd never diddle around with someone to begin with if they weren't a decent human at heart." Not anymore, now that I'd seen the error of my ways. I'd never go so far as to be grateful to Ralph for teaching me about human nature, but I'd sure as hell learned my lesson.

CHAPTER 50

I've heard that funerals benefit the living more than the dead. I suspect you could say the same thing for a house blessing. Bad juju is real, no doubt, though I'm not convinced that it clings to wood and brick, asphalt and concrete, as tenaciously as my PsyCop buddies think. But Vic would exude such relief whenever I shored up the cannery's psychic defenses, I decided the best course of action was to keep my mouth shut and take the sweaty wads of bills he pressed into my hand.

I'm not big on prayers—they're too much like begging, for my taste. But I did approach the monthly smudging with as much intention as I could muster. Starting at the front door, I got my sage bundle smoldering and walked the perimeter of the main floor. Their loft was spotless, as usual, though the giant "temporary" tent in the living room was still there, with a fine sifting of dust across the top that would send the clean freak into a tiz if he ever noticed it.

Vic skulked around while I worked, edging away like he was afraid of contaminating the proceedings. It would be useless to tell him his ramped-up energy wasn't inherently flawed. He wouldn't believe me. And besides, who was I to rob him of his hard-earned discomfort?

While he hovered around the dining room table, I made the rounds—kitchen, bath, basement and stairwell—then headed upstairs, where the normal-height ceilings felt cramped compared to the wide open spaces down below. Jacob was parked in front of his desktop with the screensaver running, working instead on a small, dated laptop he'd planted where the keyboard normally went. I didn't ask.

Back downstairs, I skirted the nylon dome and joined Vic at the dining room table, where he was shaving some cardboard off a jigsaw piece with a pair of dull, plastic-handled scissors.

"Two years is nothing." He didn't look up from his arts-n-crafts as he spoke, but there was no doubt his attention was on me. "I've been in the same situation before. Only I was the other guy. The jagoff who left."

Vic wasn't one to spill his secrets to just anybody, so whenever he was willing to talk, I listened. I watched him shove the piece partway into a hole, pry it back out, and start reworking another one of the tabs. I sat, and I waited. Eventually, he said, "Camp Hell. It was a shitty situation. No love triangle, but plenty of lies to go around, and veiled threats, and rumors. I ditched my boyfriend there, and it took me fourteen years to wonder what had become of him." He snorted. Gently, but a few flecks of cardboard went skittering across the tacky puzzle he was bent on destroying. "If that doesn't take the asshole trophy, I don't know what does."

"Maybe there is no trophy. Just a certificate of participation for everyone involved."

Vic rotated the piece and snapped it into place—the place it was actually supposed to go—with its mangled edges facing the jagged gap he was trying to fill. "It's not that I didn't care." He brushed some cardboard slivers into his palm, stared at them for a second, then tipped them into the pocket of his flannel shirt. "More like I had to work up to it because it was all so intense, I couldn't deal with it until I was ready."

It was definitely food for thought. Red and I, both of us had changed. It seemed inconceivable we might both be in the right place to synch up, but maybe, finally, we were. Vic dropped me off to open up the store, and I was so deep in thought, I nearly jumped out of my skin when Lydia swung open her door at the sound of me rattling my warped mailbox.

"Aha, it is you!" she said. "And who was that?"

"Who was what?"

"The one who just drove away. Your handsome new beau?"

"As if."

"About time you finally hooked up. I've been dreaming about that guy for at least a month."

She turned around and marched back into her boarded-up shop, and I followed, hot on her heels. "What guy?"

"The black guy with the technicolor hair and the cute butt." When I made a sputtering noise, she said, "What? I might be old, but I'm not dead."

"He's not a hookup."

"Booty call. Friends with benefits. Pelvic affiliate. Whatever you're going by these days—who can keep up with the vocabulary?"

"Red Turner is plenty of things to me, but fuck-buddy sure ain't one of 'em."

"Whatever you say." Lydia gave me a finger-wave and a knowing look as I escaped upstairs to open the shop with zero minutes to spare. I did my best to put the conversation out of my mind over the course of the day, but in the lulls between customers, her words kept repeating like an old episode of Clairvoyage...because in all the time I'd known her, she'd never once claimed to have dreamt anything about me, and her newfound psychic scrutiny had me spooked.

One thing you can always count on in Clairvoyage. Ten minutes before the show ends, there's a big revelation that changes everything. It might seem unrealistic that something so pivotal can happen in such a small amount of time, but it can. A quick call to a Rainbow Dharma pal yielded the name of the sangha where Red had spent the past couple of years. I plugged it into a search engine expecting to find a bunch of cheesy sayings accompanied by photos of stone stacks or bamboo. Instead, I got a stiff dose of reality.

Divine Mind Center had a bare-bones website that stretched beyond minimal, reached past utilitarian, and landed firmly in ugly. Not a single artistic stock photo to be found, just shots of a plain, drab facility.

The place itself wasn't what gave me pause, though. It was the people.

No trendy organic cotton yoga gear. The monks wore traditional ochre robes. Everyone else had on some sort of homespun beige pajamas that made them look like hospital patients or prisoners. And as much as the fakely sublime facial expressions of cover models on meditation books always irk me to no end, the blank stares of the mendicants were far more disturbing. It wasn't minimalist. It was barren.

The sangha's rules and regulations were just as extreme. Mandatory silence. Cramped cells that contained a single, narrow cot. And the food? Let's just say mushy lentils would've been extravagant. In an effort to discourage attachment, luxury items were prohibited. I'd never considered my personal idea of luxury to be particularly re-fined. The sangha didn't even allow their people a comfortable chair. Compared to Divine Mind Center, I was living like a Rockefeller.

Of course, if anyone knows how to stand for eight hours a day without breaking a sweat, it's Red. But it wasn't the physical hardship that would have gotten to him, but the dreariness. I scoured each page, attempting to place Red in the facility, but no matter how I tried, I couldn't wrap my head around it. Red was nourished by color. I was pondering how he'd managed to survive two years without it when he showed up yet again.

In light of what I'd seen on the website, the changes in Red were undeniable. His cheekbones were more prominent not because I'd misremembered them, but because he'd been living off tepid water and self-abnegation.

His changes weren't just physical. While his body was now hard-er, he felt softer inside. And maybe I was too.

I turned toward the cash drawer and started battening down the hatches with much more attention than I needed to, mostly so he couldn't see how hard I was struggling with the thought of his trans-formation costing him two solid years of hard penance. "You look like you could use something to eat."

"That sounds like an invitation," he said with cautious playfulness.

"You can't walk ten steps around here without tripping over a restaurant." I dimmed the overhead lights and grabbed my coat. "Let's go."

I followed him down the stairs, and as I passed by Lydia's door, it opened. Just a crack, but enough for me to see one of her eyes, and part of the other. She smiled and waggled her eyebrows as if to say, *I caught you with the hot guy you claim you're not screwing.*

I gave her a single "yeah, right" headshake in return, but it was great to see her smile again. As we passed the board-up on our way out, I recast the front window in my mind's eye a half-dozen times, with various shades of boho and paisley, red velvet and beads. And for the first time since the break-in, I really could imagine Lydia's shop rising from the ashes even more awesome than it was before.

Businesses reinvented themselves all the time. Take the restaurant on the corner. Since I'd opened Sticks and Stones, it had evolved from a tapas joint to an upscale cafe, and more recently, a pretentious locavore eatery. A quick glance showed the vestibule jam-packed with hipsters waiting to be seated, so the food must've been okay. But when I peered through the window, I saw meat on every plate. "Let's keep going," I said. "I'm guessing the local vegetarian option in November leaves something to be desired.

"Don't worry about me," Red said. "Pick anyplace. I'll find something to eat."

"About that. I'm on the bandwagon these days too—and I need something way more substantial than a salad." Hell, both of us did.

We paused beneath a streetlight where stray snowflakes meandered above our heads. Red turned to me and gave me his full consideration. Looking *at* me, or looking *into* me? I wanted so badly to play it cool, to hide the fact that my heart felt half-broken, but shored up with a tenuous and dangerous hope. Since he picked up different signals than I did, maybe I could even get away with it.

CHAPTER 51

When none of the half-dozen restaurants panned out, Red casually offered to cook. I casually accepted. And both of us knew damn well the invitation had nothing to do with food.

He drove an aging Camry a lot like the one he'd owned when we worked at Luscious. The inside of this car smelled of sandalwood too. How incongruous, that anything about him should be the same after all this time. Especially when I'd shed skin after skin after skin.

He threaded his way through the side streets and back to his same old neighborhood, but a different street. On the north side, there's a brick courtyard building within spitting distance of basically any-where, and I'd wager his new apartment wouldn't be much different from the old one.

Good thing I'm not the betting type. His old apartment had been minimal and uncluttered. This one? It took austerity to an entirely new level. It was a plain studio, maybe twelve by twenty, with brown woodwork, white walls, and a pale oak hardwood floor. Not a stick of real furniture to be seen, just a futon on the floor. No color to be seen, either, aside from a purple meditation cushion in the corner and a crimson duvet on the futon. Hard to say if it was restful, or just empty. Either way, it felt different from the way Sticks and Stones had after I'd sold off all my furniture. My empty room smacked of poverty. His, deliberate asceticism.

Since leaning against the wall would look ridiculous—and I wasn't willing to go sit on his bed—I took off my coat, an itchy woolen army surplus deal, then dropped it to the floor and sat on it. I couldn't tell if he felt awkward about having no place for a guest to sit. His energy was so tied up in knots, who's to say where his discomfort began or ended?

From my vantage point on the floor, his cupboards looked as bare as the rest of the place. There was a bag from Still Goods on the counter. He pulled out a saucepan and two dishes. Once he gave the pot a quick scrub, he filled it with water and put it on to boil, then began soaping up the plates. "What I told you at Rainbow Dharma was only half the truth," he said. "I did need some things. But I was hoping to run into someone I knew and trusted, someone who shopped at your store, who knew you...the way you are now. Who could tell me why, of all the businesses you could have gone into, you chose what you did."

"I've been known to wonder that myself," I admitted. "I suppose I was reacting to the stuff on the surface—the so-called Psychs churning up melodrama for their own personal gain, the dicks who use spirituality to take advantage of the vulnerable. But the opposite of love isn't hate, it's indifference. And I've never been indifferent to matters of the soul."

Red grabbed a box of spaghetti and a jar of sauce from the cupboard. The last man to make dinner for me had been Jacob—with a raft of fancy kitchen appliances, fresh pasta, and sauce from scratch. I'd never fully appreciated how two willful, intelligent, complicated men could be so very different.

He broke the noodles into the boiling water, then turned the gravity of his attention to me. "Do you know what it takes to become a monk? To embrace the spiritual and release the material? I've seen what greed and attachment can do. I've lived it. And I was sure that was what I wanted, to put all my focus on my practice. To be ordained."

My heart began to pound.

"For day-to-day living, all the men at the sangha shaved their own heads, even the laity. But there was more ceremony around the ordination, where an elder would do the trimming. Having someone else put those clippers to my head...it jogged loose a memory. A memory of you."

Water hissed as the pasta boiled over, and Red moved it to another burner.

"I stopped him and didn't go through with the ceremony. I had to figure out if I was taking vows because I had a calling, or because I was hiding behind them so I didn't have to face you again."

On Clairvoyage, whenever they show a tidal wave big enough to capsize the ship, they do it in slow motion, in CGI, with lots of dramatic lighting. That's exactly how it was, looking into Red's eyes. Just like the captain on that idiotic show, I knew how dangerous navigating these waters would be. And just like that bullheaded character, I was going to go on ahead and make the decision to drown myself.

I'd been angry with Red, when he walked away from me that fateful day, for not choosing me. I saw now that he hadn't only given up our relationship. He'd sacrificed every other thing in his life.

I'd wanted him to suffer. And he had.

He handed me a plate of spaghetti, then sat down on the floor beside me and ate. I snuck looks at his chiseled cheekbones while he sucked up the noodles, and pondered how long he'd been overworked and underfed. How long he'd been marched around barefoot and shorn.

How long he'd gone without sex.

Not all Buddhists are celibate, just like we don't all give up Big Macs and leather belts. Between the different paths and schools of thought, the specifics can really vary. But after seeing those photos, I had no doubt that all this time, Red had denied himself such basic companionship and comfort. Not just because the sangha had demanded it, but because it fed the part of his soul that kept insisting he hold himself to some unattainable standard.

I put down my half-eaten dinner and took his hand, cradled it in mine as if it was fragile—or maybe, like shards of a broken prayer candle, the gesture could cut us both if we didn't treat it gingerly.

"Let me tell *you* a story," I said. "Once upon a time I had a chip on

my shoulder and a level of entitlement that was positively sickening.
I didn't realize how good I had it. I was a decent enough person—I'd
swerve to avoid running over a squirrel, and I'd chip in when folks
collected for some random charity—but I felt pissed off and abandoned by some folks, and smothered by everyone else. Basically, I
was a spoiled brat who was used to having everything I wanted...but
I couldn't have you."

"Curtis...."

"Don't you dare apologize. I'm not done." I contorted so we were
face to face and forced him to meet my eyes. He needed to see himself the way I saw him. His own worst enemy. Beautiful and tragic,
poignant and perfect. I had no idea how his telepathy worked, but I
drummed up the best visual of him that I could and I tried to push
it through his thick skull. "You drove me insane with jealousy. Not
because I couldn't get you naked, but because you had some kind of
moral compass guiding you, while I was just floundering around in
the dark."

Words alone can be such empty things, but I wasn't just spinning
out a stream of bullshit. I backed up what I said with all the emotion
I could muster. Longing, sure. But gratitude. And sympathy. And behind it all, a deep and unshakable love. I didn't just feel these emotions, I projected them in an image for him to see for himself. Was
his brain flooded with pictures, or was it something more subtle—a
fleeting impression, a momentary sense of deja vu. A Vibe...like the
one that was now green-lighting my approach. If I pressed my lips
to Red's in that stellar moment of vulnerability where we were both
laid bare to each other in soul, it would be the perfect time to mesh
our bodies.

It might seem unfair to press my psychic advantage at a time
when he was already so exposed, and I did consider holding back.

Then I decided fairness was totally overrated.

There were a dozen ways for Red to duck out of the kiss if he
chose to, unhindered by things that would be in normal apartments,
like furniture. But the Vibe hadn't steered me wrong. When I closed
the gap between us—when I eased my mouth up against his—Red
stayed right where he was. His lips softened, and parted. And while

his kiss was cautious, only slightly wet, a hint of tongue, the emotional outpouring behind that kiss washed over me like a tidal wave.

His love wasn't anxious like my mother's, or shielded like Jacob's, but I could hardly call it pure. Red was a bundle of contrasts inside, pride warring with humility, desire awash with guilt. There was nothing to feel guilty for, though, not anymore, with both of us free. Not just from Luscious, but from whatever hurt we'd inflicted as we both detangled the situation as best we could.

I slid my mouth from his and brushed my lips along his smooth cheek, speaking against him like a caress. "We have a second chance. Let's not waste it."

Red stilled and his emotions spiked high, and for a moment I was worried that voicing the potential for forgiveness aloud had been a serious misstep. But he took a deep breath, and deliberately centered himself, and the apprehension ebbed...replaced by the warmth of hope. This time, when our lips met, it was him kissing me. And if every guy I'd shared my body with before had been a different shade of lust, Red was a stunning spectrum. Affection and love, desire and joy, his emotions simmered to the surface and played across my lips. Even the thread of his apprehension added to the overall experience when he pulled back to say, "I'm not looking for a one-night stand," against the wetness of my mouth.

"Then that makes both of us."

On the surface, Red answered with a gentle sigh. But snarled together in that subtle reaction were angst and relief and a tentative, painful longing. Probably not the best time for me to go announcing that I distinctly felt his feels, especially not faced with something he might not care to share.

He said, "You never struck me as the type of man to settle down."

"Variety might be the spice of life, but you see one dick, you've seen 'em all."

"That's not what I mean. In here," he pressed his palm to my chest, just over my heart, "it's like you were above it all—you didn't need anybody or anything. And by the time I realized you might be willing to let someone in to your heart, it was too late."

"You're the one who always encouraged me to be present." I bent my head to his, put my mouth to his ear, and whispered, "We're here now. This is what matters."

If our kiss was cautious, our initial grappling, crouched together at the foot of the futon, was even more hesitant. Red skimmed his fingers along my shoulders, trailed them down my arms in the ghost of a caress that made me squirm. And me, I held back. Because I needed him to be the one calling the shots, to keep reassuring myself that he burned for me just as much as I did for him.

Being the instigator would be so much easier, but I didn't allow myself to slip into that familiar role. I wanted to do all kinds of things to him, but I reined myself in, and focused instead on what he was doing to me.

He learned my body slowly, sides, back and waist, settling his thumbs over the crest of my pelvis where my low-slung jeans sagged and exposed some skin. With each caress, his touch became bolder. Hips and thighs now, while my dick started to ready itself and shift my body's topography. He skirted that swelling hardness and felt his way around to my ass instead, cupped a cheek in each hand and treated me to a good, solid grope. A shock of desire surged through me, maybe from my standard five senses, maybe from something deeper. Red wasn't just emotionally malnourished from his time in the sangha, he was starving for *me*. I knew it. I felt it. And that hunger awakened the same yearning inside me.

He caught the hem of my T-shirt and stripped it off, and I did the same to him. Piece by piece, our clothing landed in a mingled heap—and soon, our bodies did the same. By the time he lay me back on the futon, I was tingling all over. And then he slipped down between my legs and wrapped his lips around me.

Bliss.

When Red turned his eyes up to meet mine, it wasn't in that show-off way that lots of guys'll blow you because they know they look hot with a dick in their mouth, and he wasn't begging for attention, either. It was him wanting to see me, making sure he took in every last detail of our experience. As for me, after all this time convincing myself that any encounter with him would only happen in the realm of fantasy, I could hardly believe what I saw.

Even touching him was surreal. The texture of his hair fading to a short bristle toward the nape, the delicious smoothness of his cheek, the ropy band of muscle at the side of his neck. Each sensation should have reassured me that this thing between us was actually, finally, happening. And yet I'd never felt more like I was floating through a dream.

The heat cranked up between us fast, and I briefly wondered when the last time was I'd gotten laid—but then I decided it didn't really matter. Red was here with me now. And now was the only thing I cared about. The wetness, the suction, sure, that was all heady, but it was those big, sad eyes that got to me the most.

Before my eager dick got too carried away with itself, I coaxed Red up beside me to fit us together—arms and legs woven through each other—and the citrus and spice scent of our skin mingled deliciously in the heat trapped between our bodies. His mouth was hot when I kissed it again. I tasted myself on his tongue.

As sublime as that kiss might've been, momentum was picking up between us, a rush toward the peak that was years in the scaling. Red rolled onto his back and pulled me between his legs, and my leaking dick dropped into position like we were two halves of a whole driven to be reunited. It took all the self-control I could muster to pause long enough to grab a condom out of my coat pocket and roll it on. If he was serious about having a repeat performance, there'd be time enough in the future to go skin to skin.

I buy the most slippery condoms I can find, but even so, it was a precarious fit. As skillfully as I tried to finesse myself in, I could tell Red's pleasure was tinged with pain. He didn't get off on the hurting, not like a masochist would. And yet, I knew he'd be leery of any pleasure that wasn't adulterated with a stiff dose of reality.

We were both panting and hazed with sweat by the time I got myself sunk. I planted my hands on either side of his head and gazed down on him, cherishing the moment and reveling in the now—the crux of all that had gone before and everything that was still to be.

Tightness. Heat. That age-old rhythm, cautious at first, then harder as our arousal spiraled and pain made way for pleasure. I wouldn't last long, not now, faced with the sheer physicality of what we were finally doing, so I put all my weight on one hand and meshed our fingers together with the other, dark and fair, dark and fair. We clasped his dick together and he fucked the sweat-slicked channel we'd created.

I felt his peak a moment before he hit it. Not from any telltale clenches, but the massive surge of raw emotion pouring out. Love? Not that straightforward. Relief and lust and fear and disbelief, and the worry that maybe love wasn't quite enough—all these hues threaded through the emotional load he let loose.

I supposed love never really was one pure, simple thing, but a kaleidoscopic pattern that was constantly shifting, but always filled with a certain haunting beauty.

I came with my eyes wide open, with Red looking right back at me (for all I knew, looking *into* me) while I broke. I've been with countless men over the years, and sex isn't necessarily that big a deal, an intimate act, a sacred one.

But sometimes, it is.

CHAPTER 52

Futons suck. There's nowhere cushy for shoulders and ribs to settle. But I was way too blissed to let something as insignificant as my body's discomfort get in the way. We slept together, Red and me, limbs threaded through limbs, skin pressed against skin, breath mingling with breath, dreams swirling through dreams. And we slept soundly.

I might have gone right on sleeping, straight through my shop hours—no big loss there—if not for my phone. From somewhere in the pile of discarded clothes, it rang. And rang. And rang some more.

"You gonna get that?" Red's words played over my bare chest in a way that made answering the phone the very last priority on my list. I rolled onto him and stretched myself to cover as much of his naked body with mine as I could manage. The comforter was tangled around my thigh, my half-hard dick was trapped at an unfortunate angle and our laughter was tinged with morning breath. It was perfect.

Except for that damn phone. Which was still fucking ringing.

Regretfully, I shoved myself off Red and snagged a jeans leg from the clothing mound to drag the thing into my range without actually leaving the bed. The pile shifted and the phone made a chattering sound where it now vibrated against the hardwood. It stopped ringing for a moment, then started again.

Normally, whoever was disturbing me, I'd rip 'em a new one. But I was too chock full of endorphins and lovingkindess to do anything worse than turn on my Do Not Disturb. Before I could flip the switch, though, I saw it was Drunk Tony who'd been harshing my buzz, and I supposed I had a neighborly obligation to see if he was wasted on the landing in his underpants again. I picked up the call and said, "This had better be good."

"Oh fuck, sweet Jesus," he yelled over the whoop of a siren. "Thank God you're all right."

My bliss evaporated. In its place, an ugly calm took hold. I'm on the phone night and day, but the only call that's stuck with me over the years was the one where Maxine begged me to sit down, and her voice was all tight and funny—even more than usual—when she tried to make a joke out of asking me to come home during finals, and then dropped the bomb that the big occasion was my father's wake.

I suspected my current call would be just as memorable.

"What happened?" I managed to say.

"A fire, the whole building up in flames. Where the fuck are you?"

"Out." I put him on speakerphone, jumped up and started rooting through the clothes, though it was impossible to separate one thing from another in my panic. "What about Lydia, is she okay?"

"Yeah, she's fine—I can hear her bitching out the cops from here. Everyone was accounted for but you. Holy fuck, what a relief."

"I gotta get down there. I gotta...." I paused to take the underwear Red had pulled from the pile and struggle into it. My whole world had been knocked so far out of alignment I could barely figure out how to stick my feet in the right holes.

"Naw, don't bother," Tony said, while Red laid out my jeans and T-shirt, then started pulling on his own clothes. "It's a clusterfuck, man. Just so long as you're okay."

"What about my store?"

Sirens blared. "I dunno, man, it's—shit, they're making every-body move now—" More crowd sounds, and then the line went dead.

I stood there with my jeans half-on and stared at my phone like an idiot. Red took me by the shoulders and said, "Look at me,

Curtis—you got this. Hear? Everybody's scared of change, but that's all it is. I know you can handle change. Look how different you are now...even when I thought you couldn't be any finer. You can do this. I have faith in you."

Any other time, I'd be snickering over the fact that Red Turner had called me "fine." But at that particular moment, the best I could do was take a breath and try to stop shaking. And zip my fly. "Okay, right. Damage control. If I can't do anything down there, I can make some phone calls here."

Vic was the first one I called. Either I picked him because he's a good listener, or because he seems pretty invested in the store. Or maybe to see if Miss Mattie was okay. Which was dumb. Because it's not like he ever talked to her on the phone...at least not that I know of. I got his voicemail.

"There was a fire. The store is gone. I'm okay. I'm...yeah, I'm okay. I wasn't home." Weirdly enough, talking to the PsyCop's voicemail was not unlike talking to him directly. When Red stepped away to take a shower, beneath the sound of the running water, I said, "You know, it's funny. I thought I'd just made a great big change in my life, since I decided, What the hell? Might as well go for it. With Red, I mean. Just goes to show, my idea of change is jack squat compared to what the universe had in store."

No more Sticks and Stones. I sighed. "I'll bet it went up like a fucking bonfire. The incense, the resin, the books, the herbs, the charcoal." As I unburdened myself on Vic's voicemail, the ramifications sunk in. What would I do with myself? And Lydia—on the heels of that break-in, how would she cope? "Shit. I hope Lydia's okay."

I touched base with Carolyn next, and she did pick up—in fact, I had a hard time convincing her to stay put at work. Unfortunately, there was nothing she could do for me at Red's place, and nowhere for her to sit, either. I told her to hang tight.

When I called Jacob, I got his voicemail, naturally. And my annoyance flared up, just like it always had. If ever there was a man to drive me batshit crazy, it was him. But then Red emerged from the bathroom in a towel, all thoughtful and serious, even though he looked like he was walking onto the set of a porno. He paused as he passed me to press a soft kiss to my shoulder, and as his lips brushed my skin, I realized Jacob was no longer my problem. True, he'd played a major role in my life, and yes, we shared a lot of history. But he'd found someone who could actually tolerate him outside the bedroom, and I wished them nothing but the best.

There's a saying that gets tossed around a lot at Rainbow Dharma: forgiveness is the best revenge. Probably wouldn't have been endorsed by the Buddha, but realizing it was okay to release those resentments did make me feel somewhat better.

Maxine just about lost it when I broke the news, and I had to switch to video chat to reassure her that I was alive. In fact, I spent the rest of the morning on the phone, to the point where I used up all its juice. According to my insurance agent, if I kept my receipts, I'd be reimbursed for some basic stuff: a toothbrush, a change of clothes, and most importantly, a new phone charger. The low-battery beep interrupted her as she warned me not to replace my computer with anything more expensive than my current box unless I wanted to be stuck paying the difference, then the phone died completely as she began suggesting motels where I could temporarily relocate.

"Forget the motel." Red took the depleted phone from my hand, set it aside, and said, "Stay with me."

A man with no home falls for a man with no furniture. Sounded like the setup of a profoundly unfunny joke. But if we had each other, maybe that plain futon was all we needed.

Red and I had been an item, if that was what you could call us, for less than a day—and although we'd known each other pretty well back at Luscious, that was a long time ago. I'd changed since then. So had he. I waited for my gut to insist I make tracks to the nearest motel, but it just gave a little rumble to let me know lunch was long overdue. And since the part of me that had balked at moving in with Jacob during my last time of need was strangely silent, I meshed my fingers through Red's, and pulled him into a kiss.

CHAPTER 53

Given the overwhelming variety of stuff I needed, the fact that my plastic was nearly maxed out, and the suspicion that it might take insurance a while to churn through the pipes, we decided SaverPlus was our best bet. There was a time I'd only go there for clandestine meetings—either tossing conspiracies back and forth in the bathroom with Vic, or ogling the guy at the return counter—but oh, how the mighty had fallen. This time, I'd actually need to buy something.

Red and I made the rounds. Menswear for jeans, tees, socks and briefs. Electronics for a phone charger and a Chromebook—last year's model, surprisingly cheap. There was even a robust clearance section where, for a mere ten bucks, I scored a couple of camping chairs that folded themselves into a fabric tube. I was all for having a fresh and unencumbered start, but there'd be a staggering amount of computer time in my near future, and I wasn't about to do it seated on the floor.

I hadn't intended to buy a toy, but since Christmas was right around the corner, it was impossible to avoid the various gifty displays. A kitschy tower of retro goodies blocked my way to the checkout, and something among the Sea Moneys, Slinkys, ViewMasters and Spirographs caught my eye. Gingerly, so as not to cause an avalanche, I pulled down a purple box, asked, "Will Lydia dig this?" and turned it over to get my reply.

The inky water in the Magic 8 Ball's window bubbled, then parted, as an answer floated to the top: *Reply hazy try again.*

"Sounds just like her," I said, but I waffled about spending another six bucks on something that wasn't an absolute necessity.

Red took the box from my hand before I could wedge it back into the teetering display. "Either you act from a place of fear, or a place of love. Show your friend how much you love her. If you don't, you'll regret it...a lot more than you'll regret spending six dollars."

Coming from anyone else, that might've struck me as preachy, but I didn't take it that way, not with Red. His advice was like Carolyn's truth. An acquired taste for non-empaths, but given the emotion I now felt behind it, easy to digest for me. "C'mere." I grabbed his pleather jacket by the lapel and pulled him across the shopping cart. When I laid a kiss on him, I felt him smile. And I felt his heart swell with all sorts of giddy feelings, too.

It seemed like it should have felt pathetic, me with no home, no job, and my earthly possessions fitting in the trunk of Red's car with room to spare. But it didn't. It felt liberating. What if I was ready for a nomad's life, and all I really needed was a chair, a change of clothes, and a 2-pound laptop that cost less than I used to spend on drinks and dinner? Could be that clearing the physical slate was opening me up emotionally, too. Not that I'd ever say anything like that aloud. But it was definitely food for thought.

Once we were done at SaverPlus, we headed down to Wicker Park, but Tony hadn't been exaggerating when he described the scene at the building. In fact, I'd participated in clusterfucks that were a hell of a lot more organized. But it was clear that we wouldn't get near Sticks and Stones anytime soon, so we retreated to Red's apartment.

Our apartment.

Red and I fell into a rhythm there that was as easy as it had been two years back, when we'd toned Carolyn's hair from Orange Sherbet to Vanilla Ice. Actually, it was easier, without that dickbag Ralph between us...or, to be totally honest with myself, my own obnoxious immaturity.

Thanks to the cloud, all my records were intact, and I had receipts for all my very flammable inventory. I was in the midst of the daunting process of filling out my claim when Red's intercom buzzed. Not only was it startlingly loud in the mostly-empty room, but baffling, too. Because judging by the puzzled look on Red's face, none of his old Chicago contacts knew where he lived.

"It's probably Carolyn using her powers of detection," I told him. "She is a professional, after all."

Red leaned in to the intercom, pressed the button, and said, "Hello?"

What came through was not Carolyn's voice, not by a long shot, but the gravelly rasp of someone I usually bantered with in 144 characters or less. "I'm looking for Crash. Seen him?"

Red raised an eyebrow at me. I hesitated. Not because I was afraid of BornSkeptic—hell, he regularly sent me links to stupid goat gifs—but the sheer incongruity of it all was like spotting your high school gym teacher at a gay bar. I joined Red at the intercom and pressed the "talk" button. "Fancy meeting you here," I said into it. "To what do I owe the pleasure?"

"Can't a friend check on a friend to see how he's doing?"

"Indeed he could, though it begs the question—how, pray tell, would that friend know where to look?"

"Said friend would love to stand around shucking and jiving, but would prefer to end the day with his hide intact. Let me up and I'll fill you in."

I looked to Red for permission to let my melodrama into his life, but he just gave me one of his imperturbably cryptic looks, and said, "It's your place now too, Curtis. You do what you see fit."

With no excuse not to, I buzzed the buzzer.

Constantine is the type of guy you wouldn't mistake for anyone else. From his voice to his sense of humor to his truly brave corkscrew 'fro, he's memorable, to say the least. Backlit from the hall, his silhouette was familiar. At least until he stepped into the light, and I got a load of his face. Same ironic smirk as always, but punctuated now by a split lip and one hell of a shiner.

"I'd say you should get a load of the other guy, but since he outranked me, it wasn't worth fighting back. Well, then." He dragged in a big suitcase with a garment bag on top, parked it beside the door, and clapped his hands together. "First things first. The fire? An accident." I hadn't even considered the possibility it wasn't. Red and I exchanged a look. "How long it'll take authorities to come to that conclusion, I have no idea, especially given the way gang activity has been heating up lately. But I wanted to make sure you knew the score. Hard enough to get a good night's sleep without wondering if someone's out to torch you."

"That's...comforting." I wondered where he got his facts. And I suspected he wasn't about to volunteer his source.

"So you're safe, you're sound...let's keep it that way." He plucked the Magic 8 Ball off the counter and peered into the inky window. "No more psychic testing—you need a piece of paper proving you're psychic like you need a ten-pound shit in a five-pound bag. And your online research about anything more psychic than this?" He tossed the 8 Ball to me. "It ends. Here and now."

"So Big Brother really is out there."

"I always figured, if you can't beat 'em, join 'em. But as you can see, they turned the beating on me. Thing is, the only reason you're not popping up in the same shooting gallery is my massaging of the data. And with me out of the picture, you've got no one to cover your tracks." He took a handful of ice in a paper towel from Red. "That goes for you too, Red. Promise me neither of you will turn around and Google the FPMP the minute my back is turned."

"Can't imagine why it would interest me," I said with mock indifference. "Bunch of stuffy guys in suits pushing paper. Right?"

He laughed humorlessly into the icepack as he pressed it to his lips. "Exactly. So now that that's settled, can I hit you up for a little trim? I'm going to a wedding. Mine."

CHAPTER 54

As a rule, I'm not a weeper. But BornSkeptic whisked us off to a clandestine location for his haircut, and some big realizations sank in. He was marrying a dear friend of mine—that part was fine. But then both of them were about to go so deep into hiding, I might never see either of them again.

Tears were indeed shed.

We were holed up in a private room at a spendy restaurant, Lisa and Con, Red and me. Lisa's sister too, though she was running in and out on a constantly revolving supply run. She'd managed to procure basic equipment: brushes and combs, styling mousse and spray, shears that were at least marginally sharp, and a brand new set of hot rollers. Once I reined in my waterworks, I slotted myself in beside Red to work on setting Lisa's curls, sectioning and rolling, rolling and sectioning. And just as we had when we'd color-corrected Carolyn that fateful night so long ago, the two of us worked together like a well-oiled machine. At least until I couldn't deny that I might never run my fingers through Lisa's hair again.

"You've got the sí-no to keep you one step ahead of Big Brother," I said, "don't you? Why not just change your email addy and move to Evanston?"

She dabbed her eyes with a sodden, lace-edged hankie that I suspected was meant for decoration, and shook her head. "I haven't been tested—not even at PsyTrain. For all that everything fell apart there, at least they didn't do any of the traditional ratings. But they still took notes, so the FPMP knows I'm a precog. They just don't know how accurate. And Constantine....” She trailed off and glanced at her groom-to-be, who was hunched in the corner with a phone to his ear. I'd always figured he was kinda schlubby under all those baggy sweats and that crazy mop of hair, but I'd figured wrong. With the new close undercut I'd given him, plus his dark fitted suit, he was all angles—hard and lean, and poised to snap into action. He finished his call, ripped out the SIM card, dropped it to the floor and ground it beneath his heel. Then he snapped in a fresh card and made another call.

“That's one way to get out of your contract,” I said drily.

Lisa lowered her voice, even though Con obviously had more to do than listen to us, and said through a fresh round of tears, “He was so careful all these years. But all it takes is a single leak, and all the precautions in the world don't matter anymore.”

You'd think having Lisa at your side would make you invulnerable. Guess not, if you don't ask the right questions.

I hadn't cashed in the sí-no she owed me, and I couldn't help but wonder if I should get it now while the getting was good. This thing with Red and me—what if it was doomed to fail? Once the new endorphin rush wore off and I was faced with a stack of bills and a teetering pile of dirty dishes, I might not be ready to play house.

Then again, we only owned two dishes. We'd figure it out.

Red pinned the final roller in place, then stepped around to crouch down at Lisa's knee. Gooseflesh rippled down my arms as he assumed the position, since I could feel what was coming next.

He gathered Lisa's hands in his, and with his voice velvety low, said, “Listen, Babygirl. It's time to stop crying. You're getting married today, and you don't want your eyes all swollen up so that every time you look at your wedding pictures, you're sad all over again.” He squeezed her hands for emphasis, and she nodded. “Now think back to when you were young, and you saw yourself getting married. Really see yourself as that child fantasizing about her special day.”

Lisa's eyelids fluttered closed, and her eyes tracked beneath them like she was dreaming. Did Red need to be holding eye contact to share that dream? I didn't know. And hopefully no one at some scary government agency did, either.

Lisa's brow furrowed in thought. Whether or not Red was putting his hocus pocus on her, at least he'd stemmed the weeping. Her pause was long enough to make me wonder if she would even answer, but then, hesitantly, she said, "I remember...Vera Wang. All these...dresses."

A wordsmith, she was not. But Red had no need for words.

"Simple," she said. "You know? Straight lines. White, off-white. Totally...plain." She laughed self-consciously. "I guess it was tasteful, after the giant hair and big, poofy dresses from the eighties. But I thought those new styles were ugly. For my wedding, I wanted ruffles and lace. I wanted to look fancy. Pretty."

She blushed, and opened her eyes. Red told her, "You are, Lisa. You're beautiful." And as schmaltzy as it would've sounded coming from anyone else, from him, it was God's honest truth.

Across the room, Con glanced up at Lisa and gave her a private wink. I probably wouldn't have caught it, if I hadn't felt the currents of Vibing that ran between the two of them like laser surveillance beams.

Whatever Red saw when she told her unadorned story must've been enough. He pulled out his trusty pocket notebook and sketched out a stunning updo—classy, fresh, and a hell of a lot more complicated than it looked. He flashed it at me and said, "What do you think?"

Way beyond my skill set. But I supposed that between the two of us, we could handle it.

Over the next couple of hours, we proceeded to tease, curl, tuck, and pin our little hearts out. To be honest, Red did most of the work, while I served as the extra pair of hands and distracting banter. Lisa's big sister continued to whisk in and out of our makeshift bridal suite with the unlikeliest of things, from makeup to duct tape to a flouncy white salsa dress that thankfully looked more retro than dated. And yes, the handkerchief hem featured plenty of lace.

I heard the buzz of people from the adjacent private dining room a few minutes after I felt their budding anticipation. Vic blundered in as we were finishing Lisa's hair, and despite the fact that he was no big fan of her fiancee, he seemed calmer than I'd seen him in quite some while. But it wasn't until I caught sight of Jacob that I realized he and Vic had accessorized from the same hard-knocks catalog as Con. Vic had a raw scuff on one cheek, and Jacob had a reddish ding on his temple that would grow up to be a bruise come morning.

Jacob was by the bar, talking low to another gym rat in a suit. Jacob is striking enough on his own. With his carbon copy, he looked like he should be talking into an earpiece and escorting a high profile rock star to their limo.

So this is how it works, I thought. Have the bad judgement to rub elbows with a cop, and next thing you know, the place is crawling with FPMP. When Jacob spotted me giving him the side-eye from the other end of the bar, he abruptly cut off their conversation to hurry over. But not until it clicked with me that I'd seen his pal before.

"Thank God you're okay," Jacob said.

Which I ignored. "Did you know that when your buddy isn't out spying on psychics, he's proctoring exams?"

"What?"

The guy ignored us both and signaled the bartender for another round. I turned back to Jacob. "The world's most expensive quiz—in which I was purportedly the weakest link. Hard to forget such striking eyes. He was at my Psych screening. Doing what—making sure I failed?"

"I have no idea. Back then I was still with the police department."

"That's convenient."

"Can we not argue? Just this once? I've had a hell of a day—and without Jack's help, it would've been a lot worse."

"*You've* had a hell of a day?" When Jacob closed his eyes and shook his head in resignation, I pressed him on it. "No, please, do tell. Did you lose your home? Your livelihood? Your every last possession?"

Jacob stared into his beer for a moment, then said, "If you really want to know—I held down a dead body that was flailing around. Not recently deceased, either. Autopsied, frozen, and thawed. And when Vic finally forced the ghost to the other side where it belonged,

I think I...I felt something. A chill. Like...the grave." He drained his glass. "I touched death."

Leave it to Jacob to one-up me when my freaking house burns down. With the wind knocked out of my indignation, I said, "You okay?"

He considered his answer a long while, then said, "I don't know."

I sat with him in silence while we both considered the import of this thing he'd just shared. This was the type of stuff he'd held back, when we were dating...okay, maybe nothing quite so weird, but other stuff I might've been able to help him through, if only he'd been secure enough in our connection to confide in me. Now I could tell by a dozen visual clues that he was hurting—his expression, his rigidity, the set of his shoulders—but I still couldn't feel it. He was blocking me. Even now.

"C'mere, Big Guy," I said. "Bring it on in." I didn't embrace him with the intention of breaking down any barriers. A hug is a normal human response when someone you care about is hurting. But I couldn't help but notice that even after the hug, he was still as open to me as a window with its sash painted shut. If there was any lingering doubt as to our incompatibility, I'd just erased it.

Friends. Had to hand it to 'em. The ones I gravitated toward were never boring.

Take BornSkeptic. Most people would've cut someone a little slack on their wedding day. But given that it might be the last chance I had, I couldn't stop myself. I cornered Con out by the coat check and said, "So that blue-eyed bald guy drinking for all he's worth at the far side of the bar...he a friend of yours?"

"Now that I'm no longer his boss, I suppose he is."

"I've seen him before. In fact, back at my psychic screening, he was all over me. What gives?"

"Empaths. Takes one to know one."

"And he told you I was a shitty level one?"

Con snagged me by the sleeve before I could go knock the guy off his barstool. "Chill, AshMan, he vouched for you. But my telepath didn't think you were cut out for government work—and I'm not talking about snapping ugly photos at the DMV. You get involved in something dangerous, things heat up and you have to disappear, take off to some far-flung city with a fresh haircut and a new name, what happens to your mother?"

First thought was that I'd take her with me. Her dog too. But honestly, Dumpling would probably do better in witness protection than Maxine.

Once that consideration sunk in, Con said, "A piece of feedback about your screening that you might find useful: a good empath can move energy both ways. You weren't bad in receiving mode, but you didn't even attempt to transmit."

I thought back to the baffling room dividers. "But no one told me...oh, for fuck's sake." The guy in the bathroom who needed to calm down. The one I'd left flapping in the wind. "The random word spewing wasn't even the test, it was everything in between."

"Sadly so. But isn't life basically one big test?"

"Now you sound like the armchair philosophers at Rainbow Dharma." I tried to pick up on what he was feeling, given that he'd admitted I was actually empathic to some extent, but there was too much interference in the air. Excitement and fear, eagerness and dread, and the tweaky anxiety that comes with playing a high stakes game with everything to lose. I supposed if I couldn't read Con, I'd have to settle for asking. "Tell me something. You and me. Was any of our camaraderie real, or were you just keeping track of some stupid empath who didn't know his own strength and making sure he stayed out of trouble?"

"Let me put it this way. There's three things I'd never dream of doing. One, I won't pee into a bottle I had any chance of accidentally drinking from later. Two, I don't go around imagining telepaths naked. And three—I'd never ask someone to do my getaway makeover if I didn't consider him to be a true friend."

CHAPTER 55

As weddings went, the ceremony was pretty simple, with textbook vows and a justice of the peace. But the emotions behind it were exquisitely heightened. And there I was in the midst of it, empathic enough that the FPMP had chosen to squelch my rankings, soaking up all the emotional intensity.

Although the bartender shook a tasty Limoncello Collins, I cut myself off after two drinks. Scary to think I was high on life. But despite everything I'd lost, marinating all afternoon in my friends' happiness and knowing I'd fall into bed with Red that night, that's exactly how I felt.

It had been a marathon of a day. My third wind had just about blown itself out and Red had slipped off to grab the car when a familiar too-tall figure joined me in the vestibule. I'd been acquainted with Vic long enough to know he must have something to say, otherwise he would've invented urgent business that caused him to veer off in the opposite direction, whether or not the ruse landed him out behind the dumpsters.

While his anxiety spiked, he teetered on the verge of saying nothing, but ended up blurting out, "I'm really sorry about how things... turned out."

"Yeah, well. All the Buddhism must be doing its trick. I'm not as dismayed by the impermanence of everything as I might've been, once upon a time."

Vic shuffled his feet. "If there's anything I can do...."

I wasn't sure exactly what he was offering: money, a place to crash, or a shoulder to cry on. Unlike Jacob, Vic didn't communicate with hugs...not unless that communique was, *Can I let go now?*

So I settled for a companionable shoulder-bump instead, and told him, "Cool, thanks." Anything more would've just made his energy curdle. And I was feeling particularly merciful.

Red brought the car around and I climbed in. There was a moment of disorientation when we didn't head back toward Wicker Park, but only a moment. I hadn't been exaggerating about my propensity to accept change. And flexibility is never a bad thing.

An incoming text interrupted my contemplation of Red's profile, and I saw my inbox had actually been stacking up while Lisa and Con were getting hitched. News of the fire had spread as quickly as the fire itself, and lots of my old customers, some from as far back as the soirees, wanted to make sure I was alive.

I'd sent a dozen reassurances by the time I scrolled down far enough to see a huge block of messages were from Drunk Tony—one voicemail and multiple texts.

Call me

Call me

CALL ME

I'm no precog, but even I knew it couldn't be good. Maybe he had nowhere to sleep, maybe he needed some cash. Maybe, maybe, maybe. Half-glimpses of ideas ranging from bad to worse, devolving in the four rings it took for him to answer his phone.

And immediately start blubbering.

I put on my best calm-voice and said, "Tony, take a breath."

"I'm—so—sorry," he gasped out. "I don't know how I...I don't know."

"Seriously, dude, just breathe."

"It was, like, eight o'clock in the morning—I wasn't drunk."

"Okay. I believe you."

"I swear to God I heard her. Swear to God."

A chill raced down my spine. Red sensed something was up, and he pulled over and put his hand on my knee. I hardly felt it.

"Tony, what's going on?"

"Clear as day, I heard her, swear to God. I wasn't drunk. She was hollering at the cops, telling them it wasn't arson. And swearing, and calling 'em pigs. But mostly making sure they knew it was an accident."

There was only one person aside from me who'd say all that to a cop's face. By the time I was able to say her name, my whole body had gone numb. Anger. Dread. And the creeping realization that the reason Tony drank had nothing to do with him enjoying the taste of beer.

Red squeezed my knee and said, "What is it?"

My voice sounded hollow when, numbly, I answered.

"Lydia's dead."

CHAPTER 56

Tony was all done swearing to God—done talking at all. But his gut-wrenching sobs were all the confirmation I needed. I hung up and stared hard at the dash.

"Curtis?" Red asked gently. He squeezed my knee again and I pushed his hand away.

"Don't get too attached," I snapped. "Everything I do turns to shit. My career, my store, everything I fucking care about. Something's got it in for me. God? Karma? Who the fuck knows. Maybe you should get away now while the getting's good."

If ever I expected someone to lecture me, that person would be Red. But he didn't. He waited to see if I had anything more to say, and when I didn't, he pulled back into traffic and headed toward the apartment.

We drove in silence. When we parked and cut the engine, I demanded, "Aren't you going to tell me that suffering is a choice? That there's no permanence in this world, and grasping for things to stay the same is a surefire path to misery?"

"You lost your friend. Of course you're hurting."

We went inside, where the apartment greeted us in all its stark emptiness. The notion that we could live on a box of noodles, a futon, and bunch of good intentions felt profoundly naive.

Red closed the door behind us, then came up beside me and took my hand in his. I didn't pull away, not because I found his touch comforting, but because I was so numb, I hardly felt it. "All this time," I said, "I've been hung up on the fact that everyone and their brother has a certificate on the wall proving they've got talent. Everyone but me. And when I find out my score was rigged and these signals I've been tuned in to are real—not some cocktail of wishful thinking and coincidence—the one person I want to share my news with is dead. I'm tired, Red. Bone tired. And I don't see the point anymore. Why be psychic? What good is it to be a precog if it doesn't save you from a fire? And why be an empath, either? Just give it long enough, everything eventually turns out to be pointless."

Red walked me to the futon, sat me down, slipped an arm around me and pressed his temple to my shoulder. "Life is so fragile. It seems like too big a lesson to ever forget, and yet somehow, I always do, at least until I get a painful reminder. Say whatever you need to say, if you find comfort in the words. I can take it. And I'm not going anywhere. I don't make empty promises. I said I wasn't looking for a one-night stand, and I meant it. Relationships need to weather good times and bad. And I'm here to get you through this storm."

Red might've been willing to listen to me vent, but there was nothing more to be said. I slept in his embrace, enveloped by his concern, and I dreamed about sharing a smoke with Lydia. Hanging curtains in her waiting room. Drinking our disgusting cake-flavored vodka. If my subconscious was trying to make me feel better by reminiscing, it failed horribly. Because those memories only made my waking moment twice as painful, when the present came rushing back and I remembered she was dead, and then felt her loss all over again.

Despite the pathological lack of clutter in the apartment, I felt cooped up and restless. As Red sat for his morning meditation, I paced back and forth, back and forth. Caged and useless. Nothing to do and nowhere to go. Eventually, Red opened his eyes and said, "If you need to see the place, I'll take you there."

And so we went.

The dreams I'd woken from so cruelly felt more real than my present reality. I thought I'd been prepared for the burnt husk I

found where my home once stood, but I'd been wrong. The building looked the same, from a distance. Its shell was intact. But the
closer we got, the more details came into view: the blackened scorch
around the windows, the broken glass and wood. The police tape. I
scoped out what was left of the building from as close as I was willing
to get. Red kept an eye on me as I played chicken with the adjacent
lane of traffic. But he didn't try to stop me.

Eventually, one of those cars came to a full stop, then flipped on
its flashers. I only recognized that I'd ridden in it mere days before
when its owner got out and joined me, and it occurred to me that
Victor Bayne hadn't been talking about Sticks and Stones when, back
at the restaurant, he told me he was sorry.

"Can you give her a message?" I asked.

Vic trapped a piece of broken glass beneath his shoe, then
dragged it back and forth on the sidewalk. "It doesn't...work that way."

All the hurt and rage and despair trapped inside me ruptured,
and came pouring out before I could make sense of it. "I put up with
your conspiracy theories and your psychic emergencies, I give you
my advice and my expertise, and you're not even willing to—"

"I would if I could," he said hastily. "But I can't. She's gone."

Before I could mention it was awfully convenient his psychic
powers didn't work the minute I needed them most, he craned his
neck to see what he could of the hall, where a pile of phone books
had blackened under a wall of dented, collapsing mailboxes. "Lydia,
I mean. Yesterday, right after the fire, she was here. Really pissed off
about it, too. I talked her down, let her know...." his pale eyes shifted
into that faraway look they get when he goes internal. "I mean, it
wasn't creepy or anything. Y'know? I told her she was dead and she
was pretty cool about the whole thing. Even tried to summon a pack
of smokes."

While I might have called Vic a charlatan any number of times,
I always suspected he truly had some kind of ability. But the way he
was describing Lydia, it fit her so perfectly that any lingering shreds
of doubt disappeared. At the thought of her trying to call up spiritual
cigarettes, I actually laughed. Okay, maybe a tear or two escaped, but
mostly I was laughing.

He said, "I wish I had more to give you, but when I saw her, I was more worried about you. I didn't know you were okay. Not until she told me. And once she did, she pulled a card for me and...." Vic trailed off, then focused on something over my right shoulder. Red and I both looked, but there was nothing there. Nothing that either of us could see, anyhow. Vic cleared his throat, crammed his hands into his pockets, and started acting shiftier than usual. "Miss Mattie wants me to tell you she approves."

Gooseflesh raced down my arms. In all my concern about Lydia, I hadn't given a second thought to Mattie, since she was already dead. I wasn't sure if that was something I should feel bad about or not.

"Uh...okay," Vic mumbled. "Specifically, she says Red Turner is a fine young man. And she's happy that you're willing to let him help you, instead of trying to prove a point by doing everything alone. She says you can help each other." He paused to listen, and he didn't cock his head like someone being theatrical and proving how difficult it was to hear beyond the veil. He just stood there and stared. And then he added, "She says—aw, geez—she says she loves you very much, and she'll always look out for you, but she has to go. There's work to do. And, she says, now you're 'grown enough' to handle whatever comes next."

In all the time we'd known each other, Vic had never offered to act as the go-between, and there was so much I wanted to say to her, I hardly knew where to begin. "Tell her I love her. Tell her I miss her. Tell her I wish we could've spent more time together."

Vic made a curt, dismissive gesture. "You don't need me to tell her that, she can hear you just fine. But, wait, there's gotta be a way to make a ghost leave without projecting out of my body, right? That can't be good. Jennifer Chance nearly...yeah, but one of these days I might not snap back in. And what about the sticky repeaters? I don't think they're even technically ghosts."

How silly of me to think Victor Bayne had stopped by on my account. Strangely enough, I wasn't terribly annoyed. He'd always considered himself to be the center of the universe. I supposed, in a way, we all did.

Seeing him in action was a giant wakeup call. His abilities put one foot in each world, which left him off-balance in both. But the value was clear.

What good is it to be psychic? It's everything. In knowing all we can know—about the past, the future, or the great beyond—we come to understand ourselves.

I took Red's hand in mine, pressed my skin to his, and focused on the general direction in which Vic was still ranting. Even though my emotions were running so high I couldn't precisely name them, I'd had enough practice to center myself, and open up, and allow. My own feelings were complex, but there was no mistaking which emotions swirling around us didn't belong to me. I felt Red's sublime calm, and Vic's persistent anxiety. And beyond that, an outpouring of pure love. It always pissed me off that Vic could speak to Mattie but I couldn't.

But now, I realized, it didn't matter. I could feel her heart.

I squeezed Red's hand and basked in the love. Not just Mattie's, but his too. And Vic's. And then I realized that as a whole, the world around me subtly vibrated with love. Not as pure as Mattie's, of course, but more love than hate. It was a precarious balance, though, and it couldn't afford to lose any of us. People with real talent. Those of us willing and able to be a conduit for good.

Maybe it was time for Con and Lisa to lie low, but me? A world of possibility was now spread out in front of me. Professionally, I had nothing to lose—and nothing to hold me back, either. Thanks to Con's foresight, I was outside the system, and that was where I'd do the most good. Drunk Tony, for starters. If I could pry him off the barstool and get him to listen, we could work on his penchant for self-medication. And Carolyn...maybe she'd be willing to lend a hand. If anyone was sick of bureaucracy, it was her.

"I love you," I whispered directly to Mattie. Because, of anything we can all say to one another, isn't that the only thing that truly matters?

Vic stopped babbling mid-sentence, then huffed out a sigh. "She's gone," he told me. But I already knew. I'd felt her love enfold me in a final embrace as surely as if she'd done it in the flesh. And while I was sad when the feeling faded, I wasn't devastated. I'd see her again someday. Lydia too. And in the meantime, given my connections, I had no doubt there'd be plenty of tasty opportunities for a pair of off-the-grid Psychs like Red and me.

We all contemplated the now-empty spot for several moments, then Vic scratched the back of his neck and said, "So, if you need anything, y'know. Shoot me a text. Or whatever."

"Yeah, I'm good," I told him. And I meant it.

While he retreated to his double-parked car, Red and I stood our ground and contemplated the remains of the building. If I shifted my perception, I saw it not so much as wreckage, but as physical matter, rearranged. Transformed. Sure, I would've preferred my transformational experience to be less brutal. But I was tough. I'd survive.

"C'mon," I told Red, and tugged him toward the car. "I got what I came for."

When we settled in, Red turned to me, cradled my cheek in his hand, stroked his thumb along my cheekbone and said, "The way you felt your feelings, no excuses, no regrets, that's something I've always loved about you."

"Yeah? That's cool...but what about my butt? Cos I've really been targeting my glutes."

Red acknowledged my valiant attempt to keep from bawling with a shy smile. "Fine butt goes without saying."

"Can't hurt to tell me how much you dig it, anytime the spirit takes you."

We sat together in silence. There was nowhere specific for us to go, so I felt no burning desire to be on our way. Was that what living in the "now" was all about? It would take some getting used to.

After we'd been quiet a long moment, Red said, "Miss Mattie sounds amazing. I wish I could have met her."

"You still can." I grabbed his hand and pressed it to my chest, thought back to a memory of picking dandelions with Mattie, and looked deep into his eyes. "Let me tell you a story...."

ABOUT THIS STORY

I've always considered Crash to be Victor Bayne's "path not taken." Crash, for me, was an idea of what might have happened if Vic hadn't come into his psychic ability so early, so violently, and so vulnerably—if Vic hadn't been committed and then scooped up by Camp Hell.

But now that I've delved deep into Crash's backstory, I see it's nowhere near that simple.

Writing in the PsyCop universe through the viewpoint of a bold, confident extrovert was a lot of fun. Seeing the various side characters through the eyes of someone who isn't justifiably paranoid was interesting too. Carolyn, Dreyfuss and Jacob come off pretty differently when they're filtered through Crash as opposed to Vic. I really enjoyed showcasing aspects of their lives that Vic wouldn't have connected with or known about.

Mainly, though, I was inspired to flesh out Crash's backstory because I realized I couldn't do justice to the scope of his relationship with Red from Vic's point of view. As much as I take great satisfaction in meting out bits of info through Vic's unreliable narration, Red was too cryptic to stand any chance of making an impression without an empath to perceive him.

As much as he gets around, Crash does have meaningful relationships...mainly with women. Miss Mattie goes without saying. But

I delved into his relationship with his mother to show where he's come from—and then with Lydia, to show how he's matured. I especially enjoyed his scenes with Lisa. She could be her most authentic self around Crash without fear of being judged or scolded.

All in all, it was fun to ride around inside the head of a main character who's always up for a challenge. Interesting to view Jacob through a more critical eye, and Carolyn through a more sympathetic one. And definitely, it was fascinating to watch dozens of hair shows and talk to stylists about why they like doing what they do. But PsyCop is Vic's story, and I would definitely write about Crash and Red's further adventures in a future novella if that story needed telling, the next PsyCop novel will rejoin Vic in all his disgruntled and introverted glory.

ABOUT THE AUTHOR

Author and artist Jordan Castillo Price writes paranormal sci-fi thrillers colored by her time in the Midwest, from inner city Chicago, to various cities across southern Wisconsin. She's settled in a 1910 Cape Cod near Lake Michigan with tons of character and a plethora of bizarre spiders. Any disembodied noises, she's decided, will be blamed on the ice maker.

If you enjoyed the book, please leave a review. Even a brief review is beneficial to the author. It DOES make a difference!

Find Jordan in the following places:
jordancastilloprice.com
facebook.com/jordancastilloprice
twitter.com/jordancprice

THE PSYCOP SERIES

www.PsyCop.com

**Beautiful • Mysterious • Bizarre
fiction by Jordan Castillo Price**

Don't Miss the Next Story - Sign up for Jordan's Free Monthly
Newsletter Today!
www.psycop.com/newsletter

CPSIA information can be obtained
at www.ICGtesting.com
Printed in the USA
BVOW03s1106151017
497719BV00001B/31/P